BANGKOK 8

BANGKOK 8

JOHN BURDETT

Alfred A. Knopf New York 2003

THIS IS A BORZOI BOOK
PUBLISHED BY ALFRED A. KNOPF

Library of Congress Cataloging-in-Publication Data
Burdett, John.
Bangkok 8 / John Burdett. — 1st ed.
p. cm.
ISBN 1-4000-4044-2
1. Police—Thailand—Bangkok—Fiction.   2. Bangkok
(Thailand)—Fiction.   I. Title: Bangkok eight.   II. Title.
PR6052.U617 B36 2003
823'.914—dc21   2002040658

Manufactured in the United States of America
First Edition

For Sofia

ACKNOWLEDGMENTS

I thank Sandra Bacon for her great help and kindness in a difficult moment; Nick Wolff for sharing the burden of research;
Nong Ruamsantiah (not to be confused with any character bearing those names) for showing me Thailand at grass roots level;
and, in no particular order: Thip, Nit, Tao, Toy, Marly, Lek, Da,
Song, Mimi, Yen, Jin, Ay, Wan, Pat, Nat, without whom this book
would never have happened.

AUTHOR'S NOTE

Bangkok is one of the world's great cities, all of which own red-light districts that find their ways into the pages of novels from time to time. The sex industry in Thailand is smaller per capita than in Taiwan, the Philippines or the United States. That it is more famous is probably because Thais are less coy about it than many other people. Most visitors to the kingdom enjoy wonderful vacations without coming across any evidence of sleaze at all.

On a related topic, I am honor bound to say that on innumerable visits to Thailand I have experienced only honesty and courtesy from members of the Royal Thai Police Force. Nor have I heard any report to the contrary from other Western tourists. That said, the kingdom's valiant struggle with the kind of corruption that is endemic throughout the Far East has been the subject of numerous newspaper articles, government investigations and learned research projects by respected academics for more than a decade. A novelist is an opportunist and it will be obvious that I have not been shy to adapt many of these stories for narrative purposes, for which I trust I shall be forgiven. I hope that any Thai cop who comes across these frivolous pages will see humor rather than slight. This is an entertainment within a very Western genre, and nothing more. No offense is intended.

Like all the men of Babylon, I have been proconsul; like all, I have been a slave. I have known omnipotence, ignominy, imprisonment. Look here—my right hand has no index finger.

—Jorge Luis Borges, "The Lottery in Babylon"

In the whole world there is no one who does not welcome it like reason.

—Confucius, talking about jade

BANGKOK 8

1

The African American marine in the gray Mercedes will soon die of bites from *Naja siamensis*, but we don't know that yet, Pichai and I (the future is impenetrable, says the Buddha). We are one car behind him at the toll for the expressway from the airport to the city and this is the closest we've been for more than three hours. I watch and admire as a huge black hand with a heavy gold signet ring on the index finger extends from the window, a hundred-baht note clipped stylishly between the pinkie and what our fortune tellers call the finger of the sun. The masked woman in the booth takes the note, hands him the change and nods in recognition at something he says to her, probably in very bad Thai. I tell Pichai that only a certain kind of American *farang* attempts conversation with toll booth operators. Pichai grunts and slides down in his seat for a nap. Survey after survey has shown sleep to be my people's favorite hobby.

"He's picked someone up, a girl," I mutter casually, as if this were not a shocking piece of news and clear proof of our incompetence. Pichai opens one eye, then the other, raises himself and stretches his neck just as the Mercedes hatchback races away like a thoroughbred.

"A whore?"

"Green and orange streaks in her hair. Afro style. Black top with straps. Very dark."

"I bet you know who designed the black top?"

"It's a fake Armani. At least, Armani was the first to come out with the black semi–tank top with bootlace straps, there have been plenty of imitators since."

Pichai shakes his head. "You really know your threads. He must have picked her up at the airport, when we lost him for that half hour."

I say nothing as Pichai, my soul brother and partner in indolence, returns to his slumbers. Perhaps he is not sleeping, perhaps he is meditating. He is one of those who have had enough of the world. His disgust has driven him to be ordained and he has named me as the one who, along with his mother, will shave his head and eyebrows, which honor will permit us to fly to one of the Buddha heavens by clinging to his saffron robes at the moment of death. You see how entrenched is cronyism in our ancient culture.

In truth there is something mesmeric about the black marine's head-and-shoulder set which has consumed all my attention. At the beginning of the surveillance I watched him get out of his car at a gas station: he is a perfectly formed giant and this perfection has fascinated me for three hours, as if he were some kind of black Buddha, the Perfect Man, of whom the rest of us are merely scale models with ugly flaws. Now that I have finally noticed her, his whore looks erotically fragile beside him, as if he might crush her inadvertently like a grape against the palate, to her eternal and ecstatic gratitude (you see why I am not suitable for monkhood).

By the time I have inched up to the toll booth in our dying Toyota, he has flown to who knows what celestial bed of pleasure in his late-model Garuda.

I say to my beloved Pichai, "We've lost him," but Pichai also has flown, leaving only his uninhabited corpse, which snores in the seat beside me.

Naja siamensis is the most magnificent of our spitting cobras and might be our national mascot, for its qualities of beauty, charm, stealth and lethal bite. *Naja*, by the way, is from the Sanskrit, and a reference to the great Naja spirit of the earth who protected our Lord Buddha during a dreadful storm in the forest where he meditated.

2

The elevated expressway is the only road in the city where a Mercedes E series can outrun a Toyota Echo, and I drive without hope or haste (which comes from the devil; slowness comes from Buddha), just for form, feeling out of place amongst the elite vehicles whose owners can afford the toll: Mercs and BMWs, Japanese four-by-fours, plus a lot of taxis with *farangs* in the back. We fly above the brothel-hotels of the Nana district before I take a slip road into the primeval jam below.

Nobody jams like us. On Sukhumvit at the junction with Soi 4 the traffic is solid in four directions. There is a sentry box here for the traffic cops who are supposed to deal with the problem, but how do two underpaid cops move a million cars packed like mangoes for export? The cops are asleep behind their glass and the drivers have given up honking their horns. It is too hot and humid to honk. I spy our guns and holsters in a tangle at Pichai's feet, along with the radio and the portable siren to clamp on the roof when we finally go into action. I nudge Pichai.

"Better call him, tell him we lost the mark."

Pichai already has the monkish capacity to hear and understand whilst asleep. He groans, passes a hand through the condemned jet-black locks which I have always envied and bends double to retrieve the Korean short-wave radio. An exchange of static and the unsurprising intelligence that Police Colonel Vikorn, chief of District 8, cannot be located.

"Call him on his mobile."

Pichai fishes his own mobile out of a pocket and presses the autodial button. He speaks to our Colonel in terms too respectful for modern English to carry (somewhere between "sire" and "my lord"), listens for a moment, then slips the Nokia back in his pocket. "He's going to ask Traffic to cooperate. If the black *farang* shows up, Traffic will call us on the radio." I turn up the air-conditioning and wind the seat back. I try to practice the insight meditation I learned long ago in my teens and have practiced intermittently ever since. The trick is to catch the aggregates as they speed through the mind without grasping them. Every thought is a hook, and if we can only avoid those hooks we might achieve nirvana in one or two lifetimes, instead of this endless torture of incarnation after incarnation. I am interrupted by more static from the radio (I register *static, static, static* before emerging from the meditation). *Black* farang *in gray Mercedes reported stopped at Dao Phrya, on the slip road under the bridge.* Pichai calls the Colonel, who authorizes the siren.

I wait while Pichai slips out of the car, clamps the siren to the roof, where it flashes and wails to no effect on the gridlock, and walks over to the sentry box, where the traffic cops are dozing. At the same time he is strapping on his holster and gun and reaching in his pocket for his police ID. A more advanced soul than I, he gives no sign of the disgust he feels at being trapped in this pollution called life on earth. He would not wish to poison anyone else's mind. Nevertheless, he smacks his hand somewhat violently against the glass of the sentry box and yells at them to wake the fuck up. Smiles and a gentlemanly discussion before the boys in donkey brown (the uniform can appear bottle green in some lights) emerge to take charge. They come up to me in the car and there is the usual double-take when they see what I am. The Vietnam War left plenty of half-castes in Krung Thep, but few of us turned into cops.

There are several inches of slack within which every car can shunt, and our colleagues show considerable skill and cunning in making a space. In no time at all I am able to drive up onto the sidewalk, where the siren terrorizes the pedestrians. Pichai grins. I am skilled at very danger-ous driving from the days when we used to take drugs and steal cars together, a golden age which came to an end when Pichai murdered our *yaa baa* dealer and we had to seek refuge in the Three Jewels of the

Buddha, the dharma and the sangha. There will be time in this chronicle to explain *yaa baa*.

While I practice close encounters with cooked-food stalls, sex traders and oncoming traffic, wheel spins, split-second lurches and even one hand-brake spin, I try to remember what Dao Phrya Bridge is famous for. Why have I heard of it at all?

We are very happy. *Sabai* means feeling good and *sanuk* means having fun. We are both as we race toward the bridge in demonic haste, with Pichai chanting in Pali, the ancient language of the Gautama Buddha, for protection from accidents. He asks also of the Buddhist saints that we do not accidentally kill anyone who does not deserve it, a touchy point with Pichai.

Krung Thep means City of Angels, but we are happy to call it Bangkok if it helps to separate a *farang* from his money.

3

I remembered what Dao Phrya Bridge was famous for.

"Squatters, a whole village. They've been there for more than twenty years. They are all tribespeople from the northwest, Karen. They have a big still. Gambling and whisky are their main industries, with a little prostitution, begging and theft to make ends meet."

"They must pay protection. What district is it?"

I shrug. "Fourteenth, fifteenth?"

"The fifteenth is Suvit's. He's a bastard."

I nod. "He will be reborn as a louse in the anus of a dog."

"Not before he's spent eighty-two thousand years as a hungry ghost."

"Is it eighty-two?"

"That is the standard sentence for men like him."

I furrow my brow. Pichai's meditation is way ahead of mine, but his mastery of the scriptures is often shaky.

The gray Mercedes can be seen from the bridge as we pass over the canal, which surprises me. It is more than two hours since Traffic told us where it had been sighted, perhaps by one of the squatters. Why would a squatter call Traffic?

Like many things in my country, the slip road from the bridge to the riverbank peters out without contributing to the economy. It is just there, like us. I crunch to a halt on the gravel, which has abruptly replaced the tarmac, about thirty yards from the Mercedes, which is surrounded by men, women and children. They are hunched, ragged, and have automatically assumed the self-effacing postures of the poor when cops arrive. Some of them own the smeared eyes and crooked mouths of the permanently drunk. We will never know which one of them made the call. They will never tell us anything. They are my people.

Pichai gets out of the car first. He is still wearing his gun, which rides on his left buttock as I hurry to follow him, clipping on my own holster as we stride across the gravel toward the crowd, which makes way for us.

"What happened? What are you all staring at?" Not a murmur, not even a nod, but a woman in a torn T-shirt and sarong, barefoot, far advanced in alcoholic poisoning, raises her head toward the bridge and howls. At the same time I hear Pichai grunt in the way a brave man grunts when another might scream. Despite himself he steps back from the car, enabling me to see. I also grunt, but it is my way of muffling fear. I look at Pichai, who is a better shot than I. Pichai says: "Look at the door."

The Mercedes is a five-door elongated hatchback and someone has slipped a C-shaped piece of steel, of the kind used in reinforced concrete, over the handles of the front and rear doors on the driver's side. Anyone, even a child, could simply roll down the window, remove the crude device and escape, but it would take time, time to work out what was jamming the doors, time to roll down the window. It would also take a mind not clouded by terror.

Many Americans are afraid of snakes, even marines. The Vietcong used them as weapons in the tunnels of Cu Chi to great effect. This one, an enormous python, has wrapped itself around the black man's shoulders and neck and is trying to swallow his great head. I note that pythons do not normally shake like that, nor do they normally ride in Mercedes. Is the black man shaking the serpent, or vice versa?

I order the people to move away while Pichai takes out his gun. "The bullet might ricochet, it could go anywhere, go back under the bridge."

When they have done so Pichai crouches at the driver's window, but is unsatisfied with the angle of his shot. He does not want to hit the marine, who might still be alive, but how to tell if the glass will alter the trajectory of the bullet? He walks quickly and soberly around the car before returning to his original position. "Someone jammed the other doors as well."

He has mastered himself and I know what is going through his mind.

He has vowed to erase the appalling karma which must follow his murder of the *yaa baa* dealer by becoming a Buddhist saint, an *arhat*, in this lifetime. An *arhat* does not hesitate to lay down his life when duty so requires. An *arhat* masters fear.

He crouches, takes careful aim and fires. Good shot! Three-quarters of the python's head is blown away. Pichai slips the metal clip from the door and opens it, but the huge marine is top-heavy, with the snake now slack around his head, and falls onto the door, which is too much for Pichai to hold. Before I can rush to help, the marine and python have fallen onto my dear friend, pinning him to the ground. I assume that his scream is simply from fright as I go to him, at first not seeing (not believing) the small cobra which has attached itself passionately to his left eye. With a great wrench I drag him from under the marine, take out my gun and lay down beside him while he writhes with the cobra in one hand.

Another characteristic of *Naja siamensis* is that it never lets go. I shoot it through the throat and it is only then that I understand what Pichai is trying to explain through his agony. There are dozens of them, a virtual cascade, shivering strangely and spitting as they pour out of the car. One peeps between buttons on the black man's shirt, which is alive with undulations.

"Don't let them reach the people. Shoot them. They must have been drugged to shake like that."

He is telling me he is as good as dead, that there is no point radioing for help. Even if they sent a helicopter it would be too late. No one survives a cobra bite in the eye. Already the eye is the size of a golf ball and about to pop, and the snakes are approaching in a narcotic frenzy. Numb at that moment, I start to shoot them, becoming frenzied myself. I rush to the Toyota for more ammunition and change clips perhaps as many as seven times. With anguish contorting my features I lie in wait for the snakes which are trapped in the black man's clothes. One by one they writhe out of him and I shoot them on the ground. I am still shooting long after all the snakes are dead.

4

After we murdered the *yaa baa* dealer our mothers secured us an interview with the abbot of a forest monastery in the far north, who told us we were the lowest form of life in the ten thousand universes. Pichai had thrust the broken bottle into the jugular of humanity, and therefore of the Buddha himself, while I giggled. After six months of mosquitoes and meditation, remorse had gouged our hearts. Six months after that the abbot told us we were going to mend our karma by becoming cops. His youngest brother was a police colonel named Vikorn, chief of District 8. Corruption was forbidden to us, however. If we wanted to escape the murderer's hell we would have to be honest cops. More, we would have to be *arhat* cops. The abbot is undoubtedly an *arhat* himself, a fully realized man who voluntarily pauses on the shore of nirvana, postponing his total release in order to teach his wisdom to wretches like us. He knows everything. Pichai is with him now, while I am stranded here in the pollution called life on earth. I must try harder with my meditation.

5

I waited by the car for the van after covering Pichai with my jacket. A police cruiser came with the van and a team began collecting the dead snakes and taking video shots of the scene. It took four men to carry the python, which kept slipping from their shoulders until they learned to handle it. I sat with Pichai and the black American in the back of the van while it raced to the morgue and stood by while the attendants stripped my friend and I tried not to look at the left side of his face. The giant Negro lay nearby on a gurney, his naked body covered in soot-colored buboes and drops of water from melted ice which shone like diamonds under the lights. He wore three pearls in one ear, no earrings at all in the other.

I signed for the small plastic bag of Pichai's personal effects, which included his Buddha necklace and a larger bag of clothes, and went home to the hovel I rent in a suburb by the river. Under the rules I should have gone directly to the police station and begun to make my report, fill in forms, but I was too heartsick and didn't want to face the other cops with my grief. There had been much jealousy at the closeness of my friendship with Pichai.

The dharma teaches us the impermanence of all phenomena, but you cannot prepare yourself for the loss of the phenomenon you love more than yourself.

Pichai's cell phone ran out of prepaid units when I tried to call my mother from my room. There is no telephone in any of the rooms in my project, but on each floor, there is an office belonging to the management company where a telephone is available. Under the eye of the fat female clerk, who is addicted to shrimp-flavored rice puffs, I call my mother, who lives in the steaming plains about three hundred kilometers north of Krung Thep in a place called Phetchabun. She and Pichai's mother are former colleagues, close friends who retired to their hometown together, bought a plot of land and built two gaudy palaces on it; that is to say, the two-story houses with green-tiled roofs and covered balconies are palatial by country standards. While I wait I hear the *crunch-crunch-crunch* of Fat Som plowing through her puffs, and the burden of her attention is like a hundred sacks of rice on my shoulders, for she has seen my devastation.

I feel like a coward for not telling Pichai's mother myself, but I cannot face this chore or trust myself not to break down when I speak to her. Nong, my mother, will make a much better job of it than I.

I listen to the ringing tone on my mother's mobile telephone. She changes the model every two years because she always wants the smallest. Now she owns a Motorola so tiny she is able to keep it in her cleavage. I think about it ringing and vibrating between my mother's breasts. She always answers cautiously, never knowing if it will be a former lover, perhaps a *farang* from Europe or America, who has woken up in the middle of the night longing for her. The loneliness of *farangs* can be a fatal disease which distorts their minds and tortures them until they snap. When they begin to sink they grasp at any straw, even a Bangkok whore they had for a week on a sex vacation long ago.

My mother has been retired for more than ten years, but the calls still come from time to time. It is her own fault, because she always arranges for calls to her old mobiles to be patched forward to the new one. Maybe she is still waiting for that special call? Maybe she's addicted to the power she wields over desperate white men?

"Helloo?"

I tell her and for once she has nothing to say. I listen to her breathe, her silence, her love, this woman who sold her body to bring me up.

"I'm so sorry, Sonchai," she says finally. "You want me to tell Pichai's mother for you?"

"Yes, I don't think I could face her grief right now."

"Not as great as yours, my love. D'you want to come up? Stay with me a few days?"

"No. I'm going to kill the people who did it."

Silence. "I know you will. But be careful, darling. This thing seems very big. You'll come to the funeral, of course?"

I have thought about this on the way home from the morgue. "No, I don't think so."

"Sonchai?"

"Country funerals."

Pichai's body will sit in its decorated coffin under a pavilion in the grounds of the local wat, with a band playing funeral dirges all afternoon. Then at sundown the music will liven up, Pichai's mother will have succumbed to community pressure to throw a party. There will be crates of beer and whisky, dancing, a professional singer, gambling, perhaps a fight or two. Dealers will arrive on motorbikes, selling *yaa baa*. Worst of all will be the incinerator. In that remote place it looks like something from the early days of steam, with a long chimney, rusting, shaped just large enough to accommodate the coffin, with a tray for a wood fire underneath. The smell of Pichai's roasting flesh will fill the air for days. My soul brother's flesh is my flesh.

"They'll burn him in that thing, won't they?"

My mother sighs. "Yes, I expect so. Come up soon, darling. Or d'you want me to come down to you?"

"No, no, I'll come. After it's all over."

Fat Som is slack-jawed for once when I replace the receiver, a bunch of pink puffs half eaten between her teeth. She wants to say she is sorry, but doesn't know me well enough. The nature of her karma is that she cannot communicate feelings, because of some defilement from a previous lifetime, and is therefore condemned to be fat and resentful. She tries, though, with some futile wrinkling of the brow, which I do not acknowledge as I leave the room. I hear the telephone ringing in the office as I stride down the corridor, and think that Fat Som will have to finish her mouthful of puffs before she answers it. I am on the point of inserting my key into the padlock on my door, which so much resembles the door of a cell, when I hear her calling and, turning, see that she has emerged from her office and is rolling toward me breathlessly, her flesh rippling under her cotton dress. "It's for you."

Astonished, for nobody calls me here, I think that it is some mistake and that I will not take the call, but Fat Som is insistent. When I reenter the office she is weeping like a child. I wonder if perhaps my tragedy has snapped her karma, if she will be liberated now, if Pichai died an *arhat* after all and has the power to heal from where he waits on the shores of nirvana? I smile at her (for which she is almost unbearably grateful) as I pick up the receiver.

A man, an American, speaks English into my ear. "May I speak with Detective Sonchai Jipeecheap please?"

It takes me a moment to realize he has attempted to pronounce my family name. "Speaking."

My English is almost free from a Thai accent, although it contains shades of many others, from Florida to Paris, reflecting a childhood spent in the wake of my mother's career. I am told that when stressed I speak English with Germanic precision and a Bavarian accent. I will tell you about Fritz soon enough.

"Detective, I'm very sorry to be calling you at home at this time. My name's Nape, I'm the deputy FBI legal attaché at the American embassy in Wireless Road. We've just been contacted by a Colonel Vikorn who has informed us of the death of William Bradley, a Marine sergeant who was attached to the embassy here. We understand you are investigating?"

"That is correct." Shock has distorted my perspective. I wonder if this conversation is taking place on some other planet, or in hell, or even in one of the heavens? I have no sense of gripping this unreality.

"I understand your partner and close friend Detective Pichai Apiradee also died, and I want to extend my sincerest condolences."

"Yes."

"You probably know that under a protocol we have with the government of Thailand we have the privilege of access to information you may come by in your investigation of the death of American service personnel in such circumstances, and by the same token we would be willing to share FBI forensic resources with you. When would be convenient for you to come to the embassy to discuss information-sharing—or would you prefer we come to you?"

I want to laugh cynically at the thought of entertaining the FBI in my tiny hovel without chairs.

"I'll come, but you must give me a little time for the traffic."

"I understand, Detective. I'd offer to send a car, but I'm afraid that wouldn't solve the problem."

"No. I'll come. I'll come soon."

Without returning to my room I descend the concrete staircase to the ground floor. Outside, a makeshift shop leans against the wall of the building, with a long green awning which extends almost to the ground. Under the awning louts with many tattoos and almost as many earrings lounge on camp beds, smoking and drinking beer, their numbered jackets slung on the ground beside them. These are the licensed motorbike taxis, Krung Thep's most dangerous form of public transport, and its fastest.

"American embassy, Wireless Road," I snap at one of the louts, and kick the side of his camp bed. "Now."

The louts are local suppliers of *yaa baa*. They are intermittent users, too. From time to time I have toyed with the idea of busting them, but if I bust them someone else will take over the trade and perhaps expand it beyond the scope of these boys. Hit dirt with a stick and you will certainly spread it. Anyway, they buy a lot of their *yaa baa* from police confiscations, so there would be professional consequences for me. Colleagues would complain I'd taken the bread out of their children's mouths.

The motorcyclist whose bed I kicked jumps to attention and then runs to his bike, a 200 cc Suzuki, which must have been very sexy when new, with sculpted lines which run from the teardrop fuel tank to the upturned twin exhausts. Krung Thep has a way of punishing elegance, though, and it looks shabby now, with quite a few dents, mud on the footrests, rusting exhausts, a torn seat. The driver offers me a helmet but I refuse. Helmets for passengers are one of our many unenforceable laws; most people prefer the risk of head injury to the sensation of having one's brains boiled.

"You really in a hurry?" the kid asks.

I think about it. Not really, but anything to distract my mind, which is starting to implode. "Yes, it's an emergency." The kid's eyes gleam as he presses the start button.

I enjoy the ride because I'm sure the kid is on some drug or other—if not *yaa baa*, then ganja—and on quite a few occasions I am certain I am about to die and join Pichai sooner than expected. It is with disappointment and some surprise that I see the white walls of the American embassy as we turn off Phloen Chit, and find myself still in the prison of the body.

I pay the boy, then make his eyes widen when I say: "Get me some *yaa baa*. Come to my room tonight." Excited all over again, he makes wheel squeals as he rides away. Now I am face to face with a bronze eagle in a plaster medallion, a stainless steel turnstile and some heavily armed Thai cops lounging against the walls. I show my ID and tell them I have an interview with the FBI. This is relayed to the American behind the bulletproof glass at the turnstile, who takes my name and makes a call.

In meditation there is a point where the world literally collapses, providing a glimpse of the reality which lies behind. I am experiencing the collapse but not the salvation. The city falls and rebuilds itself over and over while I wait in the heat. I wonder if this is a message from Pichai? Meditation masters prepare us for the shock when we finally experience the fragility of the great out-there. It is supposed to be a very good sign, although for the untrained it presages certain madness.

Fritz was a bastard whom my mother and I both loved for a moment. The others were kinder but somehow we never managed to love them.

6

While I wait I remember the embassy was rebuilt in 1998, soon after the bombings of the American embassies in Kenya and Tanzania. The ambassador appeared on TV to explain, in not-bad Thai, that although America saw no threat from the Thai people, she feared those long porous borders with Cambodia and Myanmar where explosives and heavy armaments could be bought by just about anyone. Now the walls are massive reinforced concrete, capable of withstanding an assault by a ten-wheel truck, and if the truck did succeed in breaching the walls, there is a moat. In the twenty-first century the American ambassador works in a medieval castle. What is the karma of America?

Suddenly the American in the cabin, who might be a marine in plain clothes, decides to let me through the turnstile. One has to adjust to the jerkiness of *farangs*; this one has replaced his first jerk of suspicion with a jerk of hospitality. Through his microphone he says: "The Bureau is expecting you. D'you want to wait in here, in the air-conditioning?"

Something bleeps as I cross the threshold and I see a colorful image of myself and every metal object in my pockets displayed on a monitor on the desk. In the cabin I shiver at the blast of cold air. The young man at the desk, his hair so close-cropped he is almost bald, stares at the monitor for a moment, then asks me for my ID, the number of which he taps into his computer. I see my name appear on the screen. The marine grunts. "You've never been here before." This is not a question, it is what the computer says. "Next time we won't have to go through all this rigmarole." As he speaks he nods in the direction of the main buildings as if it were the rigmarole who is now walking mannishly toward us, a gigantic ID tag swinging from between her small breasts. Even from this distance I see that the rigmarole's name is Katherine White, deputy chief of security. About thirty, brunette, intense, athletic, frowning. I feel very Thai, despite my straw-colored hair and sharp nose.

"You have Detective, lemme see, Jiplecreap, for the FBI legal attaché?" Her voice is squeaky over the voice transmission system.

"Yep."

"I wasn't expecting him to be in there. Do I come in or do you bring him out? I forget which."

"I guess I can bring him out. Probably he could make it out all on his own."

The woman nods gravely. "Okay, let's do it."

The marine raises his eyebrows, I nod, the young man opens the door of the cabin and I step out onto the moon.

"You are Detective Jiteecheap of the Royal Thai Police? Can I see your ID please? Sorry about this, but I have to sign for you. Thanks." She establishes that I have not been substituted by someone else in the past five minutes and leads me across the forecourt toward the main buildings.

Katherine White is blithely unaware that she once accompanied me across a courtyard of startlingly similar dimensions, thousands of years ago. My Egyptian incarnation is the furthest I've been able to trace my lineage. A priest who abuses his power pays the heaviest karmic price. I spent three thousand years locked in stone before emerging as the most wretched slave in Byzantium. Pichai also recalled those far-off days when travel to the other side and back was commonplace. We occasionally relived those power-filled moments together: the escape from the body, the black night under our wings, the wonder of Orion.

7

Now I am standing in the office of the FBI legal attaché and his assistant, Jack Nape, who has just given me one of those gigantic smiles which are hard to believe in, and make one feel guilty for not believing in. Surely this is exactly how a man should be: positive, generous, optimistic, with a smile to swallow the world? He is average height for an American. I am tall for a Thai, so we are pretty much eye to eye.

"That was pretty fast. I wasn't expecting you for another hour."

"Bangkok helicopter." I look around the office. There are two desks of identical size facing each other next to a window, a computer monitor on each, a set of filing cabinets with an American football on one, bookshelves against one wall with a set of dark legal tomes, a sofa, a coffee table, some spare chairs against a wall, an American flag standing in a corner. I've seen this office before, surely, hundreds of times, in movies?

"Jack?" A voice calls out from behind a door. "That detective here?"

"Yep, just arrived."

A sound of water in a washbasin, and the door opens. This man is older, perhaps in his mid-forties, with graying hair, broad shoulders, a heavy walk as he crosses the floor with his hand out. "Congratulations, I don't think I've ever known anyone cross town so quickly. Tod Rosen. How d'you do it?"

"He got the Bangkok helicopter," Jack Nape says.

"Bangkok helicopter, huh?" Rosen looks uncertainly at Nape, who shrugs.

A moment of silence. Too late I realize I am supposed to explain. Unforgivably, I let the beat pass without doing so. Jack Nape comes to the rescue. "Could it have been a motorbike?"

"Yes," I say brightly.

Still Nape has to rescue the moment. He turns to Rosen. "Sounds crude but those motorbike taxis really do beat the traffic."

"Oh, right." Now I understand that Rosen is new to Krung Thep. "Whatever works, I guess. Great city, lousy traffic."

Again I miss the beat. Normally I do better than this. The problem is that suddenly I cannot look at a man without seeing a cobra gnawing at his left eye. I'm sure if I looked in a mirror I would see the same thing. This vision has wrecked my social skills.

"Well, ah, let's sit down, shall we? Can I get you a coffee?" I say no. I don't ever want to eat or drink again. "I want you to know how much we appreciate your coming to see us at a time like this," Rosen adds.

"That's right," Nape echoes. "If my partner had just been killed, I don't know how I'd feel."

"You'd feel pretty damn shitty."

"I guess so." Nape shakes his head in wonder. I swivel my head from one to the other.

"Not that we don't feel badly ourselves."

"That's right."

"I didn't know Sergeant Bradley personally, but I hear he was a fine man."

"A fine man, a great marine and a fine athlete."

"Served all over the world, mostly on security in embassies."

"We haven't told his buddies yet. There's gonna be some very sore marines when they hear what happened."

"That's right."

Both men peer at me for a moment, then Rosen says, "Damned cuts." He looks at Nape.

"Yep." Nape shakes his head.

"If this had happened in the seventies, a charter jumbo would have

left Washington already with ten Bureau investigators and a mobile forensic lab."

"If it had happened in the eighties we would at least have gotten five
agents on a scheduled flight."

"Right. Now what do we get?"

Nape looks at me. "Tod's been on the telephone yelling at Washington ever since we got the news."

"Not that it's doing me much good."

"What's the score now, Tod? How many do we get to investigate the
violent death of a loyal long-term serviceman?" Rosen holds up his index
finger and makes a face of exaggerated misery. "One? I can't believe it."

"Of course, if it looked like terrorism, that would be different."

Suddenly they are both looking at me with curiosity and intensity.
I admire the way they have come to the point so quickly. Who says
Americans are not subtle?

"I understand."

For some reason this statement surprises them. "You do?"

"If it's not terrorism, it must be the other thing, no?"

Nape sighs with relief while Rosen looks stonily at the floor. When he
looks up again it is with a smile so false it is almost offensive. "The other
thing?"

Nape and I exchange glances. Rosen really is very new and Nape
wants to apologize, but there is no opportunity. Rosen is expecting me to
answer his question. It seems that we're done with subtlety. I wait for
Nape's nod before I proceed.

"Bradley was in his mid-forties," I begin.

"Forty-seven," Nape confirms, clearly hoping that will be enough
explanation, but Rosen is still staring at me.

"Close to retirement?"

"He had almost exactly one year to go."

"Perhaps he had been here awhile?"

"Five years. Much longer than normal, but he fitted in."

"Liked the city?"

"He was a very private man, but the word is, yes, he loved it."

"Enjoyed a privileged lifestyle and intended to stay after retirement?"
I raise my eyes.

Finally, Rosen gives a nod of recognition. "I guess we're thinking
along the same lines, Detective. I just wanted to be sure. You think he
double-crossed his wholesalers, huh?"

"That would be the first hypothesis."

"You ever hear of them doing it with snakes before?"

"Actually, no. Never. But it is not unusual for an aggrieved party to make an example of the source of his grievance. *Pour encourager les autres.*" I did not mean to be pretentious. The French came to the top of my head as it does from time to time. I am relieved that Rosen smiles.

"That's a pretty good accent. I did a stint in Paris myself. 'To encourage the others.' Yep, it sure looks like that, doesn't it?" He shakes his head. "One hell of a way for a man to die, though." He's looking at me: Who is this half-caste Third World cop who speaks English and French? Nape has guessed. He is an old hand in Krung Thep. Just a tinge of Anglo-Saxon contempt in his expression now, for the son of a whore.

All of a sudden Rosen gets up, talking as he moves. "To tell you the truth, I don't know how hard Washington wants to push this one. They're sending a woman out—a special agent—but it might be just for appearances. How's a special agent with no Thai and no knowledge of the city supposed to investigate something like this?" Half to himself: "Maybe she screwed up Stateside and they're moving her sideways. In the meantime, though, in the interests of information-sharing, I want to ask you how you think this might fit with your hypothesis. We found it in his locker. There was nothing else of any interest, only this."

He goes to his desk, unlocks a drawer, comes back with a ball of newspaper. As he unravels the ball I notice the newspaper is in a foreign script. Not Thai and not English. Under the newspaper, a brown and black piece of rock roughly the shape of a pyramid about six inches high. I peer at the rock, then use a piece of the newspaper to hold it up and turn it over. Most of the rock is covered in mud, lichen and jungle scum, but there are some scrape marks on the bottom of it, exposing a greenish tint of core.

"Jade. The scrape marks are from potential buyers testing the hardness." I examine the newspaper. "Laotian script, very close to Thai but not the same."

"Can you read the date?"

"No."

"Okay, we'll make a copy and e-mail it to Quantico. We should have an answer in a couple of days."

"May I also have a copy?"

Nape takes the newspaper and goes off to get copies. Rosen and I look at each other. I say: "Did Bradley have an apartment in the city?"

Rosen rubs the back of his ear with his thumb. "Long-termers gener-ally rent a room or even an apartment, usually for R and R purposes, even though officially they live at the embassy. The only condition is that they tell us where it is. Bradley filed an address on Soi 21 off Sukhumvit, but when we checked a couple of hours ago, we discovered he hadn't been there for four years." I digest this in silence. "So I guess we don't know where he lived." I nod while Rosen looks away, toward the football on the filing cabinet. "If I received hints that Washington doesn't really want too deep an investigation . . ."

I shrug. "Detective Pichai Apiradee was my soul brother." This infor-mation apparently does not answer Rosen's question. I try again. "I'm going to kill whoever did it. There won't be a trial."

Fortunately, at that moment Nape returns with the photocopies, one of which he hands to me, the other to Rosen, whose mouth is hanging open. I stand up and force a smile. "How about a wager, gentlemen? A thousand baht says that I will find out the date of the newspaper before you do."

Nape grins and shakes his head. "Not me. I know you'll win."

Rosen looks at him as if he has committed treason. "Bullshit. I'll tell them it's urgent. We'll have an answer by five tonight, Thai time."

At least I've found a way of closing the interview with reasonable ele-gance. Nape accompanies me to the gate of the embassy and returns me safely to Thailand. The big smile has gone from his face. He looks older in the cloying heat, less pure. As we stand on either side of the turnstile, he licks his lips and says: "You're gonna snuff 'em, aren't you?" I stare at him for a moment, then turn to look for a motorbike taxi. It is two minutes before 3 p.m.

Monsieur Truffaut was probably my favorite. We were unable to love him because he was so old, but with hindsight it is clear that of all of them, he alone gave more than he took. He gave us Paris, after all, and a smattering of French.

8

I told the kid on the bike to take me to Nana Entertainment Plaza, a short ride away. It was eleven minutes past 3 p.m. when we arrived, and the plaza was still sleeping off the night before.

Pichai would always make fun of the way I could not stand to work Vice. I guess his background didn't affect him the way it affected me, but just now, with the courtyard mostly empty and the three tiers of bars, short-time hotels and brothels quiet in the hot afternoon, I appreciated the feeling of familiarity that came over me. I may not like it, as someone may not like the street where they were brought up, but there's no denying the depth of understanding, the knowledge, the intimacy. Maybe on such a black day this was the one place that might bring some relief?

A few girls were already hanging out at the street-level bars, chatting about the night before, comparing stories of the men who paid their bar fines and took them back to their rooms, moaning about the ones who just flirted and groped, then disappeared without buying them a drink. I knew how they liked to talk about the quirks of *farangs* whose preferences can be so different from our own. Great macho men who only want to suck big toes, or even be whipped. Men who cry and talk about their wives. Men who, fully clothed, look like the very best the West has to offer, yet somehow collapse at the sight of a naked brown girl waiting on a hotel bed. I knew every story, every nuance, every trick of the trade in which I have never partaken, not once, not even when Pichai went through his whoring phase. I paused to watch the girls coming to work, each of whom raised her hands in prayer to her forehead in order to mindfully *wai* the Buddha shrine which stands festooned with marigolds and orchids in the north corner of the courtyard, and I could not help thinking of my mother; then I climbed the stairs to the second tier.

I was looking for one of the larger bars which had already opened their doors and found Hollywood 2, one of its double doors propped open with a wastebin, houselights bright inside while women in overalls wiped the tables and mopped the floors. The aroma of pine cleaning fluid blended with stale beer, cigarettes and cheap perfume. There was a big two-level turntable with stainless steel uprights for the girls to cavort around while it turned, but it was empty and motionless at that time. I walked in and knew that the woman who was replenishing the beers on the shelves behind one of the bars was the mamasan who organizes the girls, advises them on every aspect of the trade, even the most intimate, who listens to their problems, helps them when they fall pregnant or contemplate suicide. She would tell the girls to walk out if the client refused to use a condom, and to demand extra for unusual services—or decline (Italians, French and Americans especially are known for their sodomizing ways). A good mamasan looks ahead to when the girls will have to retire in their mid-thirties, if not before; some of them even teach the girls English and pay for secretarial courses, although such enlightenment is rare. It was not enlightenment which shone from this woman's eyes: broad, tough, about fifty with a nut-brown face and a permanent scowl.

"We shut. Come back sik o'clock."

She had taken me for a *farang*. "I'm a cop," I said in Thai, flashing my ID. A change of attitude, but not much.

"What you want, Khun Cop? The boss pays protection, you can't hassle me."

"This isn't a bust."

She looked around for more cops. Finding none, she sneered. "The girls aren't ready yet. The ones upstairs are still asleep and the others haven't arrived. Why have you come so early? You want a free fuck, just because you're a cop? What if my boss tells his protector?"

"I just want a favor."

"Sure. Every man wants a favor."

"I want a Lao girl."

She smirked. "Lao girl? We got thirty percent Lao girl. What kind you want? Tall, short, big tits, small tits—no blondes, though." She cackled at her own joke. "No blond Laos here. If you want blonde you got to have Russian."

"I want one who can read and write. Actually, read is good enough."

"You mean not a tribeswoman straight out of the jungle—we have a few of those, like all the bars do." She frowned. "What you up to, Khun Cop?"

"Can you help, yes or no?"

The mamasan shrugged and yelled out the name of a girl. Someone yelled back, and a young woman appeared dressed in a white towel tucked under her arms, her long brown legs ending in bare feet. "Get Dou, she's in room three," the mamasan told her.

Ten minutes later Dou appeared in a cotton frock, a pleasant-faced young woman about twenty years old, with a broad, friendly smile and a thick Laotian accent. She was excited, thinking me an early customer. I smiled back, showed her a hundred-baht note and the photocopy Nape gave me. She scanned it quizzically. "I only want to know the date on it."

She made big eyes. This was the easiest hundred baht she had ever earned. "2539 May 17." She read it off in the order in which it was printed.

"Thanks." I handed over the hundred baht.

I told the mamasan to dig out her telephone, which she produced from behind the bar. In my head I worked out the year in the Christian era; *farangs* never like to realize we are five hundred years ahead of them.

Rosen had given me his business card with his mobile telephone number. I dialed the number and when he answered said: "May 17, 1996."

A pause. "If Quantico confirms, I owe you a thousand." Another pause. "Did you say 1996?"

I confirmed and hung up. It was 3:31 p.m.

Out on the street I made my way through the heat to the sky train station, past stalls selling rip-offs of designer handbags, T-shirts, jeans, shorts, swimwear. This stretch of stalls was owned and run by deaf-mutes who communicated across the pavement in their vivacious sign language as I passed. There were illegal copies of CDs, DVDs, videos and tapes, too. The whole street is a mecca for anyone seriously interested in law enforcement, but the deaf-mutes never seem to worry.

9

Like a lot of people, I'm a fan of the sky train on the rare occasions when it's of any use to me. The logic of the system is unimpeachable: to beat the traffic, rise above it. It was one of those ventures founded on foreign capital and foreign expertise for which our politicians developed a suspicious passion. For what felt like decades whole sections of the city's roads were clogged or shut off while armies of men and women in yellow plastic hats built their concrete pillars and their state-of-the-art elevated tracks. Now the project is complete in its first phase and the gigantic city has swallowed it up as if it weren't there at all. We all scratched our heads. All that for only two lines?

Riding it is a distinct pleasure, though. You get a great view of the city from a flying compartment with glacial air-conditioning. It's also a study in bankruptcy if you take note of the great skeletons of unfinished high-rises that loom out of the chaos from time to time, monuments to a building frenzy that chilled with the Asian financial crisis in 1998 and never heated up again. Now these new Stonehenges are home to beggars and bag people. From the train you can see their hammocks, their dogs and their washing in the honeycombs of concrete caves, sometimes a monk meditating in his saffron robes. Even though a taxi would have been cheaper, I ride the train all the way to Saphan Taksin and get a boat to take me the rest of the way up the Chao Phraya River to Dao Phrya Bridge. The river is noisy and busy with barges and longtail boats and I cannot help but remember the fun we used to have on it, Pichai and I . . .

It is early evening by the time I reach the bridge. The Mercedes is cordoned off by means of iron stakes and orange tape, guarded by two young constables who sit on the car, one on the hood, the other on the roof. The one on the hood sits cross-legged and stares as I approach. I snap at him to get off the car and look like a real policeman. Now the two cops are scrambling to *wai* me, placing their palms together mindfully near their foreheads and bowing. "How long have you been here?"

"Eight hours."

"Anybody come to take statements from the squatters under the bridge?"

The boys shake their heads. I make a quick tour of the car, looking in from the outside only. I notice that the back seat has been folded to make a clear flat surface from the hatchback door to the backs of the front seats. A cell phone lies abandoned on the floor by the front passenger seat. Nevertheless, the car will have to wait. The car will not deteriorate as fast as people's memories.

The wasteland between the Mercedes and the squatter huts is intermittently illuminated by lights from traffic passing overhead. Under the bridge, there is a homely glow from electric lights crudely hooked up to the power cables which run under the arch. People are sitting on bamboo mats eating. There are some brilliantly lit cooking pots with women squatting over them, men dressed only in shorts sitting cross-legged on the ground and playing cards, drinking from plastic cups. There are a couple of televisions, too, flickering with their ever-changing images on trestle tables on which women are preparing food.

I cross the wasteland and squat beside one of the circles of men, who take no notice of me. A stack of banknotes waits beside each man, held down by a stone. I pick up one of the plastic cups and sniff. Rice moonshine. I look around to try to locate the still. I guess it will be in one of the larger huts, lost in darkness further under the bridge.

"Tell me, brother, who is the headman?"

The card player grunts, and nods toward a large hut. I walk over, knock on the door. I smell the heavy, sweet odor of fermented rice cooking. An aggressive yell from inside the hut, to which I reply: "Please open the door, brother."

The door opens and a balding man in his fifties stands there. Behind him, the massive terra-cotta urn standing over a small charcoal fire, a pipe sticking out three-quarters of the way up, an aluminum dish full of water covering the urn. The alcohol would condense on the underside of the dish, be caught and drip out through the pipe. The pipe leads to a crude cloth filter. I show my police ID.

The man shrugs. "We pay protection."

"I'm sure. And for the gambling?"

"No one gambles here."

I nod gravely. "Who do you pay your protection to?"

The man draws himself up straight. "Police Colonel Suvit, superintendent of District 15."

"That's good. Do you think the Colonel would like to be investigated by the American FBI?"

"The who?"

"I come in peace, but I need your help. I'm not going to write anything down. An American was murdered today, a black *farang*."

"He died of snake bites. It happens."

"Murdered. The snakes also killed my soul brother, the detective who was my partner."

The man looks me up and down with more interest, now that a matter of the heart has been mentioned. "Your soul brother? I'm sorry. You're going to avenge him?"

"Of course."

"I think you'll have trouble. I wasn't here, but I've heard a gang came. Young men on motorbikes."

"Who says so?"

"Old Tou. He was sitting smoking when the car arrived, followed by the motorbikes."

"I have to speak to Old Tou."

The headman struggles with a smirk. "I think you'll have trouble." He beckons for me to follow and we trudge over the uneven ground to the least well-appointed of all the huts. Some thatch made of leaves on a bamboo frame rests on walls of battered aluminum steamer trunks no higher than four feet. I have to wonder if a truck dropped the trunks over the bridge one fine day, when Tou was young. "Help me."

I help him lift the entire roof and set it on the ground. Between the walls an old man, gaunt and gray, snores from deep in his throat. "Too much moonshine," the headman says, as if speaking of a noxious substance beyond his knowledge. "Want me to wake him?" The headman pulls away one of the trunks and kicks Old Tou in the calf without interrupting the snoring. He tries a few kicks to the rump, each one harder than the last, before I say: "That's enough." We replace the old man's roof. "When does he wake up, if ever?"

"He generally appears about midday—that's when he starts on the moonshine. He carries on drinking until he's like this. I guess he'll be dead soon."

"I'll come back tomorrow at noon. I want him sober—don't give him any moonshine. Okay?" The man nods, a slight smile on his face. "Didn't anyone else see anything?" The headman looks away, toward the canal. "Ask them." He waves a hand toward the groups of card players and the women squatting over their cooking pots. I know it is hopeless. Only a drunk who expected to die within the week might tell the truth to the police. I start back toward the road. "Make sure he's sober," I tell the headman. "I don't think your Colonel Suvit wants a team of FBI agents crawling over the place, checking on the moonshine and the gambling—and the *yaa baa*."

"Nobody here does *yaa baa*," the headman says reproachfully. "That's a killer drug."

I take a cab to the river and ride back to my project in a small longtail boat empty except for me, the boatman and two monks; we roar past other longtails and rice barges almost invisible in the night. I let the monks go first when we arrive, watching the older one carefully arrange his robes so they do not catch as he clambers onto the ancient wooden jetty which lies in darkness except for a single gas lamp blazing from one of the woodpiles. The monks pass through this magic circle of white light and disappear into the darkness beyond. I walk on unpaved paths between squatter settlements until I reach my project.

The kid is there lounging under the awning, but one of his friends speaks to him when he sees me coming. The kid immediately jumps up and follows me into the building. I pay him twelve hundred baht for three *yaa baa* pills, even though he offers to give me them for free. I tell him I'm not that kind of cop as I hand over the money. Outside, there is a roar of a bike more powerful than anything the motorbike chauffeurs own, and

the kid and I both step out. The kid's jaw drops at this vision of an equivalent tribesman from the distant future. The rider is all in black leather
with upholstered knee and shoulder pads and a tinted full-face helmet
that looks like he bought it this morning, on a 1,200 cc Yamaha that
probably does a hundred in second gear. His back bears the Day-Glo
insignia of Federal Express. He doesn't need to say anything as he gets off
the bike and pulls off his helmet, he *is* the man. A little of his glory rubs off
on me when he makes it clear that I'm the reason he's here.

The bubblepack I sign for is A4 size and comes from the United
States Embassy. Inside, a thousand-baht note wrapped around a Motorola
cell phone with its battery charger and manual and six three-by-five photos of Bradley. On the back of one of his cards Rosen had written: "Date
confirmed. Figured you and I would both benefit from the cell phone
and I guess you forgot to ask for the pix. The new help arrives tomorrow.
Keep the phone with you. Tod."

The kid says: "Check how many units it's got." I don't know how to do
that so I give it to him. He presses a few buttons and shrugs. "Only eight
hundred baht. Don't call San Francisco." I try to kick him but miss as he
walks back to his sun bed.

10

Back in my room, the desolation hits me like a brick in the face. I stand in front of my picture of His Beloved Majesty the King and burst into tears.

Why did Pichai decide to ordain? While he was alive I never asked myself this question, his progress on the Path seemed so natural, like a tree growing. And yet, even in Thailand it is not common to lose a cop to Buddha. Now that I am looking back at his life I see the pattern.

Sons of whores learn about manhood from our mothers, especially *farang* manhood. For my mother the *farang* was a Discovery Channel of exotic foreign travel, cuisine so mysteriously bland you had to concentrate to taste anything at all, and above all a great experiment in psycho-sexual manipulation which she perfected to a form of high art, eventually achieving through an almost imperceptible alteration of tone the kind of cash bonus that in lesser practitioners would have required at least a tantrum.

Not so Wanna. More traditionally Thai than Nong, Pichai's mother went to work in the bars soon after dumping Pichai's Thai father for being a "butterfly" (a technical expression amongst our women meaning he screwed anything that moved). She vomited the first time she slept with a *farang* and beheld that whacking great erection more suitable for a female water buffalo than a woman, and never really developed her skills to their full potential. Nong teased her that she belonged to the "dead body" school of seduction. Not that it mattered. Petite with pale flesh that was a gourmet delight to the touch, Wanna was—still is—exquisite to look at, and your *farang* is a sucker for the visuals.

Pichai divided his mother's customers into Masters and Slaves. What was peculiar, in his eyes, and gave rise to a profound doubt as to the soundness of the *farang* mind, was that his mother never altered her attitude of unconquerable indifference. A White Master who sought to protect her and dominate her (with assurances that her life was now saved) she rewarded with exactly the same shortlist of grunts and moans as a White Slave who would declare himself on the brink of salvation when she permitted him—quite literally—to lick her ass.

As her English improved she reported back to Pichai the substance of her customers' love babble. To look for nirvana in someone's crotch, now that really is dumb. For Pichai the horror was that these spiritual dwarfs were taking over the world. I think it was the profound disillusionment which arose from these insights that drove him onto the Path. He had about him the noble soul's willingness to act on even its most bitter perceptions; unlike me, he was never afraid to slash at the bonds, once he saw them for what they were. Maybe he didn't love me as much as I loved him?

11

Don't ask me when I first mastered the obvious. Here I am back on Sukhumvit in an Internet café, having tapped out "Bradley/jade" on the AltaVista search engine. The web site is called "Fatima and Bill's Jade Window" and consists of a black background with white text, a slowly turning jade artifact in an oval in the center of the screen. One William Bradley confesses to being owner of the site.

The artifact is a parabolic phallus which glows softly with a green-gold light, a perfectly balanced shape rising from crude rock, tapering elegantly until it reaches a smoothly polished head. There is nothing more to Bradley's web page except an e-mail address and a short text extolling the mystic qualities of jade. The same text appears in Thai, above the English.

It is the finest penis I have ever seen, whether in stone or flesh. Now Bradley is beginning to intrigue me. Jade is the most spiritual of stones. Properly worked and polished, it gives a mystic glow which seems to come from its heart, an echo of nirvana. How would an American marine understand such a thing? True jade lovers tend to be Chinese.

It is easy to trace the Internet service provider, who is based on the other side of town, in Kaoshan Road, but it is three minutes to midnight on the day of Pichai's death and I need to drown myself in people. In the narrow *soi* outside the Internet café tarot readers sit cross-legged over the cards which their clients—invariably anxious girls who are not having much luck tonight—have drawn. I walk smartly past them to Nana Plaza, which is transformed. I cannot believe that Bradley was not a regular here, and who would forget a man like him?

"Handsome man, I want to go with yooo," a girl in a black tank top calls as she leans over the palisade of the first bar, when I'm turning into the Nana courtyard from Soi 4. The plaza is flooded with white men and brown girls. Australians with guts so huge they look about to give birth stand grinning with arms around girls no bigger than their legs. Americans reminisce loudly about the night before, Germans keep saying *ja, ja* and Dutch walk around like old hands. There are plenty of East Europeans and Russians, too; Siberia is directly north of my country, and ever since the fall of the USSR there has been a steady stream of men and women with pale skins and heavy vodka habits. The men come to buy and the women to sell.

"I don't like work here, but papa me have car accident, must send money," a girl is saying to a tall, skinny Englishman. "Oh, that's awful," he says, as he pats her butt.

The atmosphere is something between a festival and a hunting lodge. It's that time in the evening when the girls make an extra effort, before the 2 a.m. curfew when the cops close the place down, and the men sense the increase in intensity, like wildebeests sniffing lion. Everyone is drinking Singha or Kloster beer ice cold straight from the bottle, and wherever you look there are television monitors. Larry King's suspenders scream from a lot of them. Even the guy who sells fried grasshoppers from a stall near the Buddha shrine owns a TV monitor on which he plays old Muhammad Ali fights and scenes from the siege of Stalingrad. Mostly, though, the screens show Manchester United playing Leeds to the boom of every kind of music from a thousand speakers.

I squeeze past some excited Italian men to climb the stairs to the second tier, which is a U-shaped collection of go-go bars looking down on the courtyard. As I pass each bar a curtain is whipped aside to show naked or near-naked girls dancing on elevated platforms, usually to Thai pop. Girls in bikinis try to drag me in, but I'm focused now on the Carousel, which is one of the biggest.

There are two revolving platforms, and all the girls dancing on them are naked. At one of the stand-up bars a *farang* is arguing with a girl in traditional Thai costume.

"I tell you I tired, no have power mek boom-boom."

The man cocks an eye at me, then back to the girl. "And may I ask why you are so tired tonight?" The accent is Swiss German. With a twist of his head the man adds: "Why do I torture myself with such questions?"

I order a beer and watch the girl pull a sulky face. Gaunt and petite, about twenty-four, although to a *farang* she might seem sixteen. She catches my gaze and shrugs: *farangs* never understand anything.

"She was probably looking after her baby all night," I offer. Bar girls are rarely exhausted by twenty minutes of sex with a customer. The *farang*'s eyes brighten.

"You have a child?" To me: "She never told me this."

Don't ask me why, but almost all the girls have one child, usually at age eighteen.

"Of course I have baby."

I watch the Swiss. Perhaps he took the girl out a couple of nights ago, made love to her casually—and finds himself haunted by her. His calculations so far have had to do with the practicalities of taking her back to Switzerland: the envy of his friends set against the disapproval of his mother; the pleasure of her body beside him every night against the social problem. And what about table manners? She probably sits cross-legged on most chairs and eats with a combination of fork, spoon and fingers.

As she turns the back of her head to me, I smile. Most of the girls are forever wrestling with their thick black hair. Often they tie it back in a ponytail, and a lot of them have taken to ripping the rings off condoms and using them as heavy-duty elastic bands, which is exactly what this girl has done; not a trick likely to win approval at the dinner tables of Zurich.

Now the Swiss has to factor in a child. But perhaps the child would not come with her?

"How old? Boy or girl?"

"Boy, him six." She beams proudly.

The Swiss looks at me with suspicion. "You know this girl?"

"Never seen her before." The Swiss is in his late thirties, balding and hurt. His face carries all the pain of a recent failure. Why has he come to Bangkok? To demonstrate continuing virility? For the simplicity of hired flesh? Now, within less than a week of landing, he is planning a relationship far more complicated than anything he's tried before.

"At least let me pay your bar fine and take you out to dinner," he tells the girl. "I want to talk to you. I want to know something."

"What you want to know?"

He stares at her, blinking self-consciously behind his thick spectacles. "I want to know why I've been thinking about you for the past forty-eight hours."

The girl brightens. "You think of me? Me too, I think of you." Not a bad performance. Nong would have made more of the moment, though, I reflect loyally. My mother still possesses the trick of projecting instant warmth. She would never have allowed herself to get as skinny as this girl, who looks like a *yaa baa* fiend, nor would she have been so slow to see an opportunity for an overseas trip.

I give the man a congratulatory nod. You wanted her, now you've got her. What more could one possibly ask of life?

I take a photograph of Bradley out of my pocket and watch while the mamasan tells the Swiss how much he has to pay for the beer and the girl.

"It's strange the way they call it a bar *fine*," he shares with me, "as if one is doing something wrong."

When the Swiss has paid up the mamasan takes his five-hundred-baht note and brushes all her girls with it, for luck. I nod to the mamasan to come over. She looks at the picture. Not a man one could easily forget: huge, black, shaved head, good bone structure, a pleasant mouth and a brilliant smile. American, not African. No, she's never seen him before, she's sure she would have remembered, but she's not been here all that long.

Turnover of labor is going to be a problem. Bradley was in Bangkok five years and had probably made his own private arrangements with women a long time ago. Men grow tired of Nana surprisingly quickly. Girls come and go.

I doggedly try all the bars, showing Bradley's picture to mostly older mamasans who look as if they've been around for a while. No one remembers Bradley and I'm tiring by the time I return to the Carousel. The huge bar is packed with the usual collection of Caucasian men and Asian women. On a TV monitor on a wall bracket two white women are serving a gigantic black phallus. On the big screen which covers one wall Manchester United are playing Real Madrid. Those girls who are not attending to a client are watching the football. There's a yell of female approval as Beckham scores from an impossible angle for the second time in five minutes.

All the men are watching the show on the largest revolving stage, where a woman in her early forties, naked except for a pair of cowboy boots, lies on the floor shooting darts from an aluminum tube she has inserted in her vagina. Customers hold up balloons for her to hit, and she rarely misses. Her name is Kat, a friend of my mother who lived with us for a while when I was young. When her act is over she makes a tour of the bar, still naked but holding a cowboy hat upside down for tips. The hat is full with twenty-, fifty- and hundred-baht notes by the time she reaches me. I toss a fifty into the hat.

"Can I talk to you backstage?"

She smiles. "I have another show at the Hollywood in twenty minutes. Come round to the changing room as soon as I've finished here."

I watch her finish her tour, which she completes with great dignity, as if she were doing a job of work as valid as brain surgery—or law enforcement. As soon as she has disappeared through the artistes' door, I follow, pushing my way through a crowd of naked women who are waiting to go on. By the time I reach the changing room Kat is already dressed in jeans and T-shirt, a tiny pack on her back, that same professional expression on her face.

"How is your mother? I keep meaning to visit, but Phetchabun is so far away."

"Five hot hours in the bus. I don't go as often as I should myself." I take the photograph of Bradley out of my pocket and hold it up. I'm sure I see a flash of recognition before the inscrutable professional mask returns. "You know him?"

She purses her lips, shakes her head. "No, I don't think so. I'm sure I would have remembered a face like that."

I put the photo back in my pocket. "That's what everyone is saying, everywhere I go."

"What happened, did he murder someone?"

"The other way around."

A tensing of her facial muscles. "Ah! An American?"

"A marine."

"Then the FBI will be all over the city. You can sit back and relax, let them do all the work."

"They have to work in conjunction with me. They don't have any investigative rights in Thailand."

"You could have fooled me. I thought America bought the country years ago, it's just that no one's told us yet. Well, you must excuse me, Sonchai, fame and fortune await me at the Hollywood."

I follow her out of the dressing room and back down the corridor full of breasts and buttocks. I continue to follow her out of the bar onto the terrace and call her name. She turns and I make a face. Her features harden, but she delves into her black backpack and takes out a card. Without looking at me she scribbles an address on the card and gives it to me. She turns to smile. "I live way out in the sticks these days—city rents were killing me." She walks quickly away from me.

The card is printed in Thai and English and reads: "Kat Walk Enterprises, Private Entertainment, Floor Shows, Cabaret with a Difference." There is a telephone number which carries the local prefix and is probably that of her agent, and her web page address. The address she has scribbled on the back is of a very distant suburb, hardly Krung Thep at all.

I walk along the balcony which looks over the courtyard. The bar on the corner is dedicated to transsexuals, who like to make up in public at mirrors on a table on the balcony. I catch a glimpse of a long feminine neck, softly molded moon face, hard bitchy eyes as I slip past and down the stairs to the courtyard. There are so many half-naked bodies now, white male and brown female, it is difficult to move. "Hello darlin', how are you? Are you lonely?" It is one of the transsexuals, full-bosomed and pouting. I shake my head.

Lonely? An incurable state, unfortunately. I push past sweat-drenched T-shirts to the street, consider with weariness the task which lies ahead. Nana Plaza is only the seed at the center of the mango; there are thousands of bars in side *sois* and disused lots in every direction, particularly on the other side of Sukhumvit all the way to Asok, which is to say one stop on the sky train: about five acres of brown flesh for rent to a similar quantity of white. East meets West. How can I disapprove when I owe my existence to this conjunction?

It is forty-one minutes past 1 a.m., hot, muggy. With resignation I take one of the *yaa baa* pills from my pocket. I've lost touch with the market, but as far as I can remember the blue pills tend to be laced with heroin and give a pleasant, opiated high. The crimson ones are mixed with fertilizer and produce a lot of energy at the expense of making you more than a little crazy, with a poisonous hangover the next day.

I return to the plaza to order a bottle of Singha beer, which I use to swallow the pill. It's crimson. There's a lot of night left.

12

They came from the north and the south, the east and the west. Krung Thep was not only the biggest city, until recently it was the only modern city we had. They came from the plains and the hills. Most were ethnic Thai but many were tribespeople from the north, Muslims from the south, Khmer who sneaked over from Cambodia, and plenty were technically Burmese who lived on the border and never paid it any mind. They were part of the greatest diaspora in history, the migration of half of Asia from country to town, and it was happening at an accelerated speed during the last third of the twentieth century. Men with iron muscles and the dogged heroism of unmechanized agricultural labor, women with bodies ravaged by continual pregnancies, they possessed in full measure all the guts, all the enthusiasm, all the naïveté, all the hope, all the desperation necessary to make it in the big city. The only thing they left out of account was time, of which they knew very little apart from the rhythms of nature. The sadistic vivisection of life into hours, minutes, seconds was one of the few hardships never inflicted by the soil. Deadlines, especially, were the source of a new kind of anxiety. Stress? Its urban version was strange, alien, insidious and something they had no way of dealing with. *Yaa baa* was a poison whose time had come.

The fishing industry was the first to succumb. No longer a question of bringing fish to predawn markets for people to take home and cook, these days the fight to net the fish was only the first step in a semi-industrial process that required critical timing to ice it, pack it, freight it; the most lucrative fish were those kept alive and flown to restaurants in Japan and Hong Kong, Vancouver and San Francisco. The job of scaling fish for local restaurants was another of those peculiarly stressful tasks which had to be completed between 1 and 5 a.m., just when your body rhythms told you it was time to sleep. The job couldn't be done without *yaa baa*.

Truck drivers were next. The brave new world required nonstop driving the length and breadth of the country, with Bangkok as a hub, and sometimes interminable journeys down south, over the border and down through Malaysia as far as Kuala Lumpur—a journey of more than a thousand miles. Nobody thought of doing it without *yaa baa*. Construction workers, too, felt the call. Hard work was not the problem, it was the pressure, the deadlines, the relentless weight of money that pressed on all projects, the night work, the dangers at high levels, welding with gas at night on the thirtieth floor of some new office or luxury apartment building. Safety regulations were primitive and not well enforced, you had to stay awake to stay alive.

Other industries followed. Bar girls whose job it was to dance from 8 p.m. into the small hours of the morning, policemen on night duty, students needing to stay awake for exams—this stress was alien to the Thai way, and required chemical treatment.

Now progress took the form of inexplicable homicides. In Krung Thep a group of construction workers mutilated passersby in a rabid slashing spree. In the northeast an addicted monk raped and killed a tourist. Truck drivers drove ten-wheelers into ditches, pedestrians and each other.

The official figure is about a million addicted to the drug, but I guess the reality to be double that. Many employers openly admit they have to purchase *yaa baa* at wholesale prices in order to distribute it to their workforces, who could not afford the retail price and could not work without it.

Yaa baa means "mad drug" and refers to methamphetamine produced from ephedrine. It hits the blood in a rush and shoots into the brain stem. When it is smoked its effect is even more powerful—often violent.

Yaa baa is much easier to produce than heroin, an amateur can learn the chemistry in an hour. In a day he can use a pill compress to produce a hundred thousand pills, usually from a mobile factory. All he needs is the raw ephedrine, which is usually smuggled in from Laos, or Burma, or Cambodia. Do you have a private army perpetually in need of a war chest? Khun Sha does, lord of the United Wa. So does the Red Wa, so does the official Burmese army itself, come to that. Well, here's what you do. You build a *yaa baa* factory right on the Thai border, guard it with your troops, most of whom are already addicted to the drug, staff it with uneducated peasants and local tribespeople to pull the handles and press the buttons, and—here is the delicate part—find the right connection in Thailand to take care of the distribution.

Which explains why I am dancing in a club in Pat Pong at 3:29 a.m.

This is the most venerable of our red-light districts, where my mother worked most of the bars at one time or another, changing employment regularly according to her luck in finding customers, her relationship with the boss and the mamasan, or simply out of boredom. This is home, which I suppose is why I've come for comfort, as I used to as a kid. Often I would come in the early evening before she changed into her hideous bar-girl costumes (I loved her most in blue jeans and T-shirt, she looked so young and sexy). Or sometimes in the early hours of the morning when I'd been unable to sleep, because of the ghosts. Then I would take a motorcycle taxi all the way from home, racing through the night. If Nong was busy with a customer, the mamasan would find me a place to sit, some food and a beer.

The police shut down the market, bars and clubs an hour and a half ago, but the street knows me from the old days. Somehow they already know that Pichai is dead and it's like being that kid all over again. I'm mothered by a hundred whores. There is a price to pay, though. I have to dance.

"*Sonchai, Sonchai, Sonchai.*" They clap steadily, insistently, and motion at the stage with their chins. This is what I used to do, to earn my supper. Day after day at home I watched my mother practicing her erotic bum-thrusts and tit-wobbles to the disco music of her time, and she never realized how well I'd learned until she came in one night from a session with a client to see me all alone up on the stage, a twelve-year-old boy-whore dancing for life.

I'm pretty far gone, of course. The *yaa baa* has fried my brains, and on top there has been beer and ganja. The mamasan turns the music up real loud and I'm dancing a blue streak. Dancing like a tart. Dancing like Nong the goddess, Nong the whore. I'm better than Jagger in his prime, better than Travolta, maybe even better than Nong. The mamasan plays Tina Turner's "The Best" on the sound system and everyone screams, "Sonchai, Sonchai, Sonchai . . ." The girls, mostly dressed in jeans and T-shirts and ready to go home, roar and clap me on and on into the oblivion I've been searching for all night.

> *I call you, I need you, my heart's on fire*
> *You come to me, come to me wild and wired*
> *Give me a lifetime of promises and a world of dreams*
> *Speak the language of love like you know what it means*
> *Mmm, it can't be wrong*
> *Take my heart and make it strong*
> *You're simply the best, better than all the rest . . .*

Pichai.

Nobody remembers Bradley, or if they do I don't remember them remembering. I am very very stoned.

13

Needless to say, the *yaa baa* was a serious failure and I find myself in Kaoshan Road at about eight-thirty the next day, not having slept at all. I am sitting in a café opposite the offices of the Internet server, drinking black coffee, while the kaleidoscopic night replays in my head. I seem to remember talking to five hundred women, none of whom remembered Bradley. I remember my dancing in Pat Pong with extreme embarrassment. Now, with the sun already hot, it is as if the night were repeating itself. The street is filling with white-skinned foreigners.

This is a different scene from Sukhumvit. Indeed, the place is so bizarre it is hardly Krung Thep at all. Thais themselves come here as tourists, to gawk and judge.

Here the *farangs* are often in couples, girls and boys, far younger than the clientele of places like Nana Plaza, kids on their so-called gap year between school and university, or university and reality.

Kaoshan offers the cheapest accommodation in the city, dormitory beds for a few dollars a night in conditions even I would find squalid. Here the feeling of party-party-party never dies, not even in early morning. The street is lined with stalls selling pirated DVDs, videos and CDs, and travel guides to Southeast Asia, cooked-food stalls, junk stalls, sandal stalls,

T-shirt stalls. Between the stalls and the cafés there is hardly room to walk; tourists with massive backpacks turn and twist to pass, having just arrived on some long-haul flight from Europe or America, in search of the very cheapest accommodation, hoping to preserve their funds for the duration of their vacation, perhaps as long as a year. Remember the Chinatown scenes in *Blade Runner*? My people quickly learned how to produce Balinese masks, Cambodian sculptures, puppets from Burma, batik from Indonesia—even Australian didgeridoos. You can change money, have your body pierced, play bongo drums, watch a video or check your e-mail. It is a long way from Thailand.

A black man looking for a low profile would be smart to choose Kaoshan Road.

Now a Thai arrives on a motorbike to open the offices of the Internet server. I give him a few minutes before crossing the street.

This man is in his early thirties, clearly one of that industrious, switched-on new generation of Thais who have seen the opportunity offered by the Internet technology. He gives me a swift glance and knows immediately I am a cop. I show the photograph of Bradley.

The man recognizes him immediately and leads upstairs to where his machines sit on trestle tables and buzz and whir from all sides of the room. Anyone renting an Internet service is legally obliged to fill in a form issued by the government under the Telecommunications Act, and the man takes a file out from one of the filing cabinets and quickly finds Bradley's form. The form is printed only in Thai script, and most of the information supplied by Bradley is also in Thai.

"You helped him fill in the form?"

"No. He took it away and brought it back like this."

"Did he speak Thai?"

"Only a little. I don't think he could write in Thai."

"Ever see anyone with him?"

"He only came to the shop twice, once to collect the form, once to bring it back. He was alone both times." The man hesitates. I encourage him with a nod. "I think I saw him once, though, walking down the street. He was hard to miss. He was with a woman." I nod again. "Well, I mean, quite a woman. At first I thought she was African American like him, then I saw she had eyes like us, and her skin was more brown than black and her hair was basically straight, even though she'd frizzed it out a bit. Tall, much taller than most Thais, but not as tall as him of course. She came up to his shoulder." The man grins. "I came up to his rib cage."

"What was her hair like?"

"Dyed different colors, green, orange, you know? But well done, the two of them sauntering down the street was like a fashion show. She was incredibly sexy, like something out of a film. Everyone turned their heads, I think people wondered if two film stars had arrived from the United States. She looked like she was enjoying the attention."

"And him?"

"I think he was a serious guy. He looked like a serious American, you know? She looked more frivolous. But as I say, I only saw them once, and from a distance, it might not even have been him. I think it was because there aren't many like that in Krung Thep."

This is my first real lead and I want to reward this man. I copy down Bradley's address as it is written in Thai on the form and say: "Listen, sooner or later some agents from the FBI will come here asking to see this form and asking the kind of questions I just asked."

"So?"

"They have no investigative powers here. You're not obliged to tell them anything."

"What d'you want me to do?"

I smile. "If I were you, I would let them bribe you."

The man nods. The suggestion does not surprise him at all. "What would be a good price?"

I think about it. I am strongly in favor of redistribution of global wealth from West to East. "If I were you I might hold out for a thousand dollars." He makes an instant calculation: forty-five thousand baht, not a fortune but a considerable windfall. He places his palms together near his forehead and *wais*. "Thank you, Detective."

"You're welcome. And if you ever see the woman again, you'll let me know."

Out on the street I suddenly feel faint. The meth has leached every nutrient from my blood, and I'm failing rapidly. My brain thuds with the rhythms from a nearby music store and I believe I'm going to vomit. The world is inclining by about thirty degrees by the time I find the narrow *soi* where Bradley's apartment is supposed to be.

14

To my surprise, Bradley's address is not an apartment but an old teak house on stilts. I kick my shoes off, climb the wooden staircase to the main door and examine a bellpull. It is old, brass—an antique curiosity, perhaps seventy or more years old. Underneath, a name also in brass: William Bradley.

I wait five minutes before pulling the bell again. I seem to hear the slap of bare feet on teak boards, but it's hard to be sure because of distant traffic noise and the interminable *thump-thump-thump* from speakers on Koashan Road. I try once more. On the third pull I realize I'm being watched from an open window by a woman in her sixties with the fearful eyes of the incurably shy. I give her my best smile.

"Khun Bradley around?" She stares. "I'm a police officer." I fish for my ID and flash it at her, aware that she is probably illiterate. She continues to stare so I try: "Mother, I have your wages for last week."

A smile breaks out on her face: naïve, country, joyful. A bright pink tongue and gums set off the pure ebony of a few remaining stumps. It seems the house even boasts an authentic grandmother with an authentic betel habit. She disappears and with surprising speed the front door opens. She is less than five feet tall with black hair drawn back in a ponytail which reaches the base of her spine; not a trace of gray. She wears a sarong and a cream-colored shirt, a gold chain with an oval in gold displaying a former king of Thailand. She presses her palms together and makes a deep *wai*. Now that she has decided to trust me she lets another smile reveal the untouched soul behind her eyes.

As I enter the house she leans over the stair rail and emits a stream of rich vermilion fluid which hits a specific target on the ground.

"Remind me, mother, how much do we pay you each week?"

"Four hundred and fifty baht."

I pull a roll of notes out of my pocket. "Sorry to be so late."

"Not late, today is payday."

"When did you last see them?"

"Two days ago. But she came back sometime and took her things. It must have been yesterday, when I was with my daughter in Nakhon Sawan."

"Yesterday was your day off?"

"Yes."

"You sleep here?"

"Yes."

I squat down in order not to tower above her. She immediately squats also, so as not to keep her eyes above mine. I take out the picture of Bradley. "This is Khun Bradley, no?" She nods her head vigorously. "I'm sorry I don't have a picture of Madame Bradley. Do you?" She shakes her head. "Could you describe her?" The question only raises a moment's doubt in her eyes; she has decided I'm a good man and a few strange questions will not shake her faith now.

"Tall, oh! Very tall. I never saw such a tall woman."

"As tall as him?"

"As him? Nobody is as tall as him. He is a giant."

"Who gave you your orders?"

"She."

"Did she speak Thai like you and me?" The question confuses her. "She *farang* or not?"

"No, not *farang*. She's Thai, speaks, talks, same as us. At first I thought she was African"—the woman makes a shape around her head indicating big hair, and raises her hand to show height—"but she's Thai."

"What did you call her?"

"Madame Bradley."

Silly question. "Mother, I want to look around, okay?" She shrugs. How could she stop me? I cast an eye over a large downstairs room which takes up the whole of the first floor, with two teak pillars equidistant from the walls. The floor of long narrow boards is highly polished, even more so than is usual in these houses, and reflects light with a dull, antique glow. Brightly colored throw cushions and futons are scattered over the floor. The cushion covers are silk, in electric shades of green, orange and purple, contrasting well with the old wood of the walls and floor. Panels in the walls are picked out in gold leaf and midnight blue and there is a sunken teak table about ten feet long with a hidden well for legs and feet. The table is laid with a homespun blue cloth, rattan napkin holders with yellow homespun napkins, celadon plates and bowls, citronella candles in coconut shells.

I'm not an expert on the American military, but it occurs to me that this is not the kind of home an average marine would be inclined to show his comrades. The choice of a teak house to live in is eccentric even by Thai standards. They tend to be inhabited by oddball foreigners or Thais of the arty type who have spent a lot of time overseas in places like Paris or New York. When I look more closely, I notice great varnished grain storage baskets of the kind which have become so fashionable, and the futons are all in gold print silk which is only produced by the Khomapastr Corporation, which exports to royalty and billionaires worldwide. Wall brackets hold what seem to be priceless antiques: kendi water jars, reliquary urns with lotus-bud handles, ceramic medicine jars. Everything is Thai, everything is alien. The whole room is begging to be photographed by *farangs*.

To reach the next floor it's necessary to leave the house and return to the external staircase. The entrance to the second floor is locked and I have to go downstairs again to find the old woman. "Mother, I've forgotten my key, can I use yours?" She fishes under her shirt and I catch a glimpse of a modern money wallet of the kind favored by backpackers. She draws out a large brass key and hands it to me. Upstairs again I open the lock with the big key, and gratefully enter the cool of the old house.

15

The slatted shutters on the windows (there is no glass) allow air to circulate, and the teak walls are good insulators. It's dark apart from the brilliant outline of the doorway, and I find a light switch, then close the door. The lighting seems to come from nowhere, directed upward from behind a teak panel which runs the length of a corridor I'm standing in.

On the walls hang six twelve-by-eighteen-inch studies of the same woman's face; they are the same print in different colors, in exactly the style of famous Warhol portraits of Marilyn Monroe. The woman is definitely half Thai, half Negro, which puts her into a specific category in my feudal society. If she is in her thirties she would have been born in the late sixties or early seventies, when the city was permanently flooded with American servicemen on leave from the war in Vietnam. It is notorious that America sent a disproportionate number of African Americans to the war, and many of their female offspring now work the Bangkok bars. My racist people tend to marginalize them, and their lot can be a tough one. I open a door which gives on to the master bedroom, where homage turns into obsession.

The woman is everywhere, in oils, watercolors, black-and-white photographic studies, color photos, sometimes full length, sometimes in portrait. There is a huge nude study in oils, opposite the bed, tastefully done, with her pelvis turned slightly to one side; no pubic hair visible, perfect brown breasts with black areolas and nipples, a long fine neck, multi-colored hair artfully chaotic and not really African: I think that with the color and frizz washed out it must be straight and black. Somehow the eye travels most naturally not to her face but to a jade ball set in a short gold stick which diagonally pierces her navel in two places.

I sit on the bed mesmerized by the extraordinary beauty of this woman, her long shapely legs, high buttocks, elegant arms, finely tapered hands turned in the style of a Thai dancer, those alluring oval eyes, almost hollow cheeks, full lips smiling ironically, perhaps a reference to her nakedness, a fine straight nose which must have come from some Cau-casian cross in her blood. I put my hands behind my neck and recline full length on the bed, to think about Bradley.

Suppose a man for whom no other man had ever been a challenge, an accomplished athlete and soldier, himself of pure African blood, hetero-sexual and surely a connoisseur of the female form as it appears all over the world, a man on the brink of middle age and retirement but more vigorous than a man half his age, stationed in Bangkok and perhaps addicted to the city, as often happens, a frequent visitor to the bars of Nana Plaza, search-ing as he has searched over decades for that perfect female form?

Surely this man was no ordinary soldier? This man was born with an instinct for visual beauty as another of his tribe might be born with a genius for jazz. I wonder how it might have happened, that such a man should ever have dreamed of becoming a soldier? Perhaps his exquisite taste developed later in life, when his career path had already been set, maybe in his late twenties? How irksome to find himself permanently sur-rounded by the ugly functionality of the military world; might one assume a continual dissatisfaction pressing on consciousness, a vow repeated minute to minute, with increasing urgency as the years passed, that *after retirement I will* . . . A meticulously planned retirement, as befits a career soldier, with the foundations in place long in advance of the due date: the most beautiful woman he has ever seen, in a beautiful house, a serious hobby in precious stones with a web page featuring a jade phallus of great elegance. Should we impute an element of narcissism? How could such a man not love himself to some degree, however stern his professional dis-cipline? Even when he was laid out on a gurney in the morgue with the flabbiness of death and his flesh disfigured by snake bites, did I not witness a stupendous example of manhood?

Imagine the moment when Bradley first set eyes on this woman. Instant armlock? A stranglehold this warrior could not escape? The kind of woman lesser men might find too dangerous to touch, who had perhaps been waiting herself for someone larger than life? But where had she been hiding? If she had danced in the bars of Nana or Pat Pong, I surely would have heard of her. Such a woman would be famous throughout the city the moment she began gyrating around one of those stainless steel poles.

I stand up to approach the painting, and admit to an aristocratic note in her pose; she doesn't look like a woman who would ever dance naked in public. But if she was the bastard child of a black American serviceman, how else would she have earned a living? If her mother was a bar girl her education would have been basic, her technical qualifications zero, her contacts outside of the bar scene very few.

I try to relate her to the rest of the house, which is not difficult. The two seem to go together, as if selected by a fine eye from different brochures. This isn't a home, not to me, it is an environment, a barricade against the ugliness of the city, a deliberate and very Western attempt to build a separate, personal reality.

A very big part of which is erotic. Who could help envisioning their passionate embrace, like two black tigers mating? I imagine elaborate lovemaking of a kind I have never experienced, a whole evening set aside as if for a private banquet, the prolongation of lust, the postponement of climax, the man's slow relentless savoring of his prize, the woman's ecstasy underneath her black god. Sure enough, in the bathroom on a shelf I find a pharmacist's collection of scents, perfumes and aromatic oils, some local but many imported, bearing the name and address of a shop in San Francisco.

My exhausted body cannot tolerate such stimulation. What of the other side to the marine? I find the computer in a small room which clearly served as an office, a desktop tower with a big nineteen-inch monitor. The office is stark, free of mementos of the woman: bare teak walls and floor, a shelf with a modest collection of books including some very large ones which look like photographic collections, and a single art object in a place of honor alone on a high shelf: a jade horse and rider. I assume an imitation. Who keeps real jade in a wooden house, even a wooden house like this?

I press the power button on the computer tower and the monitor creaks and flickers its way into Windows Millennium Edition. I click on "programs" and find a long list, perhaps as many as thirty or forty different applications. In addition to the word processors in both English and Thai, there are astrology and astronomy, gemology, a tutorial on mathematics, use of English, a Thai translation program, the *Encyclopaedia Britannica, Webster's New World Dictionary, How to Write a Winning Business Plan*—it's like a self-improvement regime for someone who intended to leap from ignorance to erudition with no gap in between.

It is 12:46 p.m. and my problem has progressed from no data to too much. Proper examination of the computer and Bradley's web surfing will take days. I call up Word for Windows, type "Welcome, Khun Rosen and Khun Nape," switch the screen off but leave the computer running.

I return to Kaoshan Road, to have a copy made of the key to the upstairs rooms, buy a cardboard camera with flash and return to take pictures of the portraits of the woman, the jade horseman and the computer. I lock the door, return the original key to the old lady, who squats on the teak floor downstairs, near a window convenient for spitting. She is chewing her betel. She seems to have forgotten about me, for she gives a start when I approach, then replaces the key in her money bag without looking at me. Outside in the street I find a motorcycle taxi.

16

At Dao Phrya Bridge the Mercedes was gone, no doubt taken away by police. I paused for a moment to examine something which must have been under the car. The corpses of two cobras, which had been beaten to death, not shot.

Even as I got off the bike to pay the fare, I had heard a noise from the squatter huts which was only half human. Striding across the wasteland, I became aware of a man's full-throated roar originating from deep in his chest, like the bellowing of an enraged bull. "Fuck you, fuck the FBI, fuck the FBI's mother, I AM THIRSTY."

The headman came to meet me with a worried look as I reached the edge of the settlement. "You're late. You said noon, it's one-thirty."

"I had a busy morning. What's going on?" They had tied Old Tou upright to a plank with rope which encircled his arms, trunk and legs in a continuous binding of bright orange. Only the old man's neck and head were free. They had leaned him against one of the sturdier huts. The cords on his neck stood out when he roared.

"You said you wanted him sober. This was the only way."

"Can't you give him water?"

"We've given him gallons. He's not thirsty for water."

"Untie him."

"Are you kidding? I'm not untying him till we've got him drunk again. If he goes on the rampage he'll destroy the whole settlement. D'you want to interrogate him or not?"

The old man glared at me with bloodshot eyes. "Are you the police bastard they keep telling me about? I'm going to tear your nose off with my teeth."

"I just want to ask you a few questions."

"Fuck your questions. I want whisky. Rice whisky."

I nodded to the headman, who brought a plastic bottle filled to the brim with transparent fluid. "Give him a little, not too much."

The headman poured a couple of inches into a plastic cup. The old man held his head up like a bird while the headman poured the alcohol down his throat. "More."

"Just answer some questions, and you can go on killing yourself as fast as you like."

The old man licked his lips. "When they let me go I'm going to kill *you*. What fucking questions?"

"Yesterday, you saw the Mercedes arrive with the black *farang*?"

He spat. "Of course I saw, I was sitting against the wall of the bridge having a drink. I saw everything."

"What did you see?"

"I saw Khmer Rouge."

Guffaws from the audience. I sighed. "You were in the Cambodian civil war?"

"Idiot, I wasn't in any fucking war. A couple of weeks ago someone brought a DVD here about some stupid American journalist in Cambodia who got his friend into trouble—a boring fucking film but I liked the bit where he slits the side of a buffalo with a razor and drinks the blood. I never would have thought of that, those Cambodians are rough trade."

"So what about Khmer Rouge?"

"In the film the Khmer Rouge all wear red checkered scarves around their stupid heads, that's what they were wearing yesterday."

"He's right about the film," the headman said. "We all watched it. I remember the scarves too."

"Who was wearing the scarves?"

"The motorcycle yobs. There were about six of them, nasty pieces of work as far as I could see."

"They arrived after the Mercedes, or before?"

"About the same time. They surrounded it."

"You see any of them open the door?"

Old Tou laughed. "No, they did the same as you and your partner. They got off the bikes, went to the car and kind of ogled and grunted, then they started jabbering. I don't think they were as tough as they made out. Then they all got together for some kind of powwow, and ran back to their bikes and left."

"Were they speaking Thai or Khmer?"

"Too far away to tell. Anyway, how the fuck would I know if they were speaking fucking Khmer or Chiu Chow Chinese?"

"Was any of them female?"

"Give me another drink, asshole." I motioned to the headman, who poured some more whisky down Old Tou's throat. "Female? No, these were swaggering boys, you know the type, probably on *yaa baa* or ganja, no true manhood, they couldn't stomach the scene in the car. After they'd gone I went over to see what all the fuss was about. That black *farang* was being eaten alive by that python. There were cobras, too."

"What did you do?"

Old Tou licked his lips. "Well, I couldn't be sure, you know." The way he said it made some of the audience crack up. Several squatted in order to laugh harder.

"Couldn't be sure? How's that?" More laughter.

"I get visions." Hilarity now from the audience. Two men and a woman lay down in order to enjoy a really good laugh. Some people leaned against a hut, overcome by giggles.

The headman grinned broadly. "He hallucinates a lot of the time. He sees snakes, mostly."

"That's right. That's why I couldn't be sure. When they told me I'd seen real snakes I had to have a drink."

"There was no woman in the car?"

"Don't be an idiot. If there'd been anyone else in the car they'd be as dead as that black man."

"You didn't see a woman at all, tall, half Negro, half Thai, maybe leaving the car before the motorcycles arrived?"

"No. A woman I would have remembered. I never hallucinate women. Why should I, I haven't had an erection in thirty years." Guffaws, people shaking their heads, the headman turning away to laugh.

"Okay." I turned to the audience. "Anyone else see the motorcycles?"

People directed their gaze at the headman. "The motorcycles were real, he didn't hallucinate them, but nobody wants to give evidence. They think this was a gang killing, they don't want to get involved."

"Generally, do people anonymously agree with what he just said, strictly on a nonattributable basis?"

"Nonattributable sounds good, whatever it means. Anonymously? Yes, quite a few saw the bikes, and Old Tou walk to the car and look in the window and then he started banging his head against the car. We all watched that. A group of people walked over to the car. You saw them when you and your partner arrived."

The headman poured more whisky down Old Tou's throat. The man's capacity was amazing. He drained the plastic bottle of moonshine before the headman judged him drunk enough to be untied. As a precaution, though, they placed another bottle nearby and stood away after the ropes were loosened. The old man made straight for the bottle and upturned it into his mouth.

I thanked the headman.

"So you won't be sending the FBI to investigate us? Moonshine is our main source of income, we'd be destitute without it."

This was the first sign of weakness and I needed to exploit it. It took only an exchange of glances and a jerk of the chin on his part for me to follow him back to his hut, where the whisky was distilling, trickling slowly out of its cloth filter into an urn. The headman took a bottle from a corner and found a couple of plastic cups. We wished each other good luck, then the raw alcohol hit the back of my throat and wormed its way into my stomach. It was cozy in the hut, with the fumes from the mash cooking over the charcoal embers.

"You're from District 8, aren't you?"

I gazed steadily at him. "So?"

A shrug. "Your Colonel is famous. Vikorn, isn't it?"

"You know him?"

A cautious pursing of the lips. "No, not personally. Like I say, he's very famous."

"Do you want to talk to him directly?"

A disarming smile. "I wasn't insinuating anything. Look, we don't want this FBI, whatever it is, coming round asking questions. The people really don't know anything. They were either drunk or playing cards. Old Tou hardly has a brain cell left in his head."

"Maybe you saw something?"

A hesitation. "Well, I did happen to be near the top of the slip road when the Mercedes arrived."

"When I asked you before, you said you weren't here."

A shrug. "I was returning from business on the other side of town."

"And?"

"It was more or less as Old Tou described, except that the Mercedes stopped at the top of the slip road, then some bikers arrived. Someone got out of the car and onto one of the bikes, but it was on the far side of the car so I couldn't see so well. One of the bikes rode off with this passenger."

Only more moonshine would develop his story. I'd had less than one-third of a cup, but already the fumes were filling my head. He poured two more cups, knocked some back like a professional and smacked his lips. I tried to maintain concentration while I gazed at him through a blur. "What else?"

A wry grin. "You're good, aren't you?" He finished the cup. "The bikers had guns. They looked like those little automatic machine guns you see in movies. They were pointing them at the car. It looked as though that black *farang* was being hijacked." He engaged my eyes. "Naturally . . ."

"Naturally you turned away. The last thing you needed was to be a witness to a crime and have to give evidence."

The headman detected no note of irony. He beamed with obvious relief. "Thanks for your understanding."

I finished the whisky and stood up. "I don't think the FBI cares about your moonshine. They might come. If they do, set Old Tou onto them. Don't worry."

"D'you want money?" the headman asked. "I can give you a little from the sales last week. The people will understand."

I shook my head. "Good luck to you, brother."

The headman gave his most convincing smile. "Thank you, brother. May you avenge your partner and live in peace."

I acknowledged with a nod.

I had told my motorcycle chauffeur to wait, and I could see him loitering by his motorbike near the bridge. I could not put it off any longer. It was time to face the Colonel.

17

A Third World police station, which is to say a two-story reinforced concrete structure festooned with our flag and busts of our deeply beloved King, with a large reception area occupying most of the ground floor, open for the length of the building as if one wall had been left out. In this open area there are many rows of heavy-duty plastic chairs joined by beams under the seats; the business a citizen may have here is infinite.

You have to remember we're Buddhist. Compassion is an obligation, even if corruption is inevitable. The poor come for money and food, the illiterate come for help with filling in forms, those without connections come for character references and help in getting jobs, tourists come with their problems, children come because they are lost, women come because they are tired of being beaten by their husbands, husbands come because their wives have deserted with the family savings. Prostitutes come with problems with their mamasans, feuding families come with complaints and threats. It is not unusual for an avenging brother or father to tell the police of his blood vow to kill the bastard who caused offense to wife or sister, perhaps seeking some indication that in the circumstances the police will turn a blind eye to the proposed assassination, for a fee of course. Sometimes young people come to try to find out who they are, for we are often a polygamous society in which babies are sometimes given to close relatives or friends for life and it is not always clear who belongs to whom. Drunks and beggars come to sit in the chairs, a monk in saffron robes waits his turn for help and advice.

Now here is the local leper who begs by holding a brass bowl between his stumps and who for ten baht will contort his face into something really pathetic. If the prospects are better he will let out a heartrending wail and bang his head on the floor until one of the cops threatens to shoot him. And there's the tattooist who plies his trade on the street corner with two very long needles and a limited palette (anything so long as it's black). When it rains the duty officer sometimes allows him to bring his victims here into the reception area, where he tortures them in one of the chairs. He is important, this tattooist who is half body artist, half shaman. Boxers and high-rise construction workers are in particular need of the protection afforded by the full astrological chart on back and solar plexus.

My junior colleagues who man the desks have developed a posture of stern kindliness, a willingness to help tempered by long exposure to the ruses of the poor, for District 8 is the very essence of Krung Thep, its heart and its armpit. I can hardly believe that my brother Pichai will no longer be here to share it with me, for this is where we both came of age, where Pichai built on his noble disgust and where I first fell in love with the polluted beauty of human life. It is here, too, that I learned to forgive my mother and to honor her, for against the backdrop of District 8 Nong's life has been a brilliant success and a shining example. If only every woman could be like her.

My colleagues look away when I enter the station. Every man has ordained as a monk for at least three months of his life, meaning that every man has seriously contemplated the inevitability of his own death, the corruption of the body, the worms, the disintegration, the meaninglessness of everything except the Way of the Buddha. We do not look on death the way you do, *farang*. My closest colleagues grasp my arm and one or two embrace me. No one says sorry. Would you be sorry about a sunset? No one doubts that I have sworn to avenge Pichai's death. There are limits to Buddhism when honor is at stake.

"Detective Jitpleecheep, the Colonel wants to see you." The diminutive woman in short-sleeved blue shirt, black belt and blue skirt is a junior police officer who acts as the Colonel's secretary and aide-de-camp. She is also his eyes and ears in the station, his antennae, for there is no such thing as a nonpolitical appointment in our kingdom. I nod, climb some stairs, walk through a wooden door into a bare passage at the end of which I knock on another wooden door no more impressive than the first, except that the architecture of the building suggests that this office will be larger than the rest, with a better view.

At the far end of the room, across a floor of bare boards, a man in his early sixties is waiting. He is wearing the working uniform of a colonel of police, who is also superintendent of this district. His peaked cap hangs from a nail in the wall to his left, a gold-framed picture of the King hangs on his right. His wooden desk is bare except for an old-fashioned blotter, a plastic receptacle for ballpoint pens, and a picture of him standing with some elderly monks, one of whom is a famous abbot of a local monastery. The occasion was the police execution without trial of fifteen *yaa baa* smugglers, which required the subsequent blessing of the abbot to square it with local opinion, which had been irresponsibly inflamed by bleeding-heart journalists (who had blatantly insinuated that the dead smugglers had belonged to a notorious army syndicate in competition with Vikorn's notorious police syndicate). With a little help from the abbot our robust citizens saw immediately that such defamation, even if justified, did not detract from the justice of the Colonel's prompt dispatch of the villains, thus saving a small fortune in trial and prison costs. Not long afterward, the Colonel financed a new dormitory wing to the abbot's monastery, complete with electricity and running water, where novice monks might meditate in peace and tranquillity.

The Colonel owns the military bearing, strong jaw and frank unblinking eyes of a truly accomplished crook. Nobody knows the extent of his wealth; he probably has no idea himself. Apart from the million-dollar yacht he confiscated from a Dutch smuggler and subsequently bought for ten thousand baht at an auction at which he was the sole bidder (because no one else was invited), there are large tracts of land in the northeast along the edge of the Mekong, a hundred bungalows on Ko Samui which he lets to tourists, a country mansion near Chiang Mai in the northwest. In Krung Thep he lives in modest accommodation as befits a humble cop, with wife number one and the youngest of their five children. Why do I love this man?

For reasons unfathomable to me, the Colonel has hung on the wall behind his desk a map of Thailand issued by the Crime Suppression

Division, which shows the geographical areas in which police conniving in organized crime is supposed to be at its worst. Arrows of different colors point almost everywhere. Along the Lao and Cambodian borders the police help smuggle drugs and endangered species destined for China; along the Burmese border we help bring in enough methamphetamines weekly to keep the entire population awake for a month. All along the coast the police work hand in hand with Customs and Excise to assist the clandestine oil trade, for which most of the country's fishing fleet has adapted its boats: they sail out to offshore tankers most nights, receiving the contraband diesel into their specially designed stainless steel tanks; more than 12 percent of Thailand's diesel oil is contraband. All around the edges of Krung Thep and in hundreds of rural locations the police protect illegal gambling dens, mostly from other police and the army, which is always trying to muscle in. At street level the police commercial genius produces some of the best cooked-food stalls in the city, owned and run by young constables who are immune to prosecution for illegal hawking. The map is a mind-boggling maze of red, green, yellow and orange arrows designating the different infractions indigenous to each area, with Day-Glo cross-hatching, dire warnings in boxes, pessimistic footnotes and stark headers. I am not the first to observe that the Colonel is the only person in the room not to have it in his field of vision.

I have gazed at this map many times. Taking into account that the police are generally facilitating someone else's scam, it begins to look as if 61 million people are engaged in a successful criminal enterprise of one sort or another. No wonder my people smile a lot.

My Colonel, a born leader, stands up while I approach his desk. I place my palms together near my forehead and *wai* courteously. The Colonel comes around his desk to embrace me. A firm, manly, warmhearted hug which starts tears in my eyes.

"Are you going to kill me, Sonchai?" He gestures to the chair by the desk.

I sit as the Colonel does so. "Should I?"

The Colonel shrugs. "It all depends on whether I set you up or not, doesn't it? If I did, then by all means, shoot me. I would in your place."

"Did you set us up?"

The Colonel rubs his chin. "I feel guilty of negligence—but that is my only crime." I nod. It is somewhat the answer I had expected. "Sonchai, I've been waiting for you all morning and I haven't eaten. We are

going to eat at my bar." He lifts the receiver of an old-style telephone/
intercom, presses a button and speaks. "We're going across town to Pat
Pong—call the bar and tell them to keep it closed. If they've opened
already tell them to clear it. And I want an escort, I don't want to spend
the rest of the day in traffic." He replaces the receiver. "Shall we?"

18

The Colonel's car today is an old white Datsun, but it could have been the royal limo for the way it beats the traffic. It helps having a two-man motorcycle escort with sirens screaming. We approach Pat Pong from the Sarawong side, and the driver stops outside the Princess Club, which stands in a side *soi* off the main street of Pat Pong. The Colonel knows that my mother worked this street and I wonder if he is making some kind of point. As we pause to enter the bar, I see myself as I must have been more than twenty years ago: a skinny boy bewildered and intrigued by the business of flesh.

The mamasan and half a dozen girls in jeans and T-shirts *wai* to the Colonel as we enter. They have set up a table in the seating area, with a tablecloth, forks, spoons. They immediately begin bringing an array of dishes from the restaurants and food stalls round about.

"D'you want to start with beer or shall we go straight into the whisky? Let's have a beer, we sell Kloster for the tourists, which I have to admit gives a cleaner taste. It goes so well with chili too."

I've eaten at the Colonel's banquets before, it is one of the old man's favorite ways of cementing the esprit de corps (trips on his boat are another), but never as the sole guest. I find it a little eerie to be served by girls who will be selling their bodies in a few hours' time, as if they were a team of virginal housemaids. They go out of their way to please the Colonel, *wai*ing and giving him their best innocent smiles. I know it is my duty to get drunk in pace with the Colonel, but I'm not sure how my body will react to alcohol after the ravages of the *yaa baa* the night before and more than twenty-four hours without sleep, not to mention those two cups of moonshine which sat in my stomach like burning coals. I sip at my Kloster, which I drink straight from the bottle, as does the Colonel. I watch him dip into a small wicker basket and bring out a portion of sticky rice which he makes into a compact ball and dips into a papaya salad, nodding to me to follow suit. Perhaps you have tormented your stomach with papaya pok-pok, *farang*, on one of your visits to my country? It is made with twelve chilies, ground up with the sauce so you cannot escape them. Even my Colonel is sniffing after the first mouthful. I let the pepper inflame my mouth slowly, before it trickles like fresh lava down to my empty stomach. I sip some more beer and immediately experience the delicious clash of the ice-cold beer with the fire of the chili. The Colonel is watching me closely. It is my duty to demonstrate heartiness.

I sample some tom-yum soup, which is almost as spicy as the salad, then start on the braised chicken with oyster sauce, which is more a Chinese dish than a Thai one, but popular with the Colonel. The fish is sea bass simply but expertly fried, with an excellent sauce of chili and fish paste, and the raw minced toad has been well prepared with spring onions and, of course, more chili. Deep in my empty, *yaa baa*–flayed stomach it is as if the chili were oozing over a wound, setting it alight. I quickly down the rest of my beer and one of the girls immediately brings another. I ask for water, too, raising a grin on the Colonel's face. Now a girl brings a large tureen of fat snails, cooked in their own juice with a brown sauce. The Colonel wipes up some of the sauce with a ball of sticky rice, then starts sucking loudly on the end of the snail until the body pops out into his mouth. I follow suit, trying not to gag.

My master finishes his beer, calls for another and opens the bottle of Mekong whisky the girls have left on the table. He pours two beakers and adds ice from a bucket. "So, Sonchai, why don't you tell me your views on the case so far?" This is not an innocent question.

"I've only had a day." I suck on a snail for punctuation. "Nothing significant yet. By the way, why did you order us to follow the black *farang*?"

He tuts disapprovingly and shakes his head. "Why must you always come straight to the point? Is it your *farang* blood? No wonder you're so unpopular."

"I'm unpopular because I don't take money."

"That too. Neither you nor your late partner made one contribution to the common pot in ten years. You were like monks on a permanent alms trek."

"Why did you put up with us?"

"My brother asked me to."

"I think you want to make merit. We might be the only good thing you ever did."

"Don't flatter yourself. Because of my brother I shielded you from a prosecution for homicide. What's so good about that?"

What can I say? I look into the tom-yum and its bright crimson fragments of chili. "You won't tell me why we were following Bradley?"

"Do you think perhaps the FBI asked me to have him followed?"

I shake my head. "The FBI didn't know anything until yesterday. They didn't even know where he was living."

"You're talking about the FBI at the embassy. I'm talking about the FBI in Washington."

"You talk to them?"

"Of course not. They talk to someone who talks to me."

"Really?"

"Because the CIA talk to the FBI. At least, from time to time. And guess who the CIA talk to?" I shrug. "The same people we talk to, on the ground in Laos, Burma, Cambodia. The CIA pays in cash, we pay in immunity from prosecution for Customs and Excise violations. In the end, we get the same information." He prods the sticky rice. "Something to do with jade." He adds this tentatively, to try me out.

"Don't believe it. Why would jade traders use snakes to kill the competition? Anyway, how could a black *farang* get into the jade trade in a serious way? It's dominated by Chiu Chow Chinese. They trade in a secret sign language. And why would the FBI care?"

He frowns. "Okay, so it wasn't jade."

"*Yaa baa?*"

"Why *yaa baa*? Why not heroin?"

I force-swallow a ball of rice to soak up the fire. "Because the DEA is all over the opium trade. Heroin is for desperadoes. *Yaa baa* is safer and the market is growing all the time."

He opens his hands. "So, you've solved the case. It was *yaa baa* for sure."

"You've told me nothing."

"It's my job to tell you things? You're the detective, I'm just the guy in the office."

"Colonel, sir, my partner died yesterday. I want to know why we were following the black *farang*." A moment of truth as our eyes lock. No one doubts the Colonel has strong ties to the *yaa baa* trade.

He toys with the idea of staring me out, which he knows well how to do, but decides on a posture of meekness and looks away. "I'm sorry, Sonchai, I'm really really sorry. The truth is I don't know why you were following Bradley. I just passed the order on down the line. Was it the FBI? Was it our Crime Suppression Division? Was it someone else? Who knows?"

"You're the chief of District 8. No one gives you orders without explanation."

"I was told his visa had expired." I want to laugh, but the Colonel has assumed a somber expression bordering on the pompous. "It's a grave offense for a member of a foreign armed force to overstay. It's not like a civilian."

"You're serious?"

He nods. "That was the official reason. I'll show you the file if you like." He leans forward. "I'm not like you, Sonchai, I don't ask indiscreet questions. That is why I'm a colonel and you will never be more than a detective."

"So whoever gave you the order was important enough for you to need to be discreet?" He shakes his head. Clearly I'm a hopeless case. Then suddenly he switches it on, the amazing charm and candor, that two-thousand-volt charisma which I can never resist. His humility and compassion are totally convincing. "I promise you, Sonchai, I had no idea Bradley was going to die yesterday. And I won't stand in your way, no matter where the investigation leads." To my question-mark gaze he adds: "I promised my brother I would take care of the two of you. Losing one is bad enough. My brother is an *arhat*. One keeps one's promise to such a man, especially when he is a blood relation. You have my word. Anyway, whatever Bradley was up to, it had nothing to do with me."

An awkward moment, before we resume eating and drinking. I say casually: "I found out Bradley's address through the Internet. I went to his house."

The Colonel raises his eyes. "You did? Find anything?"

"If I ask you a question to do with the case, will you be straight with me? Or am I a pawn in some game you're playing with the CIA in Laos, or the FBI in Washington, or the American embassy?"

"Sonchai, I swear to you, may Buddha kill me if I lie."

"A stunning woman in her early thirties or late twenties, half Negro, half Thai, very tall, maybe as tall as six feet, beautiful long legs, full firm bust, great face, hair dyed all the colors of the rainbow, a discreet little piercing in her navel for a jade ball set in a gold stick. Who is she?"

The Colonel sips his whisky. "I'm supposed to know?"

"This is your bar, right in the middle of the red-light district. Girls move around between here and Nana, they try everywhere to see if they can get a better deal—you know the skin trade like the back of your hand."

"You're saying she's a prostitute?"

"What is the likelihood she's not?"

"She's a suspect?"

"She's a possible accomplice. No woman acting alone could organize something like that. I still have no idea how it was done. How does anyone drug a full-size python and twenty cobras and get them to bite the right guy at the right moment? It must have taken an incredible organization involving a lot of people. The snake aspect is simply incomprehensible to me at the moment. Who is she?"

19

"What am I, an idiot?" The Colonel is drunk and has launched into his favorite topic—the difference between East and West—without answering my question.

"Don't I know I'm vulnerable to an inquiry anytime? Don't I know that some army bastard or muckraking journalist, or some asshole who wants my job, can start digging anytime and find stuff—my boat, my little house up north, my handful of bungalows on Samui—and start pointing the finger? Wouldn't I be happier with less assets and more peace of mind? Why d'you think I keep that stuff where everyone can see it, when I could just sell up and put the money in a bank in Switzerland? Why?"

"Because this is Asia."

"Exactly! If I'm to do my job properly I have to have face. And my enemies have to see the war chest. You just don't survive at the top of the greasy pole if you're a humble little cop piously shuffling files around. Someone's bound to defame you, and then what d'you do if you don't have the money to pay lawyers? If you don't have money to buy senators and M.P.s, how the hell are you going to defend yourself? How are you going to fight back at all?"

"Very difficult."

"I envied you and your late partner from the start, because you guys made a decision never to rise in the force—how could you if you never take money? I admired it. You made no contribution to the common pot, but I put up with that. I defended you against those who said you're not pulling your weight. I said: Look, every district needs at least one cop who doesn't take money, we're lucky, we've got two. We can wheel them out as shining examples, pure Buddhists, half monks, half cops. Besides, I said, Sonchai speaks perfect English, what a prize for a district like ours to show off to the foreign press. How many times have you spoken to the foreign media?"

"Hundreds." Dozens anyway. Every time there's a big enough scandal in District 8 to fascinate people overseas—the extravagant execution of those fifteen traffickers was a good example—the Colonel drags me out in front of the cameras to send my mug zinging around the international networks.

"And you do it brilliantly. What's that favorite phrase of yours? I love it."

"*Whilst Thailand is a humane Buddhist society committed to human rights and the dignity of its citizens, the wealthier countries of the world must appreciate we do not always have the resources to meet those high standards of law enforcement which, frankly, are a luxury afforded only by those countries which industrialized first.*"

The Colonel claps his hands in delight. "Brilliant. Did I ever tell you the Director of Police himself said what a good front man you are?"

"Yes, you told me. But it won't get me a promotion. You told me that too."

My Colonel sighs. "Sonchai, the difference between us, the only real difference, is that you are a man of the future, I am a man of the present. The present is still, unfortunately—" He cuts himself off to watch a girl who brings more Mekong, more snails, more sticky rice, a whole chicken fried in honey and chili sauce and shredded, two bottles of Kloster clouded with condensation. She *wais* respectfully, and slightly flirtatiously, to the Colonel. She is the most beautiful of the bar's girls and the one who most frequently serves her boss, who waves a hand toward her and laughs before he continues. "The present is as it is. It's not only your enemies you have to have face for, it's your friends, too, perhaps even more than your enemies. What kind of district do we serve? Is it populated with upwardly mobile yuppies, Internet fiends, law-abiding sandwich-class lawyers, doctors and dentists?"

I miss my cue because I'm cramming chicken into my mouth with large quantities of sticky rice. The chicken is to supply nutrients, the sticky rice to absorb the alcohol and chili. I have never felt so surely on the point of being dangerously ill.

"No, it's not. It's a sewer and the rules which apply to sewer workers are not the same as those which apply to stockbrokers. My people would never forgive me for being as small as life. Of course, I do not fool a man of your intelligence, I don't try to, I'm not a superman, but my people need a superman and that requires—" A yacht, a hundred bungalows, et cetera—I recite the list to myself as he falls into a rant. "There are gangsters who give millions to the poor, honest people who talk compassion and give nothing. Tell me, wise one, who do the poor prefer?"

"The gangsters," I manage to croak. I'm so drunk now, the feeling in my stomach so lethal, that I'm afraid I'm going to have to make a dash for the toilet before the punch line. It comes just as I'm standing up. "Sonchai, I swear to you I know no woman of the description you gave to me. If I did, if she was as good as you say, I would have invited her for a week on my boat—you know me." The old man grins and waves a hand to excuse me. As I rush toward the sign marked GENTLEMEN I look back once and catch an image of an attractive military figure brimming with health and contentment as he pats the backside of his favorite, who jumped to fill his glass as soon as I left the table.

I am a long time in the toilet, and when I return to the bar the old man has gone. It is like the Colonel to offer this subtle compassion, just when one least expects it; he has cut short the lunch which he was clearly enjoying and given orders for me to be taken upstairs to the room the girls use to service their short-time clients. I don't want to sleep here, don't want to look on this girl showing me the way up the stairs and see my mother twenty-five years ago, but I know I couldn't make it out in the street. Fearing I might soil the bed in my sleep, I lie down on the floor in the upstairs room and fall asleep there, just like a whore. After such a banquet what would I dream of if not Paris?

At a big café near the Opéra, with a glass extension that took up three-quarters of the sidewalk and waiters even ruder and more arrogant than elsewhere in the city, my mother said: "If only he were a hundred years younger."

Only a slight exaggeration. I had watched Monsieur Truffaut in the mornings as he crossed the great spaces of his Cinquième Arrondissement mansion flat in his paisley dressing gown, looking exactly like the undead. It was as if he'd left his mind in the grave during the night and did not catch up with the fact of being alive until after twelve o'clock, when he swallowed his collection of pills.

Nong reported that her bedtime duties were not heavy. He was one of those Frenchmen who had enjoyed a young female body next to him in bed all his life and saw no reason to give up the habit merely because his biology was failing.

It was hardly a strain to fit in with the old man's rituals. Nong and I had the mornings to ourselves. The old man would spend the hour between 12 and 1 p.m. digesting his pills and the daily newspapers with increasing vigor as the drugs took hold, then we would march off to one of the world-class restaurants at which he was treated like the *Roi-Soleil*. Maxim's, Lucas Carton, the restaurant at Fauchon, Le Robuchon; these shrines from the gospels of cuisine were everyday events for the bar girl and her son. With true Parisian discretion, the waiters neither nodded nor winked behind the old man's back. They called Nong "Madame" in reverential tones, and I was "Monsieur."

Truffaut's afternoon vigor lasted long enough to give me an English lesson, interspersed with French, and here was revelation. To the old man the only reason for learning English was to win arguments with Englishmen and Americans, preferably without their noticing it. He taught the finer points of the language: the effective use of sarcasm, the acid two-word cap on a bore's monologue, how to tell the other guy he was a jerk in a way that everyone except the jerk understood; it was the English of a fencing master, and I loved it.

He also taught pleasure. A lunch or dinner at a place like Lucas Carton was to be approached with reverence, as one would seduce a beautiful woman. The pleasure of food was more reliable than sex—a wink at Nong, ironic and self-mocking, which made her smile. "Paris is an old whore, but a five-star one."

One took a stroll before the meal, then an aperitif at one of the pavement cafés. "Choose a place full of life, for god's sake, full of intrigue and adultery. Then make your way slowly to the temple of pleasure."

Everything about the old man told me what I was going to miss out on: urbanity, the cultivated conversation of the demimonde, that special sort of job which was an extension of one's social contacts. Like the

Colonel, whom I had not yet met, Truffaut was one of life's golden ones, a member of a special tribe to which I knew even then I would never belong. There was something else about him, though, an authenticity to which Vikorn would never aspire. Every day after my English lesson Truffaut, in a state of rapture, read two pages from a book by someone called Marcel Proust. Nong noticed it too—the authenticity, not the Proust. I think she would have settled for twenty years younger, for they shared a passion for life cleansed of illusion. More than once I saw her reach out, but they both knew there just was not enough of him left. Oh yes, we could have been happy in Paris, and for several months we were.

The inevitable happened during our fifteenth week. In the middle of the night my mother felt obliged to call a number the old man had given her, and the emergency services arrived with oxygen and drips.

It was not a serious stroke, but it brought a small army of bequest-minded relatives, one of whom was delegated to tell Nong it was time for her to go. The old man had been persuaded to agree—he was hardly in a condition to argue—but true to his code, he insisted that mother and son return to Thailand in style on a first-class ticket on Air France, with whom he had family connections. An Air France official met Nong and me at the airport and during the flight we were treated as if we were Siamese celebrities, perhaps of a new generation of brown-skinned billionaire entrepreneurs. Nong groaned when we emerged into the muggy heat of Krung Thep and joined the taxi line. Going back to the bars was going to be especially tough after Paris.

I awake to a familiar ghost gnawing at my feet.

20

It is male, about nine feet tall with the round shape of a tic, tiny feet and legs. His mouth is the size of the eye of a needle, just as the tales stipulate. I have seen his kind too often to be truly frightened, but the echo of my childhood is infuriating to me, as if I've got nowhere in all these years. From downstairs there is the muffled boom of the club's sound system, but we are all alone in a primeval space, this hungry ghost and I. He is the spirit of one who was greedy and selfish in his lifetime and must spend a thousand years with that tiny mouth which can never take in enough food for that huge body.

The hungry ghosts are the most common of our indigenous ghouls, of which there are many varieties, and I'm not entirely surprised to find him in a go-go club, for they feed on every kind of vice. We all believe in them, by the way, even those who would deny it to foreigners. To many people, especially in the country, the undead are a serious pest. One of their more disgusting tricks is to appear late at night on quiet lanes holding their heads under their arms, although the more common posture is a dead-eyed, flabby-lipped stare from the foot of the bed. They bring bad luck and the only repellent is a visit to the temple and some expensive exorcism by the monks. They can be a hazard to prostitution. Every bar has its own story of the girl who contracted to spend the night with a client, only to flee in the middle of it because the ignorant *farang* had chosen an old run-down hotel infested with these filthy spirits. Even Nong, above averagely robust in most respects, once woke, with her middle-aged customer snoring peacefully beside her, to see an apparition greedily licking at the used condom which the *farang* had been too lazy to dispose of. She too had dressed hurriedly and departed, vowing never to visit that particular hotel again. I deal with this one by reciting the Four Noble Truths to myself in Pali. I watch while he vanishes, and with him the dull gray space he inhabits. I stand up and open the door.

The music and roar of voices from the bar is suddenly deafening. The burning in my stomach is ferocious and the sourness in my mouth makes me nauseous. I grope my way down the stairs and enter the bar.

It is twenty minutes past midnight, just the hour when the great game reaches a climax. Shy men who have been saying no all night find their wills sapped by drink and the ceaseless attention of near-naked young women; all of a sudden the prospect of going back to the hotel alone is more appalling—and somehow more immoral, a crime against life, even—than congress with a prostitute. Skillfully, the girls build a dream world of fantasy in the Western mind, a world which is mysteriously difficult to let go of. And the girls, too, have their fantasies: of finding the *farang* who would support them for life, or, failing that, take them to the West and relieve them, for a year or two, of this living hand to mouth, not to mention the indignity of their trade. The bar is packed.

A gang of brutal-looking young men, their heads shaved like pink coconuts, ears pincushions of ironmongery, tattoos glowing at the edges of cutaway singlets, sit mesmerized around the bar, which is in near darkness. It is the paint act. The girls on the platform are naked except for streaks of luminescent paint asymmetrically applied the length of their bodies. Under the ultraviolet spots the effect is eerie: erotic pink and mauve shapes move sinuously to the music, a Thai pop song with the usual upbeat rhythm. Other men sit in padded booths surrounded by attentive girls and staring at the show. The floor is flooded, too, by Englishmen telling each other it is the cheapest bar in Pat Pong. As I pass a booth I hear: "I want to take you out, I'll pay your bar fine."

"I don't know. Cork you too big."

"I tip big too."

"Oh, okay."

Outside the street is no less crowded. Here the forces of capitalism produce a strange conjunction. Families on their first trip to the Orient, sleepless with jet lag, browse the dense lanes of clothes stalls. Women and girls make oohs and aahs as they translate the prices into their own currency while their men acquire rubber necks. The moral impropriety of designer rip-offs seems not to trouble the respectable bourgeois conscience as they cram plastic bags with Calvin Klein T-shirts, Tommy Bahama jeans, fake Rolexes.

"Well, if you're tempted, Terry, go ahead and get it off your chest," a stout woman is saying in bitter tones as she holds the hand of a wide-eyed boy of about seven. "Just remember to use protection, and don't expect us to be waiting in the hotel when you've finished."

"I didn't say I was tempted, darling," the man says (also stout, balding, haggard), "I merely said you can see how some blokes might be tempted."

"Well, I have to say I can't see what's so tempting, I hate to be racist, but this *is* the Third World."

I am in a hurry to escape this street full of sad memories, but it doesn't do to try to rush. The place is so crowded, the night so hot, the music so loud, the ten thousand television monitors so insistent, you have to adjust to the prevailing rhythm: somnambulant rather than relaxed, as if these were not real people so much as dream-bodies the true owners of which are tucked up between crisp sheets in one of the safe clean suburbs of the West. I eventually make it out to Silom, where still more stalls line the road for more than a mile. I hail a cab.

It takes more than an hour to reach Kaoshan in the dense midnight traffic. When I arrive the music is even louder. The taxi cannot penetrate the crowds in the street who are carousing, swigging from beer and whisky bottles and checking out pirated tapes and CDs on the stalls. I pay the driver and, once again squeezing between hot damp Caucasian bodies, find the *soi* where the teak house stands in near darkness.

I imagine the black man doing this: escaping the insanity-with-soundtrack of Kaoshan, escaping the light, escaping the city, escaping the world to retreat with a sigh to his private and perfect world in the nostalgic wooden house of yesteryear. At the top of the stairs leading to the first floor I slip off my shoes and gingerly try the door. It yields to my push and I slip inside like a shadow.

It takes a moment to realize the lights are switched on. The glow they give is so soft, hardly more than that of safety lights. The old lady sits cross-legged in one of the dark corners, softly murmuring.

She is perhaps the last survivor of her generation in the village where she was born and brought up—probably somewhere in the northeast in the area we call Isaan, near the Lao border—and she is talking to all those friends and relatives who have already passed over to the other side. They are as real to her—realer—than the living. She must do this every night, no doubt longing for her own liberation from a world she has never understood and never will. I take the key from my pocket and slip out the front door, climbing up the external wooden staircase to the upper floor where the twenty-first century awaits.

The computer is as I left it, still running with the screen turned off. When I press the button to illuminate the screen, it reads:

Thank you, Detective, congratulations on getting here before us. A thousand bucks is a little steep but Uncle Sam can take it. We would like you to meet Special Agent Kimberley Jones as soon as possible. Regards, Khun Rosen and Khun Nape.

I nod at such gracious tones from a superpower, and delve into Bradley's software. It is difficult at first to find a common theme amongst it all, the marine was nothing if not eclectic. Little by little a surprising statistic emerges. In addition to Webster's dictionary there are three medical dictionaries, each more extensive than the last, as if Bradley started off with the simpler version and found his needs to be more complex. Similarly there are three separate programs which deal with human anatomy, the biggest occupying three gigabytes. I enter it to find stunning graphics demonstrating every aspect of the human body, from skeletal details to musculature, to highly colored representations of every organ. From the way Bradley has customized the program it seems as if his favorite page is a map of the female form with a point-and-click facility. I point to the left ear, click, and instantly find myself looking at a gigantic Technicolor ear, with a detailed explanation of the hearing faculty in text at the bottom of the screen and an invitation to examine different details more closely. I blink at the great lion-colored mountain range of the outer ear, ruthlessly cut away to reveal a temporal bone in leopard-skin crosshatching, a tympanic membrane in wet-look mauve, a snail-like cochlea in cornflower blue.

In a flash of inspiration, I check the program for bookmarks, find several and double-click on one of them. I find myself staring at a brilliantly colored breast. The bulk of the pendulous mound is sandstone, with a fiery inner core from which lead the volcanic lactiferous ducts to the towering summit. A footnote explains that the whole hangs between the second and sixth rib from those ocher pectorals. A sound like a soft thud penetrates the floorboards from below.

I close down the computer, switch off the light and slip out of the office into the corridor. The steps on the wooden staircase are so soft they would have been undetectable except for two creaks which I noticed on the way up. I sense rather than hear a body on the other side of the door, then the unmistakable squirt of betel spit.

I open the door wide and the little old lady flies in, knocking me down. Under her, I squirm in a sticky mess, trying to gain a footing, thrusting her to one side to send her skidding across the polished floor while I roll over to avoid the blow and spring to my feet. A meat cleaver sticks in the floor at an angle while its owner, dressed in black with black motorcycle helmet and tinted visor, pulls out a knife. The visor, clearly, is an irritating impediment to my assassination; he thrusts it roughly upward, revealing a Southeast Asian face, from the Thai ethnic group, otherwise anonymous in the spherical frame of the helmet.

I manage to stand up but he has me pinned with my back against the wall near the entrance. Forensically observant to the last, I see the knife has a serrated section on the back, a channel for the flow of blood so as to avoid those vulgar sucking sounds when withdrawn from the corpse, with an elegant parabolic curve toward the tip which catches the light nicely and is about twelve inches long. My dilemma is simple: if he lunges for my heart and I evade him by dodging to the right, I shall have about a minute more to live than if I don't dodge at all, or, equally possible, if he, reading my mind like the professional he clearly is, lunges with a slight bias to the left, he should do me in with approximately a thirty-degree penetration wound, probably with an upward thrust to take in as much lung, ventricle and aorta as humanly possible with one blade. We are reading each other's minds, he with the amusement of one who has already won, me with the clarity of thought legendary in the doomed. An infinitesimal twitch in his left eyebrow tells me he will lunge in the next second. I stake my chips on a jump to the left. A mighty leap causes the wooden house to shake and ends with the knife stuck in the panel and his visor clopping back over his face. Compared to my own problems, his next decision is hardly taxing: whether to wrestle the knife out of the wall with visor up or down? I watch fascinated while he attempts both at the same time, pushing the annoying visor up with the left while he pulls at the knife with the right. That thrust of his was quite something; the knife is stuck so fast between planks he needs a foot to press against the wall to pull it out, which requires two hands; whoops, that visor again. I have the feeling that things are not quite as urgent as I had thought, but decide to try a charge anyway. No time like the present, and I use the back wall to thrust myself forward. I manage to launch myself into the air, a mistake because once launched I find I have lost control over my direction and he eludes me by stepping sideways with a contemptuous grunt, leaving me winded facedown on the boards while he goes back to his chore with the knife, which finally yields to his efforts.

I try to stand to run for the door, but slide on the slippery surface and collapse painfully back onto my knees. I twist to the right, in a gamble that Mr. Black will lunge to the left. Wrong, I feel the knife slice up the right side of my rib cage as I fling myself facedown onto the floor. Not the best defensive position. I manage a quick flip onto my back as Mr. Cleaver leaps on top of me, visor up. I raise my left foot and for a split second keep it there. An astonished groan peculiar to the male of our species as my honorable opponent's testicles hit my heel and the visor slowly closes over his agony. A hardy fellow, I have to admit, as he rolls over and over to the open door, apparently having trouble standing, breathing and thinking. I hear him tick off the stairs on the way down to the ground on his backside and fancy I can hear that visor clopping as he goes.

My knees are all but paralyzed from the way I fell on the floor and my own blood is pooling with the old lady's. I am skidding and flailing in a slippery pond when the motorbike starts up and roars away.

I crawl to the old lady, whose throat has been slashed back to the vertebra, then grope my way to my feet using the wall and feel my way to the master bedroom. As I switch on the light I feel her eyes on me. This time the ironic twist to her lips must be especially for me. The gold-stick-with-jade in her navel gives me pause as I pass by.

In the shower I watch my blood slipping away in pink solution and feel myself weakening.

Moment of truth: Who do I distrust least? Put another way, who is likely to be both punctual and equipped for a medical emergency? There is really no contest, the Colonel is probably carousing at one of his clubs and has certainly turned off his mobile. Nor is there any point in calling for an ambulance, since in Krung Thep there are none. I pick Rosen's card out of my pocket and call him from the telephone in the bedroom. I speak in short sentences punctuated by convincing gasps of pain, and replace the receiver.

I lie on the bed while life slips away. It is not an unpleasant sensation, although one remains tormented by the question of what happens next.

21

Fritz von Staffen was certainly different, I had to give him that. For a start he was not middle-aged; he was in his mid-thirties. Nor was he discernibly inadequate in any other way. He was tall, slim and handsome, from the south of Germany where people are as likely to have brown hair as blond. His was almost black and his skin pale. His only affectation, apart from being an elegant dresser, was to smoke English cigarettes from an amber cigarette holder, but this he did well.

It was my first experience of flying. Fourteen hours in the belly of a huge machine, then a nervous trip from the airport in a big white Mercedes taxi, my mother making appropriate sounds of wonder with the tall German's arm around her while I gazed at wide empty streets as black as her hair.

We arrived at night, so the voyage of discovery began the next day, when we stepped out into the air. And what air! I had never experienced air in a city which smelled fresh, just as though you were in the country. Deciduous trees exploding in sprays of greens! I had never seen the pyramids on horse chestnuts before, apple blossom, chestnut blossom, the first roses. You had to wonder if this was really a city, or a gigantic park on which a few housing estates had encroached. *Garten* were everywhere.

There was the Englischer Garten, the Finanzgarten, the Hofgarten, the Botanischer Garten—it seemed that *Garten* were to Munich what traffic was to Krung Thep. And attached to each of these *Garten*, sometimes bang in the middle, you invariably came across another kind of *Garten*, the *Biergarten*, and equally inevitably you came across one or more of Fritz's many friends and acquaintances. They seemed like a small army at first, until they narrowed down to three couples who always seemed to be there drinking huge steins of beer, which I could hardly lift, and eating potato salad, chicken, ribs from paper plates while a Bavarian band in lederhosen played Strauss. Not that I could tell Strauss from Gershwin until Fritz explained music, as he explained many other things that a young boy needs to know.

Fritz's friends passed our tests admirably, even Nong said so. Not the slightest Teutonic coldness toward the brown-skinned woman and her half-caste son, not a hint in the eyes that they had discussed between them (as they surely had) the likely nature of her profession. The women of the three couples were especially attentive and told my mother how delighted they were that dear Fritz had finally found a mate whom he and his friends could love. Nong told me that Germans were special people, not afflicted by the narrow-mindedness that caused so much racism in other Western countries. Germans were people of the world who could cut through cultural barriers and look into the hearts of those from the other side of the earth. If only Thais were more like that.

We had arrived in May and by July Fritz pronounced my English way in advance of that of any German boy. Nong's English, too, had improved measurably, for Fritz had a clever way of teasing her: "Darling, I really love the way you pronounce your *r*'s, we used to have a comedian who did that—he was hilarious, earned a fortune on the stage and on TV."

My mother put in the time and never made an *r* sound like an *l* again, except for satirical purposes, when she wanted to show her sophistication by making fun of the bar-girl accent (other improvements were no less dramatic, though even Fritz took some time to convince her that "boom-boom" was not standard English for sexual intercourse, but rather a device by which some gifted predecessor had first pierced the language barrier on this crucial point).

In June I caught a summer cold and Nong learned her first complete phrase in German: "*Was ist los, bist Du erkaeltert?*"

During the third week of July my mother took me for a walk in the

Englischer Garten, sat down with me on a bench under a chestnut tree, held my hand tightly and burst into tears. She laughed as she cried. "Darling, I can't believe how happy I am, I'm crying with relief that the nightmare is over—I don't have to—you know—work at night anymore. I don't have to go to Pat Pong ever again in my life if I don't want to." I too felt the sense of religious redemption: I would have her with me every night from now on, until we died.

The letdown was vertiginous. The first I knew of it was an explosion of Thai expletives from the bedroom next door, a "Calm down, darling, please, calm down" from Fritz, more Thai expletives, the sound of something being thrown, a "You little savage" from Fritz, the word *Scheisser* repeated over and over again by Nong, a flood of tears not of the joyful variety, an "Ouch, you fucking bitch" from Fritz, and "I'll make you pay for that, you vile little monkey," the bedroom door opening and closing with a slam, Nong running downstairs, the garden door opening and slamming. Silence.

I figured a late-night dash to the airport was in the cards and prepared myself for fourteen hours with a furious mother, followed by Krung Thep in late July—not the sweetest prospect on earth. Obviously, Fritz kept a tall blond mistress somewhere and Nong had come across the evidence, probably after a diligent search of his pockets.

But the call to flee did not come that night, and Fritz really wasn't fooling around.

In my hospital bed I reflect on my mother's most defining moment with a pride that has grown with the years.

The next day she appeared alone in my bedroom, still boiling. She told me to pack my things, leaving out every single toy, game or book that Fritz had given me, while she did the same. Fritz insisted on driving us to the airport in his BMW. A telling line of dialogue broke the silence: Fritz: "I wasn't going to put you in any danger, you know." Nong: "So why don't you bring the suitcases from Bangkok yourself, if it's so safe?"

At the airport Nong ostentatiously opened our two suitcases and examined every item, even squeezing toothpaste and shaking cakes of soap and knocking on the cases to check for false bottoms. Fritz, with a sarcastic aside about her level of education and the Thai intellect in general, pointed out that no one exports illegal drugs from the West *into* Thailand. She ignored him with true Thai stubbornness, and when she was through checked herself and her son onto the flight to Bangkok without a single backward glance. Fritz was history.

Well, not quite. Fritz was not unknown in the Bangkok bar scene and the efficient bush telegraph passed its message to Nong a few years later: Fritz had chosen the wrong girl again, this time with disastrous consequences for him. She had informed the police in Bangkok, who had mounted a sting operation, and now he was in the dreaded Bang Kwan prison on the Chao Phraya River. I was for going to see him. Nong wouldn't hear of the idea. I insisted. Fritz might be rotten to the core, but for a number of months he had been the best surrogate father a boy could wish for. We fought, I won. One fine morning we went down to the river and took the boat as far as the last jetty, from where we trekked in the heat to the prison.

Bang Kwan was even grimmer than I expected. A fortress with a watchtower and guards armed with machine guns, surrounded by double perimeter walls, the stench of raw sewage as we passed through the first gate, and the spiritual stench of violence, sadism and rotting souls as we passed into the inhabited part of the prison. Fritz's head was shaved, he was very thin in a threadbare prison shirt and shorts. The prison blacksmith had welded iron rings around his ankles joined by a heavy chain, but he greeted my mother and me with the same Old World charm, thanked us for coming to see him, and said: "I would like to apologize for the way I behaved at the airport that last day in Munich." Nong maintained a relentlessly hard face, gave brittle answers to his questions. The interview lasted less than ten minutes.

On the way home from the prison, my mother admitted it had been a good idea to make the visit. In her eyes the Buddha had avenged her by sending Fritz to jail and humiliating him in front of her. When I sneezed from the pollution she said: *"Was ist los, bist Du erkaeltert?"*

The phrase has come into my mind because she is repeating it now as she leans over me, smiling. I grab her hand like a hungry lover, but I'm almost too weak to talk.

She has filled out somewhat in retirement, her bust is fuller and her shoulders broader, she is fifty now, and has not lost her effortless talent for projecting sex.

Not that she tries to lose it. She is wearing a crimson dress which exposes her brown shoulders and some of her cleavage, black and crimson patent leather shoes with fairly high heels, a gold Buddha on a heavy gold chain around her neck, a black and crimson handbag which is an illegal copy of a Gucci, a heavy gold bracelet, gold teardrop earrings, wet-look red lipstick, heavy mascara and that perfume I remember from Paris, mostly because Nong's personal cannot-do-without budget doubled after that trip.

There is not a trace of gray in her hair, which is curled in a plait asymmetrically on one side of her head, with the end left to flop, giving her the appearance of—an expensive tart. She sits in a chair next to my bed and lights a Marlboro Red. "D'you want a puff?" I shake my head. "Is it really bad, darling? I rushed here as soon as I could when the Colonel told me what had happened. What were you doing in that house all alone late at night anyway?" She shudders, then puts a hand on mine where it lies on the sheet. "You're going to be all right, though, the surgeon told me—he's really charming, isn't he? The longest scar in Krung Thep, but basically superficial, that's what he said." She looks at me fondly, as if I fell off a ladder during some juvenile prank. "Is there anything I can get you? Anything you want?"

I gaze into her eyes. "Mother, I've been dreaming and hallucinating with all the drugs they gave me. I want you to tell me who my father was."

I have asked this question exactly ten times, this being the tenth. I remember the other nine times as vividly as I will remember this. The question takes courage, and requires the emotional intensity of a special occasion—a near-fatal attack by a would-be assassin should do.

She pats my hand. "As soon as you're out of here, let's you and me spend a few days at my house in Phetchabun, no? We'll get in some beer, I'll invite some people, we'll play hi-lo, I can get you some ganja if you want—I know how much Pichai's death must be affecting you."

"Mother—"

Another pat on the hand. "I'm building up the courage, darling. Really I am."

I sigh and allow her an indulgent smile. At least she has come to the hospital and plans to stay the week in Bangkok so she can be near me. She smokes another cigarette, tells me about Pichai's funeral, which went exactly as expected—the police had to be called to break up a fight between two *yaa baa* dealers—and leaves me to fall back to sleep. I awake a few minutes later to find the FBI trying to open a window to let out the cigarette smoke. "Please leave it," I tell her, "I like the smell of Marlboro."

"Do you and your mother normally speak to each other in German?"

"Now and then. When we feel like it."

"Do Thais usually learn German?"

"My mother and I learned a little from one of my professors," I reply with a smile.

I want you to tell me who my father was. I still wonder about him almost daily, although my obsession has bedded down to some subconscious layer. I still stare rudely at middle-aged white American men who seem to fit the bill, but I no longer suffer from the unhealthy fanaticism of my teens. In my thirteenth year I took over one corner of our hovel and forced my mother to witness my yearning, month by month, while I plastered the walls with old Vietnam War clippings. For one week I was certain he was one of those who fought with superhuman courage in the tunnels of Cu Chi. For more than six weeks he was an aviator, imprisoned and tortured in the Hanoi Hilton, until I discovered that those heroes were not released until after I was born. Where was he during the Tet Offensive? Was he one of those of troubled conscience in the photograph where disillusioned GIs are smoking ganja through the barrels of their rifles? I think I was sixteen when I finally realized that America had lost the war, despite my anonymous father's best efforts. But by then confusion had already divided my mind. After all, despite his undoubted qualities he must have been one of those white men from far away whose mission it was to kill brown men racially indistinguishable from my mother, her father and her brothers (some years later I realized Vietnam was not a race war but a war of religion). And what about the atrocities? My only overseas trip without Nong consisted of a week in Vietnam, where I searched for him in Cu Chi, Da Nang, Hanoi and the Museum of American War Atrocities in Ho Chi Minh City. And all that time she watched in agony. Sometimes her lips would tremble as if she were about to speak his name, but she never did. What terrible secret was she keeping? Was he "special forces"—one of the torturers?

22

The FBI has a good figure, blue eyes, light blond hair, peaches-and-cream complexion, the pleasant odor of honest soap. No Parisian perfume for her. She tells me her name is Kimberley Jones. I think she's about twenty-eight and a worrier. She is a little gaunt. I suspect overexercise.

I am in a hospital such as I have never seen: a private room like a room in a five-star hotel, with a window which looks out on palms and banana plants, orchids and bougainvillea, hibiscus and the infinitely enticing *whish-whish* of an automatic irrigation system. When I last regained consciousness the FBI was already here. She said: "You lost a lot of blood, pilgrim, we only just got to you in time." She could almost be a nurse, the way she takes my pulse from time to time and plumps the bed.

When I reemerged the second time from the depths of delicious oblivion, where I'm sure I encountered my brother Pichai, the seat by my bed was occupied not by the FBI but by a more military figure.

"All this for a scratch? The Buddha must really love you."

"How do I look?" I had been afraid to ask this question of a foreign woman.

"Without the nose? On you, an improvement." To my startled glance, the Colonel added: "Joking, joking." He leaned forward conspiratorially.

"But just tell me this, it won't go any further I promise: Why did you have to kill the old lady? Was she coming on to you?"

I lay back on my pillow and returned to oblivion, just so I could tell Pichai about that one.

It seems that my mother met the Colonel in the corridor today. There's a gleam in her eye as she draws up her chair.

"He's very charming, isn't he? I think he must be very rich."

"No, Mother."

"He asked me out on his yacht. Is it true it's one of those huge things with a captain and crew, swimming platform, all that?"

"No, please, don't."

"Oh, I don't care for myself, but it would be good for you. You deserve promotion more than any cop on the force, and you'll never get it without developing connections. He even hinted—"

"If I was offered promotion that way, I would refuse it."

She sighs and pats my hand. "Well, you can't say I don't try. You're such a moral boy, I don't know where you get it from."

"Of course you know *who* I get it from, obviously not from you. *I* don't know who I get it from because you won't tell me."

Nervous laughter as she reaches for her Marlboro. "I will, darling, one day, I just need a little time, that's all."

23

Random-access memory: an island in the Andaman Sea reserved for nature and forbidden to everyone except high-ranking cops with luxury yachts; more girls than I could count, their perfect young bodies permanently sparkling with droplets from incessant diving off the swimming platform (the girls really had fun that trip); Pichai and I uncomfortable and aloof, taking a lot of flak: to refuse bribes was bad enough, to refuse free sex was downright seditious. It was an office outing, a bonding binge soon after the assassination of those *yaa baa* smugglers, intended to cement the esprit de corps, just in case anyone was getting cold feet (no one was). The other cops were all too keen to bed the girls, leaving Vikorn, Pichai and me to drink beer together and stare at the stars. I guess the old man felt secure there on his boat, with the velvet night around him—and maybe he loved us, Pichai and me. On the boat's stereo system Vikorn was playing "The Ride of the Valkyries," the only piece of Western music of which he showed any awareness. In a lull in the conversation Pichai finally asked what no one else had dared to ask: *What the hell was that weird music?*

Even at his drunkest Vikorn's war stories were veiled in secrecy. He might seem to lose control of his tongue altogether, but there was something as hard as diamond, some heavily guarded safe room in his mind that he dare not enter in company. The only real clues he gave us consisted of single words: REMFs; Ravens; O-1s; the Other Theater; American Breakfast; eggs over easy; Pat Black.

24

As soon as Nong has gone the FBI returns with a frown on her face. She cannot speak Thai, but I think she saw my mother and the Colonel flirting in the corridor. Perhaps she is suffering from advanced culture shock? I already know she and the Colonel are not going to get along.

She brings the news that Bradley's computer has arrived, and a few minutes later she begins organizing a bridge over the bed, cables, even an Internet connection. Kimberley Jones does not flirt, indeed I think she must have taken an antiflirting course at Quantico, so there is a stiffness in the way she leans over me every few minutes. When we have the computer up and running, it is even more awkward. Half the time I have her bosom in my face, which often causes her to blush. Did American culture go back in time about a hundred years? I'm sure all those movies from the Vietnam era showed a more relaxed people. Not that it matters. We become quite excited, in a professional sense, once we enter Bradley's e-mail files.

Pretty soon we are joined by Rosen and Nape, who look over my shoulder at the monitor. Everything is affable and even jolly until I say: "This guy, Sylvester Warren, does anyone know who he is?" Silence from the rest of the team. I search out Kimberley Jones' eyes. She looks away. Rosen coughs.

"You have a way of coming straight to the point, Detective, I'll give you that."

Nape comes to the rescue. "I don't think we'd want to let it be known we're even reading e-mails from Mr. Warren. Not unless we get something concrete we can use."

Rosen agrees with a vigorous nod. "That's right. If what we have is a revenge killing in a narcotics feud, we don't want to drag Warren into it. Not if all he's doing here is keeping up an erudite correspondence with Bradley on some obscure aspect of the jade trade."

I make big eyes from one to the other in the most charming and humble manner. Nape grins. "Warren's a big shot. Actually, he's a big shot here as well as in New York. He comes to Bangkok every month, gets invited to receptions at the embassy. He mixes extensively with local high society, especially the Chinese. He's a jeweler and art dealer, big-time. He has shops in Manhattan, Los Angeles, Paris, London—and here. His passion is jade. It's not surprising he would have contacts with Bradley, who's coming across as a gifted amateur, living here in Bangkok, and a fellow American."

"What a wonderful, democratic society you have, that a sergeant in the Marines hobnobs with a baron like this Warren."

All three check my face for sarcasm, which I did not intend. I have managed to produce an awkward silence. Rosen says: "Well, Americans talk to each other. We still do that. Especially if there's a profit to be made."

I think I get the point and use the program to select some of Warren's e-mails and Bradley's replies to him. Helplessness radiates from my American colleagues as I read aloud.

> Bill, your piece arrived yesterday FedEx. The boys are getting the point, I agree, but there's still a long way to go.

> Bill, look, this is good work which I can sell anywhere, but it's not what we discussed. I'm arriving on a Thai Airways flight next Tues. We'll talk.

> Bill, I have to tell you I was very impressed with the latest piece. It's not quite there, but it's damn close. I'm going to release the second tranche today. Keep it up.

I interrupt my reading to search the three sets of eyes around the bed, until Rosen says to Nape: "Tell him."

He clears his throat. "Sylvester Warren is a very well-connected man. He knows senators, congressmen. He probably fits out thirty percent of America's richest women and a lot of our richest men with their jewelry, thanks to his gift for finding the best original designers. Basically, he knows everyone with real money, donates huge amounts to the Republican Party and somewhat less to the Democrats. He's occasionally invited to the White House. He knows judges, senior lawyers. He's also been under surveillance by the FBI for years. We suspect him of art frauds, but he's just too smart to catch. Also, we don't have a whole lot of specialists in imperial jade and he's probably the world's leading expert. It's his hobby, his passion as well as his profession. If he's a crook, he's only ripping off the rich, and the rich don't like to admit to being ripped off. There's a limit to how many resources the Bureau wants to put into something like this, given our other priorities."

I click my tongue. "Would I be right in thinking his collection of imperial jade is one of the biggest outside of museums?"

"Yes."

"And he sells off a piece every now and then, probably at an auction?"

"Usually privately, but every now and then Christie's or Sotheby's gets a piece of the action. When they do, it's a special occasion. People you thought had been dead for years come out of the woodwork. Of course, the bidding is done by proxies, the public doesn't know who the real bidders are."

Rosen, frowning, takes up the story. "Washington's not keen on collecting evidence against Warren, not unless it's so good all his friends will be forced to disown him, and he's too smart for there to be evidence like that. Another problem, frankly, is that if there is evidence, it's likely to originate here in Thailand, and—do I have to go on?"

"He's too well connected here for such evidence to survive a day after it comes to light?" Nods from the FBI. "How old is Mr. Warren?"

"He's sixty-two and looks like a young forty."

"And began his career in his twenties?"

"Got a master's in gemology and another in Chinese studies, specializing in the late imperial period. He speaks Mandarin well and his Thai is very good." A pause while Nape moves his finger around the edge of the monitor. "He also speaks the Swatow dialect. That say anything to you?"

"Swatow? Where the Chiu Chow come from? Chiu Chow run Thailand," I say. "They run our banks, all major businesses. They have Thai names, but they're Chiu Chow."

"I think you've got the point," Rosen says.

Nape pauses to check my expression, which I have rendered studious. He coughs and continues. "A possible hypothesis which we don't want to go into print looks like this. A relatively crass black sergeant in the Marines, with an unexpected eye for beauty, starts a web page shortly after making a trip to Laos, where he bought an experimental lump or two of unprocessed jade sometime after May 17, 1996, probably just a few months after his arrival. Sylvester Warren sees the exhibit on the web page, notes the apparent quality of the workmanship, whatever he might think of the theme, and looks up Sergeant Bradley on one of his visits to Bangkok. Bradley is probably overwhelmed and astonished that his little venture has drawn such a distinguished eye. He also sees an opportunity to put money aside for his retirement. What he's got that Warren wants is direct on-the-ground contact with local craftsmen, who are probably of Chinese extraction, probably the artistic inheritors of world-class jade workers who fled the Communists in 1949. Warren has his own craftsmen, of course, the best in the world, but he can't use them for anything illegal. Bradley can provide both a firewall and American-style quality control. We're talking fakes. Every time a museum or private collector comes out with a catalogue, there are people all over the world who copy the best pieces and sell them. There's no scientific way to prove a fake jade—carbon-14 dating doesn't work, neither does thermoluminescence"—to Rosen—"I checked all this out yesterday."

I look up. "For Bradley's craftsmen to copy Warren's pieces properly, they would have to have the original?"

"We thought of that," Kimberley Jones says. "We talked about Bradley absconding with some priceless piece from the Warren Collection, but it just doesn't fit. There was nowhere Bradley could hide from Warren, and probably nowhere he could have sold the piece at a halfway decent price. These artifacts are matters of public record, experts know who owns what down to the date of purchase. Only Warren could sell something from the Warren Collection, real or fake."

"Anyway," Nape adds, "is Warren going to use snakes in a revenge killing? With his money and contacts here, he could have snuffed Bradley and made it look like natural causes. Why would he want the heat?"

A moment of communal reflection. I say: "What does the word 'tranche' mean?"

"Slice. What it probably means here is that Warren was financing the experiment, giving Bradley installments of cash through one of his agents in Bangkok. Like a lot of very wealthy people, Warren is notoriously tight with money. We don't think he was giving much away. Big bucks was the carrot he was offering only when Bradley had produced a perfect copy of one of Warren's pieces."

"A strange game for Warren to play, if he's so rich."

Rosen rumbles, "Welcome to American capitalism. It's a great system, except that no one ever has enough."

I say, "The horse and rider?" and draw only blank expressions. My strength is fading. I allow myself the luxury of forsaking human consciousness for the bosom of the Buddha.

25

Using the Net and station gossip as tools, it wasn't too difficult for Pichai and me to piece together our Colonel's drunken ramblings, even though their deeper meaning continued to elude us.

REMFs were Rear Echelon Mother Fuckers—a standard epithet used by U.S. combat troops for the despised officers who stayed back in Saigon and ran the disastrous war. *The Other Theater* was Laos, where America was forbidden by international treaty from waging war, and where it waged the most ferocious bombing campaign in history. *Ravens* were exceptionally gifted American aviators who had come to loathe REMFs and volunteered to fly O-1 spotter planes on secret missions out of Long Tien in the green Laotian mountains to locate the positions of the North Vietnamese regular army, which was steadily encroaching into Laos. The more obscure references to *American Breakfast, eggs over easy* and *Pat Black* proved impossible to track down.

Somehow Vikorn had made a small fortune in Long Tien. A good part of this money he used to buy his commission in the Royal Thai Police Force. There were rumors of contacts in the CIA, dark secrets known to our Colonel which the Americans didn't want to get out.

* * *

It takes more than two hours for Nape and Jones to reach Bradley's teak house and call Rosen to report that the horse and rider is gone. Rosen thrusts his hands in his pockets and goes to the window. "Looks like we found the motive for the attack on you."

"But he didn't get away with the horse and rider. He never got further than the corridor."

Rosen shrugs. "Because you kicked him in the balls. So he came back later, or sent someone else."

I know what Rosen is thinking. If the horse and rider is an original that Bradley was copying, it's going to be difficult to keep Warren out of the case. I see the weight of a controversial investigation bear down on his thick shoulders, sloping them still further, driving him more deeply into the negative karma which dogs him. I say: "Did you take pictures, or would you like to borrow mine?"

He makes a face. "Sure, we took pictures."

By the afternoon my hospital room is turning into a library. Somehow the FBI have got hold of every illustrated book on jade available in Krung Thep. They have also e-mailed the picture of the horse and rider to Quantico. A wonderful hush envelops my room, the hush of concentrated minds following clues as we work carefully through the books, checking the color plates against our photograph of the horse and rider. Is investigation normally like this in the West? I have never done things this way before and I'm finding a subtle pleasure in this novel approach to law enforcement, with no one to shoot, intimidate or bribe.

Almost at the same time Nape and Jones emit deliciously triumphant aahs. Trying not to let his enthusiasm run away with him, Nape shows Rosen a page from the book he is using, while Jones tries to show him hers. Rosen looks at both and turns to me. "What did I tell you?" He shows me the page in Nape's book, which is a beautiful picture of the piece carrying the cryptic caption: *Horse and Rider from the Warren Collection, formerly from the Hutton Collection, believed to be one of the pieces the last Emperor Henry Pu Yi took with him when he fled the Forbidden City. Procured for Hutton by Abe Gump.*

At that very moment, Rosen's mobile starts to ring. I note that he has chosen the theme tune from *Star Wars* for his ringing tone, whereas I myself opted for "The Blue Danube" (thereby demonstrating that I am no more than an impostor in Western culture, a naïve tourist anyway, with the musical taste of a grandmother; I can't think why I didn't choose *Star*

Wars, which I actually prefer). The voice on the other end is someone he calls "sir"; it causes a gray and haggard look to dominate his features.

"We're not investigating him, sir . . . That's correct, we did e-mail that picture, which was taken from the scene of a murder attempt on the local detective who is investigating . . . I know the Bradley case looks like a narcotics vendetta but . . . The piece was stolen from Bradley's home, sir . . . Mr. Warren exchanged a number of e-mails with Bradley . . . No, there's not necessarily any connection . . . No, I don't want another screwup . . . That's right, I agree, neither I nor the Bureau need the heat . . . Well, I don't know that I can do that, we don't have any investigative powers here . . . Leave it to the local police? That's exactly what I am doing, sir . . . Goodbye sir." He folds the telephone and his eyes are glittering when he looks at me. "Quantico has no comment on the picture. They say it didn't come out clearly enough on the e-mail."

Cynicism has distorted Nape's face, but I'm most sorry for Kimberley Jones, who looks ashamed and cannot meet my gaze. She says to Rosen in a quiet voice: "This man nearly died."

"But I'm not American," I say with a cute twist of my lips.

A long pause. Rosen says: "Looks like you're on your own. Kimberley here will accompany you whenever you feel you need her. She'll . . . she'll help with anything that doesn't lead to Warren." He shrugs.

"Can I at least have a picture of Warren?"

Three furrowed brows. Kimberley Jones says cautiously: "Sure, we can get you one of those. There's probably a thousand in the public domain. He's been photographed at the White House scores of times. Right?"

"Yeah, right," Rosen agrees. "But don't make it obvious it came from us."

"I'll use a brown paper envelope," Jones says with heavy sarcasm. A *Do I need this?* look from Rosen.

26

Nong sits and watches while the nurse changes my dressing. She holds herself together while the nurse is in the room, then bursts into tears. Drying her eyes: "The person who did this to you will not make a good death."

I'll have to explain that, won't I? Look at it this way: you're facing old age, your sins have been mounting steadily, but you cannot for the life of you see how you could have reacted differently, given the pathetic cards Fate handed you at birth, and now you have to consider the inevitable karmic bill: You think *this* lifetime has been tough? See that legless guy on his atrocious trolley begging on the sidewalk? Last time around he wasn't nearly as bad as you've been, why, he was a saint compared to you.

With us the lifting of the egoic veil at the moment of death reveals the workings of karma in all its pitiless majesty: see that clubfoot in your next life, that's from when you fouled your best friend on the football pitch; see those buckteeth the size of gravestones, that's your cynical sense of humor; see that early death from leukemia, that's your greed.

To make a good death is to proceed gracefully into a better body and a better life. The consequences of a bad death are hard to look at. *You will not make a good death* is a power curse; it makes *Fuck you* sound like a benediction.

. . .

Nong stays with me while they carefully help me into a wheelchair and push me down the corridor to the lift, which takes us down to the garden. This is my first outing and I insist on sitting near the deliciously swishing irrigation system. I like the intermittent spray on my face, the return to infancy in more luxurious surroundings than I ever knew. Is it just me or are we all hardwired to expect our first years to be spent surrounded by flowers in a magic garden? I'm surprised that my mother seems to read my thoughts, holds my hand and smiles. Over the wall the harsh city claws away like an animal. I experience the invalid's repugnance toward return: two more days and they will let me out. I suppose it would be unmanly to ask to stay a little longer?

A hospital orderly brings some of the art books and sets them on a table near my chair, then a few minutes later Rosen comes with a complex expression on his face where shame does battle with career-path paranoia. On the one hand, he gives me the photographs himself in broad daylight in front of my mother; on the other, they are in a brown paper envelope on which no eagle or other identification appears. He departs rather abruptly, too. After a while Nong takes her leave with some unconvincing excuse. She is bored and a little repulsed by the anodyne atmosphere. She belongs on the other side of the wall, in the lusty, clawing city.

Now that I've had a chance to examine the pix (as the FBI call them), I wonder if Rosen is making a point: Warren with the first Bush, Warren with Clinton (twice), Warren with the second Bush, looking older and sleeker. I was not expecting a jeweler to be a man of steel, but that's how he comes across, as if it was sheer willpower that got him into the Rose Garden every time. Clinton was tall, and Warren is the same height, but leaner. Gray-blue eyes, thinning light brown hair turning elegantly gray. He looks so much more sophisticated than the President, with his even tan, filigree gold chain on his left wrist, the posture of a man who has no need to insist. You can almost smell the cologne. He will outlast this President, his smile says; every time. I put him down on top of one of the art books, feeling my strength start to fade. I doze off for a couple of minutes and wake to find him still there, staring at me. I pick him up again. Perhaps it is the power of the White House that triggers an old appetite for the art of detection. Often when we are sick the mind is temporarily released from its prison in the body and floats freely. During this afternoon I sense my own begin to dock again with its destiny.

"What's the matter?" Kimberley Jones asks me when she comes up behind my chair and catches me staring at Warren for the thousandth time. "You were frowning as if you know him."

How to explain? I dare not mention the dark figure that, spiritually speaking, I see standing behind him in each of those pix and whom I seem to recognize.

27

In Kat's modest home the scent is mostly sandalwood, from her joss sticks. Like me, she lives in one room which our national optimism leads us to call an apartment, although hers is inches bigger. Her picture of our beloved King hangs in exactly the same position as mine, and her Buddha shrine sits on a high shelf near the door. I watch her bow to the Buddha three times with the incense held in a bunch between her hands. She concentrates mindfully, no doubt praying for luck. She is wearing a baggy housecoat and, I suspect, nothing else.

"I'm going to have to practice, Sonchai, I missed five balloons last night. You don't mind? It'll be like old times. Did you ever tell your mother how you helped me? I didn't, I was afraid she might be angry with me for corrupting your young mind." She walks to a slim cupboard in the opposite corner and takes out a plastic lunch box.

"I told her a few years ago. She thought it was funny. She wanted to know if it ever got any further than helping with your act. It didn't, did it?"

"Sonchai, you were ten years old and I'm not that kind of woman."

"My mother said no wonder I had a wild adolescence, when my first experience of a woman's private part was darts shooting out of it."

"Not totally misleading, if you listen to the way some men talk about women. D'you hate women?"

"No. But you hate men."

"Let's not go into that. I hate men in the abstract. You I like. You helped me perfect my act." She has taken an aluminum tube out of the lunch box together with a pack of condoms. She hands me the condoms while she lies on a futon on the floor. While she is fitting the tube, I cross the room and blow up the condom until it is about a foot long, then I tie the end and hold it out. Kat has prudishly arranged her dress so that she can shoot the darts without flashing me, like an archer from a fortress. I hold the condom as far from my face as I can while she fits a dart into the tube. Suddenly, without any sign of movement from Kat, the cock-shaped balloon bursts and a dart sticks in the plaster. There are pinpricks and chips all over the plaster.

"I never understood why you couldn't use a dartboard."

"The customers always move the balloons a little bit. I think I make them nervous. I need to know how to hit something wobbly." She giggles. "Anyway, there's a certain satisfaction in killing cocks."

"Was it Bradley made you hate men?"

"Shit." The dart had missed and now it was stuck in the wooden door, really some distance away. I had noticed a slight movement in her lower abdomen this time, in the region of her ovaries. "My first and only husband made me hate men. I'm the jealous, possessive type and he was a motorcycle taxi driver. All over the city, especially to the bars and massage parlors. I don't think there was a whore he didn't screw. I was seventeen years old, for god's sake. Thai men claim to like women, but they only like fucking. Not even that, they love anything forbidden, new, unused. They're terrible for underage girls, far worse than any *farang*. He was like that. I'm a one-heart woman. I give it once, then I don't have it anymore. So I decided I would never have another man. I learned to shoot darts from my pussy instead. I shoot down a whole army of inflated dicks just for practice. Of course, there's always another army waiting to be shot down."

"But you did know Bradley?"

"Yes, I didn't want to talk about it in Nana. Yes, I knew him. An American marine. It's a little painful to talk about. He persuaded me to give men a second chance, after all that time. Five years ago he was a regular visitor to Nana. You know, one of those foreigners who come and can't believe their eyes, get addicted for a few months, then the charm starts to wear off. He was quite a character, though. A man like that, magnificent and very black—who could forget him? He told me he was different. I'm a sucker, aren't I? I'm surprised you didn't find anyone else who recognized his photograph."

"How many women stay five years in the bars? Tell me how he was different."

"He was respectful. He didn't have that mixture of lust, fear and contempt. He really seemed to like us women, as if we were people he could be friends with. He was very popular in all the bars."

"He picked you up? He paid your bar fine?"

Bang. A good shot! I saw the dart pierce the center of the condom and impale it against the wall, from which it now hangs shriveled and flaccid, all passion dead.

"Certainly not. I told you, I don't go with men, not even to sell my body. This was different. I do private parties, that's how I really make my money, the floor show is just my shopwindow. I use an agent, and the agent tells the clients: 'Look, don't touch. This lady is not for sale. She does her act, she'll socialize, maybe even sit on your lap if you really want, but that's it.' Usually the agent is very strong about that, really makes sure the client has understood. Anyway, it happened five years ago that the agent called me to say he had a party for me, and the money was double what I usually charge. He didn't say why it was double, so I was suspicious. I said: 'Farangs?' and he said: 'No.' I said: 'You told them no sex?' And he said: 'Yes, yes, all understood, no sex.' "

I've got into the swing of it now. The inflated condom was already in my hand, at arm's length. Kat paused and sat up slightly. "It was in the Dusit Thani Hotel. The suite on the third floor is for hire for private functions. Very expensive, I would imagine. That's where the party was. They even rigged up a revolving stage for me. This was soon after the first time they showed me on *farang* TV, and I think this party wanted the live version, exactly as they'd shown it on the documentary—it was the BBC, I think. So I do my act without paying too much attention to the clients. I have to concentrate on the balloons, after all. But how could I help but notice that a giant black man is there, with a lot of peasants?"

She uttered the word with contempt. "Not even peasants, hill people. Tribesmen down from the mountains, getting filthy drunk and out of hand. When one tried to come up to the stage to touch me, I started looking for the way out. One of the tribesmen had a familiar face, as if I'd seen him somewhere, but I didn't know where, maybe the newspapers, I think he was one of those drug lords from the borderlands. He was the leader, he had this way of barking, and when he barked the others stopped what-ever they were doing and listened. It was exactly like a movie, with some chief thug trying to control the other thugs. Two of them got so drunk, though, they were out of control, and their leader didn't seem to care too much—they were talking about, you know, having me onstage together while the thing was going round. In all my years in this game, I'd never allowed myself to get into such a situation, and I thought: Oh no, here we go. Mentally, I prepared myself for gang rape—it's a professional hazard and I thought it had to happen sooner or later."

Another condom, another bang. "When they took out their guns and started comparing, I knew I was in for a brutal night. Then the black man stands up, comes to the stage, takes off his shirt—it was one of those tropi-cal things, with pineapples and mangoes all over, and obviously it's enor-mous. He puts it around my shoulders and it comes down to my ankles." She laughed. "Then he says to the boys: 'She's mine, fellas, okay?' "

She reached in the lunch box for more darts. "And these Stone Age creeps just looked at him. No one was going to mess with this black giant. He takes me into the dressing room and says, really gently: 'Better get out of here—how about a date tomorrow?' " She laughed again. "I'm not the swooning type, but I was thirty-six and wondering if I hadn't been a little hard on the opposite sex for the past twenty years. He had saved me from a nightmare, and he was just—well, frankly, irresistible."

The practice was over apparently. She stood up to pack away the darts, the condoms and the aluminum tube.

"How was it?"

"How was it? Strange was how it was. I thought he was a real gentle-man, he took me to dinner, treated me like a lady. He didn't seem in any hurry to go to bed with me. It was as though he wanted to find out something—I think maybe he was still trying to find out about Thai women—what makes us tick. We didn't go to bed together until the third date." She pursed her lips.

"Would you mind telling me about that?"

"About the sex? Is that a part of your investigation? I think he was disappointed. Like most men, he assumed I was something very special between the sheets, you know, as if I was going to have two vaginas or something? I kept hinting, explaining: Look, I developed the act exactly because I'm shy and not very good in bed—I don't know how to please a man at all—I don't know what men want."

"But for you, how was it?"

"Not like anything I've known before, but I'm not an expert. The girls say most men just want to get it in, have their little spurt, then get it out again. Well, he certainly wasn't like that."

"Could you try to be a little more specific?"

Kat gives me a dirty look. "This turning you on, Sonchai? Want to know what it's like for a woman to be underneath a man like that? Actually, I think he must have been used to being adored. He lay there and seemed to expect me to do all the work. I think he was used to women drooling and lusting after him. Or maybe it's the way Americans have sex, I don't know."

"How big was his penis?"

She put a hand over her mouth. "Sonchai! It was normal size, I mean, if it was in proportion to him he would have torn me in two. Normal size, Sonchai, bigger than Thai men, same as a *farang*."

"But you did make love?"

"Of course. But only once, and I didn't enjoy it because I was dealing with this feeling that I'd disappointed him, that he was looking for some kind of extra-exotic, freaky sex—I felt inadequate, I suppose." She sighed. "Afterwards, just to please him, I asked if he wanted me to shoot darts." She laughed. "I must have suspected that's what he wanted, or I wouldn't have brought my darts, would I? A woman like me, you never know exactly what men expect. I got the feeling he wanted me to perform for him, to be his sex toy, but he never asked me to do anything. He wanted me to know what to do. He was being like a woman, in a way. Shooting darts is the only thing I do that interests men."

"Did you perform for him? Did he say yes?"

She nods sadly. "Yes. He came alive then. It turned out that he'd planned it. He'd even bought a dartboard and he positioned me on the bed—and he made a video, with close-ups and everything. He'd planned everything beforehand, but he hadn't wanted to ask me. I don't know if he was a gentleman or some kind of strange romantic. Everything had to be perfect, though, the lighting, the position of the camera—everything. That's when he got most excited, but we didn't make love again." A pause. "What I remember most was the silk."

"Silk?"

"Yes. Everything was silk, really nice quality with beautiful colors, and he tied a silk headscarf around my head, and tied one around his own head. He kept saying how good it felt on the skin, wanted me to feel it. It was quite nice on the skin, but it was just silk—it didn't turn me on. It was like some Middle Eastern show, him being so black in this purple scarf, and when I left he gave me the scarf. He wanted to give me money, but I refused. I was pretty depressed—I suppose I was in love with him, and wanted it to go on a bit longer—and I was disappointed, you know, that he wanted to make that video, that he was like the others, only more so, in a way."

I take a photograph out of my pocket and hold it for her. Kat winces. "I've never met her, but I've heard about her. I mean, you know what people are like, they love to see you suffer? About two years after that night with Bradley, people started telling me about this woman he'd been seen with. The way they described her, that must be her. There can't be more than one in Krung Thep like that. What a body! You can't blame him for preferring her to me, can you? I can say it, now that it's so long ago: that's a fantastic-looking whore."

"You never heard where she worked, what she did?" She shook her head.

I'm about to leave when a whim makes me fish out the pictures of Warren. I show her the most recent: Warren with George W. Bush at a reception in the Rose Garden. Her eyes flicker between me and the photograph. Fear? More like consternation. She put a hand on my arm. "Is he involved? Sonchai, if he is you better forget about this case."

"Why?"

"Did you ever hear the phrase 'a special job'?"

"Of course. He's one of those?"

"He's the original special job. He used to be very well known in the bars. He would arrive once a month and the word would go round. He paid top dollar for any girl who would go with him, but none of them ever wanted to go a second time. They wouldn't talk about it, but you can guess. *Farangs* don't understand us Thais. They think if a girl sells her body, then she has no dignity, no limits. Actually, the opposite is often the truth. Women like your mother are very free spirits. Could you imagine Nong ever holding down a normal job? Or putting up with abuse from a man? A woman might sell her body because it's more dignified and safer than being married to a violent drunk who goes whoring without protection. Well, anyway, nobody went with him twice, at least that was what I heard."

"And he stopped going to the bars, all of a sudden?"

"In the middle of the nineties all those Russian women started appearing, from Siberia. The story was they would go with him time after time and put up with his things, whatever they were. They knew all about special jobs. Their pimps contacted him, so he didn't need the bars anymore. Those Siberians are real tough women. Must be the weather up there."

Kat's hovel belongs to a project almost identical to my own, except that it is not near the river, or anything else of interest to the eye. I stand at the edge of a man-made desert, waiting for a cab, wondering if this wasteland is another Western import. Have we, in our headstrong grabbing of all things Western, inadvertently bought up pieces of the Sahara? Fortunately, I have brought my Walkman with me and listen to Pisit Sritabot's phone-in radio show while I wait. A female professor of sociology is talking in such authoritative tones about prostitution that Pisit for once forgets to interrupt.

"It's an unfortunate word in that everyone has a different definition. These days a huge percentage of young women studying at university and colleges are subsidized by so-called sugar daddies—men, often *farangs* but usually Thai, who pay their expenses, even a kind of salary, in exchange for the right to sleep with the students whenever they choose. It is not illegal, but the girl is certainly selling her body. If the sugar daddy isn't rich enough to pay all her expenses, she'll have to take on another, perhaps as many as three. Often the girl will own three separate mobile telephones, one for each lover so she doesn't get the name wrong when one of them calls. Then you have the very naïve rice grower from Isaan who has heard about the money to be made in the big city, who spends a weekend hanging out at the bars on Sukhumvit, perhaps finds a man or two who hire her, only to discover she has not the slightest clue about foreign men, speaks not a word of English. She may be horrified and mystified by the very idea of oral sex and catches the next bus home to her farm in the far north, never to visit the big city again. Then you have experts, very talented and attractive women who can literally wrap men around their fingers. Such girls often receive income from three or more foreign men, who live overseas and of course are unaware of each other, who are paying her to stay out of the bars until they arrive for their vacations. Of course, she continues to sell her body every night and is probably receiving a total income in excess of any middle-ranking professional, such as a lawyer or doctor. Then you have the girls who travel, often on false pass-ports supplied by our local mafia, who also procure visas for countries like Britain and the U.S. Such girls, if they are gifted in their profession, may make as much as U.S.$180,000 a year in cities like London, Los Angeles, New York, Chicago, Paris, Hong Kong, Berlin, Tokyo, Singapore. Of course they never pay tax, and usually they save a significant amount, so within a few years they return to join our wealthier classes. Then there is the girl who is caught in some loan scam, usually in order to pay medical bills for her mother or father, who finds herself trapped in a brothel in the country, or in Malaysia, who is in reality a sex slave all of whose earnings go to pay off the original loan, who may be required to service a man every twenty minutes while she is on duty, which may be for as long as twelve hours a day. Then there are the pool hustlers. Our girls cannot compete with Filipinas, who are world class, but they're improving all the time."

"What's pool got to do with prostitution?"

"Thai pool. The game is used as a hook. Not every *farang* likes go-go bars or wants to spend an evening drinking beer. Pool mops up the remainder of the market—shy men like it too, it provides a lead-in, a hobby in common. It can seem almost like a holiday romance, which happens to last an evening instead of the usual week."

"I see."

"There is really no comparison between the destinies, mind-sets or lifestyles of these different women, but because they are all prostitutes we inadvertently find ourselves talking about them as if they were in the same plight, which they are not. The truth is that prostitution fulfills many functions. It is a substitute for social welfare, medical insurance, student loans, a profitable hobby as well as being the path to that wealth which many modern women expect from life. It also brings an enormous amount of foreign currency to our country, which means the government is never serious about suppressing it."

"I see," Pisit says again, in an unusually somber mood. "And we are talking about a significant proportion of Thai women?"

"Huge. When you consider that many women are ineligible by rea-son of age, or lack of physical charms, it begins to look as if perhaps twenty percent of women in Krung Thep who are in a position to sell their bod-ies do so. If you include the sugar daddy phenomenon and the overseas industry, which is very very big, the figure must be even higher."

"Are we as a nation dependent on this trade?"

"I don't want to exaggerate or paint these women as heroes, but it's true that without their work we would all be a little bit poorer."

"Is there something about Thai women that leads them so easily into the trade?"

Laughing: "Well, *farangs* especially say how beautiful we are and we don't seem to have the same hang-ups as many Western women. The West tries to turn the act of sex into a religious experience, when to us it is no more than scratching an itch. I'm afraid we're not as romantic as we seem. And perhaps we are a little strange. In other countries such as Japan and South Korea, prostitution declined dramatically as the economy improved. When our economy improves, the number of prostitutes tends to go up rather than down."

I switch Pisit and his guest off when the cab arrives but find myself haunted for a moment by the rice grower from Isaan. I can see her, uncomfortable without her sarong in the short skirt or black leggings and black tank top which are almost a uniform of the trade. Perhaps her legs are short and muscular, her ass a little on the wide side, her expectations wildly out of whack with reality as she stares at passing white men, wondering which of them will be her savior. She owns the broad open face and smudge nose of the northern tribes. I experience her astonishment when her first customer tries to initiate her into the black art of fellatio, her disbelief that he could be serious, that people really did that sort of thing. In my mind's eye I follow her all the way to the terminus, share her disgust with the city while she waits for the bus home. I find I love her, though I've never met her. If we are to be saved it will be by the likes of her.

On the way to my own hovel I meditate on my penis. Not only mine, my thoughts encompass every owner. Sooner or later one comes to a forked path: make it the centerpiece of your life, or put it away to be used in tumescent mode only on special occasions. Those who take the first option must surely reach a point where the sole function of one's lovers is to serve the organ in all its glory? You might put it anywhere, share it with anyone, so long as it's running the show. I find I'm not thinking about my cock at all, I'm thinking of Bradley's: the man who sported a perfect phallus on his web page. And what of his strange bedfellow Sylvester Warren, the man who played so rough only Siberians would partner him?

28

I was twenty-one and already a cop when I visited Fritz for the second time. I went alone and never told Nong of what was to be an ongoing mission of mercy. By then he had been in the jail for more than eleven years and the transformation from suave young European to wizened sewer survivor was complete. He was entirely bald apart from a couple of tufts, with wrinkles which crossed his white shiny dome. A hypersensitivity to nuances of body language gave the impression of extreme cunning bordering on insanity. If I touched my ear, rubbed my nose, coughed or looked at the ceiling I triggered responses vital to his survival. I had come on a whim, no doubt in my usual pathetic search for a father; he emerged in chains from behind the endless warren of bars into his side of the visitors' room in the hope of finding a savior who might somehow get him out of there. No two men have ever disappointed each other more; after five minutes we were laughing like drains. His family had disowned him, his close friends had been rounded up in Germany after his bust and prosecuted for trafficking in heroin. Their incarcerations had passed more quickly than his—he was in for life—but none of them wanted to visit him. I came away with the clear certainty that I was the only person in the world who could save his mind.

Eleven years later I am making my sixty-first visit. Just before we reach the watchtower I have the cabdriver stop for me to buy six packs of two hundred cigarettes. Fritz smokes local brands himself, but 555s are the more valuable currency in the prison economy. In addition I buy a packet of Marlboro Reds and have the driver stop again near the prison while I work in the back of the cab. Fritz has money—by Thai standards he's quite wealthy—but translating this into prison power is not so easy as all that. Every prisoner can open a prison account if he likes, but the amount he can take out of that account from day to day is strictly limited. At first I brought Fritz some of his own money in the form of thousand-baht notes folded and compressed so small I was able to simply flick a couple through the bars in the visiting area whenever I came to see him. The problem here was that in the jail he needed small denominations. A thousand-baht note was unmanageable and made the temptation to murder him and steal it irresistible to some of the inmates. Now I clean out the insides of ten Marlboros, slide a few tightly rolled hundred-baht notes inside each one, pack the end with tobacco and play the rest by ear. We've never failed yet. At the prison my police ID lets me get away with a light frisk. Other visitors, especially *farangs*, are body-searched.

There is always a moment of suspense while I wait in the visitors' room for the duty guard to look for him. Is he still alive, or did the last beating finish him off? Is he sick in the hospital building, perhaps with HIV from sharing a needle, or from one or other of the fatal maladies that affect the inmates? Has the King agreed to pardon him this year? Here he comes, holding up the heavy chain of his leg irons with a piece of string in his left hand, as if he were taking a dog for a walk. Officially there are no leg irons in Bang Kwan anymore, but the message never seems to have reached the guards on Fritz's block. He sits in a chair on the other side of the bars and drops the chain with a dull clank on the floor.

Amazingly, he has heard about Pichai and tells me how sorry he is. The aging process which accelerated so dramatically in the first years of his imprisonment came to an abrupt halt some time ago, as if it were aiming for a specific state of reptilian cunning. Now he is a wrinkled tortoise, anywhere between fifty and two hundred years old. He thanks me for the 555s, which the guard has already inspected and handed over, and scans my face. I know that he is not an ordinary man, will never be an ordinary man again, much as he would love to be one of the millions of middle-aged mediocrities living nondescript lives whom he once despised. I feel him probing me with that hyperalertness and know that he has read my mind, not through any supernatural power but simply through having developed the ability to read faces to a monstrous degree.

"I knew you were coming today. I saw a white bird through a crack in the ceiling and I knew it was you. I've become totally Thai, haven't I?"

"How have you been?"

He pulls the string to rattle the chain a little. "Fantastic. I've been promoted—how about that!"

"A blue boy? A trusty?"

He snorts. "Do I look like a snitcher? No, they finally realized they had a use for Germanic efficiency and attention to detail—I'm in charge of our little red-light district."

"They're bringing girls in now?"

A shudder. He speaks with incredible rapidity in a loud whisper, like some kind of eccentric genius—or a madman. "There are still things about your country you don't know. Of course they're not letting girls in— they'd be torn apart. I'm talking about the pig farm. Your people are genu- inely homophobic, did you know that? A female pig rents for twenty-five times what a male will rent for—short time, by the half hour. They've given me the books to keep and of course I'm scrupulous about the time and the money both. I've even rigged up a little electric buzzer so the john knows when it's five minutes before withdrawal time." He holds up his hands. "What can I say? It's an honor—last year they let me run the cockroach project, and I increased production by a thousand percent— the improvement in the standard of nutrition and general health of the prison population was immeasurable, and of course I've always been the upwardly mobile type."

I give him the nod—something so slight that in the beginning I could not believe anyone could notice such an infinitesimal movement—and he rubs the back of his ear. This means the guard sitting in the chair in the corner will turn a blind eye. Perhaps Fritz has bribed him with a few 555s. I take out the pack of Marlboro, select one of the cigarettes I worked on, light it, then make a questioning gesture to the guard, who nods. I hand the lighted cigarette to Fritz through the bars, he takes a couple of drags, then pinches it out. With a faint smile: "I'll save it for later."

I tell him that this time there is something he can do for me and he listens with his usual paranoid alertness while I tell him about Bradley and Dao Phrya Bridge. It is a matter of choice whether to speak in English or Thai, since he is now fluent in both and knows more prison slang than I do. When I've finished I light up another cigarette and pass it to him. This time the guard seems not to notice. Fritz takes a couple of tokes and pinches the end, as before.

He knows nothing about Bradley or the squatters under the bridge but he agrees there must certainly be someone in Bang Kwan with the information I need. He is full of his usual twitches and restless hand movements and his eyes pierce me, asking for more information. I find myself describing the woman in Bradley's oil painting, which does not seem to trigger any response until I add a reference to the Khmer. His eyes light up for such a tiny fraction of time I would never have noticed if I had not been trained in prison semaphore. I stop in mid-sentence. I have been speaking in Thai, but now he switches to English.

"I've heard of her. Everyone in here has, she's a legend because of those Khmer. Even the Thai thugs are scared of them. She runs some kind of *yaa baa* operation and uses the Khmer as protection—that's the story anyway. The reason she's so respected is she's managed to turn herself into a religious figure for them. You know how *jungle* Khmer are at the best of times, but apparently they would literally die for her. That's the legend, anyway. I haven't paid any attention to it until now. I'll see what I can do."

He asks politely after my mother and we discuss his chances of a pardon this year. By the time I leave I have passed him all the cigarettes stuffed with banknotes. This is the cash flow which has kept him alive all these years. Someone in Germany wires the money into my account once a month.

The road from the grim prison buildings to the outside world is very long and very straight and ends in a public garden overflowing with hibiscus, bougainvillea, orchids and the luscious green leaves of the Tropics. How could a meditator not see it as a proxy for the axis of the mind?

Back in my cave I find my spirit has exhausted its capacity to deal with the world and I'm in agony from the wound. A meditation aid is called for, as always after a visit to Fritz.

Ganja is, of course, much frowned upon by mainline Buddhist tradition and indeed the Greatest of Men expressly forbade intoxication in any form. On the other hand, Buddhism (I explain to myself) was never intended to consist of a static set of rules boilerplated for all time. It is an organic Way, which automatically adapts itself to the present moment. I keep it under the futon.

I roll a fat spliff, light up, inhale heartily. Now all of a sudden I'm distilling grief. I'm ripping off every Band-Aid, I'm daring to bleed, and I'm concentrating the pain (sweet Buddha, how I loved that boy!). I don't want relief, I want him. With my agony carefully located right between the eyes, I take another toke, hold it as long as I can, repeat the process. I don't want enlightenment, I want him. Sorry, Buddha, I loved him more than you.

29

Anyone in the business will tell you: detection is a mundane task of putting two and two together. Very often the mind will do this automatically, like a software program running offscreen, and the answer will pop into your head as if by magic, when there is really no magic about it, merely the organization of a hundred subliminal clues, hints, words dropped inadvertently or perhaps deliberately by someone who has not the moral fiber to tell the truth to your face. The suspicions had been forming long before my week in hospital, but when she told me she had business in town I experienced that sinking feeling deep down, similar to a lover who expects the worst.

She had been complaining about the boredom of country life for quite some time, and her harebrained moneymaking schemes encompassed everything except narcotics, of which she disapproves, although she has developed a taste for ganja in middle life. I've discouraged her from illegal immigrants, endangered species, a country brothel, a casino and trying to join a syndicate dedicated to fixing the national lottery.

Over the telephone recently the hints have multiplied without blossoming into a confession, although the sinister word "premises" has begun to recur with alarming frequency. Now she has had to confess the address because she needs help. Still in pain from the stitches, I take a taxi to Soi Cowboy. The "premises" consist of a small parcel of land between the Wetlips Club and Ride 'Em Bronco, two enormous fun houses employing several hundred go-go dancers in high season. The squashed little pub in between belonged to an Englishman who had inexplicably refused to allow prostitutes on the premises and—my mother explains without looking me in the eye—therefore lost his license because he could not pay the police protection.

She is wearing black leggings which hug her crotch and bum, a white short-sleeved shirt and a crimson neckerchief. Her hair is in a glistening black plait with a flowery decoration at the tail. Gold hangs from her ears and matches the Buddha who swings from her neck as she yanks at a crate of Singha beer out on the street. She looks fantastic when she smiles at me and smells just like that shop Truffaut used to take us to in the Place Vendôme.

"But why would he need police protection if he wasn't running prostitutes?"

My mother tuts disapprovingly. "You have to maximize profits in this street. Run your money hard, make it work for you. You can't pursue a romantic dream, that's the surest way to bankruptcy."

I puff out my cheeks and scratch my head. The vocabulary is familiar, but not in her mouth. "You've been up to something?"

"I did a short course in business management. I didn't tell you because I didn't need you to mock me and because you don't have a head for business so you wouldn't understand."

"A course? How?"

"On the Net, darling. Didn't I tell you we have broadband now in Phetchabun? A woman doesn't need to feel in prison at home anymore, she can reach the world with a couple of clicks."

I push open the door and see that the building is deeper than it looks from outside. There is a long bar to the right and that atmosphere of dank melancholy which the British like to get drunk in. There is Guinness and a range of English ales on tap behind the bar, nowhere to dance and a romantically old-fashioned jukebox, small tables where balding Anglo-Saxons can have their one-to-ones over their mugs of dark beer and the inevitable dartboard at the end of the room. I know there are such pubs all over Krung Thep and they usually do very well. Not only the British but Dutch and Germans also like to retreat from the flesh trade from time to time into exactly these kinds of oases. On the other hand, it's true that the rents in Soi Cowboy are amongst the highest in the city, because the street is so successful. My suspicions are mounting all the time.

"How long did the Englishman run this place, Mother?"

"Ages. About thirty years. He was ready for retirement."

"Just when you were looking for premises?"

"I've been praying to the Buddha for luck for ages. I went to the wat ten times last month and I've been burning incense every day." She looks up at me. "We were gentle with him. Compassionate."

"Who's backing you and what did you do for it?"

"Sonchai, please, I'm a respectable retired woman. What I did in the past to make ends meet and give you an education is way behind me, you know that."

"So how can you afford the rent?"

A brisk smile and avoidance of eye contact. "I have a partner. A business partner."

"Who?"

"I'd rather not say just at the moment. Can't you see I'm busy?"

"Well, I can't help, can I? I've got stitches."

She stands up straight after dragging the case of Singha into the bar. Now I see this was a symbolic gesture designed to provoke feelings of tenderness in a loyal son's heart. A young man in shorts, his bare chest glistening with sweat, emerges from the back of the pub and commences dragging in the rest of the crates which are lined up in the street. "I don't want you to help with the beer, I want you to help with the plans. They have to be approved by the local police colonel after being endorsed by someone responsible who knows me and can vouch for me. So I thought: Who better than Krung Thep's most brilliant detective to sign them for me? You know, maybe with a nice stamp or something from District 8."

"What's the use of a stamp from District 8 when this is District 6—" I stop in mid-sentence because I've understood. "Why can't Vikorn sign the plans if someone from District 8 is what you want?"

She is backing away down the bar as I advance toward her. "He doesn't want his name appearing directly—everyone will understand when they see—you know—that you're my son and that you're in District 8."

"Which happens to be where your new business partner is the colonel in charge. Muscle, in other words. Did this all get negotiated in the corridor of the hospital by any chance?"

Touching her hair. "Of course not. We were both so worried about you, and he would call me up when he couldn't get to the hospital himself."

"Which was every day except one."

"Well, you see how precious you are to both of us." Tossing her head. "I told him I was looking for a business opportunity in town and he told me he had some money to invest, venture capital is what they call it, you know. It was *symbiotic*." She uses the English word a little tentatively.

"What course were you on, exactly?"

"It was some special thing run by the *Wall Street Journal*. You can enroll over the Net."

I might not have a head for business but I know the street well enough to doubt there really is room for another girlie bar. I also know Vikorn well enough to doubt he would invest in anything that wasn't guaranteed to succeed. I decide to proceed artfully. "So what d'you want me to do?"

Enthusiastically: "Well, darling, you know the trade as well as I do. I thought we'd rip out all this nonsense, go for some color, interesting lighting, a nostalgia theme, we could have a little stage right at the end . . ."

She trails off, at the same time giving me an adoring beam. I'm understanding a little better minute by minute. "You're going to have an upstairs, aren't you?"

Touching her hair again. "Well, it would be silly not to, don't you think? With this kind of protection, who's going to bust me?"

"The police colonel in charge of District 6, that's who."

"My partner advises that that is unlikely, but thank you for worrying about me."

"Unlikely? Why? Oh, I know why." I have remembered that Colonel Predee, who runs the very lucrative District 6, owns a piece of a casino in District 8 and is therefore dependent on Vikorn's grace. No wonder Vikorn was able to muscle the Englishman out of his license.

"Yes, well, I don't know anything about the politics of course. I suppose the two colonels are just very good friends."

She follows me up some narrow winding stairs to the second floor, and now I see there is a third floor. "How many rooms were you thinking of?"

"Ten on each floor."

"*Ten?*"

"Too cramped?"

I measure out the length of the corridor, off which there are only three rooms at present. "Mother, they will have to be on top of each other before they enter the rooms. You're going to have about five feet from wall to wall. The rooms are going to be all bed."

"What else, darling? If you think ten is too many, I suppose I'll settle for nine."

"Seven. I'm not putting my name to plans with more than seven. That still only leaves seven feet of width for each room. You have to give them space to undress. You can't have them stripping in the corridor, this isn't the country, you know."

"I suppose." With a sigh: "Very well, let's settle for seven. I'll tell the Colonel you insisted on seven. He's not going to be exactly delighted, you've just cut the profits by thirty percent."

I clamber up to the third floor, which is a chaos of old mattresses, plastic beer crates, some aluminum beer barrels and musty-looking books. We make our way down the stairs back to the bar. I am shaking my head. "What am I doing, signing plans for a brothel? I hate brothels."

"I know, my love, but it's still the number one business. I'd love to have an Internet café or something, but they just don't pay. Imagine, you have a room full of *farangs* who could be renting girls at a thousand baht an hour and instead they're tapping at keyboards for forty baht an hour. It just doesn't stack up."

"I suppose. What are you going to call it?"

"Ah! I've a surprise for you. We're calling it the Old Man's Club."

"The what?"

"You wouldn't understand, my love, we've studied the market. We're going for a niche. We won't bother to compete with those glitzy things next door, they can have the thirty-to-fifty crowd. We're going for the retirement funds. You'll see. I explained it all to the Colonel after I finished my course—I got the best grades by the way. He went away and thought about it and he agrees. In fact, he thinks I'm brilliant."

I've been backing away from her as we speak, an obvious subconscious reaction—Is this really happening? Am I really doing this?—and now she has shepherded me into the street where the light is better. I can see it in her face now, I am witnessing that metamorphosis that women's books sometimes talk about: for more than ten years she has led a peaceful, idyllic life in the country, with all the unbearable boredom that implies, while a great reservoir of ambition has slowly risen in her, co-

inciding with the onset of middle age. Her jaw is set, there will be no stopping her now. She is working the strings, I am the puppet. She still looks
terrific. She knows she has won by the way I kiss her on the cheek.

From Soi Cowboy I ride a motorcycle taxi to the Hilton International,
where the FBI has summoned me. I take the elevator to her suite on the
twenty-second floor, where she is working at her desk on a collection
of metallic objects which, I realize after some concentration, are the insides of a gun. The barrel and stock sit calmly in one of the massive armchairs, presiding over their own disembowelment, and she sits me down
in the other. The gun and I—I think it is a Heckler & Koch submachine
gun, about eighteen inches long with a forged steel stock and parabolic
magazine—stare at each other while she talks. On the hotel blotter she
takes apart the subassembly and hammer mechanism and stares at them
for a moment, before reaching for the ice cream. Mesmerized by the gun,
I did not notice the pint of Häagen-Dazs macadamia nut brittle on the
corner of the desk. Such is her training that she is able to poke at the
mechanism with one finger whilst dipping a plastic spoon into the ice
cream with the other hand. To eat alone is a sad and pathetic condition in
my country, evidence of social and emotional dispossession. To do so in
front of another without offering to share is an obscenity and almost
impossible for me to watch. I feel the blood draining from my face as she
gulps down a miniature Everest.

"What's the matter, you scared of guns?" She takes a small can of gun
oil from the desk drawer and expertly allows a single drop to fall on the
subassembly. "Oh, I get it, you don't think I've got a license, right? No
need to worry, Rosen discussed it with one of your *capo di capi*, I'm
allowed to keep it so long as I use it with discretion. If I do have to use it,
there'll be one of those Thai cover-ups which you know all about. You
sure you're okay? I didn't think a gun would disgust you all that much. It's
a sprayer, I know, but so are most short barrels, the H and K MP-5K is
about the best. Anything larger and I'm going to look conspicuous, aren't
I?" A couple more drops for the hammer base, then she reaches for the
barrel and stock and begins to slide the subassembly into the guides of
the receiver. "See, I haven't taken it out since I picked it up from the
embassy—they had to send it over for me in a diplomatic bag and you
never know how well they treated it. One thing they always tell you at
Quantico, look after your piece." More ice cream. "Anyway, what I
wanted to talk to you about is, generally, how do you see the case shaping up?"

I watch, nauseated, while she eats more macadamia nut brittle, picks up the completed gun, hangs it round her neck from the cord and stands in front of a full-length mirror. From a loose hanging position she is able to aim and fire and perforate herself with a thousand shots in less than— oh, I don't know, nanoseconds anyway. Quantico meets Hollywood. The unexpected drama triggers one of my perceptions and I see a whole string of previous incarnations standing behind her. American cops are identical to Thai cops at least in one respect. We're all reincarnations of crooks.

She catches my gaze. "This really isn't turning you on, is it? Okay, no more guns, we'll go for a walk. There's something in the garden I need you to explain to me." She strides over to the Häagen-Dazs for a couple more mouthfuls, catches herself. "You want some?"

"No, thank you," I reply with relief, feeling as if something very unpleasant has been removed from the carpet.

"Didn't think you did. Ice cream really isn't you, is it? No chili, no lemongrass, no rice, just a pile of Western junk like sugar and dairy products with a ton of artificial flavoring. Tastes great, though." The Häagen-Dazs goes into the small fridge under the credenza. From a wardrobe she takes out a black fiberglass briefcase which turns out to be custom-molded on the inside for the H&K. She slips the magazine out of the gun, places it in its hollow, then does the same for the gun itself. I see two people here: a girl who loves ice cream, and a consummate professional taking loving care of the tool of her trade.

Now that the gun and the ice cream are out of sight I take in the view while she disappears into her bedroom. It's not a New York or Hong Kong skyline, although it's a modern city these days. I'm put in mind more of Mexico or South America in the way soaring tubes of steel and glass preside over ragged bits of park, hovels, shacks and squatter dwellings. Its true signature, however, is the permanent skeletons of unfinished buildings, their bare bones turning black in the pollution, as if the Buddha is reminding us that even buildings die. It takes training to see the metaphysics behind a failed construction project, though, and I decide not to share my insight with the FBI, who emerges wearing white linen shorts and a white and navy tennis shirt with a YSL label which may or may not be a fake. We ride the lift down to the lobby (Kimberley, the gun and I), and I wait while she checks the black briefcase into the hotel vault.

Kimberley returns minus the gun with her blond hair bouncing and a smile which could almost make her sixteen. She indicates that we are to descend into the well of the lobby with the subtlest brush of her fingers against my forearm, and we walk side by side out into the swimming pool area. Adjacent to the pool is a canal which is part of the hotel grounds and which leads to a large spirit house festooned with marigolds.

"Okay," says the FBI, "could you tell me what these are all doing in the grounds of the Hilton hotel?"

There may be as many as three hundred of them, ranging from six inches in length to one which is all of ten feet tall. They are arranged in a semicircle around the spirit house and even form a kind of low fencing around the flower beds. They are parabolic with bulbous glans, a tiny slit at the top, and some are on gun carriages with balls hanging down. Some are stone, at least three are concrete and most are wood. Some are painted lurid reds and greens. To the left is a gigantic ficus tree, its aerial roots tangled in passionate embraces.

"The spirit house is dedicated to the spirit of the tree, which happens to be male."

"And this is a Buddhist country?"

"Buddhist with a lot of Hinduism and animism underneath."

"I'm surprised the Hilton management put up with it."

"They wouldn't have had any choice. You don't destroy important shrines—it's incredibly unlucky. No one wants bad luck, especially not senior management of international corporations."

"So who brings all these cocks? Who adorns them with fresh marigolds?"

"Local women."

The FBI walks up to one and stares at it. "Women bring giant dildos to dedicate to the male spirit of the ficus tree? Hmm, food for thought." She extends a finger and traces the loop of the glans where it meets the shaft. She checks me with a half smile. I think the effects of that antiflirting course are wearing off. I decide not to return the smile, not even my half of it, and am shocked by the anger-cloud which passes over her face. She recovers in an instant and now we are walking briskly back to the lobby and the coffee shop. I'm thinking about the Heckler & Koch when she snaps: "There's a meeting at the embassy tomorrow, Bradley's senior officer is going to tell us what he knows, if anything. In the interests of information-sharing, you're invited to attend. I'll tell Rosen you're coming."

I think I'm being dismissed, without discovering why I was summoned in the first place. Despite decades of study, I still find the Western mind hard to take, close-up. The expectation that the world should respond to every passing whim (ice cream, cock, target practice) is shocking to this son of a whore. Like most primitive people, I believe that morality arises from a state of primeval innocence to which we must try to be faithful if we are not to be lost altogether. I fear such a conviction would be quaint and pathetic to the FBI, if I ever dared to express it. In Western terms Jones and Fritz are poles apart; to me they are almost identical: two infantile bundles of appetites—except that one is a catcher and the other got caught.

30

I'm late for the meeting and racing to the embassy on the back of a Honda 125, listening to Pisit on my Walkman. He is doing his daily rundown of the Thai-language dailies.

The tabloid *Thai Rath* has resurrected the old story of the cop's wife who chopped off her husband's penis (the standard penalty for overuse outside the home) and attached it to a helium balloon to send it sailing over the city. The significance of the balloon was that it made it impossible for Police Sergeant Purachai Sorasuchart to retrieve his organ within the vital nine-hour minimum for our skilled surgeons to reattach it. The organ was never recovered. *Thai Rath* reports that new evidence from neighbors now suggests that the helium balloon was a sensationalist invention (probably by *Thai Rath*), for Mrs. Purachai was seen on the day of the severance behind her house prodding about tearfully in the rubbish heap, which was unfortunately much visited by rats who doubtless got there before her. Pisit insinuates that the new evidence itself was stimulated into life by *Thai Rath*, who wanted an excuse to replay the story which Pisit is now replaying. Now Dr. Muratai comes on the program to be jollied into giving the usual lurid details of the reattachment surgery and why Thai surgeons are the best in the world in this field: they get more practice. "So, gentlemen, if your philandering results in a visit from the knife in the night, whatever you do, retrieve the missing piece and don't forget the ice."

Pisit reminds us, Thai-style, that the story had the happiest of endings: Sergeant Purachai retired from the force and ordained as a monk in a forest monastery, from which lofty viewpoint he is able to look back on his erstwhile philandering and his former organ with equal indifference. He claims to be grateful to his wife for propelling him onto the Eightfold Path.

I pull off my headphones as we approach the embassy and realize that I'm ten minutes late for the meeting, which I interrupt when I'm finally through the security and allowed to enter Rosen and Nape's office.

A lean, fair man in his forties in a buff military uniform, bursting with health, is talking to a rapt audience. "I was Bill Bradley's superior officer for most of the five years he spent here. He came in March 1996, posted at his own request. I arrived in late November of the same year. He was older than me by five years and he was the kind of sergeant you leave alone, if you're a smart captain. He was a long-service man and he knew his job inside out. He knew what he had to do better than I could have told him, and he also knew the rule book cover to cover. Frankly, with a sergeant like that under your command your worst fear is he'll make you look inferior, but Bradley knew how to handle that, too. He was always extremely respectful, especially when there were other servicemen around. I guess you would say he was the perfect sergeant and that perfection made him impenetrable from a personal point of view. If I have any insight at all that I would care to share, it would be that he was a man who sought perfection, of himself and his environment. My guess would be that was why he never tried to rise higher. A good sergeant like him is in total control of his world, even though it's a small one. Join the officer class, and other forces come to bear on you, forces which are never entirely under your control no matter how good you are. A perfect sergeant, on the other hand, is that rare animal in the military: an almost free man, in command of his turf."

Rosen said: "Anything in his service record you would like to draw our attention to, Captain?"

"His record was perfect. He was serving at the embassy in Yemen at the time of the attack by a local mob with AK-47s, rifles and other firearms. He risked his life bringing back another marine from the roof of the embassy while the roof was under fire. There was talk of a medal, but it never came through."

"What about his private life?"

"Like I say, this was an impenetrable man. He did his duty and gave a hundred and ten percent while he was here, but off duty we hardly saw him. He came to those functions he had to attend, when a colleague retired or left Bangkok, for example, but didn't socialize."

"Isn't that unusual for a marine?"

"In a younger man it might have been cause for concern, but Bradley was middle-aged, coming to the end of his thirty-year term. A lot of men value their privacy in those circumstances, and no one was about to cross-examine him about what he did in his spare time."

"He was a bachelor. Any love interest you know of?"

"Only a very old rumor that he had a relationship with a particularly exotic local woman. I don't think anyone here knows if that was true or not, because he never brought her here to introduce her. He always came alone to functions and celebrations."

"Do you know anything about a hobby or interest he might have had in jade?"

"Jade? No, I don't know anything about that." A pause. "I did watch him once, in the locker room after a basketball game. He had the kind of physique you just can't help but stare at. He'd arrived in uniform but now he put on civilian clothes. It was like watching a metamorphosis. Jewelry he could never wear on parade: earrings, rings for his fingers, a gold Buddha pendant. He put on a bright purple Hawaiian silk shirt that only looks good on black skin. That's about the most intimate I got with the sergeant. Everybody goes through a transformation when they get out of uniform, but I've never seen anything that complete before. He just didn't look like a career soldier. He even stopped walking like one, as soon as he put on that shirt."

"Thank you, Captain," Rosen said, and Nape echoed his words. "Oh, just one last thing, Captain. You did say that Bradley's posting here was at his own request?"

"That's right. It's in his file, which I reread when I heard about what had happened."

When the captain had gone, everyone looked at me, so I said: "Thank you for allowing me to attend, it has been very useful."

"Useless you mean," Jones said. "Did the captain tell us one thing we didn't know already?"

"That Bradley was pathologically secretive," Nape said. "And led a double life."

"Not so unusual in long-term soldiers," Rosen said. "You tend to hang on to what little privacy the service permits."

"And that he was a control freak," Nape added.

"All successful men are control freaks," Jones said.

"D'you want to correct that to 'all successful people'?" Nape demanded with a glare.

Jones shrank a little under his gaze. "I guess."

Rosen jerked his chin at them and grimaced toward me. "So, did you speak to your Colonel, Detective?"

"I made a written request that I be permitted to interview Sylvester Warren on his next visit to Thailand, which is today."

"And?"

"I think I will not receive an answer until after he has left."

Rosen opened his hands generously. "Like I said, a well-connected man."

My stitches are healing nicely, but I allow Jones to accompany me to the gate of the embassy with one arm locked in mine, I suppose for support. The marine behind the glass is an old friend these days and he waves me through the turnstile.

31

The *Matichon* daily reports that an unusual number of ghouls have been sighted at the notorious junction of Rama VI and Traimit. This is an accident black spot and experts opine that the ghouls are the spirits of the dead who lost their lives in crashes and are now intent on causing still more fatal accidents for the sake of companionship. In death as in life, it seems, my people love to party.

Reluctantly, I pull off my headphones. This is the moment I've set myself to visit Pichai's old room.

It is in the same project as my own, an identical room in an identical building half a mile away. At least, the architecture of the room is identical to mine. Pichai owned a TV which he left on all the time when he was at home, and a very modest stereo system on which he played Thai rock (especially Carabao) and sermons from eminent Buddhist abbots.

A superficial observer might have expected me to be the one who took the decision to ordain, but this is to leave out of account the decisiveness required to step onto the spiritual escalator called the Eightfold Path. True, it was Pichai, not I, who killed that dealer, but that only goes to show he was capable of making a decision. I, on the other hand, find myself to be one of life's ditherers. Was the Buddha really a transcendent genius who pointed out all that time ago that Nothing was even more inevitable than death and taxes? Or was he a third-century B.C. dropout who could not cope with the rigors of statecraft? His dad the King certainly thought so and refused to talk to him, post enlightenment. Is it my *farang* blood which fills my mind with such sacrilegious thoughts from time to time? And why should I be thinking this in Pichai's room? I've actually come for his silk short-sleeved shirt and his Fila loafers, which he won't need anymore, but find that they are gone, along with the TV and the stereo. There is no one to blame; soon after he decided to ordain he stopped locking his room, claiming that anyone desperate enough to steal from him was welcome to whatever they could carry away. Nobody stole anything for months, but after his death I guess his property was seen as fair game. I return sadly to my own room. In my absence someone has slid a piece of toilet tissue under my door. It is gray with grime and folded in a way which makes it difficult to open out. When I do so I find a short phrase in English: *Must see you. Fritz.* I know it is my duty to destroy the evidence, which I do by dropping it down the hole in the corner of my room.

When Pichai was alive I never felt the smallness of my home, its squalor. Working with *farangs* has not helped. Even the poorest of them have windows. I wonder if a miracle of modern technology will help me in my hour of need? I take out the Motorola that Rosen gave me and decide to change the ringing tune. I work steadily through the instructions in the manual and find that I have been given a choice of fifteen different tunes which includes the American national anthem but not that of any other country. *Star Wars* is the only attractive option, but I hesitate to copy Rosen. Angrily I realize that Motorola has led me down a labyrinth of apparent choice leading to a dead end. I have found the perfect paradigm of Western culture, but without Pichai to share it with, who gives a shit anyway? I return the tune to the factory setting, a perfectly acceptable *bleep*. The exercise has not improved my sense of well-being.

I am still in a maudlin mood and looking at Pichai's Buddha necklace as I pass it from hand to hand like a fistful of sand when there is a knock on my door. Nobody ever visits me here, so the knock is obviously a message from Pichai, proof that he is looking after me from the other side. I cross the room in one stride and pull back the bolt.

The FBI has reinvented herself. Jones is wearing a T-shirt with the headline SO MANY MEN SO LITTLE TIME screaming from her bosom, denims cut off just a little below her crotch, sandals with Velcro fastenings. She has dyed her hair the color of a carrot and cropped it in some spiky boyish style and is wearing a smile I've not seen on her before. Wet-look lipstick. I do not conceal my astonishment.

"Hi. Ah, am I disturbing you? This isn't a good moment, right?"

"How did you know where I lived?"

"I looked it up on the computer. Look, this obviously isn't—"

"I meant, how did you find the project?"

"Oh, right. Well, I've hired a car with driver. It's incredibly inexpensive here. The Bureau's paying, anyway. It's part of my job to look after you, but I'll go if this is a bad moment."

She is looking over my shoulder. I step aside. "Come in."

She takes the step over the threshold. "This is . . ."

"This is where I live."

It is not difficult for me to see with her eyes. My cave is a windowless box ten feet by eight feet with a flimsy shacklike structure at one end to conceal the hole in the ground. Ventilation comes from a black hole in the rear wall which gives onto a shaft which services all the other apartments. On a windy day I know what every one of my neighbors is having for lunch. There is a picture of the King on one wall, and a narrow set of bookshelves where any normal person would have placed a television. The books are all in Thai script, so I explain to Jones, who tries to examine them: "Buddhism. I'm a Buddhist bookworm."

The only furniture is a futon on the floor. Jones is clearly dumbfounded. To her credit she makes no attempt at concealment. "I . . . I don't know what to say, Sonchai. I've never seen . . . I mean . . ."

"You've never seen such a hovel?" I feel hard toward her. I would like to rub her nose in this reality, but my depression has miraculously disappeared.

She looks me in the eye. "No, I've never seen such a hovel. I'm sorry."

"Welcome to the Third World."

Sex is an odd thing, isn't it? A power that can transform your mood like a drug. She stands there, glowing with health and some kind of anticipation, and the images of immediate coupling are surely flooding her mind as well as mine. We both cough at the same time. She smiles with those vivid wet-look lips.

"I figured you might need some cheering up, so I bought two tickets for the kickboxing at Lumpini Stadium tonight. It's Saturday. I hear there's a big fight. Maybe you want to take me? I see it as part of my orientation. If you don't want to, though, if you'd rather stay here and get suicidal . . ."

The car is a white Mercedes. In the back seat Jones says: "I tried watching Thai TV last night. I think I got a soap, but not a soap like I've ever seen before. People kept dying and being reborn and carrying on the conversation they were having just before they died, and there were ghosts and a bunch of wizards who could defy gravity and lived in some enchanted land about five miles above the earth. Would you say that represents the Thai mind?"

"Five miles high is about right. But you left out the skeleton."

"That's right, there was a nifty human skeleton following the lead couple all over the place. What was he doing?"

"You have to bear in mind we are a holistic people. We cannot take little bits of life, like lovers walking off into the sunset, and pretend that's the final word."

On the way to Lumpini I feel the need for a cultural lecture: "You shouldn't call it kickboxing. Kickboxing is a synthetic sport that had to be invented after those Bruce Lee movies. *Muay Thai* is something else."

"Oh, it is? What are the rules?"

"Actually, there are none."

A grunt from Jones. "Why am I not surprised?"

"At least there weren't, until we had to invent some to make it acceptable to international television. Now the boxers wear those ridiculous gloves. In the old days a boxer would dip pieces of gauze in a pot of glue, then wrap them around his fists and drizzle ground glass over them."

"Nice."

"We're talking about national defense. Until relatively recently our wars with Burma—we're always going to war with Burma—consisted mostly of hand-to-hand combat. Primitive in the extreme, no? On the other hand, there were no civilian casualties, no deaths from friendly fire, nobody lost their home. In fact, it was rare for more than a thousand or so men on either side to die in a full-scale war."

"I get the point. The world has come a long way since then, right?" She leans back, sinking down into the seat like a kid.

"*Muay Thai* really came into its own in the seventies when martial arts black belts from Japan, Taiwan and Hong Kong challenged our boys. The cream of karate, kung fu, judo and all the others came over for a grand tournament." I pause for effect.

"Okay, I'm hooked. What happened? I guess the other guys lost, or you wouldn't have that look on your face."

"None of the other guys lasted a full minute in the ring with a Thai boxer. They just weren't used to being kicked in the face. Our boys get kicked in the face from the age of six, when they first start to train. The other guys looked more like dancing masters than fighters."

"Let me guess the moral. Don't mess with a Thai, right?"

"It's a mistake to make us mad."

We fall into silence for a full five minutes. My mood starts to revert.

"Want to talk about it?" Jones asks without looking at me. "In the States we always say it's good to talk about things that are weighing on your mind. I'll be straight with you, Sonchai, you really freaked out Tod Rosen with your little comment when you first met him. He would feel a lot better if you and I got to know each other."

"I did? Did I make some social faux pas?"

"You said you were going to snuff out whoever was responsible for the death of your partner. That didn't matter so much when it looked like a local gangland murder. Now that the hallowed name of Sylvester Warren has come up, Tod's nervous."

"Do American cells have windows?"

"You don't give a shit, do you? I've never yet met a man I couldn't figure out. But you . . ." She shakes her head.

"I think Rosen is nervous about many things. Why is he here? Bangkok isn't exactly a good career move for a man like him. He screwed up, didn't he?"

"His third marriage failed and he developed a drinking problem. He's a good man, very fair, and people like to work for him."

"And Nape?"

"Nape? Jack Nape is one of those Western men who arrive in Bangkok one day and by the next have vowed never to leave. I guess you could call him a refugee from feminism. He married a local woman, and the minute the Bureau recalls him Stateside is the minute he resigns. He'll probably get a job with some American law firm with an office here. He's very bright, knows a lot about your country. They say his Thai isn't bad."

I do not explain that Rosen was a doctor last time around, who suffered an appalling nervous breakdown which he is still trying to deal with. Nape was a woman, a housewife who poisoned her husband. Jones was a man, a gangster and womanizer of enormous appetite. He was the one Nape poisoned, which is why they have come across each other again this time around, with much of the previous hostility.

"And you?"

"Me?"

"Why have you changed your image? I thought you were committed to American pie?"

A hostile look from Jones. "You want to know? I got tired of being invisible in this damn town. Girls have egos, that's the main message of the twenty-first century, so better get used to it."

"You weren't turning any heads?"

A smoldering pause. "I don't entirely blame the Western men over here. I met Nape's wife last night. She's stunning and walks like her parents paid a million dollars for comportment classes. But then, most of the women here move like that, don't they? Even the ones with no education at all."

"Have the haircut and the T-shirt helped?"

"Nope. Can we talk about you now?"

"I'm a career inadequate. Ask my Colonel. In ten years I've made no useful contribution to the force."

"You feel guilty about not taking bribes?"

"You must understand, the Royal Thai Police Force has always been way ahead of its time. It's run like a modern industry, every cop is a profit center."

"Yes, I've heard about that. I guess a cop enjoys immunity from prosecution for just about everything, right?"

I have to think about that one. "Cops giving evidence against cops in open court would not be good for the esprit de corps. Transgressions are dealt with internally."

"Oh yeah? What happens to the bad apples, they're barred from taking bribes for a week?"

"Something like that, unless they're really bad." I've piqued her interest. She smells blood and a damn good story for the guys back home.

"C'mon, let me have it, what medieval punishment for the ones who really piss off the colonels?"

"Mandatory suicide," I mutter. "We are a gentlemanly service and extreme transgressors are expected to act like men, after due process."

"A kangaroo court?"

An image flashes before my mind. I'm not the type who is normally invited to these secret proceedings. It has only happened to me once: a somber mood in a large bare room full of chairs, cops of all ranks selected from every district in Krung Thep, a very scared sergeant sitting in the defendant's chair, a small table in front of him with a service revolver and a glass of water. I want to change the subject. "It's not all bad. Take a young *farang* who's caught with some ganja. He pays five thousand baht to the cop who caught him, which is a reasonable sum. He gets off with a lesson and a fright. If he were prosecuted and sent to jail in Bang Kwan, his life would certainly be ruined. He would risk all kinds of diseases, probably incur a serious drug addiction. Our system is humane and compassionate. It is also cost effective. The cop receives a bonus without any extra burden on the taxpayer. Police salaries have been at starvation level forever."

Jones cannot decide if I'm serious or not. "Well, that's a long way from the American viewpoint. It's a given that our laws are applied evenly to every citizen—the alternative is total sleaze."

"In that case, why aren't we investigating Sylvester Warren?"

Her head snaps away and she is looking out the window. "Cute, aren't you?"

A long silence. Finally, she slowly turns her head back toward me. "Actually, that's exactly what we're doing. Only don't tell anyone."

32

We are sliding past the American embassy on Wireless Road in moderate traffic, heading toward Lumpini. Jones and I both spare a glance at the thick white walls. It was the King's birthday a few days ago, and one of the gates to the embassy carries a banner which reads LONG LIVE THE KING. It's the kind of touch we appreciate from Uncle Sam.

Jones shifts her gaze away from the embassy. "Every time anyone dusts off the file on Warren, Warren himself gets to hear about it. Pressure and heat. Memos and e-mails demanding to know why resources are being wasted on a case consisting of innuendo and gossip. Once a station chief was shifted sideways. But we have our cops of integrity, just like you. A small team is secretly dedicated to the Warren case. That's why I'm here. Rosen doesn't know, neither does Nape. They think I screwed up somewhere and got myself a punishment posting. That's fine. That's what I want them to think. So don't you open your mouth. I'm telling you because you're going to help me. I've spent a chunk of my career on this and it's going to get me promotion. I know all about Warren and his jade."

"Tell me."

"Does the name Barbara Hutton mean anything to you? How about Woolworth? Her daddy built the tallest skyscraper in Manhattan until

Chrysler went higher. The Sassoons? They were very big in Shanghai before the Chinese revolution. The list is almost endless and includes Madame Chiang Kai-shek, Edda Ciano, who was Benito Mussolini's daughter, Edwina Mountbatten, the mother of the Queen of England, all the way up to Henry Pu Yi. You've heard of him?" I shake my head. "Better known as the last Emperor of China." A reverent pause. "What do all these people have in common? They were major players in global finance before anyone called it that. They *were* the swinging thirties, the roaring forties. And they started a new fashion in gems. Before them only the Chinese and a few Western specialists really appreciated jade. After them, if you didn't have at least a few pieces of 'the stone of heaven' to flash at dinner parties, you didn't get invited to the dinner parties. Of course, they're all dead now, or too old to care about jade, but jade was their passion, it was a common theme. You can't look into their private lives without it leaping out at you. And they all have heirs, who are pretty damned old themselves.

"You may as well know that Warren studied under someone called Abe Gump. He was an antique dealer in San Francisco who got interested in Oriental art when all his Italian marble, French clocks and just about everything else was destroyed in the San Francisco earthquake. He was blind but one hell of a connoisseur. He was a legend in the thirties for being able to value a piece of jade just by feeling it. He was Barbara Hutton's tutor when she wanted to learn about jade.

"So when the great families of the prewar period came out of the war and the various communist revolutions relatively poor, perhaps even destitute, they thought about selling their jade to people like Abe Gump and then later to Sylvester Warren. There's an old Chinese proverb: *Better to invest than to work, better to hoard than to invest.* You've probably heard it? Well, Sylvester Warren learned that lesson. He's one hell of a hoarder. But even hoarders have to know when to sell. You might say a signal flashed around the world to all jade hoarders in September 1994 when Barbara Hutton's jadeite wedding necklace was sold at auction in Christie's Hong Kong for U.S.$4.3 million. Madame Chiang Kai-shek made a bid but lost. She wanted the necklace for her hundredth birthday. She bid by telephone from her apartment in Gracie Square on the Upper East Side. All of a sudden jade was the biggest news again in the gem industry, but with one catch. The necklace was imperial jade, the highest quality that exists, from the Kachin Hills in Burma, and could be traced back to the Forbidden City. Without that cachet, the stones might not have fetched a tenth of that amount. It's like Elvis Presley's guitar. Without the illustrious pedigree it's just a very good secondhand guitar."

"You think Warren was using Bradley to fake these pieces?"

"We just don't know. It's a hypothesis, like Nape said. Unlike what Nape said, I work with people in Washington who are very interested in Warren. I've studied him and his business more or less nonstop for three years. I even know all about Far Eastern art. Test me."

"What are the six postures of the Buddha usually represented in religious sculpture?"

"*Vitarka mudra*—seated with thumb and forefinger of right hand touching; seated in the lotus with one hand on top of the other in his lap; seated with one hand on his lap, the other on his knee; seated with right hand touching the earth; standing with palms up facing outward; standing with one palm up, the other pointing to the earth, known as *restraining the waters*."

"That's good. Very good. Want to test me on Western culture?"

"What are the names of the Seven Dwarfs?"

I feel I know the answer to this question, but cannot retrieve it without the aid of meditation.

We have ground to a halt in a jam where Wireless Road meets Rama IV. Immediately in front, a small red light swings to and fro at about ten feet above the ground. "Am I seeing what I think I'm seeing?"

"They have to use taillights at night. It's the law."

"I'm feasting my eyes. That must be the only law in Bangkok that's seriously enforced."

We drive around the elephant to turn left into Rama IV, and the stadium is only a few hundred yards further down. Jones' driver lets us out and drives off. The courtyard in front of the stadium is crammed with cooked-food stalls and people eating and drinking, while behind them a crowd roars. Jones flashes her ringside tickets, and we walk through a tunnel which leads directly to the ring, which we walk around. Seats are not numbered, there are a couple of spaces in one corner. The stadium is packed while two fighters are slugging it out. We've arrived halfway through the fight and both men are exhausted. Now I recognize Mhongchai, who is up against his old enemy Klairput. No wonder there is such excitement. In *Muay Thai* fighters kick when Western boxers jab. Both men are bruised on both sides of their rib cages, and Mhongchai's eyebrow has opened up. It is his main weakness, otherwise he is the stronger fighter. Klairput is too slow with a head kick, which allows Mhongchai to twist his foot between his gloves. The normal tactic is to send him flying to the floor or across the ring, but Mhongchai, the genius, adapts the move by spinning him round and coming in from behind with an elbow smash to the head. Now Klairput is laid out on the mat and the referee is counting. Klairput doesn't bother to get up, he's lost on points anyway so why take more punishment? A great roar from the crowd as the referee declares Mhongchai the winner. In the stalls, people rush to claim their money from the bookies, who stand with wads of banknotes clipped between their fingers, using their knuckles as an abacus. I've always admired the speed of ringside bookies. I used to be one about seventy years ago.

Jones orders a Coke while we wait for the next fight. She sucks a straw while she looks around the stadium and places her spare hand on my thigh. She leaves it there for a provocative thirty seconds before leaning toward me and whispering out of the side of her mouth: "Behind you, at ten to twelve. Wait a minute, then make it smooth and casual." I do as I'm told and scan the seats behind long enough to catch Sergeant William Bradley and his paramour. I sit back in my seat and close my eyes to re-create the image of a huge Negro eating from an American-size tub of popcorn, and the dazzling woman beside him. She has taken the colors and frizz out of her hair and is wearing a green silk blouse, purple shorts. On reflection it is not William Bradley resurrected. This man is not quite so tall and is in poorer shape, gray in his hair. There is a substantial gut under the Hawaiian shirt, his face is puffy and he is slouching. I doubt that William Bradley was a sloucher. The resemblance, though, is uncanny. I look accusingly at Jones.

"It's his older brother. We've been watching him for a couple of days. He took an American Airlines flight to Paris, then Air France to Bangkok, so he's trying to be invisible. I found out from his hotel he was coming here tonight—the hotel sold him the tickets. I never hoped for a double whammy with the woman, though. She probably needs an escort as huge as that, men can't keep their eyes off her. Shit."

What I thought was pique turns out to be professional guilt. Jones looked over her shoulder once too often. Her eyes locked with the black man's for a second, and the giant was on his feet, leading the woman through the stalls and up the aisle to the exit with unexpected agility.

There is no way to get to the stalls from the ringside seats, so we rush back through the tunnel and watch while the Negro holds a cab door open for the woman to get in, then ducks in himself, smoothly and quickly. The cab is already driving down Rama IV by the time we reach the curbside. Jones curses. "I never figured he would sit in the stalls. A guy like that always sits ringside."

"Did he recognize you?"

"No, he doesn't know who I am. But he's a professional. He's done a lot of time, he doesn't take chances. That wasn't a runner he did, he was just taking precautions."

Yet another persona is inhabiting Jones' body. She is taut, focused, disciplined. The T-shirt and hot pants belong to the woman she was ten minutes ago and are now redundant as she dials her driver from her mobile to tell him to pick us up. She folds the mobile and says: "Okay, here's what we do. We go to Bradley's house now and hang out there. There's no way Elijah flies fifteen thousand miles without checking out his brother's house, and I'm sure he hasn't done that yet. He'll go at night, try to be incognito. He probably came to the kickboxing to pass the time until he figures it's the moment to go to the house."

"*Muay Thai*," I correct as we get in the Mercedes.

In the back of the car, Jones says: "They're both Harlem boys, William and Elijah, who chose radically different paths. Elijah has run ice, snow, crack, smack—big-time. He started as a teen and by the time he was twenty he was a millionaire with his own gang. Somehow William wasn't even tempted. A very private personality, very straight. It seemed like he would use sport to get him out of the slum, but he was one of those men who are brilliant all-rounders but don't have a specialization. He was just too big and slow for heavyweight boxing, not lithe enough for professional basketball, too big for anything else. He joined the army at age seventeen and seemed to find his element. He was one of those men who just naturally take to the military life when young, maybe without foreseeing the downside. He was ashamed of big brother Elijah and we think they didn't communicate for more than a decade. William mellowed, though, got disillusioned with the Marines. They talked over the telephone a lot the past few years."

"Elijah is under surveillance?"

"More or less full-time. I managed to get some of the transcripts by e-mail this morning."

"But there was no e-mail between the two on Bradley's files."

"I know, which makes me all the more suspicious. The telephone conversations are mostly bland and carefully nonincriminating. They were up to something. They probably used e-mail addresses we don't know about through Internet cafés. There are just a couple of moments in the telephone conversations when Bill lets his guard down. That guy was seriously worried about income after his retirement. He talks a lot about how expensive his lifestyle is, wonders how he's going to make ends meet—there's a very authentic tone of worry in the early conversations which reaches a pitch when some loan sharks start to threaten him. Then the fear disappears. It's the voice of a man who sees why his big brother did what he did. A man very very disillusioned with the system he's served all his life. Then all of a sudden the tone changes, the sun has come out, William Bradley is happy again."

"Did that coincide with contact with Warren?"

She nods her head slowly and profoundly. "Pretty much."

It takes more than an hour to reach Kaoshan in the traffic. As we approach from the river side I say: "Doc, Happy, Sneezy, Dopey, Bashful, Grumpy, Sleepy."

"Good," Jones says, distracted.

We force our way down Kaoshan and slip into the narrow *soi* which leads to Bradley's house. I'm impressed that Jones knows to take off her shoes on the outside steps, and even more impressed that she has a key to the downstairs. She opens the door softly and motions for me to follow her inside. We pad across the room, which is in near-total darkness, and arrange some cushions on the floor. She props herself up against a wall while I squat, waiting for my eyes to adjust. A click when Elijah Bradley switches the lights on.

I take in the big Negro, then my mind automatically discounts him as it focuses on his two companions, who wear red checkered headscarves around their necks. Bradley is seating himself uncomfortably in one of the leather chairs after crossing the room from the light switch, while the two Khmer squat on either side. One of the Khmer is holding a machine pistol which could be an Uzi, the other stares at Kimberley Jones. Jones is staring at Elijah, who is staring at me. Slowly Elijah reaches into his enormous shirt and takes out a stiff brown envelope, which he throws to me. I open it and pull out a legal document in Thai script, which I read. Jones glances at me.

"It's the last will and testament of William Bradley, who bequeaths all property located in Thailand, including this house, to his brother Elijah."

"Which means you all are trespassing, right? Don't you think a little explanation is in order, before we throw you out?" His voice is deep and heavy. I'm surprised at the mild note of hurt.

In Thai I explain to the man with the Uzi that I'm going to reach into my pocket for my police ID, and wait for a consenting nod before I do so. I show Bradley. "And who's the lady?"

"FBI," Jones says.

Elijah nods slowly, frowning. "Well, well, well. I just knew you were all wrong the moment I set eyes on you at the boxing. You don't have any legal right to be here at all, do you?"

"No, no I don't," Jones admits.

"The Thai cop don't have no right either, except a cop can do anything he likes in this town."

I'm fascinated by the cultural divide. For Bradley and Jones I've ceased to exist, just as for me the two Americans have no immediate claim on my attention. I do not take my eyes off the Uzi except to check the other Khmer, who has undressed Jones about twenty times already. Elijah spends a long moment thinking, staring at Jones, biting his lower lip, shaking his head.

"Okay, here's what we do. The cop leaves, you and I have a good old American-style rap and see if we can explore some common interest. Right?"

"Okay," Jones says.

"No," I say. The two Americans gaze at me.

"It's all right," Jones says. "He's saying you'll be my security. Who's going to try anything with you on the outside? You could have an army of cops here in ten minutes, and you know who this man is." She explains the situation kindly, as if to a child. "There's no danger, really."

Culture clash. "How long have you known your friends?" I ask Elijah. "A couple of hours?"

He glances at them slowly, on either side. "I don't need to know them more than a couple of hours, they're my late brother's loyal employees."

"Or jailers. Khmer don't work for anyone except themselves."

"In that case, I let you go and you come back with a couple of your colleagues and arrest them, if you feel so strongly about it."

"You don't understand." My eyes revert to the Khmer who is devouring Jones' legs. Elijah follows my gaze with a frown. "It'll be all over, and they'll be back in the jungles of Cambodia while you're facing a charge of rape and murder, assuming they leave you alive."

Light illuminates Elijah's eyes. He looks at the man with the Uzi, whose boredom might be reaching the limits of tolerance. "They kind of picked me up," Elijah admits. "I know who they are, though."

I am concerned because of where these two have come from, spiritually speaking. There are pits, and pits below pits, pits so deep only the unspeakable survives there.

"Maybe you don't. These are fanatics from out of the jungle who believe history started at year zero in 1978. The worst things you ever saw in Harlem would be light comedy to them. There's nothing I've got that would scare them. A Thai jail is like a five-star hotel compared to what they're used to."

The man with the Uzi yawns loudly and exchanges a glance with his companion, who nods and slides a knife out of a sheath under his shirt. "Aw," Elijah says.

"Don't think you want that kind of rap, Elijah," Jones says. She is holding herself together, but the blood has drained from her face. "They're your boys and the Bureau will extradite you."

"Their English ain't worth a dime," Elijah says. "Not if we talk fast. I can't make enemies of them, though. I have business in this town. Maybe Miss FBI here leaves and you and I talk?"

"That would be a much better idea."

Jones shakes her head and makes a face. "Sure hate to be the girl."

"It's a function of biology," Elijah explains, "and this ain't an equal opportunity situation. Better skit. I don't want the heat and I don't reckon I can control these guys, now that your man has explained them to me." Elijah's eyes have begun to dance from me to the Khmer, to Jones. "Don't suppose you all had the foresight to bring a firearm, did you?"

Jones and I look at each other and shrug. I don't think the Khmer have understood a word, now that we're speaking so fast, but they've seen Elijah's shift of allegiance. A dangerous moment. I stand up and start to shout angrily. I rip off my shirt to show them the long ladder of stitches on the left side of my rib cage, from just under my arm all the way to my thigh. "Did you do this?" I'm yelling. "Did one of you do this?" The man with the knife stands up to take a closer look while Jones makes for the door. He jabbers at his friend in Khmer, and they burst out laughing.

Suddenly the man with the knife is hugging me around the shoulders. "It wasn't us," he explains. "The guy who did it had to go back to Cambodia, he could hardly walk." He glances at Jones as she opens the door to leave, but makes no move to stop her. He's fascinated by my stitches and runs a finger up and down them, shaking his head. I am looking at him with clairvoyant vision now: the elongated snout, the leathery wings. He poisons my wound as he prods.

"Nice work," Elijah says, nodding sagely. "Maybe you and I can do business. You being such a switched-on denizen of these parts, maybe you've got some idea how I might get rid of these goons without bringing the ghost of Pol Pot down on my shoulders?"

"Pay them off."

"Now why didn't I think of that? Would you like to do the negotiating? I'm tired of hand signals."

I explain that the black *farang* wants to do business alone with the Royal Thai Police Force and would like to thank them for their help and assistance. The one with the Uzi plays with it while he talks about the risk of carrying a firearm in Krung Thep, which needs to be compensated for. Maybe they've been out of the jungles longer than I thought, their sense of an itemized account is surprisingly advanced. The final figure is four hundred dollars, which Elijah pays in hundred-dollar bills. We watch them go and Elijah says, "Let's get out of this museum. How about a walk in a street?"

Kaoshan is hopping as usual while we walk side by side. Elijah doesn't draw more than a glance or two, despite his size. Except for his eyes, he could be an overweight middle-aged American on vacation. His eyes never stop scanning. We stop in a bar halfway down the street and he shakes his head as I order two beers.

"That's quite a street. I ain't seen a street like that since the sixties. Harlem is real quiet in comparison. See the two dope deals? What was it, ganja?"

"Probably."

"Both those dealers were cops, right?"

"How did you know that?"

"Too relaxed, too complacent to be ordinary dealers. Every dealer ever worked for me had to suffer from controlled paranoia or I wouldn't use him. Those guys had protection. Do the cops have a bust-and-bribe scam and resell the dope?"

"It's a cottage industry."

The beers arrive and Elijah turns his up and pours it into his mouth until the bottle is empty. He burps and shakes his head. "My next incarnation I'm gonna put in for Thai cop. Pal, you gotta have the best job in the world."

I think of my hovel, my yard-long scar and the snake in Pichai's eye. "Yes," I agree.

33

"Brother Bill was different. He and I shared the same dad, so there ain't no rational explanation how we ended up like oil and water, and I'm not talking about him being a soldier and me being in the pharmaceutical industry. I'm talking about soul. I don't wish to bad-mouth my dead kin, but I have to tell you, since we're talking so intimate here, and you got me so damn drunk, Bill's soul was not the biggest you ever come across. Great souls are great sinners, like me. Small souls commit small sins and become sergeants, mayors, presidents. When he was a kid about fifteen I took him under my wing and tried to educate him. I would walk him down a street just like we did tonight and test him afterwards. 'Did you see those two crack deals go down?' I would say. 'Did you see the iron that wop was packing? Did you notice, brother dear, that members of the Boyz Love Money gang were mingling on the corner of 115th and Lexington, which is the sovereign territory of the Hoover Crips gang? Some serious violence about to go down tonight. And did it even occur to you, Mr. Universe, that the cute nigger bitch who was coming on to you outside that hamburger joint and massaging your fantasies till the whole world could see your erection was a smack fiend and after your dough, not your cock?' Young Billy never saw anything in other people except the effect of his amazing body. He was neat and tidy, a Goody Two-shoes, which is always a cause for concern. A born peacetime soldier. A born sergeant."

I cast my eyes over the ten bottles of Kloster all lined up around the table and order another. I stopped drinking about an hour ago. "He was brave under fire."

"You talking about that thing at the embassy in Yemen? He called me afterwards, about the first time in ten years. He was shaking and could hardly talk. Frankly, he was scared shitless. Sure, he acted brave, but it was his training took over. Why d'you think they put marines through that kind of torture in boot camp? Exactly so as they'll react like robots. I was proud of him, so was Mother, but he was *frightened*. That was the only time I heard him talk about getting out early. I think he kind of traded his medal for a long-term posting out here. He had his eye on your town for a long time before they finally consented to let him come."

"Why?"

"Why does any man want to be posted here? Billy was all about sex. That was his thing. Don't get me wrong, I ain't no prude, I just don't think it's appropriate for a middle-aged man to have it on his mind all the time. With Billy it was a kind of sickness. Somehow it went with him being so neat and tidy, so damn perfect. Know what I mean? I told him, 'Billy, in this world money has got to come first. Put anything you like second, but if you don't master dough, it sure as hell will master you.' He saw the light about five years ago, when he first started thinking about life after retirement."

"With a girlfriend like that, a lot of men might have it on the mind full-time."

Elijah eyes me sideways. "Fatima, she turn you on?"

"That's really her name? Fatima?"

"That's the one she gave." A slow, careful nod. "Too exotic for me. I like a more earthy mama, someone you can drink beer and watch TV with, who don't care if you fart. She kind of spooked me."

"He must have talked about her a lot."

Elijah downed another bottle. "Nope, not once. I guess he knew I thought he was kinda weird about that sort of thing. I had no idea who she was or what she looked like or even that she existed. All I had was a mobile number he sent me over the e-mail one time. I called it from New York after they told me he was dead. It was his mobile, but I figured someone might be using it. She answered and told me she'd meet me at the hotel after I landed. It was her idea to go to the boxing."

"You don't have an address?"

"Not even a phone number. I tried calling her again before you guys showed up, and there's a Thai voice telling me in English that the number's no longer available."

"First you were with her, the next thing you're with some Khmer?"

"She called them when I freaked a little at the boxing. I knew that friend of yours was wrong, Miss FBI. I have street instinct. Three of them arrived on bikes. She goes off with one of them and leaves the other two to mind me. They weren't such bad fellas. Maybe a little undisciplined."

"I can guarantee no problems for you if you want to talk a little about what your brother was up to. It might help find his killers."

"Been waiting for you to say that. Actually, I don't have a problem because I wasn't involved, whatever Miss Hot Pants might have insinuated. These days I work in a hermetically sealed environment. I don't risk contamination from anyone, not even blood relations. I sure don't risk doing business with a beginner, which was what Bill was. I just gave him some advice, that's all, the kind I hoped would keep him out of trouble. Guess he didn't take it, huh?"

"What kind of advice?"

Elijah is not as drunk as he claims. His vast body has now absorbed twelve bottles of beer, without much effect on his alertness. "Well, I guess he's dead, right? Nothing can hurt him now. He had some idea that meth could be safely imported into the States. What's that crazy name you got for it over here?"

"*Yaa baa.*"

"Right. Great name, maybe *we* should call it that. He had all these detailed plans on how to smuggle *yaa baa*, through Hong Kong, through Shanghai, even through Tokyo. He was a real details man. He believed he had some special insight because of all his work at embassies and knowledge of how diplomatic immunity works. He talked just like any amateur who gets the bug. He got all excited because he had some contacts here, people who could bring in unlimited quantities at knockdown prices. I explained to him, I says: 'Billy, don't matter that you're not moving heroin, you're in the region of the Golden Triangle, you got more FBI, CIA, DEA per square inch out there than anywhere in the world. Not a good idea, Billy. Forget it.' When I saw he wasn't going to forget it, I made a few inquiries. I called him to give him some names and addresses of people out here with experience of moving stuff. I explain business to him. I say, 'Look, settle for a five percent handler's fee here in Bangkok, don't get involved in the overseas shipping, just move the stuff from address A in Bangkok to address B in Bangkok. So it doesn't make you rich overnight, you still get a good income, given the quantities you're talking about, and you sleep better at night. Maybe when you've been in the business a few years, maybe then you can think about something a little more ambitious.' I thought he got the point, but obviously I was wrong."

"Why d'you say that?"

"Sonchai, my man, he fucked up, didn't he? My kid brother did what any dumb, middle-aged desperado does who don't want to go on another learning curve. He jumped into the snake pit thinking he was going to solve his cash flow problem in one fell swoop. I seen it happen so often it's boring. The only fell swoops that work are the ones that have structure, that have been set up over a period of years, maybe decades. I know, I sat at the feet of black professors in the university of the penitentiary. But you can't explain that to a guy who secretly thinks he's superman, who spends his whole life looking in a mirror. And just so as we can remain friends, you and I, I'm going to anticipate your next question. No, I ain't gonna tell you who I told him to get in touch with out here."

"I wasn't going to ask," I say, hurt.

Another bottle empties into his mouth, with just a little spilling from the corners. "No, come to think of it, I don't believe you were. Accept my apologies for offending your professional pride. Where would you recommend to eat around here? Don't give me anything with chili, I'm a New Yorker."

Elijah is the reincarnation of a southern planter who treated his slaves well but was unable to transcend the racism of his times. He spent two incarnations as an African American, neither of them illustrious. Deep resentment toward the system carried over from those lifetimes and drove him to crime in this one. These perceptions came to me while he was cramming some stuffed potato skins into his mouth at a diner off Sukhumvit. We've come all the way across the city because this is the only New York–style deli I know. It is 3:21 a.m., but Elijah's jet lag makes him as fresh as a daisy. The deli, come to think of it, is not New York. It is sand floor and potted plants and there is chili on the menu, but Elijah has not noticed as he tucks into a forkful of quesadillas.

"See, I'm a child of the sixties. A black man in those far-off days had to make a decision early on in life: sport, religion, jazz or crime. Brother Billy was born five years later, and already things had started to change. It killed me at the time that my kid brother was a patriot. I still don't look on my way of earning a living as criminal. Where's the victim? I supply a demand. Can I help it if the psychology of modern America has created a demand for escape at any cost, particularly amongst the white yuppie class? Billy didn't see it that way, and the second time I went to the penitentiary he stopped talking to me. It's one of those things that just when I'm mellowing toward the good old U.S., Billy is developing a black power mentality. I guess he was always kinda slow on the uptake. He even talked about becoming a black Muslim. Maybe he did, he wouldn't have told me because I don't like Muslims and neither does Mother, who's one churchy nigger."

Elijah picked up a chicken leg and examined it for a moment. I said: "Did he talk to you about jade?"

He took a big chunk out of the thigh, chewed briefly and swallowed. "Jade? A precious stone, right, from Laos or Burma or something? He mentioned it. It was a kind of hobby of his. He wouldn't have talked about it too much to me, because I never shared his taste in jewelry. That was another thing about him. Nigger can wear gold, pearls, what the hell he likes, if he does it to strut his stuff, that's okay. But Billy was serious about jewelry from an early age. It was small, you get what I'm saying? Part of his smallness, which I didn't appreciate."

"D'you know who Sylvester Warren is?" A shake of the head while he's stripping the rest of the bone with his teeth. "A billionaire jeweler and art dealer, knows presidents. He comes here once a month."

Elijah's face is blank. He shakes his head again before starting in on the nachos. With his mouth full: "We got a lot of billionaires who have to leave America to get their kicks. It ain't like it used to be. We got media, mind police, electronic surveillance. White boy like that who knows presidents can't afford even to look at his secretary the wrong way. They ain't as broad-minded as us niggers. They really fucked themselves all up. No wonder he comes here every month, this Warren. Did he know Billy?"

"They exchanged e-mails."

"Think he was the one had him killed?"

I shrug. "No one can think of a motive."

Elijah pauses with a forkful of potato salad. "Me either. Let's face it, Billy tried all his life to be as big as his body, but at the end of the day he was a little guy. A sergeant in the Marines who liked to hire cheap pussy out of Third World go-go bars. He wasn't important enough for a rich white boy to kill."

"Tell me this. Was your brother more than averagely scared of snakes?"

"More than average? I dunno. I guess every nigger in Harlem's scared of snakes. The African jungle is quite a few generations back. Sure, he was scared of snakes, same as me. I used to tease him that if he went ahead and joined the army he would be sent to the jungles of Southeast Asia where boa constrictors roamed on the loose. Freaked him out but it seems like I was right."

"Do you intend to avenge your brother's death, Mr. Bradley?"

My question, perfectly reasonable to me, has astonished him. He puts down his fork and pushes his seat back a foot to stare at me. "You mean like a vendetta?" He scratches his head by way of answer. "Only time I had anyone rubbed out was because they double-crossed me. In the business, when that happens you don't have any choice, but to tell you the truth I been regretting it ever since. I'm not a man of violence. Most of the time, being this big, I don't need to be."

"You didn't love him?"

"I don't know. He was my brother but we weren't close. I came over to sort out his estate. I get the feeling we're dealing with a cultural difference, here, Detective. Only Sicilians do that vendetta stuff in the U.S. We blacks prefer to rely on the rule of law. What *you* gonna do when you find who did it?"

"Kill them," I say with a smile.

It is 4:32 a.m. by the time I reach my hovel. As usual, I had forgotten to take my mobile with me. It bleeps while I'm falling asleep and the screen tells me there's a message. I fumble with the controls until the message appears:

River City, 2nd level, Warren Fine Art and Jewelry. Opens 10 a.m.
See you there. K.J. P.S. Dress up.

Between the two incompatible worlds of waking and sleeping my mind reverts to the dildo garden at the Hilton. Meditation is just a way of preferring reality to fantasy, as our abbot used to say. He would not have been put out by that small forest of cocks, though he might have had a problem with the Hilton. Like many of our country abbots, he retained much of the shamanism of pagan times and liked to predict the future. Once he foretold the winning numbers in the national lottery, just for fun, but hid the paper on which he made the prediction until after the deadline for purchasing tickets, so as not to corrupt his monks. There will be a massive shift of power from West to East in the middle of the twenty-first century, caused not by war or economics but by a subtle alteration in consciousness. The new age of biotechnology will require a highly developed intuition which operates outside of logic, and anyway the internal destruction of Western society will have reached such a pass that most of your resources will be concentrated on managing loonies. There will be TV news pictures of people fleeing from supermarkets and pressing their hands to their heads, unable to take the banality anymore. The peoples of Southeast Asia, who have never been poisoned by logical thought, will find themselves in the driver's seat. It will be like old times, if your time line stretches back a few thousand years.

I was flattered that the abbot chose me rather than Pichai with whom to share this side of his enlightenment, though the finer points which enable one to predict a lottery he kept to himself (on the other hand he initiated Pichai into the deepest mysteries that exist concerning the relationship between the so-called living and the so-called dead).

There won't be another world war, but by the middle of this century every country except Iceland and New Zealand is involved in a more or less violent dispute with neighbors over water rights. Papua New Guinea beats Argentina 3–1 in the 2056 World Cup final. *How to Deal with Crazies Without Turning into One* tops the best-seller lists throughout 2038. Marijuana (universally legalized) overtakes alcohol as the recreational drug of choice in Europe, even in France where legislators rush to bring it under the *appellation contrôlée* laws (*Champagne Jaune, Bordeaux Blond, Noir de Bourgogne*, etc.).

34

This morning I woke early and spent an hour in the Emporium building on Sukhumvit, before the shops opened. I see that the explosion of color which was really started by Yves Saint Laurent has migrated to Italy, mostly to Versace and Armani, while Saint Laurent himself has returned to blacks and browns. Ermenegildo Zegna on the other hand has never abandoned the glazed beiges which work so well on his superfine wools. I spare a moment to drool over his camel double-breasted blazer with mock tortoiseshell buttons (about U.S.$1,500), but today it is the atelier of Armani which has my attention with its new collection of silk-satin woven ties, cashmere one-button sports jackets and plaid four-button double-breasted suits. It is a subtler, suaver art than the late Versace's, but who could deny the élan, the very Italian playfulness (so close to Thai), in those houndstooth check shirts, wrinkle-cotton striped dress shirts and wool crepe skirts in the Armani window? My real vice, though, is shoes, and I spend most of the time ogling the Bally collection (dull-glow mahogany slip-ons, some very daring perforated brogues with echoes of Gatsby—I saw the film—and some utterly fantastic women's stuff with heels and points no one else would get away with), not that I neglect Fila, Ferragamo, Gucci or the very exotic Baker-Benjes, which has only recently appeared in our kingdom. I would like to claim it is my *farang* contamination in the blood which is responsible for this defilement and debilitating disease, but the truth is I caught it from Truffaut and Fritz, both consummate narcissists in different ways and hypersharp dressers, who intervened in my development at a crucial juncture. The FBI's instruction to "dress up" has thrown me into a crisis of inferiority which will take some meditating to deal with. I'm fed up with being poor, at least the non-Buddhist side of me is, and feeling pretty damn low when I take the motorcycle taxi to the Hilton to meet Kimberley, who has hired her usual car to take us to River City.

In the back of the car I explain: "River City is where the rich and dumb go to buy Oriental art. You pay a hundred percent markup for the sensitive placing of the piece, the backlighting, the mincing salesperson. It's a shopping mall for art tasters and looks exactly like the one near you." The tension in my voice is a direct product of my pressed khaki shirt, white pants, polished black lace-up shoes (all items generic and the shoes particularly ugly). The FBI has relegated me to the position of Indian guide by the time we reach the car park.

Why do I have the feeling she planned this moment while she was sitting in her office in Quantico and fantasizing about the glory she would bask in when she bagged Sylvester Warren? Her hair is blond again this morning, she is wearing wraparound Gucci sunglasses, a black YSL business suit with trousers, white shirt open to a string of pearls. Tiny pearls.

"I'm here on a buying trip from New York," she explains. "You're my man Friday."

We ride the escalator to the second level and there is Warren Fine Art in triple A position, in your face as you step off. Jones was wrong about the opening time. It's the kind of shop that doesn't open until eleven, when an overdressed beautiful person will unlock it with a yawn. Smart buyers do not browse, they make an appointment. For the right smart buyer the beautiful person would open the store at midnight. We pause at the window long enough for Jones to show off her expertise.

"Some not bad stuff here. That Buddha head is definitely Khmer, someone ripped it off from Angkor Wat. If Warren didn't have connections he'd be in jail, the son of a bitch." We take the ten or so paces to the next window, which is the jewelry and jade section. It is not like any of the jewelry shops in Chinatown, or anywhere else in Krung Thep. The work is almost all jade, often mounted on gold. Gold and jade necklaces, gold and jade bracelets, earrings. Arising out of the sea of green are some of the more substantial pieces, which cleverly highlight the rest, giving the impression that the whole window was once guarded by imperial eunuchs in the Forbidden City. "Will you look at that condor plaque! See the bald head, the creases in the neck denoting the bird's spare skin in that area? Just look how accurately a Neolithic person, illiterate, probably with a vocabulary of a few hundred words, has observed a creature, stylized it and turned it into art without sacrificing accuracy. Most college graduates today couldn't do that. They wouldn't even understand what I'm talking about."

I spare her a quick glance. Here is yet another personality, and a surprising one. I have been puzzling and meditating on the karmic connection between Jones and Warren without being able to figure it out. It is certain, though, that Warren has influenced her from a distance. It could have been him talking. In her compartmentalized *farang* mind she cannot see the significance of this, she sincerely believes she has become an expert on Far Eastern art exclusively to nail Warren. She would see it as evidence of pathetic weakness on her part to acknowledge how Warren has broadened and deepened her mind, even before she ever met him. From afar he has changed her destiny forever. With whom in the Bureau could she share this new passion for Oriental art? Even her family sooner or later will think her strange, and this strangeness will be her path. I dare not warn her that she is destined to return to my country again and again. I predict the allure will work through her pussy, at least at first. The path to the *farang* heart lies invariably through the genitalia.

"Wow! That tiger is priceless," Jones explains. "It's the big come-on, the piece which tells you this guy is the king of jade." Her voice has risen an octave when she says: "See how the sculptor has bunched the muscles, giving that impression of power, and look at the harmony. Limbs, haunches, back, shoulder, stomach—synchronized, masterful, harmonious."

"It's not green," I object.

"That's the point. After about a thousand years jade loses its color. That tiger goes back to the Early Western Zhou dynasty. He would never sell it, I bet. To anyone who knows anything, it's as intimidating as hell." She shakes her head. "I'm surprised he's got the guts to show some of this stuff. Look at that crouching dragon in mutton-fat nephrite and those thrush-breast freckles—think of the genius it took to see that dragon in the crude stone. That chatelaine is impressive, too, and look at that openwork plaque with peonies. I don't know, this is more than just a collector, this is a curator of his own museum." She takes the two steps back to the center of the window. "That tiger, though, it's still the best piece on display. It's more than just a great piece, it's world class, the stone equivalent of the Mona Lisa—if you like the Mona Lisa, which I don't, personally. Oh, look, he's acknowledging his Chinese connections. See that brilliant piece of calligraphy hanging on the wall consisting of a single pictograph? That's the Chinese character *yú*."

"So what?"

"*Yú* is Mandarin for jade. Since the Chinese were the first to discover it, you could say it's the original name. Those three lines mean 'virtue, beauty and rarity,' in other words the three qualities of jade according to Confucius."

"See the piece on the shelf," I say, pointing behind the window display, into the interior of the shop.

"Well, I'll be . . ."

"It might not be the same one."

"Oh, it's the same one."

Horse and rider.

In a small café in the main complex, downstairs, while we're waiting for the shop to open, Jones says: "I did try love once. I really did. It still gets so much hype, you feel you've got to give it a chance, right? I think in the States we're way past that stage, though. It's like, in the first phase of industrialization there's still marriage as in an undeveloped agricultural economy, meaning it lasts for life. The next phase, people get married knowing they'll get divorced. One phase further on, and you find people marrying *in order to* get divorced. By the time you reach twenty-first century America, love is a blip on the career path, something that was capable of making you late for work for a week, before you got over it. The sad truth is it's incompatible with freedom, money and equality. Who the hell really wants to be stuck with their equal for life? Human beings are predators, we like to hunt and eat the weak so we can feel strong for a moment. How about you?"

The question has taken me by surprise, not least because Jones has her hand on my thigh again. This time there can be no doubt as to her meaning and I think the talk about predation must be a kind of foreplay. My inferiority in my badly tailored khaki shirt, awful pants and truly hideous black anvil-shaped shoes is evident. I should take her hand off my thigh to make it clear I don't want to be eaten, but instead cast around in my mind for an answer to her question. I think of Kat as I say: "Some people give their hearts only once. When love fails, they take up some occupation which reflects their bitterness."

Jones raises her eyebrows. "Is that what I did? Became a man-hunter because my true love betrayed me?" I expect some cynical coda. Instead she mutters, "Damned right," and takes her hand away. Jones is not a Buddhist, therefore I do not explain the endless cycle of life after life, each one a reaction against some imbalance from the one before, that reaction setting up yet another imbalance and so on and on and on . . . We are the pinballs of eternity.

At 11:20 a.m. we ride up the escalator again and I am surprised at the preindustrial feeling of anticipation in my stomach, a delicious foreboding of dangerous karma to come.

She is slightly inside the fine-art side of the shop, dusting a full-length standing Buddha from Ayutthaya with a feather duster. A gong sounds as we cross the threshold and she turns toward us, a polite smile on her face. She is wearing a simple white linen blouse from Versace with open neck projecting a delicious vulnerability, black skirt probably also by Versace to below her knees. Her string of pearls is much larger than the FBI's, but what causes my most intense suffering is her fragrance, the name of which escapes me but not the brand: it is indisputably from Van Cleef & Arpels, no doubt flown in from their store on the Place Vendôme, the very shop where Truffaut seduced my mother's nose even if the rest of her body remained beyond his failing powers. I pretend to sneeze slightly to have an excuse to inhale deeply. (*Smell is the most animal of the senses,* Truffaut advised, *and like an animal a person will fall prey to a delicious intensity when he or she truly enters the universe of fragrance.*)

The first words I ever hear her utter are *Good morning,* and I note with mounting joy how her voice—womanly, soft with Negroid timbre—so exactly matches and expresses her physical beauty.

Fatima's father was black American, mine was white American, there the difference ends. I know she is experiencing the moment in the same way while Jones, with great professionalism, conceals her surprise at seeing her in Warren's shop. I do not hear Jones' spiel about seeking out special pieces for her bijou gallery in Manhattan, and neither does the spectacular woman who was Bradley's lover. Jones' voice could be a mile away, all I hear is Fatima's polite reply: "Oh, how wonderful of you to think of us!"

I am pierced by her fragility, the sense of a recent loss of life-threatening proportions so similar to mine; pierced also by a perception which initially is mind-boggling, then blindingly obvious. Why did I not think of it before?

Clearly such mutual depth of emotion can only be the product of an intense relationship in a previous lifetime, and Jones' comment about people dying, then carrying on conversations after rebirth, echoes in my head. Jones stops in mid-sentence while I float effortlessly toward Fatima across the polished floor. I have the impression of waltzing between Buddhas while I jabber in Thai about Khmer art, of which I know nothing, and—it is obvious—neither does Fatima. She explains, with a laugh, that she does not actually work here, she is filling in for someone as a favor to the boss. Here should be my opening to insert the name of Sylvester Warren, instead I let it pass. I do not want to talk shop.

Jones tries to follow us around the salon and I am pleased to see she has no idea what is going on. We are continuing not one conversation, Fatima and I, but many, perhaps hundreds, from hundreds upon hundreds of lifetimes. She is my twin. The words we use have no correspondence to the present moment, they are merely vehicles of our excitement at meeting again at last. How long has it been? A hundred years? A thousand? Now Fatima is leading me into a remote corner, near a door. It is as if she wishes to tell me something. She has taken care to choose a moment when Jones has been left behind. I see him for a split second, a face at a doorway partially opened, before he withdraws and closes the door. It was one of the Khmer who befriended Elijah, the one with the knife. I make startled eyes at Fatima, but she shakes her head to reassure me. I nod as if I understand, even though I am now thoroughly confused.

After half an hour my poor nerves cannot take any more of this intensity and I am ready to leave the shop. Fatima's body *wais* to me at the threshold, my own body *wais* back. Thus do two dolls bow to each other while the puppet masters exchange knowing smiles from eternity. Jones follows me to the escalator. "What was that all about? You seemed to establish a rapport, anyway. Did you discover anything useful? What about Warren?"

"We didn't talk about Warren."

"Oh, but you got her number and address? Her ID? Her real name in Thai? You can get hold of her?"

"No."

"So how are you going to find her again if she doesn't really work there? Don't you want to interview her? Isn't she the last person to be seen with Bradley alive? Isn't she a suspect? Wasn't she the one in the car when you followed Bradley from the airport?" Exasperated. "Don't you want to know who did it?"

"I know who did it."

"Who?"

"Bradley did it. To himself. With help from Warren."

I am walking quickly toward Jones' hired car, in which the driver is waiting with the engine running for the air-conditioning. Jones is sweating in the heat with the effort to catch up. "Wait a minute, are you for real? Are you saying that Bradley committed suicide using—oh, I get it. We're back to the Buddha, right? It's a point about karma you're making here? You've just beamed yourself up to that point five miles above the earth where good Thai cops go when they die or get confused—or fall in love. Have you any idea how unsophisticated you looked just now? Like a teenage boy. I've never seen anything so unprofessional."

"If you didn't love crooks you would never have become a cop," I snap.

Her jaw hangs open. She is truly baffled and, for once, stumped for something to say.

We are in the back seat of the Mercedes after the FBI has slammed the door shut on her side. I am trying to find the key to our past lives, Fatima's and mine, the trigger, so to speak, that set us off on our centuries-old game of hide-and-seek.

"Shit." Jones fixes her eyes at some point out of her side window while we wait in traffic. "If I'd known I'd have gotten her number myself. This is like being a cop in ancient Egypt."

Hiding a smirk: "You remember?"

She continues to grumble in my left ear while I try to disentangle great reams of karmic information that are flashing through my head. I have never experienced this before, not with such intensity. "You have to have forgiveness," I mutter. "It's the only way back."

"Damn it, I'm going to get her number myself. If I had the right I'd bring her in for questioning. She's the link for Christ's sake. You must see that? The link between Bradley, Warren, the jade and the meth. Under the right pressure she could solve the case in five minutes and I could get the hell out of this place. Maybe nail Warren at the same time."

She has the driver turn around. I wait in the car while she rushes up the escalator to Warren's shop, close my eyes and meditate. When she returns a few minutes later her clothes are soaked in sweat and a great fury is working her jaw muscles. "The bitch closed the shop and did a runner. We've lost her again."

"Really?"

She practices deep breathing for five minutes. In a controlled voice: "Don't you have anything new to report? What about your long talk with Elijah last night? Didn't anything useful come up?"

"Actually, yes, something crucial. William Bradley never mentioned Fatima to his brother. Elijah didn't know about her until he called William's mobile after the murder."

"That's crucial?" She rubs her jaw with that disbelieving look that Americans do so well when abroad. "Tell me where you want me to drop you off, because what I need right now is a big fix of crass Western culture. I'm gonna go back to the Hilton, order American food to be brought to my big, bland, air-conditioned room and watch CNN until I remember who I am. This is a magic-ravaged land, you know that? Coming here has made me appreciate whoever it was invented logic, because before logic I think the whole world was like this."

"That's true," I agree. "Magic is preindustrial."

I stand by the curbside and watch Jones' car drive off to join the jam on Rama IV. I feel a little sorry for the FBI and her belief that there is anything logical about human existence. I suppose it must be the delusion of the West, a cultural defilement caused by all those machines they keep inventing. It's like choosing the ringing tune on one's mobile: a logical labyrinth with no meaningful outcome. Logic as distraction. Frankly, I can't wait for that global power shift the abbot talked about. My mind returns to Fatima. That Khmer, though, he is a puzzle.

The truth about human life is that for most of the time there is nothing to do and therefore the wise man—or woman—cultivates the art of doing nothing. I return to my hovel to meditate. I have to confess to a certain amount of self-love arising from having solved the case (at least in out-line), which I need to eradicate in order to progress further on the Path. There are still many loose ends, after all. The snakes and Warren continue to be enveloped in mystery. Likewise it is not apparent to me how I will find the opportunity to kill Warren. And what am I supposed to do about Fatima? I feel very near to understanding the snakes when the telephone bleeps. I have to control my irritation when I observe from the screen that it is the FBI.

"Ah, look, I want to apologize. I was way out of line. I did exactly what they tell us you should never do. I lost it and got arrogant. Guilty. I guess culture shock is more powerful than anyone realizes. I really felt like I was drowning. I've never felt like that before, like being in a place with no references. Where what you thought were references are illusions. Am I making sense here?"

"I think you're making progress. That is a spiritual experience you are describing." I do not add: *Welcome to the world.*

"You don't have to patronize me just because I patronized you. I thought we could have lunch, talk about the case."

I do not want to talk about the case. I feel a digression is called for. I say: "I have to go to Samutprakan crocodile farm tomorrow. If you like we can go in your car."

At Bang Kwan that afternoon they told me Fritz had been badly beaten the day before and was in the hospital. They refused to let me see him until I threatened them with a prosecution for obstructing justice. In a ward largely dedicated to the malnourished and terminally ill—AIDS is still a big killer here—he is propped up on a pillow with bandages around his head; his left leg and right arm are in splints. I think that this time he will not recover, that his body was too weak to take such punishment, but as I approach I'm surprised to see him smiling and apparently in good spirits.

"What happened?"

"My pardon came through."

"That's great but I meant about the beating."

"What do I care about that? Didn't you hear me? My pardon is through. The King's signed it already, it's only a matter of days now."

"I'm really pleased for you. What was it you wanted to see me about?"

He gestured as best he could to his leg and arm. "Can't tell you. Sorry."

"Don't worry, I understand."

He gestured to me to come closer. "Not because of the beating. The pardon. They said it could still be canceled. I hope you understand."

I nod vigorously. I wouldn't want to jeopardize his pardon, not for all the evidence in the world. I leave a pack of cannibalized Marlboro Reds on the table next to his bed.

35

I am lying on my futon waiting for Jones to arrive and listening to the radio on my Walkman. Pisit reports that all the newspapers are reporting that the Supreme Patriarch has approved and blessed two thousand new surnames created by senior monks. The names will be offered under a surname reservation service. Pisit's guest is a spokesman for Buddhism who clearly expects joy and delight at the news. Pisit is in a skeptical mood and asks if it is appropriate to be living in a medieval theocracy in the twenty-first century when men dressed in robes from the third century B.C., who spend their time chanting in a language which has been dead for over two thousand years, are responsible for people's names? The spokesman, a monk himself, asks—aghast—how anyone could possibly want a surname that has not been blessed? Pisit quickly gets rid of him and replaces him with a sociologist who explains that we are a superstitious people for whom anything as intimate as a name needs to possess magical powers. Pisit brightens and asks about Western names. "Usually they reflect the Western obsession with money, in that they are a statement about the work an ancestor did: Smith, Woodman, Baker, et cetera."

"So it's money with them, magic with us?"

Doubtfully: "You could say that, although it might be an over-simplification."

Pisit gets rid of him in favor of a psychiatrist who is happy to discuss Pisit's favorite topic. Why are Thai men risking their health and virility by having their penises enlarged with silicone and gel? The operation is extremely painful with side effects such as swelling and infection, and is illegal. The shrink explains that prior to the invasion of Western advertising it never occurred to Thai men to think much about size, quite rightly since the standard Thai male member is perfectly adapted to the standard Thai vagina, but with Western hard porn and cigarette adverts, there has been a serious loss of self-confidence. Ironically, the effect of this assault from the West has been to cause impotence, either because of the disastrous operation or through chronic self-doubt.

Pisit, laughing: "So on top of everything else, they're castrating us?"

Laughing: "You could say that."

On a whim, Pisit calls the monk back to ask what he thinks of all this, and Western culture in general. After his drubbing just now he is in a Zen-ish sort of mood, not to say downright sarcastic: "Actually, the West is a Culture of Emergency: twisters in Texas, earthquakes in California, windchill in Chicago, drought, flood, famine, epidemics, drugs, wars on everything—watch out for that meteor and how much longer does the sun really have? Of course, if you didn't believe you could control everything, there wouldn't be an emergency, would there?"

There is a knock on my door. The FBI has arrived.

In the back of the car again I try to explain why meditation can help in the art of detection. I'm not sure if I believe what I'm saying or not, I just happen to be in the mood to say it. I may have fallen prey to the irresistible temptation to wind her up. "To understand why someone suffers a violent death, it can be helpful to investigate their past lives. These things do not happen by accident. There are no accidents, no coincidences."

"Uh-huh?"

"For example, in olden days in America, were there many brothels?"

"In the Old West? Sure."

I nod. "Bradley's obsession with sex was surely a consequence of having traded in it." I frown. "That doesn't explain the snakes, though."

"Okay, you want to play this game, it's not so difficult. Maybe he ran a brothel that was built on a rattlesnake nest? Maybe he punished anyone who didn't pay by putting rattlers in their beds?" She shakes her head. "Can't believe I'm doing this."

"You don't understand. It's not a question of plausible hypotheses. You have to follow a vibration back through time. Bradley had a very specific vibration, very strong. My problem is his karmic origins are not Asian."

"How about Central America? Aztec, Inca, Mayan? They all had snake fetishes. They were unbelievably cruel, too."

A vision immediately flashes before my mind: the snakes, the pit, the plumed priest, the rings on his fingers, the victim's terror, the ziggurat. I beam at Jones, who turns away with her usual *Can't believe this guy* expression of terminal exasperation. After a few minutes she turns back again, having mastered her frustration—not without effort, to judge from her expression. "Okay, give me an example unrelated to the case."

"An example?"

"Yes, from your own life, a genuine past-life memory that can be corroborated for a button-down nuts-and-bolts type like me." She sniffs the air. "Your obsession with perfume, for example, I bet you can trace that back a few hundred years. It's sure got me beat, you can hardly afford to dress yourself but you wear this expensive cologne—or is it a Bangkok fake?"

"Of course it's not a fake, fake perfume stinks after being on the skin for a couple of minutes. It's just a perfectly ordinary Polo from Ralph Lauren."

"*Perfectly ordinary Polo from Ralph Lauren*," she mimics. "At about fifty bucks a bottle." She stares at me, waiting for a story to ridicule.

Her attitude has made me curl up protectively around the memory: the old Pont au Change which connected the Île de la Cité with the Right Bank, four-story buildings loaded the bridge, slap in the middle sat a perfumer's: a dark and musty workroom populated from floor to roof with chemist's jars of tincture of musk, castor, neroli, jonquil, cinnamon, tuberose, ambergris, civet, sandalwood, bergamot, vetiver, patchouli, opopanax. Nong was there in the mountainous skirts of a mid-ranking courtesan, Truffaut in his startlingly white horsehair wig. Okay, it might be fantasy and autosuggestion, but how did I know there were buildings on the Pont au Change in the eighteenth century? There are none at all now and it took me days on the Web to corroborate. I'm a Thai cop, I didn't know there ever were such things as bridges with shops on them.

I decide to tell Jones after all. She stares at me in silence, then shakes her head. "If only you weren't so damn cute. How come you know all those names of ingredients? I've never heard of half of them."

Farangs are full of surprises. It's the erudition that impresses her, not the quality of the evidence.

The FBI did not need to ask why we were going to the crocodile farm. It was not often anyone used snakes as a murder weapon, and none of our usual forensic consultants was competent to analyze the blood of reptiles. Jones knew that the python and all the cobras that had not been sent to Quantico had been dispatched to the croc farm for examination by Dr. Bhasra Trakit. The croc farm is out of town, just off the main road to Pattaya. I have allowed four hours for the journey and it is a few minutes before 8 a.m. when we set off. The sun is just visible through the haze, like a rotten orange soggy at the edges. To avoid conversation I pretend to sleep in the car, while secretly meditating.

The driveway to the small administrative building does not disclose any crocodiles or other reptiles, and I think the FBI is hopeful about not having to see any at all. Dr. Trakit wears the white coat of a medical practitioner and could have been a physician except for the pet she is playing with on her desk. "I want you to meet Bill Gates," she says with a smile in perfect English. Bill Gates looks small and cute enough, almost like a toy. He is about 20 percent mouth, with a crooked grin when the doctor gently squeezes his neck and strokes him. His underbelly is creamy white with a light gray-green coloring on the upper part of his body. Dr. Trakit smiles at Jones like a proud mother, and offers her Bill Gates. "Be careful with him."

"How old is he?"

"Only three months. They're so delicate, especially in captivity. Shall we?"

Trakit had looked tiny even behind her desk. Now that she stood, we see she is hardly more than five feet, and very slim. She puts Bill Gates in the pocket of her coat and leads the way down a corridor, out into the heat of the day.

Now we see them, immobile masses of sloping scales half submerged in swampy pools. Jones tenses. Back in the States, of course, every precaution would be taken, but here in the Third World . . . *Just my luck to be the only FBI special agent ever to be eaten alive by a crocodile while on a trip to a forensic lab.* "Please walk softly," the vet says. "They're very sensitive. If we make too much noise, they panic, and when they panic they pile up on top of each other, especially the younger ones, and the crocs underneath suffocate. They suffer from depression too."

Jones is almost walking on tiptoe. *"Depression?"* (As in manic?)

"Yes. And it's much harder to tell when a croc's depressed than a human or a dog. Crocs are motionless most of the time, whether they're depressed or not. You can only tell when they stop eating. Here we are, this is the hospital."

We enter a long low outhouse with the odor of tropical dampness and something else hard to define which includes nuances of rotting vegetation and putrefying flesh. "Excuse me one moment," the doctor says. We stand and watch while the doctor goes to a fridge and takes out what looks like a slightly chilled chicken. We follow to a white door which the vet enters with a finger to her lips. On a long table in the center of the room a crocodile is strapped around its center and tail. The reptile is about eight feet long, its short legs held by chains which wrap around protective pads. The animal's jaws are held open by stout rope and it seems to be asleep. Jones waits in the doorway. "Just one moment," the doctor says. She goes to a chopping board at the other end of the room and chops up the chicken with a meat cleaver. She places some pieces of the chicken in the croc's mouth with her tiny hand, moving them around on its tongue, until the tongue begins sluggishly to move. It must be due to a defilement of mine that I'm enjoying Jones so much: she is frozen in terminal horror.

"I want Samantha to get her appetite back. Look, her taste buds are waking up. She got depressed after we drained her pool by mistake. If the pools drain too quickly, they panic. It's a reflex from the wild. Most crocs who die prematurely do so because their water holes have dried up, so they're hardwired to panic at the first sign of drought. There, did you think we were going to let you die of exposure? Poor, poor thing. Now let's see if she's found something to live for." Trakit undoes the rope, which passes through a pulley suspended from the ceiling, releasing Samantha's upper jaw. Jones takes two steps back until she is standing in the corridor. Very very slowly, Samantha begins to munch on the chicken. "There," Trakit says. "Everything comes down to food in the end."

She leads us from the room down the corridor to a stainless steel cupboard with trays of different sizes. "Here they are," the doctor says, pulling out one of the trays. Cobra corpses. Some of them have been neatly dissected, others are whole except for the bullet holes. "They all died of gunshot wounds, of course." She glares at me. "And as I told you over the telephone, they had all been poisoned with methamphetamine—*yaa baa*." She gives the FBI a look of the utmost sincerity. "Very few reptiles are naturally aggressive, except when hungry or protecting their young. The whole of the animal and reptile kingdom has learned to fear us, they will never attack humans unless panicked, or in this case drugged."

"What kind of *yaa baa*?" I ask, trying not to sound too knowledgeable. "Was it laced?"

"With fertilizer." Trakit shudders. "I can't think of anything more cruel."

"No," I agree.

"Of course, that only means that whoever did it bought the cheapest *yaa baa* on the black market. The problem is—how was it administered? How do you give a cobra a *yaa baa* fix? There are techniques for injecting snakes, of course. We usually inject through the anus."

"A lot of work for the killer," Jones says. She is standing a pace or so back from the cupboard, but the color has returned to her cheeks. These snakes are unequivocally dead, after all.

"Exactly. And anyway, it could not have been done that way. This is a problem for a detective, I'm afraid, one with which I simply cannot help. It is this: every snake contained a different quantity of the drug, a quantity which exactly corresponded to its body weight."

"Powdered and put in food?"

"I thought of that, of course. But then you really do have a problem— the drug would have started to work very quickly on the smaller snakes— the perpetrator would have had a severe logistical problem of handling dozens of drug-crazed snakes. And even then, it doesn't really explain how each snake contained exactly the right proportion of the drug for its body weight. If you sprinkle *yaa baa* powder over food, you don't normally get an exact proportion for each piece of food consumed—not unless you are operating in laboratory conditions." Trakit shrugged. "Anyway, that's all I can tell you. A mystery, the most vicious I've ever come across." She slides the drawer back, then opens another bigger one further down. This drawer is huge, very deep and runs on wheels with a rumble. The python is curled up in several elongated spirals, one third of its head missing. "He was a beauty, about ten years old, a reticulated python five meters twenty-one centimeters long." A glance at Jones. "That's just over seventeen feet. See the splotchy way he's camouflaged? He's native to most of Southeast Asia. Funnily enough, he lives in cities as often as the jungle. He loves riverbanks. They're an endangered species, mostly because of the illegal skin trade with China, and also for food—the Chinese love them in soup. Feel the power that must have been in those muscles." I heft the python's iron tail and gesture to Jones, who leans forward from the hips and gives it a single tentative poke with an index finger. "Baffling, truly baffling. You have exactly the same phenomenon: precisely the appropriate amount of *yaa baa* found in his blood corresponding to body weight. Appropriate, that is to say, for the purpose of getting him aggressively stoned. I've never seen a reptile on amphetamine, and I hope I never shall. But it must have been quite a sight."

"Intense shivering," I confirm, while the doctor looks at me with an air of concentration. "His whole body seemed to go into convulsions—it was hard to say what was natural and what was the effect of the drug."

"A condition of drug-induced terror causing extreme aggression, I would guess. Compulsive writhing?"

"I would say so."

Trakit nods. "Poor poor thing. There's no literature on that kind of drug poisoning in reptiles, but one can imagine. The drug would have induced an intense thirst, and its nerves were all on fire. Similar to being thrown into a vat of acid. What I can't understand is how anyone could have accomplished such perfect timing. Drugging all the snakes at the same time is a feat in itself, but getting a seventeen-foot python stoned at the same time as twenty or so cobras is beyond anything I could work out for myself, even if I wanted to." She gives me an empty smile. "But then, I'm not a detective."

"That's a very big snake." I look at Jones, then back to the snake. It takes up the whole of a drawer that could easily fit a human being. "If someone did inject the meth through the anus in the usual way, how long before the drug reaches the brain?"

"With reptiles you cannot answer that question as if they were mammals. Everything depends on the temperature. A cold snake may be in hibernation mode, with almost no heartbeat, and therefore very slow circulation. The drug might take half an hour to reach the brain stem. With a warmer snake, no more than two minutes."

"Even with half an hour to spare, it's hard to see the logistics, given what we know of Bradley's schedule that day. I just can't see a bunch of guys injecting the snake and waiting for Bradley to conveniently stop the car so they can chuck it in and put those clips over the doors. Not when there are a couple dozen cobras to inject and throw in at the same time. Even if they were pointing guns at him, it's hard to see how it all panned out."

"It would take more than a bunch of amateurs to handle the python once the drug took effect. Perhaps two experienced handlers could subdue it in normal circumstances. But under the influence of *yaa baa*, I think you would need half a dozen experienced snake handlers. Even then . . . You see, there is nothing that is not muscle, and it can twist in any direction. In a toxic frenzy, it would be virtually uncontrollable."

"Then we have a virtually insoluble forensic problem," Jones concludes with a shrug.

I look from her to Trakit to the snake. "Except that the killer solved it."

On the way back to the city, Jones is experiencing a moment of euphoria caused by relief of tension: "I know what you're thinking and I agree with you."

"You do?"

"The python was obviously a drug addict in a previous lifetime, right? I would guess opium or heroin, a man with some connection to the West—maybe he shot up once on Forty-second Street, and was double-crossed by Bradley in that lifetime? But what's the connection with the Mercedes? Maybe he was a used car salesman?"

"The python?"

"Yep, had that Nixon look around what was left of his mouth, don't you think? That sloping outward from the top down?"

Apparently Jones has scored a point. I endure her triumphant leer without protest for the rest of the journey. When we hit the first of the Krung Thep traffic jams I say: "Did you get the rest of the transcripts?"

"Of the tapes of the conversations between Elijah and William Bradley? Yes, I got them, but I haven't read them all. There's a ton of stuff, and as far as I can see, extremely dull and unhelpful."

"What about the tapes themselves, can you get those?"

"The tapes? We're talking a lot of volume here. After the Bradley brothers broke the ice they talked regularly, for five years. That's quite a few hundred hours. I can get them if you like."

"I only want the ones near the beginning, where William is at his lowest."

"Okay. Any particular reason?"

"I need to hear his voice." To her cynical stare I add: "People rarely know how to lie with their voices, especially to intimate family members. People lie only with words. I want to know what he sounded like when he was pleading with his big brother for a life after retirement. The same big brother who tried to teach him how to get a life twenty years before and, to William's new way of thinking, turned out to be right after all."

"Touchy-feely," Jones says. "I'll see what I can do. In the meantime I hate to overuse my left lobe, but wouldn't an examination of the Mercedes hatchback be in order?"

I look out the window, that she might not see me wince.

36

Cops who will not take money must earn their keep in other ways. Pichai's exceptional marksmanship gained him a place on every shoot-out in District 8. Thanks to my English, *farangs* are usually shunted in my direction. We are not on any tourist circuit, so my workload in this respect is not heavy: a steady trickle of Westerners who took a wrong turn and became suddenly frightened to find themselves all alone in the Third World, a few international criminals with a specialization in narcotics, and kids like Adam Ferral.

Sergeant Ruamsantiah sent for me this morning and when I arrived in the interrogation room Ferral was already seated in one of the plastic chairs, a hatpin through his eyebrow, a silver stud through one nostril, all the usual tattoos, a succession of rings through his ears like a ring binder, and the kind of light in his eyes which often distinguishes visitors from other planets. Ruamsantiah, a decent family man with only one wife to whom he is scrupulously faithful, who really does invest his share of the bribes in his children's education, has no objection to tattoos but is known to dislike nose studs, eyebrow hatpins and obnoxious young *farangs* who do not know how to *wai* or show respect in any other way. He was smiling at Ferral as I entered the room.

The sergeant was sitting behind a wooden desk, bare except for a cellophane bag of grass about three inches square, a bright red pack of outsize Rizlas, a butane lighter and a packet of our foulest cigarettes called Krung Thip, which were surely ten times more damaging to the health than the marijuana. I had been summoned to these interrogations many times; usually the *farang* kid's fear is tangible and fills the room with a frozen paranoia. Adam Ferral, though, was unfazed, which was why Ruamsantiah was using that dangerous smile. Ruamsantiah had leaned his nightstick against a leg of the table. He jerked his chin at the kid without relaxing the smile.

"I can't work him out. Maybe you can explain it. He came into the police station on the pretext of being lost, then fished in his pockets for something and out popped the grass. It was as if he wanted to get caught. Is he a plant or a moron? Is the CIA checking us out?"

Not a serious question. Ferral was too young and the dope too trivial. I would have put Ferral at nineteen, twenty at the most.

"You have his passport?"

Ruamsantiah took a blue passport with an eagle on the front out of his pocket and handed it to me. Ferral was nineteen and a few months, a native of Santa Barbara and in his visa application gave his profession as writer.

"You publish your stuff on the Web?" I snapped at him. The question took him by surprise and fresh pink blood bloomed first in his cheeks, spreading quickly to his neck and scalp. A young nineteen surely.

"Sometimes."

"Travelers' Tales dot com?" The pink deepened to crimson. "Great site, isn't it? Some terrific stories about Bangkok? How is yours shaping up?" Now the kid was shocked and looking at me as if I possessed Oriental clairvoyance.

"What did you say to him?" Ruamsantiah wanted to know.

"There's a site on the Web for extreme tourism. It's like extreme sports only sillier. Kids like this get themselves in jams in faraway countries, nail-biting situations which could land them in a Thai jail for five years, or get them stoned to death in Saudi Arabia, or strangled by a boa constrictor in Brazil, but there's always a First World safety net of course, which makes it all quite safe really. Then they write about their heroic escapes from the jaws of disaster in a foreign land. It's a way of getting published. Getting caught with ganja in Krung Thep is a favorite. According to the Net the standard bribe is five thousand baht for this quantity of dope."

Ruamsantiah angered, Thai-style. His lips thinned, his cheeks pinched and his pupils shrunk, but as far as Adam Ferral was concerned he was still a corrupt cop with a dumb smile on his face.

"Ask him if he happens to have five thousand baht on him. I haven't checked his money."

I translated and Ferral brightened. Immediately he pulled a small money bag out from under his black T-shirt, extracted a wad of gray notes which turned out to be exactly five thousand baht in crisp bills, which he happily laid on the table, fighting a gleeful sneer.

Ruamsantiah's left hand twitched. It was the one nearest the nightstick. The sergeant is more senior than me and his anger has a killer quality which I would not want to tangle with. On the other hand, I did not want to be there while he beat the living shit out of the kid, so I began to ask if he had finished with my services.

"No. Stick around, I need you to translate. Tell him to roll a joint." As I began to translate, Ruamsantiah laid a hand on my sleeve. "I want one of those huge things they make sometimes—with half a dozen papers."

I translated. "Do you know how to do that?"

Ferral grinned and went to work. The sergeant and I watched with fascination while he moistened the strips of glue with the pink tip of his tongue and expertly patched together a long rectangle of Rizlas, licked the seam of a few Krung Thips, broke them open and poured the tobacco onto the papers. He ripped open the bag of dope with his teeth and dumped a couple of pinches on the table. The ganja was raw and matted so Ferral had to rip it up with his fingernails. Ruamsantiah picked up his nightstick and placed it very gently on the table, causing a sudden draining of blood from Ferral's face.

"Tell him I want the whole bag of dope in the joint."

Ferral's eyes darted from Ruamsantiah to me to the stick, which remained thick and black on the table. Ferral stared at it. I felt a sinking in my own stomach, though nothing that could compare with Ferral's fear, which caused a cold sweat to break out on his face. He was thinking exactly what I was thinking. To be beaten up is one thing. To be beaten up stoned is a whole other experience. Pain and terror magnified by a factor of hundreds.

"Better do as he says," I told him.

Ferral went back to work without the comfort of irony. His hands started to shake.

"You've already squashed him," I murmured in Thai.

"Not enough. He'll be laughing at us as soon as he gets back to his buddies in Kaoshan Road."

"You've got him so scared he can hardly roll the joint." In addition to the shaking, a periodic juddering caused Ferral's hands to spill grass over the table.

"Okay, tell him I promise not to hurt him if he does as he's told."

This news calmed the kid somewhat. He even returned to his earlier presumption that we were going to party together, the three of us, and this of course would make great copy on the Net. On the other hand, his eyes could not stop sneaking glances at the stick.

When he'd finished rolling the joint it resembled a crooked white chimney. He glanced at Ruamsantiah for permission to light up and the sergeant nodded. Ferral took only one toke before offering it to Ruamsantiah, who declined. I also declined, which left Ferral holding the gigantic joint with a deeply puzzled expression on his face.

"I want him to smoke all of it," Ruamsantiah said, rolling his stick to and fro under his palm, generating a kind of muffled thunder. Ferral stared at me, then the joint, but the power emanating from the black stick was too much and he took another couple of tokes.

"He's to inhale properly and hold it in his lungs."

Ferral doubled up in a genuine marijuana racking cough, then carried on.

Ruamsantiah relented only when it became clear that Ferral would puke if he took one more toke. He had consumed three-quarters of the joint by this time and acquired fascination with tiny details: a fleck of dust floating in a shaft of light, the third whorl from the top on his left index finger.

Ruamsantiah picked up the lighter and waved the flame in front of the kid's eyes. Note by note the sergeant set fire to the five thousand baht. At an exchange rate of forty-three to the U.S. dollar it amounted to about a hundred and twenty dollars. Adam Ferral was not rich. This money could keep him in Thailand for more than a week, but the wonder in his eyes told of a still deeper anguish. The West dominates through wealth; for a poor Thai cop to burn it with a look of contemptuous indifference on his face was a magical act which challenged accepted reality, especially if you happened to be young and very very stoned. Worms of fire ate through the bills, sending off weightless particles of gold; Ferral saw miniature bodhisattvas riding carpets of flame. Ruamsantiah had all his attention now, his respect and his awe. The sergeant could have stopped there and Ferral would have been smart enough to absorb the lesson, but the suggestion that he was using the Royal Thai Police Force as a platform for some frivolous literary exercise had sent Ruamsantiah into a cold rage. "I'm putting him down the hole."

"Do you need to do that?"

Ruamsantiah turned his rage on me. "Not compassionate enough for you? Okay, give him the choice, eight hours in the hole or a fair trial and Bang Kwan for five years. Ask him."

The question hardly needed to be put, but Ruamsantiah's fury had even me in awe. "The Hole?" the kid asked, giving it a capital and leaving his mouth open in an O as the sinister word wrought havoc in its progress through his psyche.

Ruamsantiah stood up and walked around the desk to grab Ferral by the back of the neck to march him out of the room. The last I saw of him was a wild and desperate backward glance at me, an inadequate link to civilization surely, but the only one in the vicinity. I sat in the interrogation room for a moment regretting my wiseass guesswork. I wished I hadn't mentioned the web site. Ruamsantiah has broken hard men in that hole of his, and Ferral is neither of those things. Stoned too, on enough dope for ten joints. May Buddha help him.

A glance at my watch reminded me that the FBI had been waiting for forty minutes and was probably working herself up into a rage of her own. I decided not to tell her about Ferral in the hole. It was going to be a difficult enough trip without that embellishment.

The smile on Jones' face where she sat in the back of her car was slightly unnatural, being the product of will, but I gave her full marks for effort.

"Sorry I'm late."

"Don't worry about it. You've got more than one case, right?"

Slightly surprised by her generosity, I agreed. The FBI was in an unusual mood. When she saw how subdued I was she became touchingly solicitous: Was it something she said yesterday? She realized she can come across as arrogant and abrasive, especially in a polite, manner-conscious Buddhist society such as ours. Or was I offended that she frankly admitted how attractive she found me? That was very American, wasn't it, to be so up-front about such a thing? People in most other cultures, especially women, would never just come out and say it like that. Or was there something else bothering me?

The Royal Thai Police tow stolen, impounded, illegal and wrecked vehicles to a fenced and guarded wasteland on the river not more than a couple of miles from my housing project. Over the years small satellite businesses—metal stamps, scrap iron dealers, car repair shops—have grown up around the compound so that anyone ignorant of Thai ways might think it a well-planned industrial zone. A stranger might even be impressed by the dedication of the police guards who patrol the perimeter with M16s at the ready, protecting citizens' property until due legal process has determined true ownership.

The FBI has brought along her own kit for lifting prints, poking behind and under upholstery, which she has dragged into the small prefabricated office. Catching sight of a door which leads to a toilet, she takes out her coveralls and disappears, returning a few minutes later alight with luminescence.

Sergeant Suriya has reigned in this riverside kingdom for longer than I can remember; he is famous for the dexterity of his paperwork, the discipline of his men and the accuracy of his memory. He is enormously popular and generally considered one of those selfless individuals who live only to help others. His face possesses an extraordinary mobility as he checks and rechecks my own.

"Mercedes E-class hatchback you say?" I nod miserably. "Impounded I think two weeks ago?"

"About that."

"Number?" I tell him the registration number in a stilted voice, like a character in a pantomime.

"And you want to inspect it this morning? Has it not already been inspected by a forensic team?"

"I believe so, but the FBI wanted to look themselves. Their forensic equipment is so much more advanced than ours."

"I see. The thing is, the forensic team moved it around a bit, you'll have to look for it."

I explain this to Jones, who shrugs while Suriya studies her face. "Okay, let's go look for it. How difficult can it be to find a new Mercedes hatchback in a police compound?"

"It's hot."

"I know. I might have to take off the coveralls and get all dirty. That's okay."

"You don't want to come back when it's cooler?"

"You mean in the middle of the night? I've been here more than three weeks now, and I haven't seen a cool day yet. It's always hot. You want to stay here in the air-conditioning? That's okay. Just lead me to the car, then I'll check it on my own."

Suriya has no English and waits for me to translate. He has seen Jones' professionalism, her kit and her coveralls and her unbending intent, and therefore understands my problem. He is a sensitive, intelligent man and I feel the depth of his compassion, which only makes me the more wretched. I look helplessly into his eyes.

"You have no idea where it might be, roughly?"

He bites his lower lip in concentration. "Maybe over there," pointing toward the river, "or there," pointing north, "or there," now the south is indicated, "but now that I think of it perhaps there," pointing west. Jones has followed his hand signals easily enough and is smiling indulgently.

"You know, I really think I'm making progress. Two weeks ago I would have just lost it if someone wasn't doing their work properly, but now I see your point. I mean, what the heck if we have to spend twenty minutes searching for it? It's not as if anyone's life depends on it. It's not a perfect world and Westerners like me should stop acting as if it ought to be. How about that, am I improving or what? So, let's go do this guy's job for him and find the car." She gives Suriya a glittering smile, which he returns. Outside in the heat, she takes my arm for a moment. "And you know something, your system works better than ours, at least on the psychological level. Be nice to incompetents and they'll be nice back. Be nasty and they'll still be incompetent, so what do you gain by making an enemy?"

"That's so true."

"Right. It even has a Buddhist ring to it, doesn't it? I feel like you've put me on some kind of spiritual learning curve. So how do you want to do this, intuitively or systematically?"

"Up to you."

"Well, since I don't have any intuition to speak of, I'll have to suggest we use a system. How about we start at the river, near the jetty, and work slowly west till we find it?"

The jetty is unexpectedly robust and modern-looking, with tubular steel piles more than two feet in diameter, a smooth reinforced concrete surface and a squat, powerful-looking gantry at the end with a heavy-duty sling. It doesn't fit with the rest of the scenery, as if visitors from the future built it on a whim, then left it for us to use. Jones doesn't pay it any mind as she turns her back to it, stretches out both arms to establish longitude and outlines the modus operandi.

I try to follow Jones' instructions to the letter, walking slowly between wrecks of cars and trucks which have been stripped to their bare rusting bones, carefully scrutinizing the lines to left and right so as not to miss a late-model Mercedes Estate. About halfway through the task Jones throws me a black look down a narrow lane between the wrecks, but we don't stop until we reach the far western end of the compound. Sweat is pouring from Jones' hairline and she is blinking from the salt. She has undone the zip on the front of her coveralls and rolled up the sleeves. She avoids my gaze while she squats against the wire fence and I squat beside her. I say: "I'm sorry, Kimberley."

A deep breath. "You know, back in my country I'm accustomed to thinking of myself as a pretty bright person. Then for a few days over here I wondered if I'd been deceiving myself, and maybe I was a pretty dumb person. I got over that when I realized I was just suffering from culture shock, that everyone is dumb outside their own frame of references. So I set myself to learn patience and even a little Buddhist compassion and for a moment I was stupid enough to be pleased with my own progress. Reality has a way of kicking us in the balls, doesn't it? Especially in Thailand, or so it seems to me."

I feel worse than ever and am unable to reply. I look at the ground instead.

"At least tell me if I have correctly understood why you've been in such a foul mood all morning."

"Yes, you have understood."

"Let's cut to the chase. What I've understood is that in Bangkok's only police car compound all the vehicles look as if they died from vehicle plague about twenty years ago. I know the standard of living is not particularly high in your country, but there are quite a few luxury cars on the roads of Bangkok, a quite surprising number of Mercedes, high-end Toyotas, Lexuses, that sort of thing. Statistically, one would expect them to be represented at least by one or two models in the car compound belonging to the Royal Thai Police Force, wouldn't one?"

"Yes."

"And oddly enough, the only new-looking, late-model, intact vehicles I've seen are two BMWs parked very close to that jetty."

"That's true, Kimberley."

"That *is* true, isn't it, Sonchai? Sonchai, you have done many things to my mind since I've teamed up with you, but I have always forgiven you because I never caught you being dishonest. I never thought you would deceive me. Why did you let us come on this wild-goose chase when you knew all along they already sold the fucking car?"

"There are cultures of guilt and cultures of shame. Yours is a culture of guilt, mine is one of shame."

"Meaning you always wait to see if the shit is really going to hit the fan?"

"That's not a bad way of putting it. The car could have been here."

"I don't think so. That sergeant in there sold it, didn't he, that Mercedes which constituted a major piece of forensic evidence in our little murder investigation?"

"It's not his fault."

"Oh, not his fault. Are we doing karma again, or did a tree spirit build that magnificent jetty and force the sergeant to use it to whisk away every damn car worth more than a thousand dollars, on one of those barges I bet, all the way to wherever cars go in Bangkok to experience rebirth, maybe a Buddhist monastery?"

"It's hard to explain to you, but it really is a good system."

"I thought you were an *arhat*, a totally noncorrupt cop?"

"I am, but you have to bear in mind relative truth. Before there were endless wars between the districts. Sometimes the colonels came close to shooting each other. The only solution seemed to be for each district to have its own compound."

"Let me get this straight. With only one compound receiving cars from all over the city, it was the district in which the compound was located that was making all the dough from selling the cars and the parts?"

"Yes. It was very bad. There were fights, shoot-outs, quite a few deaths. The profits from the cars are very good, you see, so everyone wanted a piece of it. Then we had a rank-and-file revolution. Cops from all over Krung Thep voted to appoint Sergeant Suriya as the officer in charge of the compound. He's a devout Buddhist and maybe nearly an *arhat*, so everyone trusts him. He spends the proceeds on charitable works, especially for the Police Widows and Orphans Fund, and to help cops with health problems. We've even built a new wing on the Police General Hospital."

"We?"

"We're all proud of what we've achieved here. There was a party when they finished the new jetty. That crane cost twenty million baht." I wriggle a little in the heat. "It's just a different way of doing things, I can understand why a Westerner would have a problem."

She nods sagely. I think my country is having an aging effect on her, which does not make me altogether sorry. I believe the first buds of wisdom have appeared under those blue eyes. I detect just the first touches of Thai humor around her mouth. "Wouldn't it have been easier to call the sergeant and ask him outright if he still had the car or not? Just not the Thai way of doing things, huh? No admissions until the *farang* has exhausted herself digging up the unpalatable truth. So how is it no one ever complains? An expensive car gets towed away and the owner doesn't want it back?"

"Oh, where the owner is still alive we always offer the opportunity of buyback."

"Buyback?"

"Sure. Within a specific period of time of course. After that we classify it as a wreck, which gives the government legal ownership."

"Government meaning the cops, right?"

We both stand up at the same time. It really is too hot for arguments. "Who else?"

We trudge back to the office, which is empty. From the window we watch while Suriya expertly drives one of the BMWs onto the jetty. He has already lowered the sling, and now the car sits over it, waiting to be hauled into the air. From across the river a steel barge turns against the current and makes toward the jetty. As soon as the boat is tied up, Suriya gets out of the car to work the gantry. I remember the stories of the first time he tried to work this crane; there are at least three cars drowned in the river directly under the jetty. You would never believe that now, from the great skill he exhibits in putting the car in the bottom of the barge. Merrily he skips off the seat of the gantry to fetch the second BMW. Jones is watching intently.

"New, a BMW like that costs at least thirty thousand U.S. I guess they would go for about twenty secondhand. Is that what they would fetch over here? So in ten minutes' work we've just seen the Police Widows and Orphans Fund swell by forty thousand dollars? Not bad. Does he keep any books?"

"Oh no."

"That would be incriminating, huh?"

"He doesn't cheat us."

Wonderingly: "Nope, I don't believe he does at that. Let's go back to town, Sonchai, my learning curve has been even steeper than usual this morning."

When I reach the station the public area is full with the usual assortment. Three monks are next in line, then some beggars, a bag lady, a young girl about fourteen years old looking impossibly new and bright in this worn corner of the world; perhaps as many as sixty men and women of every age in clothes just a little better than rags. Everyone is waiting patiently with their diverse problems. When I inquire at the desk I discover that no one has heard of Adam Ferral and Sergeant Ruamsantiah was called away urgently to some traffic disaster soon after I left the station and has not yet returned. When I check my watch I see that more than ten hours have passed since he put Ferral in the hole.

The hole is exactly that, a circular excavation in back of the police station originally dug for some plumbing or construction purpose, then discarded. It was Ruamsantiah who arranged for a hinged trapdoor with padlock to be cemented on top. Inhabitants are dependent on the imperfect fit of the lid for ventilation. It takes a few minutes to find the key to the padlock and someone to help me drag the kid out. When we have done so I am relieved to see that Adam Ferral can still walk. Except that it is no longer Adam Ferral who inhabits this body. He staggers around somewhat before I put my arm around him to help him into the building and out again into the public area, where he walks into the front desk, then into the monks, before I take him in hand again to lead him to some vacant chairs at the back where I sit him down. All of a sudden he bursts into chest-jarring sobs. I can think of nothing to do but pat his back and wait. Only a few of the other people in the waiting area turn to look, and then turn back again as if nothing unusual were happening. This is District 8 after all. It takes ten minutes for the sobbing to quiet, and then Ferral yanks at the hatpin through his eyebrow until it comes out and hands it to me.

"You don't have to do that."

"I'm not doing it for you or the sergeant, pal." His voice is surprisingly strong and firm and as far as I can recall hardly resembles the voice he used this morning. "When I was down your fucking hole I promised Christ, God, Krishna, Muhammad, Zeus, the Buddha and anyone else who would listen that if I got out of there with my mind halfway intact I'd get rid of it. My old man hates it, he calls it a disfigurement. I've been torturing him with it for two years. I'm keeping the nose stud, though."

"That's quite a collection of deities you were in touch with."

"More than in touch," Ferral says, looking at something on the far wall. "I been talking to them for ten fucking hours. They helped me, you know, with the other things. You know?"

"Yes," I say. "I know."

"You been there, huh?"

"Yes."

He taps my arm. "The Buddha's great, isn't he? Terrific sense of humor. He tell you any of those jokes of his?"

"No, I don't think I've ever been quite that intimate."

Ferral shakes his head. "Cracked me up, man. Really cracked me up. Well, thanks for the experience."

"I look forward to reading about it on the Web."

Ferral looks at me as if I've committed sacrilege and, pulling himself to his feet, staggers off in the direction of the street. In my hand a hatpin. I watch him go not without a tinge of envy. In nearly two decades of meditation the Buddha has not told me a single joke. Surely one would laugh for eternity?

Back in my hovel I turn Pisit on. His favorite female professor is answering the standard question from a caller about what the trade of prostitution does to a woman psychologically and what kind of wife does she make for those strange *farang* men who marry her.

"Prostitution ages women in ways they don't notice at the time. It's not the act of sex of course, which is perfectly natural and good exercise, it's the emotional stress of continual deception. After all, the customer is only kidding one person that there is any meaning at all in what he is doing: himself. But the girl has to keep up the pretense with one or more men each night. Such stress works the facial muscles, tightening them, producing that hard look prostitutes are famous for, but more important than that, a great dam of resentment builds up in her mind. The first thing a prostitute does when she finds a man willing to look after her is to give up the sex goddess role and probably the charm too. Invariably, she makes the mistake of assuming the customer wanted to marry the real her, not the fantasy, despite the fact that he is only familiar with the fantasy. Then there is a dramatic change in appearance. Many of the girls use hormones to enhance their breasts, but doctors warn them not to continue for more than a year, because of the risk of cancer. Also, there's not a whore in Bangkok who doesn't walk around in six-inch platform shoes. The return to reality can come as quite a shock: from tall, bosomy porn star to flat-chested dwarf. No, prostitutes do not make great wives as a rule, but it has nothing to do with fidelity. Usually the last thing such girls want is an extramarital affair, in which they would probably be expected to play the sex goddess all over again. What they want is the right to be irritable and charmless, which they lost the moment they started on the game."

Caller: "So such marriages do not usually last?"

"Sadly not. Most bar girls who marry their clients end up back in the bars within a couple of years."

I think of him. In my mind's eye his uniform is torn, there is blood on his sleeves and a scythe-shaped scar impressively disfigures one side of his face when he walks into the bar in Pat Pong. He came for some relaxation from the torment of war, a beer and some female company. He is a clean-living American boy, he does not hire prostitutes, not even on R&R, but three (or more) of his closest buddies died yesterday (or the day before) and a man can only take so much. He is young, for god's sake, twenty-two—no more than twenty-five at the most. The eighteen-year-old girl behind the bar is more than beautiful, she possesses something he didn't know he was searching for: she is bursting with a vitality which might be the only cure for his crippling sense of loss. It is self-preservation, not lust, that moves him to pay her bar fine and take her back to his hotel. She can play the sex goddess as well as any woman, but she read the heart of this broken young man the minute he walked into the bar. It is not fantasy he wants, but health. She uses her amazing strength to heal him until he is sure he cannot live without her. Some token of their mysterious and sacred coupling is called for. They decide to make a baby. Me.

They were not the kind of people the professor is talking about. There was a war on and it was thirty-two years ago. I dismiss Pisit and his guest as unreliable and turn them off. In the silence I think of Fatima. Surely her dream life is almost the same as mine? It is hard to think of a father figure who would have fit the bill better than Bradley.

37

"No one in the market has seen the full potential of Viagra," my mother explains over a Marlboro Red. We are sitting at a food stall after finishing a meal of tom-yum soup, fried fish, spicy cashew nut salad, three kinds of chicken and thin rice noodles on a street in Pratunam. Our table is loaded with six different dipping sauces, beer bottles, chopped ginger, fried peanuts, mouse-shit peppers and bits of lime. We are about twelve inches from the traffic jam but the stall is famous for the quality of its roast duck curry. It is so famous the police colonel in charge of the district doesn't dare to bust or squeeze it even though its tables and chairs take up most of the sidewalk and force pedestrians to risk their lives among the traffic. Thai cuisine is the most complex, subtle, variable and generally the best in the world. It knocks the socks off fussy French and flaky Chinese, although one must give credit where it is due: during Nong's one and only Japan trade (in Yokohama, a Yakuzi mobster with impeccable manners whose chronic migraine could only be relieved by more or less continuous sex): on my first bite of Kobe beef I forgave Pearl Harbor on your behalf, *farang*.

Protected by a firewall of chili, our cooking has been immune to the corruption suffered by other great cuisines due to Western influence and the best food can still be found in humble homes and, more especially, on the street. Every Thai is a natural gourmet and cops don't bust the best food stalls if they know what's good for them.

"I suppose not," I yell above the traffic noise.

"I mean, everyone knows about it and *farangs* know they can get it over the counter at any pharmacy anywhere in Thailand, but we haven't woken up to the new client potential which is coming onstream."

"It sounds as if *you* have, Mother."

"Think about it," she yells. "You're a seventy-year-old *farang* man and for the past twenty years your sex life has gone from extremely boring to nonexistent. You expect to die within the next ten years and you haven't even thought about sex for the last five. You've thought of yourself as totally out of the running and you've got used to your family and loved ones thinking of you as some decrepit old fool who ought to have the decency to pop off sooner rather than later so they can inherit the house."

My mother is remembering Florida, of course, and Miami, where everyone seemed to us to be on their way to or from an old people's home. I blink several times as certain images of Dan Rusk pass before my eyes. It must be the work of imagination that I see a hoary old hand so huge it is capable of covering the whole of my mother's backside; the trip from the airport to his "spread" in the U-Haul truck was interminable, as was the spread. A massive kitchen and other vast vacant spaces so impregnated with his solitude it felt as if we had landed on a planet with double the gravity of the earth, turning the most normal activities—conversation in particular—into a chore requiring superhuman strength of will. Rusk lasted a week before my mother called her only relation who possessed a telephone and invented a family emergency—I forget what dire accident her mother was supposed to have suffered, but it was enough for Rusk to drive us back to Miami and pay for the nonexistent hospital care. We were never so glad to be back in Krung Thep with its effortless vitality. "You've always had a positive view of human nature."

"Then one day someone at your old people's home mentions Viagra. Some old bugger even more ancient than you, who even *you* think should have the decency to pop off immediately, whispers in your ear that he recently spent a week in Bangkok and tried the blue pill and had an erection that lasted four hours which he used to sample three or four beautiful young women. Well, what would you do?"

"You've got a point."

"You'd choke on your false teeth in your rush to book the next flight to Krung Thep is what you'd do. So the market can't help but grow. There are more than fifteen million American men over the age of sixty-five, their wives and kids have treated them like shit at the best of times and after age fifty in America it is no longer the best of times no matter how much money you've got." She emphasizes these startling truths by stubbing out her cigarette. "They put up with it because they ran out of options a long time ago. At least, they think they did. I have good news for them. But do they really want disco music, techno, all that frenzy— they're probably too deaf to hear it anyway. Do they really want to watch girls in bikinis cavorting around steel poles, all that nonsense? Of course not. They want something from their own times, an environment that caters to their age group and is sensitive to their needs."

"Oxygen on tap behind the bar? An ambulance waiting in the street? Why not add a hospital wing to your brothel?"

"I wish you wouldn't call it that. I'm providing libido therapy to the aged. What I'm trying to explain is the matter of timing."

"Timing?"

"That's the thing. A young man gets an erection because a woman has aroused him, and for ten thousand years the trade has built itself around that biological fact."

"What else would it build itself around?"

"So we're still a primitive industry at the mercy of nature. We're still at the stage of hunting and gathering. But with the market we're targeting, the customer gets an erection more or less exactly one hour after taking the pill, it's the equivalent of a steak in the fridge. We've freed ourselves from Mother Nature and taken control of the timing. There's a four-hour window which he's not going to want to waste drinking beer and listening to junk music. He might want to relax later, but his main priority is to take advantage of the drug. Especially when he has probably read that it can cause heart attacks."

I blink at the apparent incongruity of this last remark. She lights another cigarette. "Don't you see, in their minds this could be their last fling? They might have decided to go out with a bang, so to speak. We could be helping them to celebrate their last days on earth. They're trading in a couple more years of limping across the linoleum and endless card games with the other arthritic goners for maybe a week of ecstatic humping with the best thing they've seen for fifty years. This is a service of compassion and enlightenment. I'm sure the Buddha will approve."

"Euthanasia by orgasm must be better than lethal injection."

"Exactly. Also, if it's your very last party on earth, why spare the expense? If your kids are all selfish jerks you may as well sell the house to spend the money on my girls. So what I'm proposing is a telephone booking service. Just like a restaurant. The customer comes to the bar the first time, sees a girl he likes, after that he calls us from his hotel, warns us that he's about to take the pill and expects to be rampant in exactly one hour. There's a plus for us, of course, since we don't have to hang around waiting for the customer to decide if and when he wants the girl. We get a fixed timetable that we can work around. I've discussed all this with the Colonel. He thinks we can't fail."

"How will you structure the advertising? Medical journals or triple X web pages?"

"Web pages, with plenty of visuals, but we think word of mouth will work for us over time. After all, there's no one else in this field at the moment." I think of geriatrics shuffling into the bar with crooked grins and bulging trousers, the missing link between sex and death. "So, Sonchai, what about it?"

"It could work," I agree with some reluctance.

"Of course it will work. The trouble is there's no way to patent it. As soon as the competition sees what we're up to there'll be a thousand similar bars springing up all over the city. We've got to move quickly, I'm not the only financial brain in the business."

I watch while two young women try to walk past us carrying about ten plastic bags each, crammed with cheap clothing. There's no room on the pavement and they walk around a taxi caught in the jam. This is where most of the sex traders buy their clothes and we have said hello to a lot of old friends today. My mother's purchases are under the table. We are in Pratunam because a couple hundred yards away lies a vast market where T-shirts, shorts, skirts, dresses, trousers, blouses indistinguishable from the products of the ateliers of Calvin Klein, Yves Saint Laurent, Armani, Zegna et al. can be purchased for as little as three dollars each. Nong has bought her season's wardrobe, which I noticed is a little more austere than usual, befitting a matriarch of industry. I call to the waitress to pay the bill, but my mother restrains me. "This is on me, darling, I want to thank you for signing those plans."

I say okay, the plans did amount to a fair amount of work because she and the Colonel kept changing them. Of course there had to be a TV in every cubicle and in the end they decided to include a full Thai massage service, so each five-by-eight room has to be equipped with a small Jacuzzi in the corner with all the plumbing that goes with it. I foresee disaster with ninety-year-old scarecrows slithering around in the soap suds and expiring during the full-body massage. At that age surely a man might be knocked out cold in a skirmish with a mammary gland? But I have to assume the Colonel knows what he's doing even if Nong has been carried away by her brief congress with the *Wall Street Journal*. I pass over the slim briefcase in which I've been carrying the plans and watch while she opens it. She takes out the plans and rifles through them with growing consternation.

"You forgot to sign them, darling."

"No I didn't."

"But you promised."

"I know."

"So what's stopping you? Here, use my pen."

"No."

"Sonchai?"

"I'm not having anything to do with this . . . Until you tell me."

It's one of those mother-and-son things. We have too much on each other not to be aware of the significance of this eye lock. I do not waver or blink. Finally she drops her gaze. "Okay, I'll tell you. Just sign the plans."

"Tell me first. I don't trust you."

"Brat." Her hand is shaking as she reaches for yet another Marlboro and lights it.

"Why is it so difficult? If you don't know who he was, if you were banging three a night that month, just say so, it's not as if I don't know what you did for a living."

"Of course if I didn't know I would have told you long ago," she snaps, and inhales rapidly. "It's not as simple as that."

"How can it be complicated? For god's sake, Mother."

I might be hallucinating, but it does seem to me that some tiny tears have appeared at the corners of my mother's eyes. "Very well, darling. But you have to promise to forgive me. Promise in advance."

I experience profound suspicion but promise anyway.

"Sonchai, did you ever wonder why I made such efforts for you to learn perfect English? Did you even notice that almost every one of those trips we went on were with someone who spoke it perfectly, even Fritz and Truffaut?"

"Of course I noticed. If I didn't notice before I would have noticed with that Harrods man. What else did he have to offer?" An image of a skinny Englishman with a huge nose through which he emitted most of his vowels and an even bigger mother problem, who derived strange pretensions from his apartment's proximity to Harrods in London—an appalling two weeks when Nong had a screaming argument with his mother, who lived in the flat upstairs, and I went through a brief shoplifting phase in the great store—passes through both our minds. "I thought you were just doing the best for my future."

"Well, I was, but it was more than that. I was full of guilt about . . . I was trying to make it up to you . . . He loved me, you see." My mother bursts into tears. "I'm sorry, I'm so very very sorry, darling"—dabbing her eyes with a tissue from her handbag—"it was all those fire engines. And the food, it was so bland, they had no idea how to cook, it was totally tasteless."

Thank Buddha I'm a detective and able to make sense of these fragile clues. Suddenly everything falls into place. A past I never had and a future I never will have flash before my eyes. My heart rate has doubled and for the first time in my life I feel like hitting her. Instead I reach for her cigarettes, take one, light it with shaking hand and order more beer. I drink in great gulps straight from the bottle. "An American?"

"Yes."

"A serviceman?"

"Yes. Very brave. He had lots of medals. He was an officer. He had a terrible war, he was in a mess psychologically for quite a while."

Inhaling deeply on the cigarette: "He took you to the States? He wanted to marry you?" A nod. "New York?"

"Manhattan. The apartment was near a fire station. There were sirens every five minutes. I thought the whole city was on fire."

"And the food was awful?"

"Have mercy, darling. I was eighteen years old for god's sake, I'd never been outside Thailand and I hardly spoke a word of English. I was terrified and I wanted my mother. I wasn't the hard-ass I became. I grew up after I had you." An exhalation. "They couldn't even cook rice properly. His parents hated me. I was brown with slit eyes, and no matter what he said they knew how we had met, what I did for a living."

"But he adored you?" A nod. "He knew you were pregnant?"

"He was crazy about you even before you existed. I had to run away.

He came back to Thailand looking for me, but I hid up in the country. I was in a state of panic after New York. I'm sorry. I talked about it with the abbot—I went up to the monastery. You never knew that I'd been up there, did you? He asked me if my American lover needed me only while he overcame his shell shock. That was a good question and I didn't know the answer, so I vowed to the Buddha that if you grew up strong and healthy and I had the luck, I would make sure you learned perfect English."

"You deprived me of a crack at the presidency of the United States because you didn't like the food? That's very Thai."

"You got a crack at nirvana instead. What kind of Buddhist would you have been if I'd stayed in America?"

I choose to ignore this brilliant riposte. "I could have been an astronaut."

"No you couldn't, you can't stand heights."

"What did he do, what was his profession, was he a drafted man?"

"Drafted. He was going to be a lawyer."

"What? American lawyers are all millionaires. I could have been a senator at least."

My mother has dried her eyes. She is a master of abrupt recovery. "Children of American lawyers all die of drug overdoses at an early age. Look what I saved you from. Anyway, if you'll only sign those damned plans we'll make a million and you can go and live there if you like. See how long you can stand to be away from Thailand."

I have smoked the whole cigarette in less than a minute, causing me to feel nausea. My heart rate is calming, though, and I'm beginning to see things with a little more focus. "What was his name?"

"Mike."

"Mike what?"

"What difference does it make? Smith. There, now you know, has it changed anything?"

I do not believe for one moment that his name was Mike Smith, but I let it pass. I surprise her by giving her a big smile and patting her hand, which seems to relax her. She drinks a glass of beer in a couple of gulps, lights another Marlboro and sits back in her chair.

"Thank you for taking it so well, darling. For thirty-two years I've lived in fear of this moment. Did I do the right thing or not? Don't you think I've been tortured by that very question? I wanted to tell you, but all the family advised me not to—what you didn't know you couldn't blame me for—that's very Thai, isn't it? Sometimes I think I must have been insane to leave America. Even if he'd divorced me after a couple of years, I probably would have got a work permit, the right to stay. But Thailand was a different place then, we were all so unworldly, so fearful of strange lands. We were prudes, too. Does that surprise you? A girl wouldn't think of selling her body unless she was desperate. My father was sick with his heart problems, my mother was hit by a car when she was riding her bike, my grandmother had to be kept—she was blind by that time—and my two brothers were in their early teens. I had a right and a duty to work in the bars. These days girls will go on the game just to save enough to put a deposit on an apartment, they sell themselves for any old excuse, because they love sex and money, though being Thai they never admit it and like to pretend they hate the work. Would you believe I'm shocked at what the trade has come to? But what can one do? This is the real world."

After I sign the plans, she pays the bill and we stand up. I embrace her warmly. She gives me a puzzled look as we say goodbye. She takes a taxi but I decide to wind my way amongst the jammed cars. *What difference does it make? He adored me even before I existed. He loved her.* I'm walking on air.

Still high, I am trying to be invisible as I make my way to Charmabutra Hospital. The complex is new and shiny and about one minute from the bars of Nana Plaza. There is a McDonald's on the ground floor and a Starbucks in the first-floor lobby, a marble and glass reception area with parabolic front desk, Internet access from computers everywhere and a telephone wherever you put your elbow. But it *is* a hospital. The brochure boasts over six hundred highly qualified physicians and a small army of Singaporean, Thai, American and European managers and talks about the Heart Center, laser correction of nearsightedness, a stroke screening package, abdominal ultrasound, a complete laboratory analysis of blood urine and stool samples, liposuction, body contouring and laser resurfacing of the face, packages which take care of everyone's travel needs from the U.S. and Europe and luxury rooms with brilliant city views. At reception I mention an interview I have arranged with Dr. Surichai. An administration official takes me in an elevator to the seventh floor, where the doctor is waiting for me. We spend about an hour together. As I am leaving the hospital a group of three large men surround me and bundle me into a waiting limo. It is a navy blue Lexus and there is plenty of room in the back for myself and two of my abductors. The third remains behind as we speed off with a corny squeal of tires which I feel is unworthy of my Colonel, who is lounging in the front passenger seat, wearing civilian clothes and dark glasses. It is his usual driver behind the wheel.

"May I ask why I'm being abducted?"

"You're not. You're being quarantined in preparation for your meeting. The last thing we need is for you to turn up in your Tommy Bahama rip-offs, flashing your police ID for every Tom, Dick and Harry to squint at."

"Turn up where?"

"Give me your ID."

I hand it over. "I would like to know where we're going."

The Colonel puts my ID in the pocket of his Zegna jacket, which is not an illegal copy, and shakes his head at my obtuseness. "Did I or did I not receive a written request at 4:33 p.m. two days ago to the effect that one Detective Jitpleecheep Sonchai be permitted to interview one Khun Warren Sylvester during his five-day stay in our country on a business trip from the United States?" He turns to look at me, raising his glasses. "*Written* request with date and time stamp?"

"I like to do things properly."

"You like to fuck things up royally is what you like to do. To whom were you going to go with your copy of your written request with date and time stamp if I refused?"

"No one. There's no one to go to. I just wanted to make it clear—"

"That in the whole of the Royal Thai Police Force there is one *arhat*, one pure, unblemished soul valiantly and heroically doing his job while the rest of us slop around in the sleaze." My jaw hangs unattractively. "Have you any idea what shit you're dragging us into? Why couldn't you pop unobtrusively into my office when no one was looking and whisper plaintively in my ear that you needed to see the great Khun if I could pull the right strings and so long as it was okay with me and everyone with his foot on my shoulder all the way up to the top of the pyramid? You do know that the most important and influential women in the kingdom get most of their rocks from this jerk? Especially the Chinese. You do know that?"

"Yes," I confess.

"You do know that when he is in Krung Thep officially he stays at the Oriental in the Somerset Maugham Suite with all its charming nostalgia and river view, and that when he is not here officially he stays somewhere quite different?"

"I did guess he might have two different preferences, as far as official and unofficial business is concerned."

"Then you did guess that in return for generous donations to the Police Widows and Orphans Fund by the great Khun, quite a lot of effort is expended by your superiors to help the Khun keep his little unofficial pleasures from the notice of the media?"

"It probably crossed my mind."

"And did it further cross your mind that any interview of the Khun by you would have to be witnessed by those qualified to deny anything incriminating he might say, in the unlikely event he says anything of importance to you at all?"

"No, I never thought of that because I never thought you'd let me talk to him."

The Colonel grunts. "Didn't you? Not even after you mentioned to your friends at the American embassy that you had made an official request to interview Warren which you expected to be turned down."

"Damn."

"Thus precipitating one of those reverse domino effects, you know the kind that makes all the pieces stand up again just when we all thought they were finally knocked flat and lying in peace?"

"There's been trouble before?"

"The Khun's a dangerous asshole. There's a whole section of our noble force assigned to making sure he doesn't go too far when he's over here. He's one of those *farangs* who think our country is a playpen for rich Western psychos who've been unfairly repressed by their First World cultures and need to reexperience humanity's primordial roots out here in the exotic Orient. How would there not have been trouble before?"

"What sort of trouble?"

"None of your business."

"I'm an investigating officer—"

"You're an investigating dickhead who will get your death wish granted while the rest of us have to clean up with our hands in the shit. You're worse than my brother. Have you any idea what a pain it is to have a fucking saint for a brother?" He turns away from me to look out a side window. "Anything went wrong was always my fault. It's going to be the same with you, I can see it coming. The media will get hold of it after your spectacularly violent death, they'll build a shrine to you, you'll be the first Thai cop ever to be martyrized for his love of truth, justice and the rule of law and I'll spend the rest of my life telling people what an honor it was to have you on the force and how difficult it is for a poor fallen wretch like me to live up to the high standard you set. Don't you think I get enough of that with having an abbot for a brother?"

"Was it whores?"

"Was what whores?"

"The trouble. He hurt one? It must have been pretty bad for anyone to even notice."

A sigh. "It was bad, okay?"

"Even so, must have been a foreign whore," I muse. "Even if he killed a Thai girl, there wouldn't have been the kind of heat you're talking about."

"No comment, and what the fuck's it got to do with Bradley? Warren didn't kill Bradley."

"I know. But that doesn't mean Warren's not the culprit, karmically speaking."

As we turn into Asok, a shake of the head: "Just like my fucking brother."

The traffic coagulates halfway down Asok. I'm pretty sure I know where we're going now, and of course the Colonel knows I know. He glances up to look at me in the rearview mirror. "Just out of interest, what were you doing at that hospital?"

"None of your business."

"Did Warren ever use it?"

"Not that I know of."

He shifts his eyes from the mirror. "Why do I not like that answer?"

38

Just as I suspected, we are heading for the Rachada Strip. Think Las Vegas with a different vice at its center. Think also neo-Oriental wedding cake architecture of blinding vulgarity. Think about wearing sunglasses after dark. In daylight the neon competes with the sun and most of the signs include the word MASSAGE. We slink into the forecourt of the Emerald Hotel where each of the Lexus's four doors is opened simultaneously by lackeys who have been trained to do that for little Japanese guys with towering bank accounts, for this is not normally a Western haunt at all. But then, I have begun to wonder if Sylvester Warren is really a Western man.

I watch and wait with my two minders while the Colonel crosses the vast lobby to speak to one of about twelve receptionists, who *wais* to him. Even over the distance one can sense the reverence when Warren's name is mentioned. A jerk of the Colonel's head brings us across the floor to the bank of lifts. We choose the one which reaches the penthouse suite, and when the LED flashes 33, we step out into another lobby. A young woman in a blue and gold silk sarong *wais* to us and leads us into a room the size of a school hall with floor-to-ceiling windows, five-seater sofas, an undergrowth of orchids in cut-glass vases and a tall slim man standing in profile to us with his hands thrust into a twenties-style padded smoking jacket. We lost the minders at the ground floor so it's just the Colonel and I who *wai* to the Khun, who to my surprise *wais* elegantly back, with the proper moment of mindfulness. Under the rules a man of his exalted status is not supposed to *wai* to minions like us at all, but the gesture has a charm which is not lost on the Colonel. For all his cursing in the car, Colonel Vikorn is all smiles and deference before this unique source of wealth and power.

"Welcome to Shangri-la," Warren says with a generous smile which contains many things, self-mockery being one of them. I feel my spirits sink at such impenetrable subtlety. His perfect poise also is intimidating, and seems to go with his perfect tan, the filigree gold chain on his left wrist which I remember from the presidential photographs, the nuance of an expensive cologne—and those implacable gray-blue eyes which seem to acknowledge that all affectation is merely a means to an end, adornment a form of jungle camouflage. We are so enthralled by the Khun's aura it takes both the Colonel and me more than a minute to realize there is someone else in the room. "You know Colonel Suvit of course, superintendent of District 15?"

I *wai* dutifully to the stocky man with shaved head in police colonel uniform while Colonel Vikorn, not entirely surprised, gives him a nod. Colonel Suvit's presence here is deeply shocking to me, not least because it amounts to an insolent confirmation of my worst fears: I will never be permitted to progress beyond this moment, professionally, even personally. I will be the bird flying against the window until I fall from exhaustion and join all the other bird corpses lying on the floor. I feel more than a little dizzy.

"I asked Colonel Suvit to come because I understand his beat covers the spot where the late William Bradley was found. The Colonel and I have known each other many years so it's also an opportunity to enjoy his company." The sentence is a little flowery because he has spoken in Thai and we're like that. At the same time I know that Warren has taken me in, absorbed the entirety of what I am, and relaxed. As he expected, I'm no threat at all. Now he looks me in the eye. "Unfortunately, my time here on this trip is very limited." He pauses and seems genuinely to hesitate between number of options. His eyes flicker across to Colonel Suvit, who remains inscrutable. I have no intuitive grasp of this American at all, even his vibrations are carefully, masterfully controlled, like those of one who lives behind a protective shield. "I wonder therefore if it would be in everyone's interests if I spoke, and then if I've left anything out, Detective Jitpleecheep can ask anything he likes?"

"I'm sure you won't leave anything out, Khun Warren, and the detective won't want to ask a single thing." Colonel Suvit does not trouble to look at me. He raises half an eyebrow at Vikorn instead, who leans his head to one side, dubiously. The hostility between these two men is my only source of comfort in this palace of privilege.

"First, I must apologize to you, Detective, I really should have contacted you directly instead of putting you to the trouble of seeking me out."

The biggest surprise here, after the apology, is that Warren has switched to English, neatly cutting out the two colonels, who are reduced to dumb observers. His accent is soft and almost British. While I'm trying to think of an elegant reply to his elegant opening, he carries elegantly on. "I heard about Bradley's death probably not long after you found him. Let me be frank and admit I have many friends in your country, many of them in high positions, and, being Thai, they look after me. They knew that Bradley and I were friends of a kind, brought together by our quite irrational passion for jade." He pauses to search my face before continuing. "As Hemingway said about big-game hunting, either you understand it or you don't. To those who don't, the jade craze must seem ridiculous in this modern world where silicon rules. To those who do, a friendship between a marine sergeant and a jeweler is not unthinkable; on the contrary. Hobbies bring people of different walks of life together—wine, horses, pigeons, falcons—gems. When people find a common passion they overlook social barriers. Not that a jeweler is necessarily an exalted personage. My trade obliges me to cultivate the truly exalted. Who will buy gems if not the rich? My friends and clients are the movers and shakers of this world, I myself am no more than a humble merchant."

This last sentence, delivered without a trace of humility, but without irony either, marks the end of the beginning. He takes a cigarette holder out of a pocket of his smoking jacket and walks to one of the coffee tables where a packet of cigarettes awaits. Ignoring the colonels, he offers me one. I refuse, speechless. I think I am receiving the kind of special treatment a condemned man receives the night before his execution. He resumes whilst fitting the cigarette, waving it to make his points. The cigarette holder is jade.

"I'll cut to the chase. The best nephrite and jadeite in the world come from an area in the Kachin Mountains in Burma and have for thousands of years. During every one of those thousands of years, the political situation in Burma has been volatile, the human cost of mining the jade appalling, the greed of the Chinese middlemen—they have always been Chinese—outrageous. This is no less the case today than it was in the warring states period. At the present time a corrupt and probably insane military junta, desperate for hard currency, sells the jade in parallel with opium and methedrine. The miners are encouraged to shoot up on heroin to help them endure the disgusting conditions, and there is a high incidence of HIV, often developing into full-blown AIDS. The mortality rate amongst the miners is extremely high, which suits the junta, who don't want the miners returning to Rangoon to gossip. Word has got out, however, and a few Western journalists have published accounts of the situation, along with the usual sort of photographs showing destitute Third World people dying in conditions of extreme squalor. Everyone has their own views about political correctness. Is it a sign of a new high-mindedness in humanity, or has it produced a society of blamers, second-guessers and tiny-minded, self-righteous bigots? You can guess where my own answer lies. In any event, as a merchant whose customers need to be seen to adhere to the highest public morality, I have to be careful. I cannot afford for it to be obvious where my jade is coming from. In a nutshell, I have not been able to visit Rangoon for nearly a decade." He shrugs. "If I cannot be seen to sell new jade, I must sell old jade. Fortunately, there is some around. Not all the stone plundered from the Forbidden City was of the highest workmanship. One can take a piece and improve it, according to demand. One can also disguise the new jade by making it look like something that has been around a long time. By imitating a piece from the imperial collection, for example. There is no fraud involved. The customer knows very well what she is buying and is delighted to be able to dodge the pseudomorality of these strange times. If she doesn't really like the design of the piece, she can always ask me to have it reworked by my craftsmen. We're not talking about whales or baby seals, after all, jade is not about to become extinct. Nor is the Burmese government about to stop selling it, so if I don't buy it while the price is really quite reasonable, my Chinese competitors certainly will. As I say, there has never been a time when a person of delicate conscience could purchase jade from Burma. I can't afford to have a delicate conscience. I made a decision early in my career that I wasn't going to try to compete with people like

De Beers, Boucheron, the whole Vendôme clique. My bag was going to be East Asia and I have spent a lot of my time and money protecting my territory. The media might pretend to follow the rules of heaven, down on the ground nothing has changed since the turf wars between Neanderthals and Sapiens. The Sapiens won because we know how to fight dirty."

He lights the cigarette and there is just the slightest shaking in his hand as he does so, a flaw probably imperceptible to a mind not sharpened by meditation and paranoia.

"A jeweler is a salesman, and all good salesmen are opportunists. When I came across Bradley's web page, I saw an opportunity. When I looked him up over here, I saw that I had not been mistaken. The symbiosis was impressive. He had already made a trip to Laos, and up into the jungle near the Burmese border, where he had purchased some lumps of jadeite for experimental purposes. His experiment was a failure. It is simply not possible to become a buyer of jadeite overnight. It is the apprenticeship of a lifetime. On the other hand, he was in desperate straits financially. His somewhat luxurious lifestyle had left him in debt. I think I do not need to explain what that word can mean in this country. The Chiu Chow loan sharks to whom he owed hardly more than a pittance were getting restless. Naturally, I paid off his loan and undertook to pay the expenses for his web page. You could say I saved his life. Later on I personally loaned him enough to buy the teak house he was renting, at a very reasonable rate of interest. I also helped him furnish it with bits and pieces from my collection. I taught him a great deal about the jade trade and introduced him to close associates of mine, all of them Chinese, who have been doing business with me for three generations. They are on the ground in Burma, Laos and Cambodia and I never make a move without seeking their advice. Part of that advice includes the best way to anonymously bring the stone into Thailand. With the border problems between Thailand and Burma the advice has sometimes been to move the stone through Laos and Cambodia and into Thailand from the east. Through Khmer country. At other times we bring it in from the northwest, through Karen country." A pause to inhale. "Bradley became my agent here, a secret agent if you like, who arranged for the stone to be deposited in one of my warehouses. He also arranged for some of the pieces from my own collection to be copied by local craftsmen. I then arranged for the finished articles to be offered to the more discerning and discreet of my customers. A good detective like you would have had no trouble tracing the lineage of the pieces, but I was confident it would have been beyond the resources of the average muckraking journalist." A shrug. "Was I Bradley's financial salvation? Not entirely or permanently. I got him out of a nasty hole and through me he supplemented his income while he was still a marine, but his services could never have earned him the kind of money he needed after retirement. Did I realize that the contacts I was providing him with could also be used for whatever illicit trade he might choose to invest in? I would have been a fool not to see that from the start. My only stipulation was that my stone should never travel in the same shipment as his own imports. A stipulation which, I fear, was not always honored." A smile. "Not that such a minor betrayal of trust would have induced me to have him killed."

I have listened enthralled while he has destroyed my case piece by piece. It has been a brilliant speech, full of cryptic references to an unspoken indictment, like that of a lawyer who confesses to a traffic violation by way of blocking a murder charge. I understand now that it was Warren who insisted on seeing me against the advice of both colonels, who have remained silent and silently offended throughout the oration. With such a thorough explanation of his conduct, I have lost the moral as well as the legal right to pursue any line of inquiry involving him; a far more effective way of neutralizing me than to have me silenced by force of authority. I have never before had the honor of meeting such an accomplished gangster who makes even my Colonel Vikorn look like an amateur. I switch to Thai to thank him for his time and beg him to forgive me if I have caused him any anxiety, which was unintended and I hope forgiven.

Relief from the two colonels when they hear this. A smile from Warren, who is nevertheless studying me for signs of insincerity. As the four of us make for the door, I see that he is not entirely convinced that I am entirely convinced. A pause while he seems to search for a way to dot the last i, then a shrug as we say goodbye.

Silence in the lift on the way down. Eventually, Vikorn says: "What did he say?" A question which turns Colonel Suvit's eyes to rivets. I tell them. "So you're satisfied? No more written requests to meet friends of our movers and shakers?"

"Satisfied," I say. I do not have the heart to mention Fatima, or that her presence in Warren's shop seems to make a mockery of everything Warren has said this morning, although I could not begin to explain why that should be so.

In the lobby I sense a reluctance on the part of the two colonels to let me go, an impression fortified by Vikorn's two minders, who stroll over to join us and block me front and back.

"Let's sit down." Vikorn gestures to four large pink sofas set around a coffee table a little smaller than the surface area of my hovel. He places his hand on my shoulder and presses me down to the sofa. I find I am sitting between two men who do not choose to take full advantage of the spaces offered by the sofa. Colonel Suvit's left arm and shoulder are pressed hard against my right side while Vikorn is squeezing from the left. I have never felt so wanted. Suvit is about fifty, ten years younger than Vikorn and a dangerous age for a Thai cop. Somehow he has not managed to make as much money as my Colonel, though not for want of trying. His is a jealous, ferocious spirit who can never understand that a good gangster spends money to make money. He squeezes too hard (that is the rumor, statistically supported by the high rate of beatings and deaths amongst his tribunes). Where Vikorn will ostentatiously contribute to poor relief as a way of ensuring local support, Suvit kills people who get in the way, a method which many consider to be bad form. Vikorn's minders sit on the sofa opposite and stare at me.

"Tell me about yourself," Suvit says. "I mean, how did a wet little creep like you ever become a cop in the first place?"

"He was an accomplice to murder."

"Not a bad start," Suvit concedes.

"His mother's father was a close follower of my brother. He and his fellow felon spent a year at my brother's monastery, after which even the Royal Thai Police Force was a relief." Vikorn sighs and takes out a slim tin of cheroots, which he does not offer to Suvit or me. He lights one and exhales with a frown. "You don't know my brother. He can dismantle your mind and rebuild it the way some people take clocks apart and put them together again. Afterwards nothing works properly, but the thing still manages to tick. That's what he did with these two."

"But you admire your brother," I say reproachfully.

Vikorn takes another toke of his cheroot and ignores me. "Then he sent them to me. It was just the same when we were kids, every time he broke something I had to fix it."

"He's fifteen years older than you," I point out.

"Exactly. You can see how unfair he was, expecting me to clean up after him. I've done what I can, but there are screws my brother loosened which I've never been able to reach. Would you believe that Sonchai here has never been with a whore?"

"He's queer?"

"Worse. He's an *arhat*. He won't take money."

"That *is* worse. I'm glad he's not on my team. There's nothing you can do?"

"You can take a horse to water . . ."

As if on a signal, the two colonels hold my two arms and raise me to my feet. It would be preferable, in a way, if they were acting in accordance with a plan, but this is unlikely. They are Thai cops after all, and I feel I am in the grip of ingrained professional reflexes as they escort me out of the hotel with the two minders following.

"Let's take a walk," Vikorn says. "It's such a nice day."

Another of his lies. It is muggy, the sun is invisible behind the pollution, and the crowds droop as they make their way along the strip, dodging from one air-conditioned refuge to another. After a couple hundred yards we reach the Consulate of the Republic of Ukraine, which gives all three of us pause for thought. What middle-ranking functionary, violently liberated from the straitjacket of socialism and brownnosing for promotion, chose this site in the center of the world's most extensive brothel area? A hundred yards more and Vikorn jerks his chin at a neon sign the size of a truck which is attached to a building which bears some resemblance to a colonial mansion, but not much, it being five stories high on a site the size of a football pitch. The sign says JADE PALACE in English, Thai, Japanese, Mandarin and Russian. The same five languages convey that a massage service is available. I start to struggle, but Suvit and Vikorn have me in an iron grip and the two minders are close enough behind to trade viruses. "Jade Palace, I like it," Vikorn says as I am marched up the steps, where the uniformed lackeys *wai* to us and open the big glass doors.

In the lobby the eye is inevitably, if not subtly, drawn to a window about a hundred feet long behind which are arranged perhaps three hundred plastic seats. It is daytime so most of the seats are empty; there are no more than about thirty beautiful young women sitting in their finery, all carefully selected for their porcelain skin, perfect bosoms and beguiling smiles. Vikorn twists my head to make sure I'm looking at them. "Aren't they fantastic? And you know what, because of the prices they charge and the tips they get, they want you as much as you want them. Which one will you have?"

I give him a wild look and shake my head. Suvit has increased his grip on my arm, while Vikorn loosens his and walks over to the reception area to say a few words to one of the men in dinner jackets. The minders close in behind me. I see Vikorn take out a credit card.

Now Vikorn has returned and we are making for the lifts. At the fifth floor a sign warns that we are entering the VIP Club, which is reserved for members only. Three young women, who have benefited from the improved diet which was available to their generation and are about my height and sure contenders for Miss Thailand, are waiting in elaborate silk bathrobes. The fourth woman is about forty, shorter, well turned out in an evening gown.

"This is Nit-nit, Noi and Nat," she explains with a deep *wai* to Vikorn and Suvit. The minders are guarding the lift.

"Where's the room?" Vikorn asks. The mamasan gestures to a padded green leather door off the reception area. He turns to me. "Your choice. Do you want the girls to strip you or shall we do it for them?" Not bothering to wait for an answer, he says to the mamasan: "Lock the door on him. Don't let him out until his time's up. How much did I pay for downstairs?"

"Three hours," she says with a curtsy and a *wai*.

The girls giggle behind me while I am taken and thrust into a gigantic bathroom, with Jacuzzi as central feature, a Sony flat plasma TV about a yard long and two feet tall, high up on a bracket, a double king-size bed with rubberized sheet, and a dazzling array of aromatic oils in bottles standing around the Jacuzzi. The door shuts, then opens again and Nit-nit, Noi and Nat stride in, grinning. The door shuts with a click. Nit-nit turns on the water in the Jacuzzi while Noi and Nat skillfully undo my shirt and pants, pull off my shoes and socks, underwear, lay me on the bed. It does not help my self-respect that my resistance is worn down by liberal application of an American product. Johnson's baby oil is a girl's best friend in these parts. I am not resisting as fiercely as I might. I am not resisting at all. In a last-ditch stand I chant softly to myself in Pali from such scriptures as I remember; unfortunately, I remember what every young monk recalls: *Monks, I owned three palaces, one for the summer, one for the winter, and one for the rainy season. During all four months of the rains, I remained inside the monsoon palace, never passing its doors; everywhere I was accompanied by courtesans who danced and played music, sang and looked to my pleasure without cease.* A seductive precedent from the Golden One in whose footsteps I endeavor to follow.

Nit-nit returns from the Jacuzzi, undresses completely and runs her finger gently along the ladder of my stitches, moaning sympathetically. It's enough to make me burst into tears.

"D'you want the TV on or off?" Nat asks sweetly while she undresses.

"I don't care. Whatever."

"You don't mind if we put the football on?"

"Is it Man U?"

"Playing Bayern Munich." Breasts dangling, she reaches for the remote.

39

The Colonel, a cybervirgin if ever there was one (mouse? double click? keystroke?), has surprised and impressed my mother by purchasing for a hefty fee from a gangster in Atlanta a specialist e-mailing list (updated every thirty minutes) which is automatically transmitted to a gangster in Phnom Penh (try nailing anyone for anything in Phnom Penh) who, for really not much money at all, will zing advertisements for the Old Man's Club at any surfer who has been so uncircumspect as to alight for a nanosecond on a web page bearing such keywords as Viagra; sex; Bangkok; go (go); porn; impotence; and prostate. There really cannot be very many sexually active men over the age of fifty using the Net who have not received my mother's cyberequivalent of *Hello sailor!*

On my way to work on the back of the motorbike this morning, listening to Pisit's phone-in: *Thai Rath* reports that car thieves have hit on a new wheeze: rent a car, drive it over the border to lawless Cambodia, sell it to a Khmer thug, report it missing to the Cambodian cops, let the hire companies claim the insurance. According to *Thai Rath*, the culprits are all Thai cops. There is the usual flood of callers complaining about police corruption before Pisit introduces his guest, an insurance expert.

Pisit, laughing: "You have to hand it to the cops, they do seem to have found a crime without a victim. I mean, who loses here?"

"Everyone, because of the rise in insurance premiums."

"Does the average Thai driver pay insurance?"

Insurance expert, laughing: "No, if he gets into an accident he bribes a cop."

Caller: "Does this mean that money which would otherwise go to insurance companies goes to the police?"

Pisit, laughing: "Looks that way, doesn't it?"

Caller: "Is this right or wrong? I mean, if the cops didn't get the money, their salaries would have to be increased, which would mean an increase in tax, wouldn't it?"

Pisit, admiringly: "That's a very Thai question."

When I arrive at the police station Jones is already there, in our work-room. I decide to begin on a dynamic note which to my fancy has a mea-sure of American aggression about it, which I think she'll appreciate.

"Kimberley, there must be something else Warren did. Why are you holding out on me?"

I take my place beside her at a crude wooden table on trestles. We are carrying on from the day before yesterday and there's a stack of cas-settes in a wooden box between us. Jones figured we would not have the facilities to play the large-spool tapes they use at Quantico, so she had them copy Elijah's telephone conversations onto the cassettes. She also figured, with equal clairvoyance, that we probably wouldn't have the facilities to play the cassettes either, so she bought a couple of cheap Walkmans on her way here, and now she's taking a break with the head-phones hanging around her neck. There's nothing on the bare boards of the tabletop apart from the Walkmans and our elbows. No pens, no paper, no computers, no files, but there is a stack of old file covers that some-one has dumped in a corner of the room and one empty chair in another corner.

"What makes you so sure he did something apart from art fraud?" She does not look at me as she speaks.

"Mostly because I don't think he does art fraud. I think you want to think that because you've got it in for him. So I ask myself why you would have it in for him, and the answer I come up with is sex. You don't resent men for being rich and powerful and owning more of the world's assets than women, you resent us for having cocks."

Wearily: "Sonchai, the myth of penis envy was put to rest in my country sometime before I was born and I'm not in the mood to relive those prehistoric battles. I made the mistake of having some Thai beer last night which has given me a splitting headache, and listening to these two drawl in deep Harlem dialect isn't helping. That's not a racist comment by the way, just a sociological observation. And on top of *that*, coming here I twisted my ankle on a manhole cover for the third time in as many days. Tell me, wise one, why do the manhole covers in your city have to be three-quarters of an inch above the pavement? I know this is a chauvinistic observation to make, but in my country we have this eccentric habit of making them *flush* with the sidewalk. If we didn't the city of New York would go bankrupt with negligence claims. I know there's got to be a reason. It's karma, right? Every Thai citizen spent a previous lifetime tripping people up, so now they have to get tripped up?"

I make a sweet smile. "We don't trip. Only *farangs* do that. It must have been you who tripped up other people in a previous lifetime."

A shake of the head. "Okay, let's drop it. Anyway, what's got you so frisky this morning?"

This is a good question. It took me five showers to get the Johnson's out of my hair and skin, but it's going to take a few more days to wear away that special glow, that phallic pride which no good meditator permits to defile his mind. I never thought I would have been able to cope with such a challenge, but I seem to have managed despite lapses of concentration on the part of the Three N's whenever Beckham scored. Such feats were never part of my egotism. I decide to talk about the case.

"I think Warren hurt a woman, probably a prostitute. And I think he covered up so well there's not a chance anyone in the whole of Quantico will ever get the evidence to bring an indictment."

"If that's the case, it would be indiscreet for me to talk about it to you, wouldn't it? Listen to this, I think this might be what you're looking for, not that I exactly follow your occult reasoning."

She hands me her Walkman and headphones.

Listen, bro', something I never mentioned so far. I borrowed money. I guess you don't know what that means out here. You borrow money, you pay back, you don't let it ride. I'm talking sharks, bro', sharks like don't exist Stateside. These cats, I mean, they don't have to threaten.

Yeah, I did kinda figure that, Billy. It did cross my mind. How much?

[Inaudible reply]

That's one fuck of a lot, kid. I don't got so much right now, and if I did I would probably have to use it for forward investment. I do business these days, I got to make my money work for me.

I ain't askin' for money exactly. I'm askin' for a way out, Eli. I got to get out of this once and for all. Just tell me what to do, like in the old days. [William is speaking in a throaty whisper, the whisper of a man collapsing inside.] *You know me and eve'y thing you ever said about me was true. I'm a second-stringer born, I'm the original second child syndrome. An' on top a that I just spent thirty years following orders. I'm damn good at doing as I'm told, Eli, you know I am. I can perfect any order you give me, down to the last detail. That's what I know. Fucked if I kin think up one original thang, tho'. Not a goddamn one.*

Billy, d'you think it's a wise thing or a foolish thing to start this kinda talk over the telephone line of a convicted felon?

Okay, okay, we'll do it the other way. I'm sorry, Eli, sorry to make you have to say that. I was wrong . . . [A very long pause, perhaps as long as five minutes, when I assume the conversation is ended and am waiting for the next one, then a wail of spiritual agony such as I've never heard from a grown man before. It lasts for more than thirty seconds.]

Hang in there, Billy. [A sigh] *I'll see what I can do.*

It's bad, bro, it's bad. I'm scared as shit.

[Tenderly] *I can tell, kid, I can tell.*

I stop the Walkman and pull off the headphones. I allow Jones a nod of appreciation. She takes back the Walkman and sets it on the table. "Okay, we'll do a deal. You tell me why you're so sure I'm so sure Warren hurt a woman and I'll tell you if he did or not."

"There was some scandal here which is making everyone nervous. It looks like half the senior cops in Bangkok were involved in covering it up. I don't know what it was, but the Colonel more or less admitted it involved a woman. I figured if he did something like that here, he might have done it in your country too."

Jones is unable to hear any reference to my Colonel without making her jaw muscles work overtime. She seems to be choosing her words carefully. "A twenty-nine-year-old prostitute who specialized in submissive sex. She would charge very large amounts of money in return for being tied up and abused by wealthy men and pretending to enjoy it. She was tough and smart and could fake orgasm the way—well, the way any woman can. She chose only those men who had too much to lose by going too far. She knew how to choose, too. She thought she could read men, at least that kind of man, and she never accepted a job without scoping the guy out. I guess she figured Sylvester Warren was about as safe a bet as she could make. I think it was the only time she misread a man."

"He hurt her?"

"The human body cannot survive with less than sixty percent skin. The problem is more water than blood. You lose moisture faster than you can replace it, even assuming you're not tied up and unable to get yourself a drink."

"She died?"

"Gladys Pierson died on February 15, 1996. She was still tied up." Jones puts her headset back on, then takes it off again. "Everyone who worked on the case knows that Warren did it, but there's no evidence, no hair and fiber, no sperm, no DNA. We think he paid a team to clean up after him, specialists who normally work for the mob."

"He used a knife?"

"A bullwhip. It's called being flayed alive." She switches the Walkman on and off, on and off. "From my profiling course I would say that the two sides of Sylvester Warren came together at that moment. I think he'd used a lot of women with that specialization before, but something about this one drove him over the edge. I think it was the most ecstatic moment of his life, something he'd subconsciously been building up to since adolescence, but was too smart, too controlled, too strong to give into until then. But it was something that sooner or later he was going to have to repeat. Usually the psychosis which has its origins in adolescence is given full expression between the ages of thirty-five and forty-five. We're talking men, white men. But Warren is a very disciplined man, the wall between the conscious ego and the seething fantasies would have been much thicker in his case. I think he came to this kind of stuff relatively late in life. Maybe he used drugs as well, but somehow I doubt it. I think he's a genuine psycho without the need for chemical assistance." A long pause; Jones is clearly moved. "You're right, when we realized we weren't going to get the evidence we needed, the others in the team gave up, but I decided he was into art fraud. It was an excuse to keep on investigating him—and to learn about Oriental art. What the hell? I was pissed, and I don't think all his transactions are legit. Art is so much more complex than murder, it's hard for anyone in the Bureau to argue with me when I say there's evidence of fraud—how would they know without reading an encyclopedia on Southeast Asian antiques? I'm gonna get him sooner or later. They got Al Capone on tax evasion for god's sake. D'you have any idea what happened over here?"

"No, except that I think it was a Russian prostitute. Do you have a photograph of your victim?"

"I can get one. I can give you a description right now. A stunning light-skinned African American, beautiful long legs, full firm bust, great face, hair dyed all the colors of the rainbow, a discreet little piercing in her navel for a jade ball set in a gold stick. She was tall, too, just under six feet. We're pretty certain she got the gold stick from Warren. Preliminary interviews are not uncommon with this kind of prostitution—after all, a lot of money changes hands. Usually the woman will ask what kind of clothes, what kind of underwear, what erotic props or fantasies the john wants. We think Warren wanted to customize her body with his gold stick and she agreed."

We stop talking as soon as the door opens. It is the Monitor.

Jones gave him this name. His real name is Detective Constable Anusorn Mutra—it and he appeared yesterday, on permanent secondment from District 15, compliments of Colonel Suvit. He sits cross-legged in chairs in corners of rooms, and except for visits to the bathroom is tied to me on an invisible leash. He owns the short brow, saggy cheeks and melancholy mouth of an idiot, but he has been expertly programmed to guide me away from any line of inquiry that might lead to Warren. The smartest thing about him is a new Nokia which he keeps in the left breast pocket of his shirt and which requires only one keystroke to join him to his master in District 15. We do not use the name "Warren" in front of him, even though he speaks no English. I have already complained to the Colonel, using arguments that do not normally fail: How could a self-respecting tribal chieftain tolerate a spy from a competitor right in the center of his camp? Vikorn replied mysteriously that if I took care of the Monitor he might yet save my life. Jones and I watch the Monitor cross the room and seat himself in his usual corner.

"Should we buy him a bowl and wicker basket?" Jones asks.

I ignore the crack because I've seen a possible fruitful line of inquiry. "Would it be easier for you or me, Kimberley"—I'm using American Polite here, even doing the smile—"to get hold of the jeweler's schedule over the past years, I mean to find out exactly what periods he spent in Bangkok?"

"Let's put it this way. If I do it and the wrong person finds out, I get reassigned to Records. If you do it, the wrong person will definitely find out and you get reassigned to your next life. I'll see what I can do. You see if you can find out how many Russian prostitutes suffered untimely deaths in Bangkok over, say, the past five years. If checking your records is indiscreet, you can always use the newspapers. You know, hardly a day passes without some police scandal of one kind or another. Must be all those profit centers working overtime."

I ignore the dig because I want to get on with the job. In particular I want to take a second look at the e-mails between Warren and William Bradley, which means hunting down Bradley's computer, which is stored in a place we call "the evidence room." I tell the Monitor to go get the key, then immediately regret this order because of the likely time lag. We watch him shuffle across the floor. The FBI puts her hand on my thigh, then immediately takes it off again. "Sorry. The fact is this town liberates all sex drives, not only white male ones. I went to that place you keep talking about, Nana? I was expecting to feel totally disgusted, but I saw your point. Those girls are born huntresses. I wouldn't say they were happy in their work, but they're not exactly suffering either. I didn't see a single one who didn't have a cell phone clipped to her belt. A lot of them, you can see it in their eyes, that combination of money and sex and the thrill of the hunt, it's addictive. I could relate, as most women could. And it's hard to witness so much unrestrained promiscuity without feeling the itch yourself. Some of the men were damned good-looking, too. They weren't all middle-aged farts like you implied. You also happen to be damned good-looking yourself, if you don't mind my saying so." She looks away when she says this, so I cannot tell if she is smirking, blushing or biting her lip in the anguish of unrequited lust.

"You have to remember where they're coming from," I say, to avoid the main issue. "Anything is better than a country brothel. Anything. *Farangs* give them a five-star experience in comparison."

She turns back to look at me. "It's true, most of the girls come from the country, don't they?"

For a moment I think about taking the FBI to a bed somewhere, but immediately I realize this is a consequence of the defilement from yesterday. This is exactly how karma is generated, through craving arising from craving arising from craving. Just because I successfully negotiated the charms of three beautiful women, with the help of JBO and an astronomical investment by my Colonel, I now feel I can fuck the FBI with impunity. But the Lord Buddha taught two thousand five hundred years ago that there is no impunity. In more elegant language than I can muster he warned that you always pay for pussy, one way or another. For example, if we go back to Jones' room at the Hilton, one of two things could happen. She could enjoy it more than I or I could enjoy it more than she. The keener one immediately becomes the slave of the other, with disastrous consequences for both. I think it likely that I would initially fall under her spell, which gets more powerful every day. Having trapped me, she would use her abrasive genius to nibble away at everything about me which is alien to her: my belief in rebirth, my spiritual dimension, my meditation, my Buddhism, my preference for huge doses of chili in everything I eat. She would not realize that she would be turning me into an American, but by the time I'm living with her in some luxurious but soulless suburb in one of those cities in America which look like all the others, conscientiously working at the sort of work immigrants work at, speaking with an American accent now and forced to go underground with my chili habit, she will have started to hate me because I will have become a millstone round her neck and the lust will have run out a long time ago. There might even be a child, which of course will make things a whole lot worse, because our mutual karma will include this third person. After death, no matter how hard we try, we will be reborn in circumstances where we will be forced to continue where we left off. We will be sworn enemies by this time, and I will probably be the dominant one now, due to the way things have to balance out in the universe. No, I am not going to fuck her today.

"Sonchai, what are you doing?"

"I am meditating."

"D'you have to do that now, in the middle of a conversation? We're supposed to be working."

See what I mean?

There is no point waiting for the Monitor, who has probably got himself lost, so I leave Jones to the cassettes and go search for the key myself.

I find that I have underestimated the Monitor, who found the key all right. It was already in the door because three young constables are in the evidence room playing some kind of Space Invader game on Bradley's computer. The polythene we used to carefully protect the evidence is on the floor and the three boys—they're between eighteen and nineteen years old—have brought in stools, and some food in Styrofoam boxes, some cans of 7UP. It looks as though they have installed themselves here for quite some time. The Monitor is standing silently behind them watching the black steel–clad invaders get knocked off by the lithe white defenders, with something that approximates to excitement.

This situation, like everything in life, is a useful conundrum to a practicing Buddhist. To scream and yell will generate more negative karma than has already been generated by the boys. On the other hand, too soft an approach on my part will lead them to continue on their downward path. What would my master the abbot do in such circumstances?

I find that I don't really give a shit, so I slam the door as hard as possible behind me. This has the effect of a scramble. Three rapid *wais*, the computer is turned off in double-quick time, the food gathered, the Styrofoam boxes closed, the polythene replaced, the 7UP drunk in a minimum of gulps, the room emptied except for me and the Monitor. My precipitate action has had the negative effect of obliging me to unwrap the computer again and turn it on, so it was not an entirely skillful strategy. I have plenty of defilements left to work on, even if I don't go to bed with the FBI.

I tell the Monitor to bring Jones, while I locate Bradley's e-mail file. Jones enters while I am reading. I find it convenient to divide the e-mails into phases.

Phase 1 [July–September 1996]:

Bill, your piece arrived yesterday FedEx. The boys are getting the point, I agree, but there's still a long way to go.

Bill, look, this is good work which I can sell anywhere, but it's not what we discussed. I'm arriving on a Thai Airways flight next Tues. We'll talk.

Bill, I have to tell you I was very impressed with the latest piece. It's not quite there, but it's damn close. I'm going to release the second tranche today. Keep it up.

Phase 2 [November 1996–July 1997]:

Bill, I have to admit you've impressed me quite considerably. I'm not entirely sure how we take it from here, but I agree you can continue to cross-refer over the Net. I think the best would be for you to e-mail me the design you have in mind, I'll come back with some general comments, you'll modify and work up the details (something you're damned good at) and we'll proceed like that until we've got an agreed set of three-dimensional designs. I'm releasing a special payment for your extra expenses. I have to tell you I'm damned excited. It's like being a kid at Christmas. Except that this is the real thing, if you see what I mean.

Bill, got the designs you sent. I fully agree that the Net has its limitations here, so you better send the hard copies FedEx. I'll continue to make general comments over the Net, with more detailed ones when we meet. I'll be in BKK end of next week. I'm at the Oriental, however, and I think I explained what that means. The Chiu Chow bosses are throwing one of their parties. I'll call you and we'll meet somewhere discreet. I do not want you to come to the Oriental. When I stay at Rachada, that's a different matter. I'm sure you understand.

Bill, received your FedEx package today and I'm more excited than ever. This new venture of ours requires a whole new outlook. They say an old dog can't learn new tricks, but I take a more Buddhist view: by learning new tricks you stop yourself from turning into an old dog!

Phase 3 [September 1997–end 1998]:

Bill, I understand your reservations about your work and its final purpose, but frankly this is hardly the moment to get cold feet. You have to finish what you start. Be a marine.

Bill, this is fantastic! Can't wait for everything to be finished! I'll be in BKK early next month and maybe you'll let me have a peek? See

you then, and I apologize if I was a little insensitive in my last
e-mail.

Jones is looking over my shoulder at the screen. I glance up at her.
She is frowning, her jaw is working. I think she is starting to realize who
did it, which will be a problem for me but, I now realize, an unavoidable
one. I watch and admire while that efficient professional side of her
comes to dominate. Sex could not be further from her mind at this
moment.

"I never read them that way. That's pretty smart of you to divide them
into phases like that. D'you want to explain what inspired you?"

"The tone of his voice on the cassettes. The totally desperate but
gifted second-stringer, the order-follower who will do anything for money
is doing just that. The symbiosis only began with jade. It went on to something quite different."

"But we don't know that Bradley knew . . . everything that might have
been on Warren's mind."

I sigh. To me it is obvious, but intuition clearly plays no part in
American law enforcement. "No, except that Bradley's knowing would
have been an overwhelming motive for killing him. Anyway, look at
the change of tone, starting with phase two. Can you imagine Warren
expressing that kind of boyish excitement if it wasn't over something really
different? This guy has been in the gem trade all his life—how is someone
like Bradley going to get him all excited about copying a jade figure like
the horse and rider?"

Jones is shaking her head. I check her eyes and realize that she has
still not plumbed the unspeakable depths, which is just as well. There is a
lot more work to do. The snakes remain a problem and I do want to know
what Warren did that Vikorn and Suvit don't want me to know about.

While Jones returns to the embassy to retrieve photos of Gladys Pierson, I
leave the station to use an Internet café to check the *Bangkok Post*, an
English-language daily which is published on the Net in its entirety and
has an excellent archive going back ten years. As I patiently click through
the thousands of articles and reports responding to the keyword "murder"
I know I'm wasting my time. I key in "Russian prostitutes," and the name
of Andreev Iamskoy immediately pops up. The ways of karma are mysteri-

ous and implacable. Convinced I will not be able to live out this lifetime without another brutal session with Iamskoy, I give up on the Internet, pay fifty baht for fifty minutes' use and while I'm waiting for change cast my eyes over the rest of the users sitting at the twenty or so monitors in the shop. They are all women between the ages of eighteen and thirty and they are helping each other out with the English. "Thank you for—*allai*?" "*Money.*" "Okay, thank you for money." "Thank you, *darling*, for money." Giggles.

Back at the station the FBI, who has mastered the art of riding the motorcycle taxis, has managed to return alive from her embassy. While the Monitor looks on with glistening eyes we compare pictures of a naked Gladys Pierson with a naked Fatima. Jones explains that Pierson used such pictures extensively as part of her marketing. We place them side by side and put a sheet of paper over their faces, which do not resemble each other. Jones and I exchange glances.

"The same!" the Monitor says. "Same body! Even same thing in her belly button." It's better than Space Invaders. Jones takes out another picture, postmortem, of Pierson lying facedown on the mortician's table. The Monitor's eyes are still glistening. I look away.

"Is it your theory that he was having sex with her while he was doing this? I thought a bullwhip was very long?"

"We made a lot of tests. You're quite right, the whip would have needed to have been at least six feet for this kind of penetration. We think he had an assistant."

"Oh," I say. "An assistant?"

"There are people who would do that. Women as well as men. And don't forget how rich the jeweler is. Also, you see how regular the ruts are? Whoever did it knew how to handle a whip. When I look at this picture I always think of the Marquis de Sade with his personal valet." Jones takes out another picture. Pierson has been turned over on the table.

"Breasts as well?"

"Correct. Can you send this creep off on an errand before I punch him?"

"Go get us some coffee," I tell the Monitor.

40

We are so accustomed to sitting together in the back of Jones' hired car, it has become our equivalent of sitting on a sofa and watching TV together. We have progressed from flirtation to sexless tolerance with no passionate coupling in between. I think this might be an example of postindustrial romance. This thought is not canceled out by the Monitor, who sits in the front passenger seat munching fat pork sausages which he made us stop for at a cooked-food stall. He is like a nightmare offspring who was pre-cipitated rather than conceived.

"If I've understood why we're going to Pattaya, I'm wondering how you intend to sideline the Monitor," Jones murmurs into my ear.

"I have a plan."

"I thought maybe you did." A yawn. "So what's he like, this Iamskoy? Another urka gangster with Cyrillic tattoos on his forehead and a sales brochure that includes weapons-quality plutonium?"

"Not quite."

Pattaya is a beach resort which would be about an hour's drive from Krung Thep if it were ever possible to make the journey without traffic snarl-ups. It is also the place where the Industry reveals itself for what it is: *the* Industry. Jones has brought her *Lonely Planet* guidebook, from which she quotes:

> The sex industry's annual turnover is nearly double the Thai government's annual budget. (Wow!) Only an estimated 2.5 percent of all Thai sex workers work in bars and 1.3 percent in massage parlors. The remaining 96.2 percent work in cafés and barbershops and brothels only rarely patronized by non-Thai clients. In fact most of the country's sex industry is invisible to the visiting foreigner and it is thought that Thai-to-non-Thai transactions represent less than 5 percent of the total.

Jones closes the book and looks at me with an expression I've never seen on her face before: humility? "Prostitution was never my bag. I studied the law on it, of course, and know how to bust a streetwalker in the States, and I know a lot about the career of Gladys Pierson, but I never really went into it sociologically. This is one hell of a phenomenon you have over here. I wonder if it's ever been this big, in the history of the world? I think it must have very complex sociological origins. I didn't tell you, but when I visited Nana that time I saw a young American man, maybe twenty-two, twenty-three, very very good-looking, a real pinup, except he'd lost both arms in an accident. The girls didn't treat him any differently than anyone else. There was nothing forced about it either, they asked how he'd lost his arms, played with his stumps—broke all the rules of social etiquette—groped him and asked if he wanted to take them to his hotel. He was grinning like a cat and at the same time there were tears in his eyes. You didn't need to be a psychology major to read his mind. He'd come halfway round the world to be treated like just another guy. I couldn't detect an atom of physical revulsion or patronizing attitude in any of the girls. It's like, I guess you don't have the same problem with physical deformity as we do? Those were young, beautiful, perfectly formed women, and they didn't bat an eye."

I don't really know how to reply, although this is an observation one hears from time to time. The amputee is a standard visitor to Nana. Not only amputees; men unacceptably short in the cultures of narcissism whence they hail will be snapped up by our accommodating women (who are likely to be as short or shorter). Chronic alcoholism might be a form of leprosy in your fastidious country, *farang*, with us it is the mildest of ailments, hardly worth a mention. Nor are buckteeth, false teeth, gray hair, no hair or clubfeet any impediment to admission to our Oriental Democracy of Flesh.

All of a sudden, just as we're coming into the suburbs of Pattaya, the conversation takes an unexpected turn. Jones lays a hand on mine. This is not a flirtatious gesture, although affectionate. I would say it was almost pitying. "Sonchai, I think I understand the case so far. Not as much as you do, but almost. You're gonna have to tell me what you expect of me with regard to what happens next. That's only fair. I've been thinking about you and about the case and about Thailand, and I'm still here. I haven't fled back to the States, or complained about you to the head of the FBI, or shot you, or even kicked you in the balls. I'm still here. If you want me to stay, you better level with me."

"You know who did it?"

"Yes."

"Then you know why she's also innocent in every human definition."

"But not in any legal definition."

"I'm talking personal morality."

"That's exactly what we're taught to avoid at the Academy. We call it getting creative. It's a no-no. It's the law that counts."

"Culture shock. It's getting creative that counts. Even Vikorn, whom you despise, he has a strong personal morality from which he never waivers. He's led me in shoot-outs which could easily have gotten him killed. He's a brave chieftain. Maybe he's a dinosaur to you, but there are reasons why we love him. We don't love cowards over here."

"You want me to keep my mouth shut?"

"Yes."

"You'll give me Warren?"

"I don't know if I can do that. Maybe he belongs to me. He didn't kill *your* partner."

"He didn't kill yours either."

"Karmically he's responsible."

"That's an easy argument to make. It's also easy to turn around. Maybe he killed me in a hundred previous lifetimes. Maybe he owes me this time. Anyone who hunts human beings will tell you, most of the time it's not personal, but sometimes there's that special chemistry. I want Warren, Sonchai. Do we have a deal?"

"I'll think about it."

We have turned into Pattaya and drift slowly in the stream of traffic along the main waterfront avenue.

"Did I really just see a bar called the Cock and Pussy Bar?" Jones wants to know. Her mood has changed dramatically, she seems angry. "Is there *anything* here not dedicated to sex?"

She has a point. Bar after bar line the street opposite the sea, and behind every bar a team of girls who will do anything you want for five hundred baht so long as it doesn't hurt. We are a peace-loving people, we don't like pain. We don't like people who inflict it, either. We do not give law, sex and death more importance than those delusions deserve, but deliberately to inflict suffering is seriously un-Buddhist.

Turning away from the bars, back to me and the case, Jones says: "Have you any explanation at all for why Fatima should be in Warren's shop?"

"No. None at all. I agree it's a puzzle."

"Like the puzzle of how the python?"

"The problem of how the python is second only to why the python."

"I know."

On Naklua Road I tell the driver to let the Monitor and me out of the car. We walk quickly in the heat toward a shop whose window is packed with pirated CDs, most of them games.

"I know why you're doing this," the Monitor confides.

"You do?"

"You're going to fuck the *farang* woman, aren't you? Are you going to a hotel?"

"I'm not sure."

"I don't want to waste your money."

"How so?"

"PlayStation 1 is totally out of date. Okay, it's cheap, but it has no value, you couldn't sell it secondhand."

"And the others?"

"Microsoft Xbox is good but it doesn't have the range of software."

"And GameCube?"

"GameCube is okay, but it's out of date."

"Leaving?"

"PlayStation 2. It's awesome. You can download from the Net, it plays everything designed for PS1, it plays DVD sex movies, DVD games."

"Do you need a computer?"

The Monitor looks at me strangely. "You plug it into a TV, like all the game consoles."

"Oh, I didn't know. How much is PS2?"

"Seventeen thousand baht."

"*Seventeen?*"

"You want me out of the way with my mouth shut, right?"

"Right."

In the store the Monitor starts into an arcane argument with a young shop assistant about the latest version of a game called Final Fantasy. The clerk, a boy about fifteen with ring-riveted eyebrows, shows disdain. It seems he favors Dragon Warrior VII, and even Paper Mario, rather than Final Fantasy, a position the Monitor cannot relate to. "Are you kidding? Paper Mario better than Final Fantasy? Final Fantasy is awesome."

A shrug from the boy. "Look, I work here, what do you think I do all day? I play the games. What do you do?"

"I'm a cop."

"So, how would you be at the same level as me? I'm telling you, DWVII is more awesome and you get a hundred hours."

The Monitor is seriously nonplussed. "What's the ending like?"

"Awesome."

"What about shoot-outs, what's the best in your opinion?"

"In my opinion? How can you do better than Unreal Championship. The guns . . ."

"Awesome?"

"Awesome."

"How many games do you throw in with the machine?"

"Usually five, but since you're a cop, you can have ten."

The Monitor explains to me that the selection is going to take some time. "What about porn?" he asks the shop assistant.

"We have everything. What do you need, straight or gay? S&M? Lesbian? Whips and candle wax? Gang bangs? What race, *farang*, Chinese, Indian, Thai, Latino?"

"Latino? What is Latino porn like?"

"Awesome."

The Monitor gives me the nod and allows the shop assistant to take him to one of the booths where a PlayStation 2 is already set up. I watch while the clerk loads a disc and the screen immediately shows a dark-eyed beauty naked on a park bench somewhere in Latin America. One by one muscular young men arrive color-coded in blond, black and auburn, no doubt to make them distinguishable. The Monitor fast-forwards like an expert, freezing moments of penetration which he examines with the eye of a connoisseur before continuing, discarding all padding. He is done with Latino porn in less than five minutes and the clerk loads the more serious entertainment of Dragon Warrior VII. The Monitor is immediately absorbed and seems to impress the clerk with his swordplay. The clerk returns to me and I pay for the machine. Outside the FBI is waiting in the car. She says: "That easy?" I nod. There was something akin to real intelligence on the Monitor's face when he was doing battle with the dragon. I think there must be some cultural moral in that, but Jones never appreciates those kinds of thoughts. "What is he watching?"

"Latino porn and Dragon Warrior VII."

"D'you think he is someone from humanity's immediate future?"

"How is it you can say things like that and I can't?"

"Are we going to have another one of those arguments?"

"No."

"How did you explain to the Monitor the reason why you wanted him out of the way?"

"I let him think I was going to fuck you."

"Doesn't your Buddhist code stipulate that you're not allowed to tell lies?"

"There's relative truth."

"Want to make it absolute?"

"We've been through that. We're culturally and spiritually incompatible."

"Meaning my abrasive American personality turns you right off, huh?"

"You are an excellent agent."

"How about if I were to soften up? I hear Johnson's baby oil can help in these kinds of situations." She turns away from my paranoid gaze with a smirk on her face. "It's the protocol," she says to the window, "information-sharing. Your Colonel is pretty selective, but then I guess so are we."

At the end of the waterfront strip we veer off to the left, then to the right. Halfway to Jomtien Beach, we take a left down a private road belonging to an upmarket block of condominiums. It's upmarket for Thailand, anyway. No one has bothered to repave the road since I was last here a few years ago, and we have to sit and wait in the car for the security to come and open the main gate.

I have timed the journey, taking the likely traffic problem into account, so that we arrive at about noon, when all good Russians are somewhere between sober and drunk. It is 12:12 p.m. when we reach the penthouse apartment on the thirty-seventh floor of the condo building and I press the buzzer. I agonized over whether to call ahead or not and finally decided not to. If Iamskoy is compromised with a half dozen Siberian women without visas, or who have overstayed their visas, or are obviously on the game, he might be that much more willing to talk. A lot will depend on how drunk he is, though. Too drunk and he will pass out, the way he did last time. Too sober and he'll be uptight, too far into him-self with his Russian melancholy to communicate at all.

I think I might be in luck because a woman answers the door. She is about twenty-six, dyed blond hair, Caucasian, thick lips and a wolfish look which she clearly believes to be irresistible. She is wearing a black dress which comes an inch or two below her crotch and reveals a lot of cleav-age. Her perfume is not up to my mother's standards, but then I don't think this woman has spent much time in Paris. She looks blank and about to close the door on us when I flash my ID.

"Andy," she calls without anxiety. Instead of Iamskoy another woman appears in shorts and T-shirt. Then another. A fourth is dressed in a long nightgown done up firmly at the neck. "Is this a bust?" the first woman asks, more with curiosity than concern.

"I don't know," I answer truthfully. "I want to speak to Andreev."

Eventually Iamskoy appears from among the small crowd of females. He is tall and gangly and has kept most of his hair, which makes him seem younger than the fifty and some years he has spent in this body. He does a double take, then grins broadly. I think he has absorbed just the right amount of alcohol when he says: "Sonchai! So long it's been! Come in, my good friend, come in."

I'm checking Jones' face as we enter, thinking she'll be surprised, because apart from the collection of women this is not like the home of a pimp at all. It is very untidy and a major contributor to the untidiness are the books. They are everywhere, on shelves on the walls, on the carpet, stacked up in corners, under the legs of collapsing armchairs.

Jones is fairly wide-eyed, but mainly because of the women, who seem to be unnerving her with their glares and snippets of harsh-sounding

Russian. In my humble opinion Jones is a lot more attractive than any of them, which could explain the glares. I don't think she has seen the books at all, so I point them out. "Andreev is the most obsessive bookworm you'll ever meet. Look at them! French novels, Russian, American, Italian, but that's just light reading. Physics is his subject. He still keeps up with the latest developments, right, Andreev?"

This is not a diplomatic question on my part. His expression turns to bitterness for a moment, then he recovers and puts a forgiving arm around me.

"Thais are actually not sensitive at all, they just have this way of covering up through ritual politeness," he explains to Jones. "If you cut away the *wais* and the other formalities, you find a people who really don't give a damn." His accent is thick, the grammar perfect.

"I think I'm finding that," Jones says. She's looking at the books now and, as I expected, warming to Iamskoy, whose eccentricities are so much more comprehensible than my own. She has read books about this stereotype, perhaps seen him in movies. Gently: "Are you really a retired physicist?"

"Unemployed. Sacked. Kicked out. Let's not mince words. The boot was looking for me even while Gorbachev was in power, that world-class loser. It got me right up the ass when the economy collapsed under the terminal drunk Yeltsin. We pick our leaders, we really pick them."

He leads us, still moaning about Gorbachev and Yeltsin, into the living room, where chaos has all but defeated order. The only unambiguous landmarks are three vodka bottles, partially consumed with the tops left off, on a large plain glass coffee table. From my last visit I remember the Russian tradition of opening more than one bottle. One bottle may be spiced, another flavored with apricot or apple; it is similar to the Thai habit of providing dipping sauces to flavor a meal. Of course, vodka is not food unless one is Russian.

Apart from the vodka, you have to spend a moment before you can visually disentangle one object from another. Books are not the only culprits. There are pieces of women's underwear, shoes, ashtrays, a vacuum cleaner with its tube snaked around the coffee table, crushed beer cans, some unopened bottles of wine, and on a side dresser such a heap of makeup products it's like a miniature rock pile. Nothing is horizontal or vertical, everything is resting crookedly on something else. And yet it is a huge apartment with five bedrooms, easily enough to accommodate twenty neat Thai girls who would surely keep the place spotless.

Two of the women have followed us into the room, the others are having an argument in the corridor. Muttering to himself in Russian, Iamskoy starts picking things up off one of the sofas and chucking them in a pile in a corner: a black bra, a volume of an encyclopedia, a bottle of shampoo, books which he examines curiously like long-lost friends before condemning them to the new pile. It takes a few minutes before we can sit down. He sits on the floor with his back resting on another sofa which has not been emptied of junk and says something to the woman in the short black dress, who finds some plastic mugs. She pours some vodka into the mugs and hands the mugs to us, without asking if we want any or not. She hands Iamskoy the bottle, then pours herself a drink from one of the other bottles. Meanwhile, the other woman leaves the room.

"Zoya has an appointment with an army general," he explains. "He's a first-time customer and she's slightly nervous. Only slightly, though. That's why she's only drinking slightly." We watch as Zoya pours more vodka into her cup and knocks it back. She says something in Russian to Iamskoy, who waves her out of the room. "Amazing, isn't it?" he asks Jones.

"What?"

"Did you see her figure under that dress? Power legs, fat ass, short strong torso, round shoulders—a form evolved over many thousands of years to survive the steppe and work the land—but the General finds her exotic. With all these brown-skinned goddesses around, he actually pays more than ten times for Zoya."

The front door slams.

"Perhaps it's love," Jones says.

Startled for a moment, Iamskoy looks at her, then breaks into a broad grin. "That's good. That's very good. Excuse me." He puts the bottle to his lips to knock the vodka back. I watch his Adam's apple move twice in full-throated swallows. "I think I must seem even more of a wreck to an American than I do to myself, no?"

"I guess I don't know how much of a wreck you seem to yourself," Jones replies. I realize that Iamskoy and I are both watching to see if she will sip any of her vodka. I take a sip of mine by way of provocation and I'm pleased to find it is from the spiced bottle. She catches me looking at her and puts the mug on the arm of the sofa.

"To myself I look more than a wreck. I'm atomized. I was a nuclear physicist so I should know. Nobody knew where my master the great Sakharov was leading us when he took his stand. He was like Christ pitting himself against the Roman Empire. How many put their money on Christ at the time? He must have drawn the longest odds in the ancient world. But then they weren't Russians. Russians love a bad bet."

"You worked with Sakharov?"

"Let's not exaggerate. I was an assistant to his assistant. More properly, an assistant to the assistant of his assistant. Communism was strangely hierarchical toward the end, a point which has been made many times." Another swig. "It's really ironic, isn't it, that the transformation in Russian society largely provoked by Sakharov the nuclear physicist has led to our atomization? It's like reality imitating a bad pun. Of course, nobody told us that's where it was all leading. We knew that capitalism makes whores of everyone, but not atomized whores. That was something we could not conceive in our theoretically logical universe. Since the fall of the Soviet Union I have become the proud owner of at least twenty different person- alities. This is necessary in the global economy. I'm a burned-out physi- cist, an intellectual snob, a drunk, a failed poet, a renegade husband, absent father, a master of unfinished novels, an incompetent business- man, a fan of Russian ballet, a bankrupt and a pimp. It is impossible to be all these things at the same time, so I must decide, moment to moment, which of these many Iamskoys I should wear. In America you must be adept at such rapid costume changes, you've had more practice. For a Russian, it's still hard."

"You must enjoy the challenge." To my surprise, Jones picks her mug up and takes a deep swallow, not a polite sip at all. She glares at me. "Which of your many parts do you find the most difficult?"

"Pimp," he replies promptly. "It's even more complex than trying to write a novel and requires much finer judgment than playing with neu- trons. You would think it would be easy, just a question of supply and demand with the added advantage that the products transport themselves of their own accord, no need for freight and delivery systems. Not with Russians. You think I run these women or they run me? They are inde- pendents. Two of them have degrees, one of them is a Ph.D., the other two are merely very well educated. They could get work in Russia if they really wanted to, but . . ." He shrugs.

"Not well paid, huh?"

"It's not money exactly. Not in the American sense."

"What is money in the Russian sense?"

"Gambling chips. They go home as poor as when they arrived, but while they're here they get to gamble for relatively big stakes in those police-protected casinos which don't officially exist. Paying their fares home after they've blown their profits is part of a Russian pimp's overhead." A glance at me. "That and paying off the Thai police of course." To Jones. "Every Thai cop apart from Sonchai is a world-class businessman. You simply can't beat them. If I'm not careful they hire the girls, then fine me the price of the girl—for trafficking in women—less ten percent for my expenses. Not Sonchai. He's an even worse businessman than me. That must be why I like him, he doesn't make me feel inferior."

"I wondered," I say, sipping more vodka.

"That and the fact that he's even more of a head case than me. You should have heard our last conversation. It was like Hindu science fiction. I guess he didn't enjoy it as much as I did, though, because he stayed away three years."

"You passed out after insulting the Buddha."

"I did? Why didn't you shoot me?"

"I didn't think you were alive."

"Anyway, what did I say?"

"You said that Gautama Buddha was the greatest salesman in history."

To Jones: "I was right. He was selling nothing. That's what 'nirvana' means: nothing. As a cure for the great cosmic disaster most of us call life, he prescribed a rigorous course of meditation and perfect living over any number of lifetimes, with nothing as its final reward. D'you think anyone on Madison Avenue could sell that? But the whole of the Indian subcontinent bought it at the time. Today there are more than three hundred million Buddhists in the world and growing."

"You also said he was right. I can't remember the argument."

"Correct. Black holes in space, which can fairly be described as pockets of nonexistence since no light or time survives there, have been seen to emit subatomic particles and reabsorb them. Life comes from nothing and returns there after all. Smoke and mirrors, just like the man said two thousand five hundred years ago. Magic. Which may yet make logic the biggest superstition since the virgin birth."

"Well, there you are," Jones says. "It only goes to show. But there's a play on words here, isn't there? He was only selling nothing if you understand nothing in a certain sense. Nothing to a Buddhist is also everything, since only nothing has any reality." A little self-consciously, she takes another glug of vodka. Iamskoy and I are both grinning at her. Iamskoy suddenly claps a few times and I feel obliged to join him. Jones blushes but I've never seen her so happy.

"You've been schooling her?" Iamskoy asks me.

"Not at all. I didn't think she was interested in Buddhism."

"Are you?" Iamskoy asks.

"I'm interested in this jerk." She points at me and takes another deep swallow of vodka. "And Buddhism is the only sure way to turn him on. At least with Buddhism you can get some conversation out of him."

"I found that too," Iamskoy says. "He has this Thai way of falling asleep at the drop of a hat, but mention rebirth or nirvana or relative truth, and he perks up. That's what I love about this country. Everyone has a spiritual dimension, even cops. Even crooks. Some of the biggest gangsters make merit by giving huge sums to the monasteries and donating to the poor. Makes you wonder."

"About what?"

"About what the past five hundred years of Western civilization have been about. If we'd remained medieval we might have been smiling as much as the Thais."

"Gimme some more vodka, will you?" Jones says to me. "I've been waiting for a conversation like this, seems like forever. It's better than school."

There are footsteps in the hall and the woman in the nightgown appears. After Iamskoy's comment I check her figure, as far as I can. She is slim and pale with hair which is almost black and very large green eyes. I could find her exotic. Jones gives her a big warm smile, woman to woman, and she smiles back.

"This is Valerya," Iamskoy says. "She's the Ph.D. You see, she heard the conversation and was irresistibly drawn to join us. That is one of our million faults, Russians are perpetual undergraduates. We still talk about life in a way the West grew out of fifty years ago."

"It's better than sucking cocks," Valerya says, walking to the coffee table and taking one of the bottles and swigging it. "But I'm not yet a Ph.D. I'm funding my thesis." Her English is less accented than Iamskoy's, with a British tone. Now that she has spoken I can see her hardness, though, the hardness of a beautiful woman who doesn't need to care. I no longer find her exotic.

"Were you funding your thesis at the casino last night?"

A shrug followed by a second swig. "You're right about Russians. We love to blow everything on a bad bet. I can't believe it. All that sex, for nothing. If I could delete the gambling I could delete the selling of my body, they cancel each other out, but I'd still need to fund my Ph.D."

"What is your subject?" Jones wants to know.

"Child psychology."

Iamskoy and I both see the look of horror cross Jones' face, but Valerya doesn't seem to as she engages Jones' eyes and speaks earnestly about how a Russian degree isn't worth a dime even in Russia, but with a Ph.D. she could probably get a teaching job in one of the American universities, using her research project into criminalized street kids, of which there is an abundance in Vladivostok, just like in New York or Los Angeles. She really wants to get to the States.

As Iamskoy predicted, the babble of semi-intelligent conversation is too tempting for the three other women, who now appear one by one, with two vodka bottles cloudy with condensation. More plastic cups appear and all of a sudden we have a party. Despite her passing disgust that a hardened prostitute should also be a child psychologist, Jones is taken with Valerya, who seems to offer intelligent female companionship, maybe something to develop while she's here, maybe she'll help Valerya get to the States and they'll be bosom buddies. They yammer away twenty to the dozen about a dazzling array of subjects while Iamskoy develops his theory about materialism being the superstition of the twentieth cen-tury, a dark age which will be replaced by an enlightenment of magic. He believes I will be seduced by this, which only goes to show he doesn't understand Buddhism, which despises magic, but I don't want to annoy him quite yet. The three other women are babbling in Russian inter-spersed with English and seem to be talking about a winning strategy at blackjack. The vodka swills and the noise level rises and I fall into silence. This is a Caucasian party. What I see is the great juggernaut of Western culture with its insane need to fill space, all of it, until there is no space or silence left. After a while I say: "Andreev, did any of your workers ever get flayed alive?"

A thundering silence. Jones is deeply embarrassed and red in the face. Valerya has stopped in mid-sentence and is boring into me with those green eyes which don't seem so beautiful anymore. Iamskoy has snapped his head away toward a wall and the three others who I didn't think spoke much English are looking down at the carpet. When Iamskoy brings his head round again to face me his mouth is crooked. "Is that what you came to ask me?"

"Yes."

"Get out!"

"Andy!" Valerya says.

"Get the fuck out of my flat!"

"Andy, you can't talk like that to a Thai cop. You're a Russian pimp in a foreign land. Stop it."

For a moment I think he is going to stand up to hit me, and he does begin to rise, but he is too drunk to make it all the way up from the floor and falls back in despair with his head resting on the seat of the sofa as if he has lost the use of his limbs. "Why?" His eyes plead with me. "Why bring that up? Didn't your people do enough? Haven't I spent enough of my life in that purgatory? Was it my fault?"

I turn to Valerya, whose cynicism might be exactly what I need, in the face of all this indecipherable Russian emotion. "You know what I'm talking about?"

"You're talking about Sonya Lyudin."

"Shut up," Iamskoy tells her.

"Don't be ridiculous, Andreev, the whole of Vladivostok still talks about it. Why shouldn't we tell him?"

"He knows already. He's just being a sly Thai."

"I don't," I say. "I don't know already. Already what?"

"If you don't know already, what are you up to? This is very hush-hush over here, you know. Very hush-hush. Oh yes." Upset, Iamskoy has lost his urbanity and control over his tongue. "You're not shupposed to talk about it, even if it's shtill the big story in Vladivostok. At leasht in the grimy circles in which I am now forced to mix." Picking up the vodka bottle and looking at it. "Grimy circles. I who once shat at the feet of the great Sakharov." He bursts into cackles. "That's good. Shat at the feet . . ."

"The story of Sonya Lyudin is tragic," Valerya explains, "but not typical. If it was typical none of us would be here. We're not orphans or street whores. We're smart women here to make a fast buck in a hard world. There's no way we would risk our bodies like that. Sonya Lyudin was different."

"How different?"

"She was a street whore. No education, born into an urka family. Hard as nails, a real Siberian. She'd do anything. She had no fear. She thought all men were dumb animals to be led by the nose. I'm not a great fan of men myself, but I think that's a dangerous attitude for a woman to take. Especially in this job." One of the women on the floor says something in Russian. "Natasha says I'm being a snob, that Sonya Lyudin was not so stupid as that. Just unlucky."

"She was supposed to have protection," Natasha explains in English. "She wasn't an independent. She was brought here by a gang of urkas. They were supposed to protect her. Andreev was just used for the introductions."

"That's true," Valerya concedes. "They took a contract out on the American's head. They'll get him sooner or later."

"They won't," Natasha says. "The American paid them off."

"No he didn't," Iamskoy says. "He tried to, but they refused. They couldn't let it go, it was a matter of credibility. Of face, as they say out here. So the American had to get protection of his own. The best protection, so I hear."

"What American?" Jones is alert now, leaning forward.

"Someone called Warren. A jeweler. A big shot in this country."

"This is known? You're telling me in Vladivostok the name of Warren is openly associated with this?"

"Oh yes. He's a kind of bogeyman amongst women like us. You know, the worst nightmare: *Be careful you don't get a Warren tonight.*"

"There's a video," Valerya says. "I've spoken to women who have seen it. A white American and an enormous black man."

"Andreev," I say, "I have to know. Do the Thai police have a copy of this video?"

He seems to have reached the passing-out stage. I think he is nodding but I can't be sure as his head falls forward, then throws itself wildly back, then falls forward again. I look at Valerya and Natasha, who avoid my eyes. Iamskoy slides inexorably into the horizontal with legs together and arms by his side. All of a sudden he's the tidiest thing in the room.

Laid out on the floor, Iamskoy opens one eye. "The Thai police bought the video from the urkas, paid a fortune for it. Of course the money came from Warren and of course the urkas promised it's the only copy. They don't care about the video, they want Warren."

"Valerya, how tall was Sonya Lyudin?" Jones is locking eyes with the child psychologist, who turns to Natasha, who turns to the woman next to her. Now everyone is looking at Iamskoy. "About six feet," he says with his eyes closed. "Slim. Very good body."

"How much time did she spend with Warren before she died? Were there a number of assignations?"

"There were two. The first was quite short and according to her nothing happened except that she stripped for him and he fondled her. He gave her a short gold stick and told her if she wore it in her navel he would set a jade stone in it. Of course, she was only too delighted to go to the nearest body piercer and wear the gold stick. She never came back from the second assignation."

"Did she mention a black American?"

"No. Only people who saw the video talk about a black man. I never saw the video."

"Often the killer in this kind of case will need a trigger," Jones explains to Valerya. "Sometimes it's racial, sometimes social, sometimes physical—only tall or small victims for example—sometimes it's social background. Usually it's something that somehow gives the killer a proprietorial feeling, some claim on the body of the victim. It looks like Warren was very particular."

"He's a jeweler," Valerya says. "He would be, wouldn't he?"

"Can anyone tell me the date when Sonya Lyudin died?" Jones wants to know.

"Twelfth December 1997, during the night, so I suppose it could have been the thirteenth," Iamskoy says. "Now get out, please."

In the back of the car again, Jones says: "Warren was in Thailand between December 5 and 15, 1997. I forgot to tell you I checked his dates."

On the way back to the Pattaya beachfront we pick up the Monitor, who is waiting outside the shop with his new PlayStation 2 under his arm. We set him up with some fried chicken and more sausages from a stall and join the traffic jams for the trip back to Krung Thep. While the Monitor is munching away Jones does it again with her hand on mine, which is resting on the seat.

"Don't you think it's time you told me about that hospital? Vikorn told Rosen you went there and asked Rosen to ask me to find out why. I'm being straight here. Those are my orders."

I look at her. I wonder if she's ready for this. I draw a breath and say okay. While I'm telling her I'm replaying the visit in my own mind.

41

No one was ever in any doubt about how Charmabutra Hospital acquired the capital to buy that fine twenty-story complex and all the state-of-the-art medical equipment it stores, even though its main product never appears on the glossy brochure.

"What is a transsexual?" Dr. Surichai asked me, raising his arms and hunching his shoulders. "Opinions differ, even in the medical profession. *Especially* in the medical profession. Is she a fully functioning human being who has finally achieved the gender identity which should have been hers at birth, or a freak, a medieval eunuch pumped full of estrogen?" Dr. Surichai placed a forefinger across his lips as if he were considering the question. His face brightened. "Some shrinks think my patients are all psycho. To them there's no such thing as a woman born in a man's body. They think what I do is criminal." With a brilliant smile: "Or ought to be."

"What is your opinion?"

A frown. "My opinion is that the whole issue is complex beyond anyone's capacity. As you would imagine, I've thought about it a lot. You have to start with the question: What is gender? There's anatomical gender: breasts, vagina, womb, ovaries, penis, testicles. Then there is chromosomal gender, which is as fundamental as you can go. Here you're talking about the nuclear building blocks of the body, but the outcome of chromosomal analysis is not without ambiguity and doesn't necessarily conform to the anatomy. You can have a chromosomal male with a woman's genitals, in other words. At the end of the day, the chromosomal approach is only really used in tests for professional sportsmen and -women—you have to have some criterion to decide if your champ is top of the men's league or the women's. Then there's hormonal sex, which is purely a matter of chemistry and can be changed simply by taking a few drugs. And there's psychological sex. In other words, what gender do you feel yourself to be? How do you respond to the world, as a man or a woman? The big question is, what comes first? For most of us, it's never an issue, we conveniently experience ourselves as being the gender of our bodies. But supposing you don't? Supposing you have a nicely functioning, full-size penis, and spend your waking life believing yourself to be a woman in the wrong body? This is not a new phenomenon, there are records from ancient times, especially in Asia, of people who were basically transsexual in an age without the technology to make the change. The only difference today is that we have developed the technology. All I do is to adapt the body, in such a case."

"What do you do exactly?"

"I cut off their cocks and balls. It's called vaginoplasty, meaning to make a vagina. I use the skin inversion technique. Basically, we skin the penis—deglove it—invert it and sew it into the vaginal cavity. All men have a vaginal cavity, by the way. We open it, line it with the skin of the penis, use the leftover skin to mold a mucosal flap for the clitoris, even give the little darling a hood and Bob's your uncle. Well, not quite, but that's the basics. There's a lot of preparatory work, mostly involving hormone injections and psychiatric tests."

"Tell me about the tests."

"Well, like I say, there are psychiatrists who just don't buy the whole 'woman in a man's body' argument, but they're considered square. The profile of a true transsexual is really pretty simple. The perception of being the wrong gender starts amazingly young—between the ages of three and five. The need, interestingly, seems not to be sexual. A lot of transsexuals are not interested in sex at all. In the M2F—sorry, male to female—category, which is the only one that really matters at the moment, the desire is simply to be accepted as a normal woman, which is almost perverse, because there is nothing more challenging to normal identities than a transsexual. They are the true revolutionaries of our time, the ones who make even gender a flexible proposition.

"It's quite sweet really. A gay queen who cross-dresses goes to pubs and clubs to show off—he's really simply a showman, an extrovert. But a true transsexual cross-dresses and takes the dog for a walk on his own—he really feels more at home in women's clothes and does all his ordinary things in them. In his dreams he is a heterosexual female, and by the time he comes to me he will do anything—absolutely anything—to live inside the body of a woman. Since these men are often husbands and fathers, the whole thing can mean giving up his kids as well as everything else he's made of his life as a man."

"It doesn't happen the other way—women who think they should be men?"

"Sure, but up to now the operation is much more complex. It's really quite easy to make an artificial vagina out of a cock, almost impossible to make a fully functioning penis. Generally F2M is pretty messy at present. I have no doubt that once we learn how to produce a full-powered dick and stick it on, they'll be lining up in the street. This is the age of dissatisfaction after all. Everyone wants to be something they're not."

The doctor didn't look as if he'd ever wanted to be anyone else. He was slightly plump, in his forties, but what impressed most was the golden glow that seemed to emanate, a man for whom poverty was not even a concept. When he spoke of his work his Thai was interspersed with Western medical terms and often American slang as well; sometimes he broke entirely into English, once he saw that I understood.

"And in this case, did she/he satisfy all the requirements?"

An almost imperceptible hesitation. "Of course." A wave of the hand. "He was shemale when he came to us."

"Shemale?"

"A horribly trendy-sounding word, I know. We've taken to using it, since everyone on the street knows what it means. Basically, a shemale is a man who has taken all the hormone treatment, started to develop breasts, but has no present intention of following through with the operation. The hormones are there to give the appearance of femininity and to make him feel feminine, but he retains his sexual organs for the purpose of orgasm. Naturally, in a homosexual relationship he would tend to take the passive role."

"And your patient—Fatima—she was in this intermediate condition when she came to you?"

"You can't call it intermediate, necessarily. A lot of men live their lives like that. They go on taking the estrogen until old age, sometimes."

"So Fatima might have fit that shemale category? She might not have intended to go through with the operation, except in very favorable circumstances?"

Dr. Surichai frowned, tapped his desk. The desk was almost the only part of the office that wasn't white or beige. Even the curtains on the windows were beige, the walls were white, Dr. Surichai wore a white coat and his sculpted plastic chairs were white. The desk was light too, of some kind of varnished pine, and the picture rails were picked out in gold. The clinic achieved perfectly the intermediate condition between a modern hospital and a world-class hotel.

"Look, I know what you're getting at, but what can one do? This is the age of access to knowledge, the Internet. More and more people come already knowing the answers to the questions—they've looked everything up on the Net and they know all that I've just told you. So someone like Fatima is bound to say: Yes, I first wanted to be a woman at the age of three, and when I cross-dress I don't go to the clubs to show off, I just go for a stroll in the park."

"But Fatima was a street kid, a male prostitute with little education?"

Dr. Surichai shrugged. "If you're asking do I think she was coached, the answer's yes."

"By whom?"

"Who d'you think? Like you say, she was a street whore, there was no way she was going to be able to afford me without help. The only way these creatures get the kind of medical treatment she got is by finding a sponsor. Thailand is the world capital of GRS—that stands for gender reassignment surgery. We have the microsurgery here, and some of the best surgeons in that field. People come from all over the world. Montreal is good and there are some fine hospitals in the States specializing in these techniques—Johns Hopkins is world class, of course, but the Anglo-Saxon world is terribly hung up and confused about this sort of thing. The psychological tests are terrifying and last three months. The whole induction process normally takes two years in the U.S. People don't necessarily want to expose themselves to the men and women in white coats for that length of time, so they come to us. As a result we get the practice. We do a thousand operations where an equivalent clinic in the West would do only a hundred. Naturally our surgeons are more practiced. Also"—a smile—"Thai doctors are rather good at cutting people up. We're the neatest in the world. Must be those Asian genes. All of which makes our clinic rather expensive to locals—dirt cheap to Westerners of course. Generally, the local business from the street goes down-market to one of the other clinics. The results in those places can be hit or miss."

"You met him, then?"

This was the first question that seemed to surprise the doctor. "Met him? You mean the marine? You're not kidding I met him." I raised my eyebrows. "I saw more of him than I saw of my patient. When he wasn't here consulting me, he was calling me up on the phone. I made the mistake of giving him my mobile number. I got calls in the middle of the night, as if I was some kind of G.P. or something."

"Is that unusual?"

"The intensity was unusual. He was a very intense man. A perfectionist. Sometimes he didn't seem like a soldier at all, but then I would think, Yes, that's exactly how the very best kind of professional soldier would be, attending to detail, never letting anything slip by him. He had an eye, though, which you don't usually find on a soldier. My god, he had an eye. He practically designed her, and I have to admit that by the end of the process, he got the perfect product. Without a doubt Fatima is my finest creation."

"Also his creation?"

"Yes, that's correct. He looked everything up on the Net, he got professional-class software for his damned computer and would come out with stuff I'd hardly heard of. He mastered all the medical Latin, understood every detail of the skin inversion technique I just told you about, and about the voice stuff too."

"The voice?"

"That's the real problem. Sexual organs are not so complex, they hardly vary between us and the other mammals, they're one of the oldest organs, been around ever since God divided the world into male and female and we know a hell of a lot about them. They're also rarely modified for social reasons. The voice is something else. I'm not a shrink, but if you want my opinion, the voice is far more important as an identity than whatever you've got between your legs. I could cut your bits off and make you the most wonderful pussy, but you wouldn't be happy if you sounded like a man every time you opened your mouth. The Adam's apple can be shaved—in Fatima's case only a little shaving was needed, just a local operation with the teeniest little incision on the anterior neck."

He pointed to his own Adam's apple and moved a thumbnail down it for a quarter of an inch. "She was a natural really, hardly much of a bulge at all. I left her with the teeniest, weeniest concealable scar—she wore necklaces at first to cover it up, but it really did fit with the natural creases when it healed. I don't think anyone would necessarily notice, or know what it was even if they did see it. But that didn't deal with the voice, of course, only the cosmetics of the anterior neck. For the voice you need therapy, perhaps combined with a rather tricky little technique called 'indirect cricothyroid approximation.' Basically, you tighten up the vocal cords to produce a slightly higher range."

A pause while Dr. Surichai seemed to examine my neck. "It's a misperception that a woman's voice needs to be higher than a man's to sound womanly, however. Some women have very deep voices and manage to sound wonderfully female. Gender identification through voice is something we start to do from an early age, there are a million subliminal instructions we absorb. It's the voice which really tells the world who and what we are, far more than genitals or even dress. Your voice, for example, Detective, is exactly modified for the purposes of your profession. You are polite and firm, you can intimidate without raising your pitch, I bet you know how to terrify merely by introducing a certain ice into your speech, no? Teaching someone to project the opposite sex through speech without sounding phony or like a drag queen is the most difficult task. Fortunately, it's not a surgical problem."

"Fatima speaks exactly like a woman, there's nothing male about her voice at all."

"Correct. You really have to admire Bradley for that above all things. Frankly, on the surgical front he was a pain in the neck. He got exactly the tits he wanted, but it took about twenty hours of discussions, drawings, diagrams, e-mails of nipple details—would you believe? To do a really good breast job you have to follow the natural contours of the torso—it's really an aesthetic problem, so you need an artist's eye. Bradley thought he was the only one who understood the laws of beauty, I was just a glorified butcher. He got on my nerves, frankly, although I have to admit he knew what he was talking about. With the voice, though, that was different. He put in a lot of work himself, used a tape recorder and sent her to a voice therapist after we tightened her vocal cords a notch. I think that's where she learned such good English, the therapist was an American. Mainly, though, either the therapist or Bradley, or probably both, understood the aural contours of the female identity and transmitted it to Fatima. That's her real secret, which people don't usually spot. They're fixated on her long legs, perfect tits and Afro-Modigliani face—they don't realize that the full force of her sexuality doesn't hit until she opens her mouth. That's the trigger and the reinforcement, the signal which says: 'This is a real woman.' It still gives me a thrill when she speaks, that Negroid texture, and very, very female."

"Please think about this question, Doctor. Did you ever have the impression that someone apart from Bradley was helping in Fatima's design?"

I watched his brow furrow while he cocked his head to one side and stared at me. "Really, that is a possibility? I never thought of that, but I did wonder where the marine was getting some of his ideas from. Sometimes he spoke more like an art dealer than a soldier."

"Any idea where the name Fatima came from?"

A bright look. "Curious, isn't it? I was present when they decided on her new name. Bradley said: 'What you gonna call yourself, honey?' And she said: 'Fatima, daughter of the Prophet.' She took us both by surprise, as you would imagine. I realized afterwards that as a Karen she would have been subjected to all sorts of missionaries, Muslims as well as Christians. Bradley said: 'You sure?' And she said yes. It was the only thing she was ever uncompromising about."

He stood up. He was unexpectedly short, no more than five-six; sitting down, he projected power and authority with a fashionably sleazy touch; standing up, he was a small guy with something to prove. "Look, if this is relevant you can have copies."

On the other side of the room Dr. Surichai kept his computer, a tower on a desk next to a twenty-inch flat screen. I caught a glimpse of a diagram of a penis while the doctor moved the mouse and made keystrokes. He went to a file manager program and called up a file named Fatima. He ran quickly through some graphics of sexual organs, Adam's apples, then stopped at a diagram of a breast.

"This is the sort of thing I mean." He nodded at the screen.

Someone had used a computer program to map out the contour of a breast against a green matrix of crisscross lines which seemed to represent a torso. "This is breast diagram number seventy-six. I'm not kidding, he numbered them and sent them to me via e-mail. They're large graphic files and clogged up my system before I got broadband. You see, this is merely the outline. If I click on the nipple, like so, I get nipple detail."

The image changed to something which might have been a broken tower from an ancient monument. The dimensions could be measured by reference to the green matrix grid. "You see, he even worked out what size nipple he wanted, how long it should be, the size of the areola. See?" Now the screen was filled with what was recognizably a giant nipple with black areola. "One thing you have to say for the guy, he wasn't hung up about being black. He was proud of his African roots, which was one thing I rather liked about him."

"The only thing?"

The doctor shrugged. "As you can imagine, I get all sorts. The fanatically involved lover is a standard character in my line of work, although he's rarely as intelligent or persistent as Bradley was. What I couldn't quite get used to, though, was a layman looking on the surgery with such a cold eye. Surgeons have to be like that, but if the patient was my lover, or some-one close to me, I don't think I'd be quite so obsessed with the aesthetics — I'd just want to make sure they achieved the gender identity they craved, on their own terms, to give them psychological relief. After all, that's what the operation is supposed to be all about. Now look."

The image changed to a full breast outline, with arrows and incision marks. "He's even working out exactly how he wants the saline bags to be placed. You see, in breast enlargement you put the saline inserts behind the mammary gland, lay them on the chest cage itself. They're kept in place by the breast, but they move a little, which gives the realism, which is why everyone these days prefers saline to those ridiculous silicone inserts which set like concrete and actually echo when you tap them!" The doctor made a face of professional revulsion.

"But Bradley here is going one stage further. He wants to measure the precise position of the saline bag, down to the tenth of a millimeter, as if he's positioning a gun emplacement or something, to achieve precisely the breast contour he's aiming for. I've never come across anything like it. Frankly, when it comes to breasts, there's a certain leeway — most patients realize that real breasts change shape all the time, depending on whether the woman is standing, sitting, lying down, et cetera, and they're happy if an enlargement more or less follows nature. But Bradley was aiming for something specific—I suppose a personal erotic image, the tit of his fantasies. Now, you see?" The image changed to a representation of a full torso against the grid, seen from side and front. "He's actually very good. This is the effect, as he explained to me many times. The breast has to be just slightly large for the torso, but only slightly, giving the appearance of a full, firm bosom, but not something too flappy—that was his word, 'flappy.' A lot of men have their own idea about tits, but I've never known anyone to analyze it in such detail. Firm, but not unnaturally so, friendly, in other words soft and yielding, large but not so as to make her look top-heavy or overblown—another of his words. I told him he was seeking the impossible—if you want soft and yielding, you have to give up on firm. If you want large and soft, you're not going to get a constant shape at all, it will change all the time. He would say, 'I know, Doctor, I know, you have to aim for the perfect balance, that's all.' We spent hours, days on her breasts. He really drove me to extremes of detail I've never gone to before. In the end we got his perfect tits, and they are rather nice, don't you think?"

Suddenly I was looking at Fatima, naked to the waist, her familiar breasts pointing at me, that slight smirk on her face as in the portrait opposite Bradley's bed. "Just tell me, Doctor, while all this was going on—what was Fatima doing? After all, it was her body you two were discussing."

" 'Passive' is too insulting a word. But she wasn't inclined to assert herself much, either. Bradley usually visited me on his own, but when she came with him, he was careful to include her. 'That okay, darling? You're gonna knock 'em out'—that sort of thing. I think she believed he genuinely wanted the best body for her, and probably had a better understanding of beauty than she did. Also, you have to bear in mind this guy was a very powerful presence. A giant and maybe even a kind of a genius in his way. It was hard for me to argue with him or contradict him. And she adored him, you could see it in her eyes. This guy, this god, came out of the night, turned her whole life around, gave her self-respect—after all, we're talking about a street prostitute who never had anything, transformed into a kind of a star. She was ready to go along with him in just about everything. I wouldn't say she was without personality, though. Not passive, just appreciative."

"You never saw them argue?"

The doctor thought about that one. He frowned. "Not argue exactly, but you have to bear in mind the cultural divide here. Fatima has jungle roots. She would talk about them having sex when it was all over, she would go right to the point of the exercise in other words, and he was a bit of an American prude. He didn't like to talk about their intimacy in front of me, which Fatima and I both thought was odd. After all, I was building the body he was going to worship, when it was all over. Fatima wanted to be sure her new vagina would satisfy him, would give the full pleasure, but he wasn't comfortable talking about that. In all our discussions, it was the visual aspect he was interested in, he hardly mentioned what the experience of sexual intercourse was going to be like."

"Is that unusual?"

He nodded. "Yes, very. The big question after 'Will the patient be able to experience orgasm?' is 'Will the vagina feel real?' The answer is yes in both cases, by the way. We use erectile tissue from the penis to provide the sensation of pleasure and orgasm. Since we use skin from the penis to form the vagina, it feels just like a real vagina, so long as a lubricant is used."

"Sorry, I forgot to ask. When Fatima came to you she had already been taking hormones—estrogen I think you said—for some time. Was this something Bradley started her on?"

That frown again. "I don't know. You'll have to ask her."

"Didn't you ask her?"

His mouth tightened. "I didn't need to. She was taking estradiol, which is a plant-based estrogen widely used in the U.S. and Europe. It's quite sophisticated. Most local estrogens are still made from the urine of pregnant cows. There's no difference in effect, but some evidence to show that the synthetics like estradiol are safer."

"In other words, left to her own devices, Fatima would have taken the local variant? It does look as if she was coached from an early stage, doesn't it, Doctor?" A grunt. "That didn't bother you?"

It seemed that I had finally succeeded in piercing the doctor's urbanity. He abandoned the intermittent English phrases and broke out in pure Thai. "Bother me? That she was the creature of her lover? You're talking like a *farang*, perhaps because you're half *farang*. Which of us isn't the creature of someone else? He was giving her a better life, the life she wanted, that was the only issue for her, and she was prepared to pay any price. Those were my patient's subliminal instructions to me, the rest is just *farang* nonsense, bullshit they cook up over there to justify an army of consultants, all of whom cost the earth. Thank god Thailand hasn't come to that yet." A swallow, then in a more temperate tone: "Do I really have to remind you what kind of life we offer to penniless illegitimate half-castes, *Negroid* half-castes, in this land of compassion?"

"Thank you, Doctor. Sorry for one last question, it really is the last: Did you have any idea how Bradley was able to afford you?"

I watched carefully for signs of insecurity and found none. Dr. Surichai simply shrugged. "He was an American. Americans have ways of getting hold of money, even if they're poor. Perhaps he had a rich relation or something? It wasn't my business to ask. He paid my bills regularly, on the dot."

"About how much? Roughly, I don't need the exact figure."

Dr. Surichai rubbed his jaw. "Well, I had to charge for all the extra time spent with Bradley, all those two-in-the-morning conversations when he'd woken up with some new idea, or some aesthetic issue that was nagging him. About one hundred thousand U.S."

"Compared with how much for a more average client with no lover to complicate things?"

"Maybe five percent of that."

"Five percent? You and Bradley really went to town on Fatima, didn't you?"

"Like I say, he was obsessed and could afford it."

Jones is quiet for a long while after I finish. We're almost at the outskirts of Krung Thep when she says: "That's what you saw the other day at Warren's shop? You took one glimpse close up and saw she was a transsexual? I'm a woman and I couldn't tell. Even now, if I didn't know and I spent a day with her, I don't think I would realize. But you saw it and understood the case right away, didn't you?"

I raise my hands, then let them drop. "The whole case, no. The outline perhaps."

"You're gonna tell me it's your meditation makes you so sharp?"

"Not meditation. I'm from the street, like her."

"Is that what it takes for a woman to turn you on, she has to be from the gutter? Don't answer that. So, we have a designer victim?"

"Yes," I say.

"And a business partnership intended to produce product after product, just like with the jade?"

"Life is cheap in this kingdom, and the life of a male whore particularly cheap."

"Take a throwaway body, turn it into the object of your fantasies, do what you like with it, then when your sponsor the big boss says it's time, let him use it in his own unique way, trash it and get ready for the next one? Play God and the devil both at the same time?"

"Yes," I say, "exactly. What could be more intoxicating for men who, in their different ways, have had the best of everything? Except it didn't work."

"You give up your gender, your genitals, turn yourself into a eunuch for the man you adore, then find out what he has in mind for you."

"By which time you have also found out he is a coward and terrified of snakes."

"Yep, I would go for the cobras."

"Me too."

"But why and how the python? According to the autopsy, the python didn't even hurt him, it just happened to be on the point of swallowing his head when you guys turned up."

"Python and Khmer?"

"Python, Khmer and a video?"

Not for the first time Jones has surprised me with her acuity. I wait for her to continue the thought, but do not want to press the point myself. I think that after all she's not as sharp as all that, when just as she's about to drop me off at my project, she says: "Makes you wonder why Warren's here at this time, doesn't it? I mean, you'd expect him to stay away at least until you've finished your investigation."

On an impulse I really ought to have suppressed, I took her hand and kissed it when I said good night. Her hand snapped over mine like a steel trap and for a moment she refused to let me go. I had to tug to escape, by which time a mean look had appeared on her face. "Don't take this the wrong way, Sonchai, I'm just trying to get a hold on local customs, but would I be right in thinking that there weren't too many professions open to you when you joined the workforce?"

"Whore or cop," I snarl as I leave her.

42

A small bribe to the registration clerk at Charmabutra Hospital avoids those weeks of delays which attend upon inquiries through official channels. Now I have a photocopy of Fatima's registration card: Ussiri Thanya, male, born in a remote village on the Burmese border in 1969, the year the Americans landed on the moon and Kissinger secretly met with North Vietnamese negotiators in Paris, desperate for a way out of the war. Ussiri's official address in Bangkok was a remote suburb way off to the east: Room 967, Floor 12, Block E, King Rama I Building . . . Even on paper it sounded like a hovel. It's the kind of journey best undertaken on a Sunday, when there's not too much traffic.

It only takes me an hour and a half to reach the blocks of reinforced concrete which stretch for acres in every direction. Housing is a specialized racket, not really suitable for police entrepreneurs, who generally leave it to the Lands Department and planners. One of the most popular scams involves using an illegally low ratio of cement to sand. The building looks fine at first, but the concrete doesn't have the resistance to the weather or, more importantly, to stresses and strains. Little by little holes appear, oxygen reaches the steel reinforcement, which starts to rust, someone in government has to decide on the optimum date for evacua-

tion: as late as possible, obviously, since there will be a few thousand people to rehouse, but not so late that a big collapse causes too many deaths
and an international scandal. I don't remember ever hearing about this
estate, which looks as if it contracted smallpox a long time ago. There are
big holes in the walls of many apartments, bare steel visible in columns
which surely must be on the point of collapse. No one has lived here officially for years, but there is a thriving community of squatters who seem to
be camped out in the car parking areas. There are the inevitable card
players sitting around cross-legged on the ground, women bent over cooking pots on gas burners, TVs hooked up somehow to the public lighting,
men conscientiously downing mugs of rice whisky this sweltering Sunday
morning, dogs with serious diseases, kids and washing. Nobody pays me
any mind as I seek and find Block E and climb dangerously decrepit concrete stairs all the way to the twelfth floor—the elevators clearly gave out
long ago. I'm breathing heavily by the time I arrive. Sweat drenches my
shirt and pants. I'm itching all over from the heat, the exertion and perhaps some bugs endemic to old rotting buildings.

Room 967 is on a corner. The door yields to a single kick and I find
myself in a familiar box. Somewhere there must be a government direc-
tive on exactly how little space a Thai can be expected to occupy without
going insane or turning communist. The dimensions are exactly the same
as my own hovel's, but Fatima enjoyed the inestimable advantage of windows on two sides. From both the urban sprawl stretches to the horizon.
The earth is flat and there are no real landmarks, only the inevitable combination of large housing developments and squatter-type shacks and
small houses with tin roofs, all of them a little unreal and insubstantial in
the haze. The room itself looks as if it was simply abandoned by the occupant, without any attempt at an orderly removal. I guess no thief was going
to climb twelve floors to check out a poor boy-whore's belongings. Fatima,
at this stage in his life, slept on a bamboo mat, smoked Marlboro Reds
and joints, and kept photographs of young men dying of AIDS. They are
studies in black and white pinned up on the walls: gaunt, skeletal, faces
and chests bearing the insignia of Kaposi's sarcoma. One of them has it in
his eye. If I squat in a corner opposite the door, I have this gallery in view
in both directions. Now I am Ussiri, long before he became Fatima, my
back against the wall, staring stoned at my inevitable future: the failure of
the immune system, chest complaints rapidly deteriorating into pneumo-
nia and lung cancer, failure of the body to heal itself inside and out, pro-

gressive loss of mental faculties, brain tumors, bewilderment: this was all for—what?

On the floor near the toilet I find a registration card for a medical clinic not far from Pat Pong. I know the clinic, which, like just about every clinic in that area, specializes in tests for sexually transmitted diseases. It's where the whores go for their monthly checkups.

In Soi 7, off Silom, I sit patiently in the small waiting room while women, men and transsexuals between the ages of eighteen and thirty come and go, either to give blood samples or to receive the results of the samples they gave yesterday. The vast majority are women. I can read their faces without strain. Only a few took risks this past month—perhaps giving in to a client who didn't want to use a condom (so many *farangs* complain it kills their erections)—or perhaps permitting some other abuse; most of the girls are quite jaunty, confident they took the right precautions: rubbers, cold-water showers before and after, Listerine mouthwash.

HIV is not that easy to catch and the girls are mostly fanatics for hygiene, now that the government has done such a good job of explaining the mechanics of contagion. Things were different ten years ago, of course, when young Ussiri Thanya took pictures of his dying friends and waited in his hovel for his own death. Then it seemed as if the mystery disease was stalking Thailand in particular—Nong and I made many sad visits to friends in those special hospitals which look like Victorian insane asylums, and which are allotted to the poor to die in. Perhaps we rubbed shoulders with Fatima without knowing it?

The clinic is owned and run by an energetic middle-aged Thai man who steps incessantly in and out of his surgery in a white coat. Everyone who deals with whores on a daily basis learns *whorecharm*, which is to say a particular way of talking to the girls which neutralizes their tendency to irritability and generally makes them feel good about themselves. The doctor has mastered this art, which no doubt explains the success of his clinic (he is known to accept payment in kind from time to time, if a girl is having a bad month). He asks them when they last "worked" in a serious tone, resonant with respect, counsels against overuse of their assets in a way that gives them the giggles, makes them promise for the thousandth time always to use protection, sells them some Listerine and contraceptive pills and congratulates them on a successful test—"See you next month." I wait until the room is empty before flashing my ID and asking for his records relating to Ussiri Thanya. To my surprise he recognizes the name immediately and takes me into his surgery, which consists of a red upholstered couch, packs of hypodermics, test tubes and bubblepacks. There is a large refrigerator in one corner.

"He's still alive?"

"That surprises you?"

A thoughtful pause. "Not exactly. Even ten years ago most people didn't actually die, though everyone on the game half expected to. He was one of those who developed a real phobia about it—it was a common reaction at that time. I remember he came for a checkup once a week at some stage. I told him, 'Look, the disease takes a while to manifest, you may as well just come once a month,' but he was neurotic. The strange thing about him was that you sometimes got the feeling he wanted to be infected. That he hated the suspense. Maybe he wanted to join his friends. The male whores got hit even worse than the girls. It was pretty bad. Nowadays not many true professionals get caught—it's the amateurs, the weekenders who don't take proper precautions, who still get infected. Generally, AIDS has had a fantastic effect on our national health. Very little syphilis or gonorrhea around here these days—not even very much herpes. And of course everyone is fanatical about the checkups."

"His results were always negative?"

"Sure. Like I say, he was neurotic. He once told me he lost half his customers because he was so obsessed with disease it turned them off. He would bring his friends to see me, the ones who were too scared to have the test without someone to hold their hand. He was almost like a medic, he learned a lot about the disease. He was intelligent, he picked up the nature of the virus and could talk about it better than I could."

"He had a death wish?"

A shrug. "That to me is a Western idea. Humans are the only animal which is aware of death, so you could say we must all have either a fascination with it or an inability to face it. If he'd had a genuine death wish he'd be dead, wouldn't he? It's not difficult for a boy whore to die in Bangkok, if that's what he wants to do."

"But he was strange?"

"Obsessed with the disease. Obsessed with not getting it, but no way was he going to change his profession, even if he could. Not a death wish, maybe a death obsession."

"In the Buddhist sense?"

"Perhaps. He told me he meditated on death. It was the only reality. I got the feeling he was on the edge, you know? How many of your friends can you watch die when you're eighteen years old?"

"When did he stop coming to see you?"

A quick glance at me, then away. "I'd have to check. I don't think I've seen him for eight or nine years. Wait, I'll check. It was before I got this damned computer, so I'll have to look in the files."

"It might not be that important. You never saw him with a black American? A very big man, a marine?"

"No. Never."

"He never told you he was changing sex?"

Raised eyebrows. "That's what he did?"

"Surprised?"

A frown. "Yes, surprised."

"Why? It's not unusual, is it?"

"No, not unusual, not around here. But you get a feeling for these creatures, the men as well as the women. They come in all shapes and sizes. Canny businesspeople some of them, on the game until they've saved enough capital to open a bar or a hairdresser's. Others are the same inadequates you see on the streets all over the world, with not only their bodies for sale but their personalities as well—slaves. They're the ones who go for the operation, generally. With no identity to speak of they have nothing to lose. He never struck me as like that. Oh, he was as gay as a lark, but he had a strong mind. A good head on his shoulders. He knew who he was."

"Not a natural for the operation?"

"Look, I'm not a shrink, what do I know? I don't even practice medicine anymore, I find it too stressful, so I only do blood tests."

"There were pictures of boys dying of AIDS on the wall of his apartment. Some of them looked already dead."

"That sounds like him."

"I think he sat in his hovel staring at them for hours on end."

"Of course he did."

Out on Silom I pass a bookstore with a new biography of Pol Pot. There are aberrations on the Buddhist Path, just like any other. Pol Pot was a monk before he decided to kill a million of his own people. Sometimes the reality of death becomes overwhelming—and compelling.

At River City I pause before taking the escalator to Warren's shop. I'm nervous, without knowing why. Well, I guess I do know why. Fatima killed

Bradley—and Pichai. I'm supposed to kill her, aren't I? How to kill that boy who sat in a hovel exactly the same size as mine, crying for his dead friends, just like me, wondering what the hell it's all about—just like me? When I steel my nerves to take the elevator, she's not there. A different assistant, a very well-groomed young man who may or may not be gay, gives me a disapproving stare as I walk in. I make my excuses and leave quickly, relieved I don't have to kill anyone today. Back in my hovel I am Ussiri again, back in *his* hovel, meditating on death. I bet he'd gone very deep into himself by the time he met Bradley.

Now the mind, in its inexplicable wandering, strikes off in a more practical direction. Monday, I use my mobile to call a clerk in the Lands Department who is amenable to persuasion. I promise him a thousand baht if he will make a few simple checks on his computer. He calls me back in half an hour with a very different address.

If you want to catch a whore at home, even a retired one, go in the morning. Old habits die hard. After more than a decade in retirement Nong, for example, never rises before eleven.

By the mid-nineties Thailand had established itself as a bona fide Asian tiger, complete with expensive roar and land prices shooting through the roof. Families who had had useless lumps of land on their hands for generations found themselves courted by estate agents and developers and became millionaires overnight. Bangkok was a hub, and there's nothing better than that for a city to be, is there? The magic words "developing economy" brought in hundreds of thousands of foreigners, all of whom needed places to live of international quality. Apartment buildings rose from steamy fields like mushrooms. Some of the best of them are to be found off Sukhumvit between Soi 33 and Soi 39, where the apartments rejoice in that attention to detail for which our Japanese cousins are justly famous. Every second restaurant and supermarket around here is Japanese, you can buy sushi, tapanyaki, tofu, harami, tempura, kushikatsu, otumani any time of the day or night. At the end of Soi 39, near Petchaburi Road, the three gigantic towers of the Supalai complex rise to kiss the muggy sky. The guard at the desk in the lobby wants to call up to the occupant of the four-thousand-square-foot penthouse, and can be dissuaded only with five hundred baht and a promise of incarceration if he gives me any more trouble.

Now I am riding the elevator to the thirtieth floor, wondering if today is the day I kill her. On the other hand, I have taken the professional precaution of bringing a small Dictaphone.

It is 10:35 a.m. and, standing outside the impressive double oak doors guarded by Chinese gods in green, red and white porcelain, I can hear the television when I press the bell. Sudden silence as the TV is switched off. Only the neurotically sensitive hearing of a cop like me could discern the soft padding of bare feet across the floor. Now I am being observed through the spyhole. Someone is giving serious thought to what to do next.

It takes five minutes, then the dull thud of a heavy bolt, a couple of clicks for the other locks, and I am face to face with an icon.

Even surprised at home at this ungodly hour, she is nothing less than magnificent. A green and red silk kimono tied up negligently at the waist, her thick black hair hanging down over her shoulders, pearls in her ears, rings on her fingers, designer flesh, modest smile — "*Sawadee ka.*"

"Good morning, Fatima. Nice apartment."

"Please come in."

It is a duplex. A polished teak staircase leads to the bedrooms upstairs whilst the eye is drawn to the floor-to-ceiling windows with a magnificent view of the city.

43

Despite her impeccable postures, I have a sense that the shell has cracked. Smiles, frowns, hand gestures—fragments of personality—come and go, as if dredged up from memory, whilst something quite different, beyond the human, seems to control her. From time to time I think she is glaring at me, until I realize there is a total blackness behind the eyes when the postures fail.

"We met on a train to Chiang Mai. I probably don't have to tell you why I was going to Chiang Mai? I was twenty-seven and sick to death of the bar scene in Bangkok. The boys had mostly stopped dying of AIDS by then, but there was no romance left. The clients were mostly just pigs, white pigs. Gay white men on the rampage in Southeast Asia are not always the considerate type. I took the train up to Chiang Mai because the scene up there was supposed to be different. Everyone was so stoned on opium and heroin, so they said, you didn't really have to work at all. That's what I was, a bum boy, a creature without self-respect, a poor, skinny, ladylike thing with a dick, one of the world's lost, just dirt in the road. How could you be anything else, being half black and brought up here? Thais are the most racist people on earth, they despise Negroes. They even look down on pure-blooded Thais if they have dark skin. And look—I'm pretty brown.

"Being that kind of gay, I'd pampered myself and spent everything I had on a first-class ticket in a sleeper that was supposed to be all my own. I'm enjoying a cigarette and contemplating suicide for the thousandth time that year when the door opens and there he was, a magnificent black giant who I would never have taken for a soldier by the way he dressed and moved, except for one of those big round green bags soldiers carry. He looked about forty, which has always been my favorite age in a man, and of course, being black, how could I not make that connection to the father I've never met? Super fit. I thought: What a wonderful country America must be, that someone so black can grow up brimming with self-respect, nonchalant, with a sense of belonging, even amongst all those white people. Of course I gave him my most seductive smile, not expecting any result. He smiled back, though, said sorry for disturbing me, he'd booked the compartment next door. I said: 'That's okay, love, anytime.' Just like a whore. I thought that would be it, because he looked so straight, you know? Usually when you talk like that to a straight guy, it turns him off, even disgusts him. He gave me this big smile, though, and asked if he could sit down for a moment. My little heart starts on the big *thump-thump-thump*."

An inhalation. "I won't bore you with the gory details of Chiang Mai. God knows why a man like him was going there at all, except that it's on the tourist circuit. God knows why he's with me. He never admitted that I was his first, you know, but I can tell this is not really a gay. Let's be honest about this, there are all different shades, and men who love sex usually experiment at some stage in their lives. I think he was like that. I think he'd had women all his life and was at that stage of wondering if it's worth it, you know? Maybe that special something missing could be supplied by a man? I thought, Fair enough, I'm having the time of my life staying in a good hotel with the man of my dreams, when it ends I'll have nothing but wonderful memories, something to carry me forward into the next disaster. I can see he's not comfortable with me socially. To tell the truth, we never leave the room together. He would go out for a meal or a drink, I would go out separately. Socially, he's very very uptight. He's a marine, after all. He's going through quite a thing, but to my surprise he didn't dump me after the first night.

"Then, after five days, he gives me my marching orders. I say: 'Of course, darling, it's been wonderful for me, just wonderful, you're the best thing that ever happened to me. And by the way, can you help me out with ten thousand baht, I'm a little short of the readies?' We made that sordid little trip to the bank machine together, he hands me the cash in a dark alley and we walk off into our separate futures — or so I thought.

"Two days later, he came looking for me. He'd searched every gay bar in the town, and found me in the end, drowning my sorrows. That's when I knew something totally appalling was happening to this beautiful man. This giant stood there with tears in his eyes, looking at me across the floor. Of course, I would have done anything for him. Anything at all. If he'd said, Take this knife and cut your throat, I would have done it. You might say that it was a first for me too: love."

"But he never got used to you being a man?"

"No. Well, put it the other way: he never got used to him being queer. He held himself together for the first few weeks, but I could see it coming. I wondered what he was going to do with my poor body when he really started to break apart. Someone like me sees it all the time, it's a professional hazard: the middle-aged man who cannot admit what he is turning into, what he's doing. I wondered if he would have a fit and kill me with those magnificent muscles of his, not that I cared. It was as good a way to go as any. What for him was something squalid and nasty was the high point of my life. He was good to me, when he remembered what a generous-spirited American he was. And I simply adored him. He liked to smoke ganja and I would get some for him. Then the drinking started. I don't think he drank much before he met me, but soon he could get through a bottle of Mekong in an hour. It's like the song says: *hate myself for loving you*." A sigh. "I think he really did love me, at the beginning. I think I was a kind of liberation, in a way. After all, he'd been chasing pussy all his life and not gotten anything out of it. At least I understood him. I had testosterone of my own in those days, I knew how a man thinks. I've sort of lost that now. He never did beat me, though. Not once. Even his sex wasn't particularly — you know — over the top. He dominated, of course, but it was more like an emperor expecting to be worshiped than a sadist demanding obedience. I hoped that things would work out. After all, he kept talking about retirement, and he wanted to retire in Bangkok, so I thought, Why not *come out*? What have you got to lose? Spend the rest of your life in love and freedom. With me. I would have looked after him. My god, would I have looked after him. But of course, it never works out that way, does it? There's always something drags us down, just when we think we're being saved."

"Was he into jade at that time?"

"Oh the jade, the jade. Yes, he was into it. I think one of his retire-ment dreams had been to go into the gems trade. I think when he was in Yemen and all those other dreadful places, he fantasized about coming to Thailand and exporting gems and jade to the States. Perhaps making his own designs. My god, that's almost like me fantasizing about becoming a marine. I'm not an expert, but in my little opinion you don't get near the gems trade out here unless you're Chinese, or very well connected to the Chinese. I wasn't going to tell him that, of course. I helped him, with a sense of foreboding I must say."

"You helped him?"

"He needed an interpreter. He was talking to all sorts of people, including tribespeople from up in the hills and including my own people, the Karen. So I was very useful. I translated into Thai and into Karen and back again into English. I had this bar-boy English at that time, nothing like as good as I speak it now. I have him to thank for that.

"We even got as far as buying a couple of lumps of jade and having them worked into little trinkets by some craftsmen in Chinatown. I had to tell him in the end they were laughing at us. The jade he'd bought was third rate, and his designs were sort of—well, not exactly world class. That penis on the web page was the best thing he did. He modeled it after his own, of course. Even I started wondering where his head was, that he thought starting a web page with a whacking great cock on it was going to change his life. Funnily enough, I think that web page was his way of coming out, his way of finally telling the world what he was: a beautiful, perfectly formed cock.

"Then things started to fall apart. He'd borrowed quite a lot of money to buy the jade and have it worked. I thought he would have borrowed from a bank or something, it didn't occur to me until it was too late that he'd borrowed from Chiu Chow loan sharks. I mean, how dumb can you get? Did he think he'd get special protection because he was a marine? Did he think the President of the United States would send an aircraft carrier if he got into trouble with the sharks? He had that very naïve streak, you see. A blind spot, I suppose you would call it. Perhaps it was from being in the Marines all those years, there were things in front of his eyes on the street he just did not see. That's when his drinking and his ganja smoking started to get out of hand. He had to get a medical certificate a couple of times because he wasn't fit for work. He was terrified of random drug tests. That's also when he started into me, telling me I'd destroyed his life, calling me all the names a bum-boy gets called when his man starts to freak. Even then, I have to tell you he never hit me. I don't think that he was a violent man by nature. Not until someone turned him violent. But I didn't know that at the time. All I knew was my luck was as bad as ever. Even though it wasn't my fault, I'd sort of brought bad luck to this man I loved. I made him pray with me. I was Christian, he was brought up a Christian—at first he didn't understand that someone like me can be a believer. So we prayed and somehow I think that might have made things go from bad to worse."

"How so?"

"Because he really got into the praying, and bought a Bible and started preaching to me about salvation. He would go on for hours, usually after he'd had a bottle of Mekong, and I used to sit at his feet and murmur adoring approval. It was like those American preachers you see on the TV sometimes, all emotion and intensity and certainty about God's grace. We Karen are religious groupies, we love everyone's God, we've had more missionaries over the years than you can count: all kinds of Christians, Buddhists, Muslims. We take them all in, believe every word and never bother about the contradictions. So I was a perfect audience for him. We would reach this peak a few times a week, after ganja and whisky, when we were certain that the doors of heaven were about to open and we would walk right in. You have to bear in mind that he was under a lot of pressure. The loan sharks were closing in. They didn't want to kill him, of course, but they were charging twenty percent a month and at that rate things get on top of you very quickly. He would get these three-in-the-morning telephone calls and the guy's English would be so bad I'd have to take the phone and have him make his threats in Thai so I could translate. It was the usual stuff, you know, what they would do to his body, his face—especially his face. They're not stupid, those people, they know a person's weakness."

"And at this time, you were still . . ."

"Still a man? Oh yes. My change came later. I would say that we decided I would start to take the estrogen together, it was a family decision which popped up quite casually. We were in bed one night, drunk, and he was caressing me and I asked him if he would like me to have tits. I don't think it had occurred to him before. He sort of jumped a bit. Maybe he saw it as a solution to at least one of his problems. If he turned me into a woman he could claim not to be queer, couldn't he? But that wasn't what

I'd had in mind. I was just suggesting the estrogen as a sort of—you know?"

"Sexual adjunct?"

"Exactly. So I got hold of some local stuff and, lo and behold, the tits start to grow. The effect on him was weird. I mean, he started obsessing about making changes to my body. I said, 'Sweetheart, I'm starting to feel like a lump of jade that's being worked on.' He laughed, but it was true. And the funny thing was that at that time, everything seemed to change for the better. He told me he'd been contacted by someone very very big in the gems trade in America and it looked like a little real business would be coming his way. Nothing big to start with, but at least there was light. And this jeweler—he never told me his name in the early days—was going to pay off Bill's debts. Boy, I mean, it was just like the clouds lifted all at once, all thanks to this big shot from America, this jeweler, who I never met until much later, but who would come to Krung Thep once a month on business and he and Bill would go somewhere—to this guy's hotel I guess—to talk business all night."

"All night?"

"That's right. I had my suspicions. I mean, it's pretty standard that someone comes from the West or Japan on a business trip and expects to be entertained in the Bangkok tradition when the talking's over. I didn't really mind. I even thought it might be healthy in a way. I mean, from what he said this jeweler seemed to like women and I thought if Bill is doing a little pussy-chasing just for form, it's probably what he needs. He was still pretty freaked out about having a serious affair with a man. Maybe he needed the balance. Anyway, the jeweler had become our number one man and anything he wanted he had to have. At the same time, all kinds of stuff started appearing in our house. Silverware, ceramics, local craft products, things which I thought were priceless in my ignorance of those days, but which turned out to be just leftover junk from the jeweler's warehouse."

"They went to the bars together?"

"I don't know about that. This guy was so big, so rich, I got the feeling they would party with some hired flesh, you know, the most expensive kind, right there in his hotel suite. Bill mentioned a Russian pimp and some Siberian women."

"How did Bill seem after those sessions?"

"At first he was kind of amused. He would say that this guy, who was so respectable, who met presidents, who knew senators and members of Parliament, was really quite a swinger. He didn't say more than that to save my feelings. Quite a swinger. Then one time he stayed away three days and when he came back he was a different man."

"Different?"

Silence.

"Totally different. He'd lost his soul. He even admitted it. He got drunk, smoked some ganja and started tearing up his Bible. He says: 'I prayed for grace and salvation, but they sent me the devil. So now we work for the devil. Maybe there's only the devil, maybe all the other nonsense is kid stuff. That's what the man told me. Kid stuff.' He looked at me when he said that. He looked at me and carried on tearing up the Bible."

"And that's when you started on the estradiol?"

"That's when my transformation went high tech. Estradiol. Computer programs, medical dictionaries, specialist news groups on the Web."

"And Dr. Surichai?"

"And after a few months, yes, Dr. Surichai. I'm watching Bill every day playing with this computer stuff with—you know—diagrams, color pictures of the anatomy of a man and a woman, and he can move the bits around, cut off this, add this, and I'm standing behind him adoring him with my arms around his neck saying: 'Yes, darling, let's give me tits like that, anything you like. You can have three tits and two pussies if you want, anything, anything.' "

"You were being designed?"

"That's right, I was being designed. What did I care? I was just so flattered, you know, that my man is obsessing about me. Who wouldn't be? I didn't care if he'd turned into the devil. What did God ever do for me?" A quick flash of those large black eyes. "What you have to appreciate, darling, is the change in me. It was as if I was born and brought up in hell, then suddenly transported to heaven. I found love, a home, a sense of belonging, for the first time ever. Somehow I think I see in your eyes you know what I'm talking about, no?"

"Yes."

"And when you experience that kind of transformation, you're walking on air. You really can't believe your luck."

"But you knew you didn't fit the usual profile of a transsexual? You didn't believe yourself to be a woman trapped in a man's body?"

"That crap? That's what *farangs* get all hung up on. Here in Krung

Thep we already have designer bodies—the boys on the street will cut anything off, add anything on, take any kind of drugs. We are the future, darling. The *farangs* will catch up. You'll see, they'll soon drop all that psychological caring stuff once they see how much money is in it."

"But you must have thought about it, that at a crucial moment the man with the knife was going to cut everything off?"

A shrug. "Not really. I was doing it for love, darling. You're a child of the street, you must know what it means to have nothing to lose? And it wasn't really a loss. He turned me into a goddess."

I switch the recorder off. In my mind echoes Dr. Surichai's question: *What is a transsexual? A medieval eunuch pumped full of estrogen?* Did Fatima ask herself that very question now and then, in her down moments? I switch the recorder back on.

"But you didn't make any connection with the jeweler?"

"No, except that that was where the money was coming from at first. Then Bill used the jeweler's contacts to get into the *yaa baa* trade, and that was where the money was supposed to be coming from after that. But you know, there wasn't much time, suddenly, to worry about anything. I'm taking the drugs, going to see the doctor, Bill's obsessing about my throat, the Adam's apple thing and what my voice is going to be like— even the whole devil thing just faded into the background after a while. I think Bill just put it into the back of his mind what he'd agreed with the jeweler."

"When did you find out?"

"Well, Bill wasn't doing as well as he expected with his *yaa baa*. The shipment came about every two months. We would go to the domestic airport to collect it. I went with him just in case there was a problem that needed a translator—his Thai never did get beyond the beginner stage. The stuff was sent by some Burmese army general who paid off everyone on the border, and a local syndicate. All Bill had to do was move it from the airport to the squatters under the bridge. They're Karen and have strong connections to the people in the jungle on the border. The syndicate didn't really need Bill except for that one link from the airport to Dao Phrya Bridge. It would have looked strange if a Karen squatter turned up to collect a big shiny steamer trunk every few months, but an American in a Mercedes sort of went with the trunk. But Bill's contribution was not exactly crucial and he wasn't indispensable, so he didn't get paid that well. I didn't know this until quite recently, that he wasn't getting that much money out of the *yaa baa* thing, despite the risk. I mean, if he'd gotten caught they would have put him in Bang Kwan for life, wouldn't they?"

"Probably. He would have been transferred to the States after five years, but he would have had to do time there as well. He was running a big risk."

"That's right, that's what I told him, a big risk for small bucks. I'm trying to be the good wise wife at this stage. I'm also getting curious. Dr. Surichai and his hospital do not come cheap, and if the *yaa baa* isn't paying that well, and the little bits and pieces he's doing for the jeweler aren't paying that well either, where's the money coming from?"

"Did you have suspicions?"

"Not of what was really going on, no. I knew there was a whole side to Bill that I didn't know about, but I had no idea what that was. For a while I really wondered if he was serious about the jeweler being the devil, or a devil worshiper, you know, if there was some kind of black magic they were into. I even wondered if Bill was blackmailing him. I asked him outright a few times, Where are you getting the money for the medicines, Dr. Surichai, the hospital, all that? He would tell me not to worry about it, the money was there."

"But you did find out, somehow?"

Silence. She is sitting on a sofa, I'm sitting in a large armchair.

"You think I killed him, darling?"

"I know you did."

"Little me? How on earth would I manage with all those snakes? Be real, Detective, it would have taken an army of experts."

Then she stands up, exactly as a woman would, elegantly and with an erotic intonation in the way she twists her buttocks, which really does seem to be unconscious. In the silence I have to admit it's eerie just how perfectly the operation seems to have worked in her case. No wonder Dr. Surichai is so proud of himself. It is only from this angle, looking almost directly up at her neck, that I can see the tiny scar he talked about. I stand up and she escorts me to the door. The idea of killing her is ridiculous at this moment. I am under her spell and she knows it. She cocks her head slightly. In a whisper: "Not going to kill me today?" The question takes me by surprise because I'm sure she read my thoughts. She leans toward me. "Let me kill the jeweler for you, then you can do what you like with me. What do I care?" Suddenly holding my chin and staring into my eyes. "You're an *arhat*, why ruin your karma on a senseless vendetta? The world needs you. Let a devil do your killing."

I try to move but she holds my shirtsleeve in a hand suddenly turned into a claw. "The first time you saw me, in the shop, you knew, didn't you? I'm the other half of what you are, darling, if one of us is in the world, so must the other be. I'm your dark side. I think you realize that. Kill me if you like, but then you kill yourself."

She opens the door and suddenly I'm outside again, between the Chinese door gods. There is no time to ask her about the apartment, which she bought outright in her own name according to the clerk in the Lands Department, or the priceless furnishings. The cost of the penthouse was twenty million baht, or half a million dollars, but the jade collection—on display on a Chinese temple table in polished blackwood—would have been worth more than that. Then there were all the other artifacts from Warren's shop, artistically placed on pedestals, antique tables, or just left on the floor where one might easily kick them by accident if one were not careful.

I am left thinking how easy it would have been to kill her. The thought that I may have failed Pichai threatens to depress me. It is only counterbalanced by the opposite possibility, that she has charmed him too.

44

Yesterday my mother sent a messenger to the station with samples, for the Colonel and me, of the new T-shirts and tank tops she has designed. The motif is identical in both cases: under the main legend in burning scarlet—THE OLD MAN'S CLUB—the subtext in black italics: *Rods of Iron*. She employed a professional cartoonist to produce a convincing caricature of senior prurience: stooped but muscular, bald but sprouting pubic hair from his chin, tongue hanging out. The Colonel sent for me to ask what I think. Filial loyalty (read: a childhood of relentless brainwashing and emotional blackmail of the lowest kind) obliges me to opine that it is the work of genius.

He takes the T-shirt in both hands and presses it against me. I have to hold it up as he stands back. "*Farangs* go for this sort of thing? It's so . . . so ugly."

"It's the way they are. If you give them a traditional Thai men's club they'll be intimidated."

"Really?" For a moment he stands confused, stranded in an alien psychology. "It's not important that some of the customers will actually look like that?"

"That's the point. It makes them feel more secure."

A slow nod of understanding, or at least acceptance. "By the way, your mother and I are giving you ten percent of the shares in the business. She wants you in as a family member, and I can see the advantage of not having you passing heavy judgments on us when you go through one of your devout phases."

"I'm afraid I cannot accept. Making money out of women in that way is expressly forbidden by the Buddha."

"So is smoking dope. Anyway, I'm ordering you. Disobeying a superior is also proscribed from the Eightfold Path."

"Then I accept."

I take off the T-shirt and fold it on his table. He unfolds it to take one more look, then, reassured—if aesthetically challenged—the Colonel nods and lets me go. After all, Mother is the one who took the *WSJ* course on the Net. When I reach the door, he calls to me. "Sorry, I forgot. This fax came through from the American embassy a couple of days ago. It's just one of those dumb profiling things they do in Quantico. I had it translated into Thai, but it's the usual crap. Stuff you would know just by thinking about it."

I find a quiet corner of the station. The profile is only three pages long and surprisingly free of technical jargon.

Report from the Department of Criminal Profiling,
Federal Bureau of Investigation, Quantico, Virginia

Category of document: Confidential, for distribution only to interested parties (permission is granted for this report to be shared with the Royal Thai Police)
Subject: Fatima, a.k.a. Ussiri Thanya, a transsexual who underwent gender reassignment in her late twenties, born and brought up in Thailand. Father an unidentified African American serviceman (probably a draftee during the Vietnam War); mother a prostitute of tribal origin in northwest Thailand, a member of the large Karen group who reside in the border areas. Within the Thai tradition, the subject is believed to have been brought up by her grandmother in the tribal area on the border with Myanmar while her mother continued to work as a prostitute in Bangkok . . .

Just as Vikorn said, the report is nothing one could not work out for oneself. I skip to the last paragraph.

Save for those who experience a deep, personal and lifelong craving for gender reassignment, the long-term effect of surgical removal of the genitals is likely to be of the most appalling psychological devastation.

The subject's suspected reaction in murdering Bradley in an elaborate, sadistic and clever manner is entirely consistent with our expectations. However, it is highly unlikely that the subject's rage has been assuaged. She turned Bradley into a savior figure, the only human being who differed sufficiently from the others to the extent of being basically benevolent. To him she sacrificed the only possessions to which the world apparently attached value: her genitals. With her betrayal by Bradley she would most likely have ceased to be capable of trust in any form. If to date her behavior (absent the murder of Bradley) has been relatively normal, we believe that she is simply acting from memory, or pursuing a plan of some kind which must be essentially sociopathic. The need to do to the world what the world did to her will be irresistible.

45

The Correctional Services and Immigration Departments collude to keep a foreigner in quarantine the moment he is released from prison, pending bundling him on a flight back to his own country. The reasons are unclear, for why would a *farang* ex-con be more of a threat to society than the hundreds of Thais who are released from jail every week? The rule is strict, though, and no amount of arguing and pleading on my part gained me access to Fritz while he waited in the Immigration building for the bureaucrats to arrange his ticket. The best I could do was to ascertain that he would be on the next Lufthansa flight to Berlin, which left at ten in the evening. Even at the airport he was fenced in by Immigration officials and police.

In a fake Armani jacket, his remaining tufts of hair carefully shaved, prison tattoos on his neck, and in white pants, he could have been just another middle-aged tourist trying to be hip in Krung Thep, except for the large Band-Aid above his left ear and the walking stick. He saw me coming long before his minders did, but instantly looked away with that prison reflex. I had to use my influence to follow him airside, where the Immigration people decided their duties were completed and disappeared. Close up, I saw how strange and brand new the world now appeared to him. I was put in mind of a creature with lightning reflexes and restless habits, perhaps a sable or a mink, panicked and fascinated by the straight lines and smooth surfaces of the human world. He sat next to me on a bench near the gate where his flight would board and his eyes scanned while he spoke: "The operation at Dao Phrya Bridge is officially moonshine. Only a few of the squatters know about the *yaa baa*. The headman uses the contacts they made for the moonshine to distribute the meth. After all, if you can metabolize that rice whisky you can probably handle *yaa baa*. They're major distributors in Bangkok and they're run by a real big shot."

"Who?"

"A cop of course. A police colonel."

"Did you get a name?"

"Vikorn."

"You're sure?"

"If the information wasn't accurate they wouldn't have needed to beat me so much, would they?"

"I guess not. Nobody mentioned Suvit? The squatters are in his district."

"No. Vikorn was the name. The way I heard it, he runs a very big operation. The squatters are only a small part of it. Maybe this Suvit works for him?"

"Anyone talk to you about the way the marine was murdered? How it was done?"

"No one knows how those snakes were organized so well, but everyone knows it was that *katoy*, the ladyboy, who did it."

"How are they so sure?"

"She was seen by one of the squatters. Some Khmer on motorbikes met the Mercedes before it drove down to that slip road. Maybe they were summoned by cell phone. The marine hardly spoke Thai, so he wouldn't have known even if she said: 'Come kill the bastard now.' She was seen going off with one of them. They actually escorted the marine down that slip road—they had guns, so probably the marine didn't dare open the door even if he could."

I shake my head. "It doesn't make sense. If the point was to kill him, why not just shoot him?"

Fritz in turn shakes *his* head. "To answer that question, just spend a few months in a Thai jail. Death is just too ordinary for most vendettas—the point is to maximize the terror."

His scanning eyes saw from a monitor that his flight was boarding. He held out a hand for me to shake. Our eyes locked. He looked away. "You're better than me. I shat on you and your mother and you saved my life. I wouldn't have bothered, but thank you. When you go to the Buddha you can tell him you cured a German of his racist superiority complex. From the bottom of my black heart, thank you" were the last words I heard Fritz utter. I left him to return to the departure lounge.

One should not exaggerate, at least two-thirds of the people waiting for flights were normal couples, singles, families: Western, Japanese, Chinese, Indian, African. The other third consisted of Western men usually over forty-five with Thai girls invariably under thirty. What we don't realize, we Thais, is just how simple life is in the West. Too simple. The most modest of contributions—a forty-hour week at the least demanding of mechanized tasks—earns one a car, an apartment, a bank account. Other gifts of the system—a spouse, a child or two, a small collection of friends—arrive automatically and gift-wrapped with support of every kind. A whole hemisphere, in other words, lies dying from event-starvation. It must be a subconscious demographic drive that sends these men to us; each one of those beauties hanging on their arms is a time bomb of demonic complications and explosive events. Hey, let's hear it for Thai Girl, selflessly taking her message of love, life and lust to a jaded world!

Complications come naturally to us, we are never without them, like our traffic jams. Like Vikorn. If only one could package him for export.

46

Last night the FBI invited me to supper at the Italian riverside restaurant at the Oriental hotel. With great compassion she told me not to dress up. She wore a generic pair of white linen shorts, open-neck white short-sleeved shirt, open sandals: simplicity itself, I gratefully observed. I ordered antipasto misto and calf's liver to follow. She copied me with the antipasto and ordered a baked lasagna for herself. When the waiter came with the wine list she gave it to me, because I had told her about Truffaut and his meticulous education of my palate. I ordered a simple Barolo and made a great fuss of holding the glass to my nose, sipping decorously, then chasing the wine round my mouth with my tongue, while the wine waiter—a Thai—stared at me, before I gave Kimberley a big wink and knocked the wine back with a vulgar gulp. It was only a Barolo after all. We both realized that this was the first time I had made her guffaw, a dangerous moment in the ritual of seduction. I am ashamed to admit I did not turn off the charm as resolutely as I ought to have done, and she muttered darkly about my being too damn cute for words. I was asking for trouble.

"Sonchai, why do you hate me?"

"I don't."

"But you pretend not to find me attractive? A stupid woman would decide you were gay—lots of women protect their egos that way—but I'm not stupid. You're not gay, sometimes you're attracted, at least on a physical level, but you veer away. Time after time. Like a wild animal that sees a trap. I'm curious."

I cast my eye over the other patrons. Three middle-aged Western couples who were probably staying at the hotel, and at least four tables consisting of a young Western man and a Thai girl. What a good life we must offer to any young *farang* with a little money. An evening spent trawling the bars will secure you that beautiful young goddess of your dreams for as long as you care to rent her, and you may play out a romantic evening or two with her in an expensive restaurant under the stars with the certainty of bedding her afterwards. And all without petulance or temperament, or obligations which stretch into the future. Tip her well and she will even come to say goodbye to you at the airport. Love à la carte must surely be an improvement on the fixed menu?

"I don't want to feel like an ice cream."

"Huh?"

"Look at them." I wave a hand at the other tables. "Those girls don't speak English as well as I do. They don't surf the Net. They've probably never been abroad. They don't realize they're a new flavor from Häagen-Dazs. Anyway, they're professionals."

Jones swallows hard. I feel sorry that I've brought her close to tears. She's tough, though. "That's how you see me? Another Western sleaze-bag, just like the *farang* men?"

I don't say anything for a beat or two. Then: "No one escapes their own culture. It's hardwired in us, from birth onward. A consumer society is a consumer society. It may start with washing machines and air-conditioning, but sooner or later we consume each other. It's happening to us too. But you see, the Buddha taught freedom from appetite."

"Him again." A sigh. Now she is determined not to let me off the hook by changing the subject, or even talking at all. I start to grin. "What are you laughing at?"

"The beauty of the Buddha. Look how perfectly he described cause and effect. Your ego is injured, so you won't talk to me. Perhaps I will retaliate by not talking to you. Then we become enemies. If we had guns perhaps we would shoot each other, over and over again, in lifetime after lifetime. Don't you see how futile it all is?" I've made her unhappy, far more than I expected. It is as if I've kicked her in the pit of her stomach, just when she was offering love. A crime against life. "Kimberley—"

"Don't."

"Kimberley, when my mother was sixteen years old she offered herself to a mamasan she'd been introduced to in Pat Pong. Nobody forced her to do so, her parents were not those kind of people. Nobody was going to stop her, though—they were dirt poor. The mamasan put her on display at her club every night, but postponed selling her until a good offer came up. Virginity is supposed to be most highly prized by Japanese and other Asian men, but the highest bid in my mother's case came from an Englishman in his forties. There are plenty of men who would under-stand the special pleasure in deflowering a child, but I don't. He paid forty thousand baht, an astronomical sum. My mother insisted that her best friend accompany her so she would not feel so terribly alone. The friend sat in the toilet while the event took place. He was kind to her, in a man-ner of speaking. He used a lubricant, tried not to hurt her too much, and burst into tears when it was over. My mother and her friend stared with great wonderment at this man who was more than twice their age. As the Third World said to the First World: If it makes you feel so bad, why do you do it? They felt sorry for him. It was my mother's blood on the sheets, but the agony was all his. He did not appear to be rich, so he must have saved up. Forty thousand baht was a lot of money, even for a Westerner. It was a very special occasion for him, a kind of feast. Perhaps it was his birthday. When we are in the grip of hunger we think only of eating. Then, when the banquet is over, we see the evidence of what we really are."

Something is happening behind her eyes. I wonder if I've succeeded in reaching her latent Buddhahood. A Thai woman would simply have thrown a tantrum and walked out, but there is American Will here, that grim hanging on.

Quietly: "You've never slept with a Western woman?"

"No."

"If you did, you would be that virgin on the bed, being raped by a pig?"

"She wasn't raped. She knew what she was doing. She was proud that she commanded such a good price. Of course, she gave almost all of it to her family. That's what innocence looks like over here."

"The legal age is eighteen in this country. In the States it would have been statutory rape. He could have been sent away for twenty years." A long silence during which the atmosphere freezes and I realize how naïve I'm being. No latent Buddhahood in the FBI, merely the cold fury of a

will deflected, an appetite frustrated: no ice cream in the fridge tonight:
damn.

"Did you ever think your meditation might not be such an asset in the
craft of detection?"

"How so?"

"Naïveté. A luxury no cop can afford, frankly. The way you see it,
Warren, Bradley, what they did to Fatima, what they did to the Russian
whore—what they planned to do to a bunch of other boys and women,
that's peculiarly Western, isn't it?" The expression on my face says: *Yes,
obviously*. "That kind of existential crime without meaning, without profit
motive, has to be just an extension of Western self-indulgence, doesn't it?
A variation on the theme of the guy who raped your mom? Let's get the
bill, I wanted us to eat here tonight for a reason. Let's say it's reality sand-
wich time for both of us."

She makes no attempt to extract the arrogance from the gesture when
she calls for the bill. She pays with a gold AmEx card and I follow almost
at a trot as she strides across the floor, leading me around by the pool
between great mountains of bougainvillea, crimson hibiscus nodding in
the evening breeze. We wind up at the Bamboo Bar, the hotel's famous
jazz venue. Jones checks her watch before leading me inside. She asks the
maître d' for a discreet table for two near the window. The seats are woven
wicker with luxurious cushions, the air-conditioning glacial, the mar-
garitas perfect with viscous ice, salt glittering around the rim of wide
glasses, generous shots of tequila. We are just in time for the first act. The
maître d' anounces "the incomparable, the spectacular, the truly magnificent Black Orchid." Enthusiastic clapping from the old hands in the audience, the small band plays a couple of bars and she walks on.

The song had to be "Bye Bye Blackbird," didn't it? Corny perhaps, but
wonderful, too, with a depth of melancholy I've never heard before. I
wouldn't have guessed she could even sing like a woman. Jones is enjoying the shock on my face.

"She's not bad. Not a professional of course, and jazz outside the
States is always a bit of a disappointment, but she's not bad."

I realize that Jones is deaf to a specific quality in Fatima's voice. Let's
call it heart: *build the fire, light the light, I'll be home late tonight, blackbird, bye bye*.

Let's *not* call it heart. The sound she is making is the sound hearts
make after they're in pieces and the fragments dissolve into the over-

whelming sadness of the universe. The power to hear it may be the only privilege of the thoroughly dispossessed. "No," I say, and sip the margarita, "not as good as an American, but not bad."

"Now look to your left at about ten o'clock. Don't move your head, just your eyes."

"I already saw them." Warren and—a triumph for Jones to judge by the expression on her face—Vikorn. She doesn't know that the short dapper Thai man sitting with them is Dr. Surichai until I tell her. Together the threee of them make a half-moon around a large round table. They are all absorbed by Fatima and have no inclination to look behind them, but the diva in the long purple silk gown and heavy pearl necklace glances in our direction. Our eyes meet for a moment and she misses a beat. Not a professional at all. She recovers quickly and the band covers her mistake, but not before that total blackness has intervened behind her eyes. A few seconds later and she's got a better idea. She cocks her head slightly to one side and engages my eyes mercilessly while she sings: *No one there to help or understand me, oh what hard-luck stories they all hand me* . . .

"I want to go," I tell Jones, sounding just like a girl who is out too late and—I'm afraid—covering a single sob by leaning over and coughing. We wait until Fatima has finished her song, when the clapping masks the noise of our departure.

"Pretty well as soon as Kennedy decided to send military advisers to Laos, the CIA realized they had a problem," Jones explains in the back of the cab. "It was the CIA who ran the war there, by the way, from beginning to end. The problem was the opium. When the French ran Indochina it didn't bother them at all, they ran it as a state monopoly, complete with bonded warehouses in Vientiane and Saigon. When America got involved the obvious knee-jerk reaction was: no more opium. Just like us to try to reinvent the wheel, right? That noble idea lasted maybe ten minutes and here's why. The Laotian armed forces had this unique characteristic: they didn't fight. Not anyone, anywhere, anytime, and most of all they didn't fight the North Vietnamese regular army, which scared the shit out of them. The only people who would fight were the Hmong, the indigenous mountain tribe up in the north, whom the Laotians were happy to see annihilated by Ho Chi Minh. Americans like guts, we love to fight and we love fighters, and the Hmong were that. They became the CIA's favorite exotic pets, but the drawback was they depended entirely on the opium crop to survive. Of course, the French would have explained all this to us if we'd asked them, but—well, we were Americans, weren't we? The only answer, though, was to help the Hmong sell their opium. Being fantastic hypocrites—like all masked avengers—we didn't want to get our hands dirty. The Agency tried to keep its involvement to a minimum. Basically they would use anyone they could disown afterwards. They preferred non-Americans. Your Colonel was hardly more than a kid at the time, but he caught on real quick. Coming from Udon Thani, he also spoke Laotian fluently, so after he'd done a stint as short-order chef he got the job of organizing the Hmong's crop up in the mountains and getting it to the airstrips. With the Hmong you have to realize we're talking Stone Age—people whose idea of commerce was trading pigs for wives. Vikorn was fine up there in the hills, but even he wasn't that sophisticated when it came to dealing with the Chinese. It was the Chinese traders—specifically the Chiu Chow clan, who originate in Swatow—who brokered the product when it reached the cities. *Of course.* The Chiu Chow are the finest businesspeople in the world, then, now, and for maybe a thousand years past. They run this country—hell, they practically run the Pacific Rim. The Agency didn't want to be in the business at all, but they had to accept that since they were in it, it was in their interests to make sure the Hmong didn't get too burned. They needed a dealer who was a match for the Chiu Chow."

"Warren."

"Sylvester Warren was born to a theatrical couple in Boston. They were the usual alcoholic narcissists who started to fade early in life. The only way they could deal with the responsibilities of parenting was to employ a Chinese maid on a minimum wage. A Chiu Chow girl from Swatow who hardly spoke English. As the parents faded out altogether, she took over the house. She ran everything, including Sylvester's education, which took on a very Chinese flavor. To survive at all the kid had to learn Chiu Chow, and this fascinated the other Chinese from Swatow who were living in Boston and particularly New York. They saw a low-risk investment. Warren has been involved with them all his life. They funded his gemology degree, set him up in his first businesses and loaned him as much money as he wanted. The price he paid was to belong to them body and soul. When the CIA found out about him he was already in the jade trade, importing into the States with a shop in Manhattan. They didn't worry too much about conflict of interest. On paper he looked like the perfect broker for the Hmong's opium when it reached Saigon and Vientiane. As a matter of fact, he didn't do too badly by the Hmong. He got halfway decent prices for their opium. At the same time he did exactly what Vikorn did. He built up connections in the Agency, and just in case the Agency should become useful in later life or—just as likely—decide to double-cross him, he collected a body of evidence showing how the heroin epidemic on the streets of New York during the sixties and seventies was largely thanks to the CIA's helping the Hmong sell their crop. I guess he and Vikorn didn't meet more than once a month, but they talked over the field radio a lot. Vikorn wouldn't learn English, so Warren, who is one of those people who can learn any language in a month, made a point of learning Thai. Vikorn has been in awe of him all his adult life. Warren did what Vikorn did, but he did it bigger and better and for a lot more money—just like a Yank is supposed to. For every million Vikorn made out of the opium, Warren made ten, but more important than that, Warren's connections in the CIA and the Bureau go all the way to the top. You didn't really think it was money alone that got him all that influence, did you?"

We're turning into Wireless Road now, on the way to the Hilton. I wonder what is going to happen next when I say: "Why didn't you tell me before?"

"Because I wasn't going to pop your naïveté until you popped mine. I kinda liked that medieval loyalty you have for your Colonel—says a lot for your heart, but not much for your head. No money no honey, isn't that what your ma always told you?"

"Fuck you." As she's getting out of the cab, I say: "Surichai? What was he doing there tonight?"

An elaborate raising of the hands and shoulders. "Did I say I knew everything?" Then: "Want me to pay for the cab, or can you manage?" Poking her head back into the car, almost going nose to nose with me: "Warren's winning, by the way. He'll have me out of here in a week or less. I'll be out of your hair."

I am in the back of the cab, racing through the night; the shock of Vikorn socializing with Warren and Surichai, of Fatima singing in a jazz club, is slowly eclipsed by a shock of my own making. I've never told the story of my mother's first sale of her body before, never really taken it out from that secret, painful place where it resides in my heart. It wasn't

Nong who told me, but Pichai. The friend who sat in the toilet was Wanna, Pichai's mother, who must have told her son, who whispered the story to me one dark night up in the monastery, when the future seemed nonexistent.

What is shocking is the way the story has marked me without my realizing it, and Jones' effortless reading of me: yes, that must be why I've never slept with a *farang* woman. If I didn't know that about myself, what else don't I know?

When I reach my room I call Jones. She is half asleep, surprised to hear from me and intrigued by the tremor in my voice. "According to the principles of profiling, how long has Fatima got?"

"Before she flips completely you mean? There's no way of knowing that. Profiling is like predicting share prices. You know what the market will do eventually, but you never know when. A day, a month, a year—who knows? Why is it suddenly so important?"

"Surichai," I say, and hang up.

There was something else too—something to which only a Thai cop would have attached significance. A couple of tables removed from Vikorn's group: five well-dressed Chinese men in business suits. Vikorn must have been aware of them. Likewise Warren.

47

Professor Beckendorf, in volume 3 of his masterwork *Thai Culture Explained*, turns almost Thai himself in the final paragraph of chapter 29 ("Fate and Fatality in Modern Siam") in the way he lurches without warning into metaphysics:

> Whereas your average Westerner does all he can to direct and control his fate, the latter-day Thai is no closer to adopting this attitude to life than were his ancestors a hundred or two hundred years ago. If there is any aspect of modern Thai psychology which continues to accept *in toto* the Buddhist doctrine of karma (so close to that Islamic fatalism often expressed by the phrase: *It is written*) it is surely in the conviction that *que sera, sera*. At first glance such fatalism may seem backward, even perverse given the dazzling spectrum of weapons Westerners now have in their arsenal against the vicissitudes of life; but anyone who spends much time in the kingdom quickly finds themselves questioning the wisdom, and even the sincerity, of Western attitudes. When he has paid up his taxes, his life insurance, his medical insurance, accident insurance, retrained himself in the latest marketable

skills, saved for his kids' education, paid alimony, bought the house and car which his status absolutely requires he buy within the rules of his particular tribe, given up alcohol abuse, nicotine, extramarital sex and recreational drugs, spent his two-week vacation on some self-improving (but safe) adventure holiday, learned to be hypercareful of what he says to or does with members of the opposite sex, the average Westerner may—and often does—wonder where his life went. He may also—and invariably does—feel cheated when he discovers existentially that all the worrying and all the insurance payments have availed him not a jot or tittle in protecting him against fire, burglary, flood, earthquake, tornado, the sack, terrorist activity, or his spouse's precipitate desertion with the kids, the car and all the spare cash in the joint bank account. True enough, in a kingdom without safety nets a citizen may well be brutally flattened by accident or illness, where a Westerner might have bought himself a measure of protection, but in between the bumps a Thai still lives his life in a state of sublime insouciance. The standard Western observation is that the Thai is living in a fool's paradise. Perhaps, but might the Thai not reply that the Westerner has built himself a fool's hell?

One cannot help but feel sorry for Beckendorf, peeping out at us from between his books, wishing to god (or Buddha) he had the guts to drop out, take some *yaa baa*, go to a disco, pick up a girl and get laid. I don't know why he has popped into my mind as I ride a motorcycle taxi on my way back to Warren Fine Art in River City. As far as I know, Warren and Beckendorf have nothing in common; indeed, you might say they represent opposite ends of the *farang* spectrum, with Beckendorf the eternal student, naïve and credulous despite all his fine long words, and Warren the ultimate cynic. But they do both *belong* to the *farang* spectrum, both spend their lives looking over the wall a little wistfully, although wistful is not the first word that comes to mind when I think of Warren. Perhaps I'm trying to make sense of a telephone conversation last night at around midnight in which Warren invited me to come "check out my wares" this Sunday morning. There was something just a shade, well, *wistful* in the voice, almost shy, as if he had something personal to share which he had trouble putting into words. He even seemed on the point of blurting something out—again, not a word I would have expected to think of in his case—when Fatima came to his rescue and asked me in Thai, in her soft, husky tones, if I could make it for around 11 a.m. She made it clear that Kimberley Jones was not invited.

I called the FBI after I put the phone down on Fatima, and Kimberley made the same point she's been making for days: Why is Fatima working for Warren, after she killed Bradley? It simply doesn't fit with our hypothesis or Fatima's mind-set when I went to see her in her apartment. In fact, it's so out of whack with our suspicions that we've discussed twenty different theories which make Fatima a hit woman for Warren, but for the life of us we cannot come up with a reason why Warren would want to rub out Bradley. It doesn't fit with the FBI profiling exercise, it doesn't fit with Fatima's declared intention to kill Warren—it doesn't fit with anything. I'm not expecting a confession when I ride the escalator up to Warren Fine Art.

The shop is shut with the chain-link curtain down, but Fatima is in there dusting the six-foot wood sculpture of the Walking Buddha. She is wearing a pearl blouse, open at the neck, her large pearl necklace and Vietnamese black three-quarter-length silk pants. I stare at her between the links. She senses my eyes behind the glass, gives me a warm smile as if I'm an old friend, and presses a button to raise the chain-link. After I enter the shop she presses another button and the chain curtain descends again. She slips me a grin, which almost seems to say: Now we're all cozy.

"I thought you were fantastic the other night," I say with total sincerity. "I've never heard that song sung so well." She laughs modestly and makes a comic little flutter with her eyelashes.

While this has been going on the Khmer who owns the Uzi appeared from a side door. He is not wearing his gun at this moment but might as well be from his attitude. He leers at me and slouches against the back wall. Fatima picks up a telephone, dials a number. "Mr. Warren, Detective Jitpleecheep is here to see you," she says with the smile of a competent P.A. "He's in the warehouse," she tells me in Thai. "He'll be along in a minute. Can I get you something to drink? Green tea? Coke, whisky, beer?"

I shake my head. We keep locking eyes, for long seconds, then breaking the contact. I am uneasy and cannot understand the nature of this meeting, this morning, this day. When I get the chance I furtively try to meditate for a second to try to plumb the depths of what is going on, but I simply cannot read her or the Khmer. Everything is wrong, unnatural. I think that perhaps the Khmer is her jailer, that Warren has proof she killed Bradley and is using this and his Khmer bodyguards to control her and ultimately to use her as he intended from the start. I know this is Kimberley's favorite theory and it certainly seems to fit the facts, if not the atmosphere. The FBI has no patience for atmosphere, of course, and Kimberley is certain I'm being set up, perhaps Warren will have me killed with Vikorn's permission? I managed to enrage Kimberley with my indifference to this possibility. After I put the phone down on her I meditated with a joint and went to bed. Pichai was there, in my dreams, glowing and smiling.

Warren enters from the door at the end of the shop, followed by the second Khmer, who is wearing the Uzi. The American is wearing a gold paisley cravat, sleeveless cream cashmere sweater, navy superfine wool sports jacket, Zegna gray-green pants and Baker-Benje slip-ons which I find too beautiful to look at. He transfers his cigarette and jade holder to his left hand in order to shake mine with his right. His gray eyes search my own. As usual I cannot read him, his protective coating is impenetrable to my Third World sorcery. His face is just a little haggard, though, and his shaving this morning has been imperfect, leaving a line of stubble under the right side of his jaw. Close up I become convinced that his fragrance is from Joël Rosenthal, the jeweler at 14 Rue de Castiglione in Paris who launched his own perfumes, and I wonder if this is not perhaps some kind of reference: jeweler turned perfumer?

"Glad you could make it," Warren says with his usual charm, and actually makes me feel as if he is pleased to see me. I do no more than nod, however, and wait. Of course he understands perfectly, and with a facial expression which is almost a wink, if a weary one, he beckons for me to follow him across the shop to where the horse and rider is sitting on a shelf. He takes the piece down, holds it up to the light, then hands it to me. As with all jade, hefting it is a sensual experience, its weight belies the lightness of the artist's design. I know very little about precious stone, but an inner voice compels me to come out with an inspired observation, which I transform into somewhat stilted English: "The piece is so transfused with light it seems as if it might fly away at any moment, then when you hold it you realize it originates in the earth after all, that the weight, coldness and darkness of the earth are still somehow locked inside it, but that a magical power has caused it also to express the airiness of the spiritual world."

This is not at all the sort of thing I normally come out with, and for a moment I wonder if I have taken too much of a chance and gone too far. Warren is in an unusual mood, though, and my outrageously pretentious words, because inspired by the Buddha, have finally penetrated his shield. I've unbalanced him for a moment, during which he stares at me with the hostility of someone who has been found out, then he recovers, touches my arm with the tenderest of gestures (I believe I feel a slight shiver on his part as he does so) and takes the piece away from me.

"Bradley was having it copied for me," he explains. "I sent someone to get it back as I had a right to do—it's mine after all. I guess I sent the wrong guy, but you have to bear in mind that Bill had very recently been murdered. I had no idea what to expect at the house, so I sent someone who knew how to be rough. I'm sorry about your injury. If the scarring is bad, I'll have someone in the States take care of it." He is gazing into my eyes as he speaks and I experience a deep need coming from him. If I didn't know better I would think it a cry for help. His eyes are watery. Fatima and the two Khmer are watching us closely.

"Fatima told me that you and the FBI woman came here last week," he says, now fully recovered, while he replaces the piece on the shelf. "So I thought you and I should talk before the Bureau gets out of control again. You probably have no idea what price you pay for success in the land of the free. You become a sitting duck for every second-guessing bureaucrat who sees you as a vehicle for promotion. I've already got some people in Washington onto it, I don't expect that Special Agent Jones will be in the kingdom for very much longer."

While he is speaking he is leading me inexorably to the front of the shop and the window display, which is protected by a second, inner chain-mail curtain. At a pad on a wall he punches in a code, presses a button and this hardened steel curtain rises. It is exactly like watching a beautiful woman undress, only to be overwhelmed by the power of her nakedness. The ancient jade glows under the lights, and now for the first time, no doubt influenced by Warren's presence, I can see the genius which underlies many of the modern settings in silver and gold.

"These are all your ideas," I say. Now that I have glimpsed his spirit I can understand his art.

" 'Ideas' is right. I hardly do any detailed design anymore, I have people who are better at it than I am. But a craftsman is not necessarily an artist. He needs that something extra that only comes from the cold heart of the universe." A faint smile and he picks up a heavy jade necklace on a gold chain. The jade is worked into large balls about three-quarters of an inch in diameter. "It was Hutton's," he says matter-of-factly. "Actually it went round the whole circuit. Henry took it with him when he fled the Forbidden City, then sold it to Koo, who sold it to her best friend Edda Ciano. Edda sold it to poor Barbara, who sold it to me the year before she died. She was so doped up by then I could have had it for a dollar, but I gave her the market price."

Fatima has crossed the room to join us, apparently drawn by the necklace. He cocks an eyebrow at her, then reaches out to remove her pearls. I see great professionalism here, the suave hands which have adorned the bodies of queens and princesses with his creations. He handles the pearls as if he is handling her body—with infinite tenderness—places them on the velvet of the window display, then—with an unexpected gesture— gives me the jade necklace. It is heavy like a collection of miniature cannon- balls as I place it around Fatima's neck. An electric chaos of glances, eye-locks and turned cheeks as I step back to admire it: sex, money, para- noia and a thousand double bluffs crackle under the lights.

"Actually jade isn't really your color, my dear," Warren says, taking out his cigarette case, selecting one, tapping it gently, fitting it to his ciga- rette holder, lighting and inhaling and taking one pace back, as he must have with a thousand women. He has become impenetrable again and Fatima seems to experience a moment of fear. "Oh, it looks spectacular around your neck, because anything would, but nothing becomes you so well as pearl. What d'you think, Detective?"

I have to agree. The jade looks fine to me, but cannot deliver the shock of the pearls on her chocolate skin. When I replace them, I realize how I missed them, even for that brief moment. The effect is almost unique in that you never quite get used to it. Take your eyes away for a moment, then let them return to the object of contemplation, and it is as if you were experiencing the effect for the first time. Fatima smiles bril- liantly, fondles the jade necklace for a moment, looks into Warren's eyes.

The hand which removes the jade holder from his lips trembles slightly. "Okay," he says gruffly. "It's yours. Keep it. The detective will be my witness."

I allow my mouth to drop open, but Fatima seems not in the least sur- prised. She nods as if at a commonplace sort of homage, carries the neck- lace to the end of the store. I'm watching in disbelief as she pours it into a black Chanel handbag. Warren is watching me. "Surprised? Actually, she can have anything she wants. What would you like from the window, my dear? Something priceless? My whole Aladdin's cave is yours. I'll be the genie."

Fatima is holding the Chanel handbag close to her stomach. A dark look comes over her face and she merely shrugs. Warren stares at her across the room for a moment, grunts, then reaches into the window to pick up the white tiger. He holds it up for me to look at and I have the uncanny feeling that he heard Kimberley when she admired it and explained it to me. *To anyone who knows anything, it's as intimidating as hell.*

"I want to take you downstairs to the warehouse," he says, handing me the tiger. I almost drop it in my astonishment that he should entrust such an icon to my hands and I believe I flashed him a look of fear. He smiles, I think in appreciation of my reverence. Immediately, I begin to wonder . . . "Oh, it's real all right," he says, reading my thoughts.

Holding the tiger in both arms like a mother, I follow him to the back of the shop, and under the eyes of the two Khmer and Fatima we walk out the back door, which I now see leads nowhere except to a single elevator which appears to have the hardened steel adornments of a bank vault. Only the hum of the Mitsubishi electric motor breaks the silence. Now Warren and I are alone in the lift, ignoring each other's eyes as people do in such close quarters, unless they are conspirators or lovers. Warren and I are neither, of course, which makes me wonder why I sense a frustrated longing on his part, a yearning, a silent pleading, even. We seem to descend to the bowels of the earth. The journey takes longer than I expected; his warehouse must lie under the lowest of the car park levels.

"This is it—the real shopwindow, you might say. Professional buyers don't bother too much with what I have upstairs. I wouldn't put it there if I didn't know I could sell it to some fool sooner or later for an inflated price. Down here, though, is where a real connoisseur might find a bargain or two. Beauty is a great mountain, Detective, and fashion only illuminates one face at a time. Sooner or later another side starts to get the attention and, bingo, the hoarder makes his killing. Hoarders are the toughest people to sell to, but also the most fun." An intense penetration of my brain by those gray eyes. "The greatest pleasure in life is to be understood, is it not? But who in the world does an artist like you or me find to understand us?"

I am about to protest, but decide instead to give the great vaulted cellar my full attention. It is far larger than anything I would have imagined from the shop, and charmingly chaotic. I calculate it must be perhaps half the size of the car parking area, with aisles running longitudinally from front to back.

"The mind cannot take in such treasures," I say in Thai, the proper language of reverence.

"Let me help," he says with a smile. I cannot understand why he should be flattered at what pathetic homage a Third World detective can render such a collection, but why would he wish to deceive me? I start when I hear the lift doors shut and the motor hum. He rests a hand on my forearm for a moment to reassure me, but this has the opposite effect. Here in his den I am able to see his strange spirit so much more clearly, experience its agony.

"You understand me, don't you, Detective?"

"I think so."

"And what is your answer to my anguish?"

"Possession in great measure requires great sacrifice, if the possession is not to destroy the possessor," the Buddha makes me reply. Warren grunts and the moment passes as he launches into a kind of sales pitch, beginning with five great stone Buddha heads standing on pallets, clearly stolen from Angkor and bearing tags, which presented themselves to us like prehistoric giants as we turned into one of the aisles.

"Special Agent Jones is bright enough," Warren says, pausing to light a cigarette, "but she's an American cop—she doesn't have your range or depth. I started buying as much stuff from Angkor as I could soon after the civil war started. As an American I felt responsible. The Pentagon bombed the shit out of the country and destabilized it, then the CIA backed the Khmer Rouge because they were the enemies of the Vietcong and we Americans are very sore losers. So, we destroy a country. Well, not quite, these ancient kingdoms don't really die, they reincarnate. But I wanted to save Khmer art, especially from Angkor, and the only way to do that was to keep buying it until things settled down. I'm sending it all back now, at my own expense." A sigh. "To be frank, nothing has changed since *The Quiet American*—when we finally destroy the whole world it will be with the very best of intentions. Meanwhile, as an American who has been deprogrammed by Asia, I'm trying to make amends. You believe me, don't you?"

"Yes."

"See, that's the difference. Jones wouldn't understand, wouldn't want to believe I can be a good guy. American cops have zero tolerance for moral ambiguity, otherwise they couldn't be American cops, could they? Not that I give a goddamn."

Step by step he takes me down the long corridor chockablock with gold Buddhas, spirit houses, ceramics, wood carvings from Ayutthaya, thirty feet of shelving from floor to ceiling dedicated to alms bowls, another section bearing hundreds of ceramic figurines—it is all amazing, priceless, wonderful. And I am still carrying the white tiger.

When we reach the end of the aisle, Warren takes it from me and sets it on a shelf. "It is the best thing I have. The phrase 'worth its weight in gold' is a cliché which really needs revision. I wouldn't sell it for ten times its weight in gold. Now explain to me, Detective, how I knew it was perfectly safe in your hands?"

I shrug modestly, then search his eyes when I hear the lift doors open at the distant end of the warehouse. Footsteps, and Fatima appears with the two Khmer. Now both are toting Uzis and Fatima looks haggard. Warren gives her a cruel, agonized glance as she approaches.

"Because you do me the honor of recognizing my integrity, so I repay the compliment." He is clearly distracted as he utters these words and beckons Fatima to approach. The two Khmer stiffen and remain where they are. Now I see it. Somehow he picked it up when my attention was distracted: a rawhide handle and yards of leather disappearing into the gloom under a shelf.

When Fatima reaches us he turns her to face the wall and places her hands gently on a shelf about two feet above her head.

I say: "Please don't."

Ignoring me, he reaches around her to undo the buttons of her blouse, which he then pulls up to tuck over her shoulders, revealing the length of her perfect back and her bra strap. He undoes the strap; now there is no impediment to the eye traveling up and down those miraculous vertebrae. "Please don't."

Taking my hand, he brushes it up and down her back, then makes me reach round to cup a breast. "To learn love, all a man need do is touch her perfect flesh, no? But to keep loving, that's a very different skill. Which of us isn't seeking that love which is as yielding as Fatima's flesh, and as resilient as stone? Which of us doesn't test love till it breaks? Am I really so weird?"

His face is quite twisted in agony now. It does not require clairvoyance to see his demon in all its black glory. I whisper hoarsely: "Whip me instead."

A leer from Warren. "Don't disappoint me, Detective. You know it's not as easy as that." He hands me the whip.

"No."

"But you'll be so much gentler than I. If you do it I promise not to lay a finger on her."

"No."

"Not for your life?"

"I don't care about my life."

A long silence during which I think the Khmer are about to execute me, then: "Okay, you win." I feel these last words are intended for Fatima. I glimpse Fatima's hands doing up her bra strap. Her shirt is still undone when she turns to take the whip from him. With a leer of extraordinary cruelty, she tells him: "I told you he's an *arhat*. You lose. Pick up the tiger and put it on your head."

I watch while Warren does as he is told. He is trembling with the priceless artifact balancing on the top of his head while she takes ten paces toward the back of the shop. I am thinking that perhaps she does not have a lot of practice when she snaps the whip to make it snake out behind her. There is a crash from the alms bowls section of the warehouse, which makes me search Warren's face. He is literally chewing his lips. Suddenly the rawhide is whistling toward us and I instinctively duck as it passes overhead. I don't think Fatima has made any attempt at accuracy, the leather comes crashing down toward Warren's face, forcing him to grab the tiger while he hunches over. The leather tears out a great swath of his jacket and sweater and the shirt underneath, and tears his flesh. Still, he does not let go of the tiger.

"You cheated," Fatima hisses. "Who told you to move?" The whip comes crashing down again, this time on the hands holding the tiger. Still he does not let go, but the leather curls around the plate and she pulls it out of his hands. It smashes to the floor in a thousand pieces. I am standing with my jaw hanging open, my eyes jerking from her to Warren to the fragments on the floor. "He cheated," she hisses at me. "You saw it?" Warren and I both duck as she whirls the whip over her head, then swings it toward us. She hits the shelf full of ceramic figurines, clearing it in a stroke. Warren is hunched, sobbing. He goes down on all fours to try to pick up the smashed plate and mutilated human figures on the floor.

I am given no time to make sense of this bizarre event. The Khmer are beside me shepherding me back to the lift, leaving Fatima and Warren in the warehouse. I am marched out of the shop into the muggy Sunday by the river, where tourists browse and droop and the longtail boats roar up and down. Jones is in the back of her hired car in the open-air car park and does not disguise her relief when she sees me.

48

We drove around aimlessly, Jones and I, while we tried to make sense of my adventure in Warren's shop. We thrashed it around in a hundred traffic jams, drove to Pattaya, lunched at a fish restaurant by the sea where Jones punished me for not sleeping with her by getting into a rant against Thai cuisine (chili in the fish: *How can you ever taste anything properly with your whole frigging mouth on fire?*), and returned to Bangkok with no explanation of the puzzle beyond a perceptive remark from the FBI: "One thing's for sure, somehow Fatima got hold of that tape Iamskoy was talking about. Take it from an American, no way Warren puts up with that kind of shit if she hasn't got the means to ruin his life."

"And the Khmer, his bodyguards?"

"Over to you, you're our tame Asian."

Night has already fallen as I close the car door on Jones and stroll across the forecourt. The common parts are poorly lit, only the illegal shop with the illegal tarpaulin is bright with lamps which illuminate the motorcycle chauffeurs who are still lolling in their beds and look stoned out of their minds. I climb the steps to my room and see that someone has busted the padlock. Burglars do not normally flatter me with their attentions, because everyone knows I have nothing, even though I'm a cop. It has happened only once before, when a neighbor's TV packed up in the middle of a soap and he broke into my room in the absolute, but false, certainty that I would have a television of my own. Standing in front of the busted lock, I wonder if someone else's TV has broken down, or should I be worrying about something more sinister? I decide that my enemies are too sophisticated to bust the lock and wait inside my room to assassinate me in my own home, but I lack the nerve to act on this comfortable conclusion until I hear a prolonged trombone fart from inside. I open the door cautiously. I cannot see him but an animal sense makes me aware of his vast bulk and I can hear his gigantic breathing. He grunts and rubs his eyes as I turn on the light. Torn cardboard six-packs are strewn around the futon, which is far too narrow for him even though he has dragged it into the center of the room. He overflows on either side, but manages to push himself up into a sitting position with some agility.

"I lied to you," he says in that throaty Harlem drawl.

"I know you did. Leave me any beer?"

He turns around and I notice a new addition to my ménage: an ice cooler. He dips his fingers in what has already turned to water and hands me a dripping can of Singha.

"That's the last one. Want me to get some more from the shop? I kinda made friends with the owner and those kids on the beds. It ain't so far from Harlem. I said: What are you on, fellas, meth or ganja? But I already knew it had to be ganja, no way they was so lethargic on meth. They offered me some meth, but I told them I don't do drugs. So they offered me some women instead, like how many did I want? Kids were ready to get on their bikes and bring me half a dozen. A nigger could feel at home in this country in no time. Poor Billy had a point after all. How'd you know I was lying and what was I lying about?"

"Your reason for being here. The FBI told me you changed planes and airlines in Paris, so you were trying to be incognito. You could have done the journey much more economically if you'd stayed with one airline all the way, and I don't think you stopped off to admire the Eiffel Tower."

A grunt. "So you figure I'm here 'cos I was involved in Billy's meth business?"

"No."

Silence. "I better go get some more beer."

By the time he's on his feet he fills my hovel. I'm reminded of a

Buddha statue in a cave that's too small. I have to stand aside to let him out the door. When he returns he is with a couple of the motorcycle kids, who are weighed down with stacks of six-packs and bags full of ice. Elijah reaches into his pocket and takes out a new padlock with keys dangling from it. "Sorry about the other one. There wasn't any comfortable lobby or anyplace I could wait."

"Never mind. How'd you break it so cleanly? I didn't see any marks on the door."

He snorts. "That little thing? I did it with my fingers. Muscle power, my friend, still opens doors from time to time."

"What did you say?" I ask, suddenly transfixed by the ice cooler.

"I adored Billy," Elijah says. "Probably because he adored me. We hardly knew our father, so I was the only role model he had. We were inseparable until I got my ass sent to reform school, just a little smack deal that went wrong. I was fifteen years old. When I came out they gave me a good probation officer, a black who understood where I was coming from and knew my mother. He says to me: 'You might have the smarts and the speed, but what you gonna do to your kid brother? You gonna destroy him? No way young Billy can take the kind of shit you're gonna take. You're dragging him down to hell without a ladder.' I didn't need to think about that because I knew he was right. I started to put some distance between me and the kid, even though it broke my heart. I can't say I was thrilled when he joined the Marines, but it was a load off my mind. It hurt when he started acting so superior and looked down on me and my wicked ways, it hurt a lot, but it was still a load off my mind. Even when he stopped calling me or talking to me, it was still a load off my mind. I felt like a father who has done better for his son than he ever could do for himself. I was so thrilled when he started calling me again, it was like ten years didn't count for nothing. We was pals again. Since he died I wake up with the sweats thinking about breaking the people who did that to him. Breaking them across my knee, one by one."

It is 2:34 a.m. and we've drunk most of the beer. Elijah has told me how to cook meth, how to set up a network, how to find cops to bribe in New York. In particular I am now an authority on glassine bags (they have to be the right size—too big and the price is too high for the average crackhead; too small and you're giving yourself too much work—above all, don't get fancy and put your own proprietorial stamp on the outside, like gold stars or something, because the courts will assume organized crime). He's told me everything I need to know if I ever want to deal in drugs in the United States, and now he has finally told me why he is in my country. He has come to tell me because he has realized his quest for vengeance is impossible. With greater speed than the FBI he has understood that crucial thing about Asia: we play by different rules and we are two-thirds of the world. He has come to say goodbye.

When he heaves himself to his feet I need help from the wall to do likewise. I have felt great love for this gigantic man with his gigantic heart, and this love has compelled me to match him beer for beer. I've never been so astonishingly drunk in my life. I am also grateful that he has helped me solve one detail of the case which has been nagging at us for weeks, the FBI and me. On rubber knees I follow him to the shop and we hug each other goodbye near the motorcycle taxis. Only the largest of their bikes, a 500 cc Honda, is strong enough to sustain him, and there is much grinning and wonderment when he sits on the back, crushing the suspension. I watch him and the driver wobble off into what is left of the night, then I stumble back to my cave, where, with superhuman concentration, I press the FBI's number into the keypad of my mobile. I wake her from a deep sleep and it takes some moments to convince her I'm not some Thai variant of a dirty phone call. She is fully awake by the time she has made sense of my drunken mumblings.

"Saw it when Elijah busted my padlock," I explain with sloppy pride.

"The cobras were in a steamer trunk? Bradley thought he was doing a standard pickup from the airport? The python was there to bust open the trunk?"

" 'Xactly."

"But what about the whole problem with injecting the snakes with *yaa baa*?"

"Weren't injected. Packed in straw between ice. Snakes hibernated. Ice smelted. Snakes woke up thirsty. Drank water from smelted ice. Water had *yaa baa* in it. *Yaa baa* drove python crazy. Bust the locks no prob." I cackle. "Must have been fucking terrifying."

"What about those two dead snakes you found—the ones that were beaten to death?"

"Squatters had to snatch trunk before we arrived. Some snakes left in back of car. Rest all over Bradley. Killed ones in back with stick or something. Steamer trunks was the way they brought in the *yaa baa* every few months—that's why Old Tou had enough to build his hut."

"Some trusted squatters snatched the trunk out the back door despite the snakes, because it would have blown their whole operation if you'd found it? Yes, I can see that. But that drunk never mentioned anything like that?"

"Maybe he wasn't so dumb. Maybe they schooled him. Who knows, he's a drunk."

A pause which I think must express wonder at my forensic brilliance, or my advanced toxicity—I'm not sure which I'm most impressed with myself.

"No kidding. Well, nice work, partner. We'll talk when you've slept it off. Maybe in a week or so?"

49

A knock on my flimsy door. Someone calls my name, trying out *Sonchai*, then *Detective Jitpleecheep*. I must have fallen asleep fully dressed on my futon. My head is killing me. It takes twenty minutes to emerge crumpled from my cave. Without windows I tend to lose all sense of time, especially when I've been pissed out of my brain. I'm traumatized by the bright sunlight. Out in the forecourt just in front of the shop and the motorbike kids I see that the Colonel has sent a car with motorcycle escort. It is the same Lexus as the one in which he recently abducted me, with a different driver at the wheel.

There are four motorbikes this time and the traffic cops have been warned to make way for us. I am surprised to find we are heading for the domestic airport, but there is nothing I can do about that. I wish they wouldn't be so gung ho with their damned sirens.

I am escorted firmly but politely from the limo to the check-in desk for flights to Chiang Mai, where one of my minders pulls out a first-class ticket in my name. The minders use their police IDs to pass through into the waiting area, where we all sit down. Even when it's time to board they accompany me as far as the airplane. The flight lasts thirty minutes and there is another limo waiting at the other end. The driver is Vikorn's usual trusted man. I'm sobering up by the minute, leaving no alcohol buffer between me and my triple-A headache.

I have never been to his house in Chiang Mai and I'm surprised at how far out of town it is. We travel parallel to the Ping River for about ten kilometers until we come to some of the best riverside property in the world. From time to time they appear for sale in the classified pages of the newspapers, these million-dollar mansions in their own leafy grounds with river access and five-car garages. Some of them are renovated teak houses, some are imitations of Thai style, but most of them are imitations of Western luxury houses, perhaps from Malibu or the suburbs of Los Angeles. Gangsters own all of them. The Colonel's is a two-story with vast sloping roofs in red shingles, white walls and floor-to-ceiling windows. Two cops with walkie-talkies stand guard at the electric gate, which opens as we approach.

Vikorn's driver gets out of the car and walks across the gravel in a relaxed mood, as if returning home after a day's work. The Colonel in a loose linen shirt, baggy black pants and old leather slippers comes to the door, looks at me waiting in the car and beckons me in. A few minor clues—the way he shuffles, a lazy left eye—tell me he is drunk. Must have been something in the stars last night.

By the time I reach the front door only the driver is there. He leads me through the house to a huge room on the river side which spans the length of the house. The wall is entirely of glass and looks onto an old wooden jetty on a bend in the river on which a couple of fishermen are paddling a small teak boat. It's like a painting from former times, the dense green of the jungle nodding over the slow-moving loop of brown water, two preindustrial fishermen with their nets and paddles, a serenity so profound it is as if time has stopped.

The room is so big I have to search for him; he is in a leather armchair at one end, smoking a cheroot and looking out. An empty bottle of Mekong whisky sits on a coffee table. I walk silently across the teak floor and take a seat in the armchair opposite his: Italian leather, cigar-colored, as soft as a baby's skin. The gun on the coffee table between us is an old-style army revolver with a barrel about twelve inches long. The Colonel does not look at me.

"You're angry with me, Sonchai?"

"You lied."

"Not really. I told you I'd never met a woman of Fatima's description. Fatima is not a woman. Not to an old-fashioned man like me, anyway."

"She was your contact for the *yaa baa* Bradley was moving?"

He raises his arms. "What could I do? I had to have someone. I had my doubts about employing a *farang*, but in some ways it made a lot of sense. As a marine at the American embassy he was never under suspicion, but how far can one trust a foreigner? I needed someone to tell me what he was up to, moment to moment. I recruited her at the same time my people agreed to use him."

I nod in my turn. This much I have understood. "What I don't understand is why you had Pichai and me follow Bradley in the first place."

"Because of what you were, the two of you. By that time I was sure she would kill Bradley and I expected the Americans to demand a full investigation. Any other cops might simply have arrested Fatima, but you two devout Buddhists, I knew you would not have the heart to prosecute once you knew what had happened. Naturally, I didn't want her in jail where she could be interrogated by my enemies. Her crazy thing with the snakes took me completely by surprise, though. I had no idea. I'd like you to believe that. I knew she would kill him, but I didn't know how."

"You *knew* she would kill him? And you used Pichai and me because you were feeling compassionate? I don't understand."

He covers his mouth to burp. "I'm getting old, Sonchai. I'm talking to my brother again these days. I sent him a mobile telephone more than six months ago. He almost never switches it on because it would disturb his meditation, but he uses it to call me now and then, when he can get someone to charge the battery at the nearest village. He doesn't have electricity in that Stone Age monastery of his. He told me I'd be lucky to be reborn in the human form at all, after the kind of life I've led. Maybe a deformed beggar was the most I could hope for, but something in the animal kingdom was more likely, or even an insect, a bug of some kind. He's pretty merciless, as you know."

"Go on."

"I asked his advice when I realized what Warren and Bradley had in mind for Fatima."

"How did you realize that?"

"That tape of Warren the Russian mafia made. They made it because they thought it would be a good idea to blackmail Warren on the basis of his sex with a prostitute. What they ended up with was a recording of a murder. Warren was desperate. He saw his whole life collapsing. He asked his good friend Colonel Suvit to get the tape for him, to deal with the Russians. The urkas have business here, they need us much more than we need them, but Suvit is not exactly a diplomat. You know what he's like. So then Warren asked me to help for old times' sake—perhaps the FBI told you about all that? So I was the one to negotiate the return of the tape. Apparently the urkas have their standards, their honor. If they say there's only one copy, then that is supposed to be reliable. I don't know, I've never dealt with them before, but they do run a lot of prostitutes here, and they move a lot of their heroin through Thailand, so they need to keep us on their side. It was smart of Warren to have us negotiate the return of the tape on his behalf. And the money they received for the tape should have been enough to shut them up. Warren paid three million dollars for it, less our commission. I saw the wire. I got the tape, but I refused to hand it over to Suvit or to Warren. Suvit was furious and so was Warren, but what could they do? I told Suvit: 'Look, we'll keep the tape to keep Warren under control. So long as we have it he'll do as he's told.' " A wave of the hand. "But then I started talking to my brother. He started to dismantle my mind, the way he does. And that tape, you know, what they did, Warren and Bradley, it's very Western, very cruel, very un-Thai." A sigh. "We've killed a lot of men, you and I, but no women as far as I can remember. And what did it amount to? We simply sent them on to their next lives a little sooner than expected, usually without pain or suffering."

"What are you saying?"

"I'm saying I couldn't let them do what they planned, not even to a bum-boy." I am still puzzled and wrinkle my brow, wondering if it is alcohol poisoning which has paralyzed my brain functions. "I decided to outline my problem to my brother and let him guide me. I didn't tell him about the tape, he knew nothing of its existence. He meditated for a day and called me. His solution was elegant, clairvoyant and radical, like Buddhism itself, and consisted of one sentence: *Give her the tape.* Call me a superstitious old man, but I gave it to her, just a few days before she murdered Bradley with those snakes. Naturally, she understood everything, once she had seen the tape and that poor Russian woman with that gold stick in her navel."

I stare at him, then can hardly resist a smile. "With that tape she controls Warren? She made him come here, to Thailand?"

"That is correct. We've all underestimated her. She's turned him into her slave. I guess you could say it is justice Thai-style."

"But what about Warren's minders, those Khmer?"

A scoffing sound from deep in his throat. "She always controlled them. Warren and Bradley hired them in a panic when the Russians started putting on the squeeze, but how could Bradley communicate except through Fatima? Those animals only speak Thai and Khmer. Sure, Warren speaks Thai, but he's not here all the time and they don't trust *farangs*. Her people are all from the jungle, she understands how those goons think. Warren and Bradley saw no danger because they underestimated Fatima. Little by little Fatima turned herself into a religious figure for those Khmer. They're all lost since the civil war, and since Pol Pot died. For them she's like a return to the old days, with transsexual shamans, apocalyptic visions—plus she's provided them all with Harley-Davidson motorbikes and Uzi machine guns. She's like a combination of Pol Pot, Father Christmas and a Hindu death goddess, all in one."

The mind likes truth. It will work quite hard to make the connections, once the pieces are all on the board. "She and Warren invited me to Warren's shop two days ago, I watched her destroy his most expensive piece of jade—a priceless piece, and a whole lot of other stuff."

"She's toying with him. I don't know what she has in mind. She's the cat, he's the mouse. She's enjoying herself. The worm has turned." He raises his eyes, the lazy one still half covered by its lid. "Actually, she's toying with all of us. An interesting situation, no?"

"You have no idea—?"

"None. I don't know what she has planned. I always kept Fatima at arm's length. I only used her to report that the shipments had arrived safely and the product duly moved across the city. Bradley was a fool if he didn't guess someone was checking up on him every minute of the day. Some of those shipments were worth twenty million dollars. And I'm not talking about the jade." A pause while he rubs the side of his nose. "Actually, I don't like the trade at all, but we have to keep our people awake somehow."

"How did she manage with those snakes?"

"She's Karen, her people sell endangered species to the Chinese all the time, and the Chinese like their snakes fresh. The Karen have become expert in the transportation of live reptiles. She simply told them what she wanted and paid them. She probably did it with a single phone call."

He raises his hands and shoulders. "Fatima is out of control, but with that tape she controls Warren. Why kill him while she's having fun using him as a slave and destroying him slowly?"

"And through Warren she controls you too? I saw you at the Bamboo Bar a few nights ago."

An old man's sly glance. "You did?"

"Dr. Surichai was there."

He swallows hard and stares at me. "Fatima wants to do to the world what the world did to her. It's not just a question of killing Warren—he didn't make the world. See? And now that she controls Warren, she controls everyone. Of course, when I was summoned I went to watch her sing. Warren insisted—he more or less went down on his knees to plead with me—because that's what Fatima wanted."

"All that fuss just to get you to go to a jazz club to watch her sing 'Bye Bye Blackbird'?"

"If you weren't such a fucking saint you'd understand. She's in control for the first time in her life, she's running the world. She's the empress, people indulge her every whim—or else. It gave her a kick to see me hop at her command."

He leans forward to turn the gun around so that the handle is pointing at me and the barrel at him. "Kill me if you have the guts. You have the right, it's my fault your partner is dead."

At that moment I turn at the sound of soft padding across the floor. This young woman's black hair is short, almost cropped, and there are three earrings in each ear. She is wearing jeans and a black top with boot-lace straps which reveal an elaborate chrysanthemum tattoo over her right breast. My first thought is that she must be one of his daughters, but I remember from the gossip that the tattoo belongs to Da, the Colonel's fourth *mia noi,* or minor wife. She hardly gives the gigantic revolver more than a glance, *wais* to me and—with a glance of contempt as she registers Vikorn's drunkenness—asks rather briskly if we need tea or drinks? If not, she would like Vikorn's driver to take her into town, where she has an appointment with a girlfriend. The Colonel irritably agrees to let her have the car and driver and we watch her pad across the floor barefoot. Vikorn makes a wobbly gesture with one hand.

"A mistake. I'm a dinosaur, Sonchai, and I didn't realize how our country has changed. In the old days when you took a *mia noi* all you had to do was to feed her and her family and give her a baby or two. Now"—he shakes his head—"self-improvement is all the rage. I've paid for hair-dressing classes, beautician classes, tattooing classes, endless aerobic classes and the latest is Internet software. She claims she's bored out of her brain at home and wants to start her own Internet café. She doesn't seem to want kids at all. She tells me we have a deal, a contract. She gives me her body whenever I have the strength, she's faithful to me, in return I finance her upward mobility. You might say she's a living fusion between East and West."

"It doesn't sound too bad a deal."

"I know, but where's the romance? She isn't even scared of me. Did you see the way she looked at that gun, as if to say: The old man is playing his games again? Yesterday she said to me: 'Are we doing sex tonight or can I watch the football?' Since when did our women get obsessed with football?"

"It's been going on for quite a while. I can confirm they often prefer it to sex."

"She's the most ambitious and the least contented of all my wives. This is liberation, to be permanently unsatisfied? What kind of a world is this? I don't think I want to hang around in it much longer. Are you going to send me to my next incarnation or not?"

The Colonel does not so much as stiffen when I lean forward to pick up the gun. I break it open to check the chambers, all of which are full. I realize that he is quite serious, that he would like me to kill him.

"You think I'm bluffing?"

"No, but I know at least one person who will doubt the gun was loaded, when I tell this story." I snap the barrel into place and put the gun back on the table.

"So, how do you know the bullets are not blanks? You've spent too much time with the FBI, my friend, you've started thinking like an American." He picks up the gun and holds it shakily in both hands. "Honor is honor," he says. The shot makes a jagged hole in the glass wall and brings his security running from four directions. Still holding the gun, he waves them back where they came from. He replaces the gun on the table with a loud clack. The bang from the shot is still echoing in my ears and there is a steady tinkle of glass from the shattered wall in which lightning-shaped cracks have appeared. It is difficult to explain why this melodrama has only deepened my love for him. He says: "I don't know why I built a *farang*-style house. When I was younger I was impressed by the West. Now I can see how far we have lost ourselves. Look at that stupid window. What kind of idiot would build a wall of glass in the Tropics? Better small windows with shutters, high ceilings, a minimum of light, teak walls, the feeling of a living, breathing space." He looks away from me. Now, in order to look at the fishermen he has to lean a little to one side. I can hear his thoughts, quite loudly, inside my head. He is talking to his brother, admitting that it would have been better to lead the life of a simple fisherman. His brother advises him not to mistake sentimentality for nirvana. Vikorn turns his attention to me with a helpless look on his face. "You heard that, didn't you? He's totally ruthless. Won't let me get away with anything."

I watch while with some difficulty he rises from the armchair and beckons me to follow. He leads me to a small private theater consisting of a gigantic TV monitor and about twenty seats facing it. He tells me to sit down, leaves the room for five minutes, then returns with a videotape. "Naturally, I made a copy." Bending like a man ten years older than himself, he slides the tape into the machine on a shelf under the TV, and immediately a grainy black-and-white image of a young white woman with blond hair and Slavic features appears. She is wearing jeans and a tight T-shirt and smiling vivaciously, apparently determined to capture the attention of someone offscreen. She nods in response to some cue and begins to undress. The T-shirt comes off first to reveal a black bra and a gold stick which perforates diagonally the circumference of her navel. She fingers it whilst making an O of her mouth and sliding her tongue around the inside of the O. She bends forward from the hips whilst undoing her bra. She wiggles her torso to make her breasts wobble, but a quick frown followed by an obedient nod tells us that this is not pleasing to the audience. In a more serious mood she pulls off her jeans. Now she is naked except for a G-string. Apparently this is not erotic to the audience either, and with a slightly frustrated expression she pulls it off to stand naked with her hands on her hips, awaiting instructions. Puzzled, she raises her hands above her head and keeps them there for several seconds. There can be no doubt that the purpose is to highlight the gold stick in her navel.

Vikorn freezes the tape at this point and turns to me with a quizzical expression. If one disregards the color of the skin, the resemblance to Fatima's body is startling. Vikorn presses the forward button. On instructions, the blond woman lowers one hand to finger the gold stick, erotically up and down, up and down, round and round, a combination of male and female masturbation.

Now she lies on a bed behind her, full length, and once again the gold stick seems to dominate the screen. Her body language indicates that each time she stops fondling it, she receives a reprimand from her client. Now she turns over onto her front. Immediately two gigantic black hands take one of her wrists, bind it quickly with tape to the iron of the headboard while other hands—white with a filigree gold bracelet hanging from one wrist—bind her on the other side. She half closes her eyes and gives a convincing impression of a woman in deep lust. The camera takes in only her face and the upper part of her body, therefore one can only guess by her facial expressions that she is experiencing penetration. Her expression abruptly changes to one of profound physical shock at the first lash, which sprays blood lightly over her cheek. I scream at Vikorn to stop the tape.

The TV screen is blank. Vikorn is looking at me with an expression of almost academic—and drunken—curiosity. "My brother talked about you and Pichai quite a lot. He said you were both very talented in different ways. He said your problem was your total lack of identity. You can be anyone you like, literally, but only for short periods of time. Who were you just then, the victim?"

"Fatima, the first time she watched the tape," I mutter, ashamed of my weakness.

To my surprise the Colonel puts his arm around me. "It's okay."

A pause. I say: "I'll have to bring her in, won't I?"

This question ages him still further. The skin under his strong jaw slackens somewhat. Now I can see the reptile in him: loose-skinned, prehistoric, cunning. This is the real punishment. Not rebirth in the body of an animal, but the eternal headache of trying to manipulate his way out of the consequences of his greed. With infinite weariness: "I suppose so."

"Want to help?"

"How can I?"

"The Chinese?"

He nods and grasps my arm. "Everything depends on them. If they choose to protect their man, we're finished, all of us. Fatima will broadcast the tape over the Internet and go ballistic. Who knows what she'll do? They took her humanity away—what has she got to lose? The Khmer will stand by her, they don't have anything to lose either. There'll be a bloodbath."

At the door he reminds me of a toad, shrunken. A helpless gesture, then he grasps my arm again and a new light comes into his eyes. "The jeweler is a sick man, but he's also a genius. You should have seen him in his prime. The Chiu Chow love him. How d'you think I did so well myself? Everything comes out of Chinatown, you know? We Thais are only good for fucking, fighting, drinking and dying. That's what Warren taught me—and his Chinese friends." A long pause. "They were great days. The mountains of Laos are true Buddha country. Green, thick with mist in the morning, we used to climb like that"—a steep gesture with the palm of his hand—"until we reached six, eight, ten thousand feet. The air starts to get thin then, and it's ice cold. Pat would start his damned tape with 'The Ride of the Valkyries'—that was the first time I realized a *farang* might love a Thai. We crash-landed twice with bullet holes all over the plane. I shit in my pants, but that American aviator was like a superman. We got back to Long Tien somehow. The Hmong were wonderful, too. How could anyone understand the innocence of the opium trade? Warren was good to the Hmong, he forced his friends the Chiu Chow to pay top dollar—how about that? Even he had honor in those days."

He stoops when he turns to go back into the house.

50

This isn't a *whodunit*, is it? More like a *whatwillshedonext*. While the FBI was here this question pressed on both of us as if it were inevitable that somehow we would reach one of those neat endings the West is so fond of, with all i's dotted and all t's crossed. Perhaps we were supposed to walk off into the sunset together, Jones and I, with no nifty Thai skeleton following us around, either? But Warren won at least that battle and I had to go to the airport to see her off last night. We were stiff, affectionate and melancholy all at the same time. Her eyes were pleading when she said, "I'm gonna miss you, Sonchai," so I had to make my eyes pleading when I said, "I'm gonna miss you too, Kimberley." Secretly, I lamented that her progress on the Path has not been as great as I might have wished. Of course she'll be back. In the meantime *whatwillfatimadonext* has turned into one of those open-ended Thai questions to which one does not necessarily expect an answer in this lifetime. Without that American impatience to drive me forward I'm not sure what, if anything, I myself will do next. Bring her in? The Colonel is reluctant and the possibility of a dastardly murder going unpunished does not enrage me as you probably think it should, *farang*. Of course I cannot forget Pichai—but did she kill him in any sense beyond the superficial? We all know who really dunit, don't we? And what, exactly, am I supposed to do about *him*, that prototypical Western man? And then, of course, there are my almost nightly conferences with my dead soul partner, which I've not told you about. These days, apparently, he is not in the least interested in matters arising from the destruction of his chemical body, which, on reflection, he is glad to be rid of. There are plenty of ways of getting in touch, he tells me mysteriously while we share the twilight zone between waking and sleeping.

For a brief moment I think the United States of America will rescue me from this dilemma after all. Out of the blue I'm invited—summoned is probably a better word—to my second home, the U.S. Embassy on Wireless Road. I do not fail to notice a subtle increase in my respect quotient as I pass my friend on security at the gate—mixed with a fairly blatant splash of curiosity, I might add. Then my old companion from ancient times Katherine White arrives with the news that I am not going to the office of the FBI legal attaché this time, but—a quick scan of my face to check that I'm fully cognizant of the honor I'm about to receive— to the ambassador's suite. A brisk march through those parts of the embassy designed to welcome kings and princes.

The ambassador and her deputy are both female and, ethnic origin aside, might have been cut from the same pattern of tall, slim women in their late forties with long arms, brisk manners and tones of voice which assume obedience. The ambassador is white and her deputy is black. I have been shown into the meeting after the massacre. I can almost see the careers of Rosen and Nape lying bloody and broken on the carpet. Nape is relying on what is left of his youth and options to see him through the meeting, but Rosen looks depressed. They are standing around a desk bigger than a king-size bed; only the ambassador is seated. Behind her the American flag hangs by a window at a slant and behind it lie the manicured gardens of the embassy. The deputy ambassador stands to one side.

Graciously, the ambassador stands as I approach and shakes my hand while Rosen makes the introductions. I wonder if her politeness is a form of reproach to the others.

"Well, I guess you know the main business of the hour, Detective?"

"Is it that Mr. Sylvester Warren has disappeared?"

"You got it. I've had faxes, phone calls and e-mails from two senators already, a call from the White House, an urgent fax from his lawyer in New York and some stuff from his staff." A glance at her watch, then at the deputy. "But I've got the Queen at noon, then I've got that flight to Tokyo. So I'm gonna leave it all to you. You can carry on in here, no point moving everyone to another room. Sorry to be leaving just when you've arrived, Detective. I sure hope you can help us. Your Colonel Vikorn was very complimentary about you over the phone this morning. He says you'll find him." A quick scan of my face. "That could be a very high priority." A last glance and nod at the deputy and she strode out of the room via a door near her desk.

"Well, I guess we can all sit down," the deputy says. We move across the room to a set of chairs and sofas around a coffee table. "Let me just run through the points the ambassador made, for the sake of the detective." A steady glance at me with two fingers raised. "Two possibilities, Detective. Either it's terrorism or it's not. We've got just a few hours to decide. On the one hand, Sylvester Warren is a high-profile American known to visit this country monthly. He's friends with presidents and heads of state and is probably as well known in Southeast Asia as he is in the States. Maybe more so. This country has a sizable Muslim population. Just south of us, in Malaysia and Indonesia, we find the most populous Muslim countries in the world, with a fair number of extremist factions. The borders are porous, anyone can enter by land or sea. I don't need to tell you the connections people are going to start making. You see the issue, Detective? It's as much diplomacy as forensic investigation. The reason we have legal attachés is that those two disciplines get confused from time to time, and we like to have a little warning when that is about to happen." A tightening of the lips as she scans the others.

We are doing American Grim, a genre with which I am unfamiliar. There is an implication, apparently, that the sterner you make your mood the more likely you are to solve the problem. But what problem? It takes me quite a while to realize that behind the façade of Grim we are acting out a pantomime with which I am thoroughly familiar. The laws of bureaucracy are much like the laws of physics it seems, they are identical in every corner of the earth. I see it now: I am here in the ambassador's splendid office for the sake of form. There will be a minute recording the fact that the ambassador herself and her deputy both personally interviewed Detective Jitpleecheep, following the alarming news of Warren's disappearance. Having satisfied themselves that no act of terrorism seemed to be implied, they had no choice but to allow the local police to investigate in their own way, in partnership with the FBI legal attachés, to whom a stern (grim) reprimand was given for their apparent laxness in failing to protect a high-profile American citizen. In parallel with the open minute, there will be a secret memo recording the fact that Warren is a psychotic sleazebag who is probably tied up in a wooden shack somewhere getting what he deserves, without risk to American security or any other U.S. citizen in Southeast Asia.

"This is a matter we are taking extremely seriously," I say slowly, in case someone wants to quote me.

The deputy is astute and gives me a surprisingly cute smile. "I'm relieved to hear it," she says, also slowly.

"We are satisfied that there are no terrorist implications in this case."

Nape almost smirks and Rosen is clearly shocked that a non-American knows how to play this game. "I can endorse that," he says, engaging the deputy's eyes with pathological sincerity.

In theory we could end it there, but it's a bit short and the meeting cries out for padding. Anyway, I'm suddenly in the mood to show off. It's been a while, but the mind-set is strangely addictive.

"Whilst Thailand is a humane Buddhist society committed to human rights and the dignity of its citizens, the wealthier countries of the world must appreciate we do not always have the resources to meet those high standards of law enforcement which, frankly, are a luxury afforded only by those countries which industrialized first."

Rapid blinks from the deputy until she has understood what I'm doing. "Can I quote you on that?"

"Absolutely."

A nod to Rosen, who nods to Nape, who takes out a ballpoint pen.

Now the interview is over and it seems everyone is delighted that the local cop is so learned in the noble art of ass-protection. Nape insists on accompanying me back to Thailand. At the gate he says: "That *katoy*'s got him, hasn't she? Think there'll be anything left by the time she's finished? Maybe a thumb and a couple of kneecaps?"

I stare at him for a long moment, then hail a motorcycle taxi.

Back in my hovel I roll a joint. It is 12:56 p.m. by the clock glyph on my mobile.

51

Waiting is difficult only for those beset by the delusion of time. Dope helps, of course. Weeks have passed, Jones has called me three times from the States, each time on a Sunday. The loneliness of *farangs* is a wasting disease for which, the FBI will sooner or later realize, Thailand may be the only cure. The sensation of somehow following in the footsteps of my mother is deeply disturbing to me, but I don't let it get me down. After all, there is plenty to do. Nong's bar has already opened unofficially and is doing astonishingly well. There are accounts to check, board meetings to attend, provisions to order. Then the call comes.

Dr. Surichai is taut and formal over the telephone, using neither his bedside manner nor his fashionably sleazy tone. I think this is the voice he uses in directors' meetings at the hospital, when the nitty-gritty of balance sheets is being discussed. He says very little, indeed I have the feeling he would rather not be making the call at all. At the request of his patient he is inviting me to his home on Soi 30 Sukhumvit, very close to the Emporium shopping mall.

It is a mansion rather than a house, with an electric gate and uniformed security. In addition to the doctor's own guards, a half dozen well-dressed Chinese men stand around looking sullen and alert. One of them barks out something in what I think is the Chiu Chow dialect when I arrive, no doubt telling the others not to reach for the bulges under their jackets. A maidservant lets me into the house and shows me into a large salon where I sit on a sofa and wait. Surichai emerges from a corridor in a sleeveless canary-yellow cardigan and slacks, with a slight frown on his face, holding a single sheet of paper on which a statement is written in Thai script, with an elegant signature in Western script at the end. I study it carefully, hand it back to him with a nod, not entirely surprised. It seems the contending parties have reached one of those Oriental solutions which would be unthinkable in the option-starved West.

"I was asked to take him in as a patient in my home. Obviously, he doesn't want to be anywhere public. I've had to bring a lot of equipment from the hospital. Now, for some reason he wants to see you. This sort of thing can cause enormous and radical personality changes. He's decided you might be the only person in the world who understands him. Has he been a close friend of yours?"

Surichai's brisk manner has irritated me and I don't bother to answer his question. "He did a deal with Fatima?"

"His friends did. These Chiu Chow who have invaded my house. You've no idea how medieval the Chinese mind can be. They're not modern people at all. The way they see it, the solution to the kind of sex problem their friend Warren has is very simple, even if the cure is somewhat radical and—dare I say—*Forbidden City–ish*. Fatima put them in a fix. If they let her kill him, it would look bad for them, even suggest they didn't have the power to protect their man. If they protected him, she would destroy him anyway by broadcasting that tape over the Net, and perhaps setting her Khmer loose. This was a compromise even Warren agreed to, as witnessed by his signature on that bit of paper. Of course, it was that or die. Fatima consented after he'd put more than half his fortune in her name. She must be the richest woman in Thailand. Maybe the wealthiest transsexual in the world. You better come through. I operated yesterday. He's still very weak, but as I say the main thing is the total personality change. Mentally I'm afraid he's very unstable. You'll see." A pause. "He went into shock immediately after I operated. I had to pump him full of tranquilizers or he would have died. Even then his vital functions were suspended for a couple of minutes." He examines my face for a moment, checking me for some kind of understanding, but I have no idea what he is hinting at.

Down a corridor surprisingly wide for a private house, on the walls of which I'm impressed to see original oil paintings of nineteenth-century Krung Thep. We take a left turn into what must be a late addition to the building and enter a solarium built of steel and glass, the views of the garden mostly obscured by wall-to-wall curtains. The head on the pillow is almost unrecognizable; not that the features have changed but because the personality inhabiting this body bears almost no resemblance to that of the former tenant. As a student of the Path this transformation is fascinating to me: the new resident has inherited a body and collection of memory cells with which it is unfamiliar, and of which it must try to make sense. A weaker spirit would have had a nervous breakdown, but this one has simply chosen to go haywire.

He motions weakly with his hand for me to sit down on a chair near the bed. "Welcome, my dear friend," he says in Thai. I'm startled almost out of my skin: that was Pichai's voice. The face smiles. In English: "It's okay, I'm still in the twilight zone. Your friend says hello. He's very talented you know. Isn't reality wonderful?"

All of a sudden he bursts into tears. *"Here lies a fool who tried to fuck the East*—d'you know who said that, Detective?"

"No."

"Kipling—the poet of that other Anglo-Saxon empire. God save us from our blindness." Weeping. "God save us." He stretches out a hand to hold mine. "Look, look at my life." A sweeping gesture. I had not yet taken in the treasures which have been sensitively placed around the room. There is the horse and rider, on an alabaster plinth. There are some priceless pieces from the Warren Collection, including jade jewelry from the Forbidden City. Indeed, jade is everywhere in its incomparable luminescence. Warren—if I may still call him that—presses a switch by his right hand and an electric motor starts to hum. With majestic slowness the curtains open, revealing a stunning garden bursting with hibiscus and bougainvillea, rhododendron, a magnificent bodhi tree with aerial roots and a wooden seat around the bowl, flower beds exploding with color.

"See"—I jump, for it is Pichai again speaking in Thai, using Warren's vocal cords—"this is his soul: life is all on the outside, on the other side of the glass. Inside there is only stone. This is your *farang* for you."

"He cut mine off, so I did the same to him." It is Fatima's voice now, hissing through his mouth. My blood runs cold and a horrible tingling passes up and down my spine, but the figure on the bed seems oblivious to his other visitors.

"Know the very last lesson a *farang* learns who tries to trick the East?"

he says in Warren's American voice. "That he's been fucked from the start. From the start. The key is not to tell him until it's too late." Gripping my hand. "You have more patience, more history, more cunning, more sorcery—and you get the sun twelve hours before we do. How could we ever win?"

"He wanted to make people like jewelry," says Fatima. "Now who will buy *him*?"

"Have compassion," urges Pichai.

"Balls," says Fatima.

"Go too deep into the West and you turn to stone yourself," says Warren. "It's almost as simple as that. Sooner or later you start trading people, one way or another. And if you're trading them, why not modify them? Ah, the demonic beauty of the human form! Who can resist working it like the finest jade, once you realize you have the power? You pass that threshold without even noticing. America is the continent of death. This has been known for thousands of years. I have been everything in the Great Cosmic Lottery, women and men, thieves, princes and slaves, and I've stayed too long on this earth. The body is a doll, but it corrupts the spirit. You think I'm the only one? This is a devil hard to beat, Detective. Enticing beyond words. I wanted a perfect form to dissolve into, but the forms kept dissolving first. That's the truth about me, take it or leave it." A quick check of my face—but who is behind those eyes? "Building designer humans out of throwaway people—d'you think we'll resist once the American empire has reached adolescence?"

When the door opens and Surichai enters the room I cannot prevent myself from throwing him a glance of utter helplessness. He nods in complete understanding.

"He's been speaking in Fatima's voice? Eerie, isn't it? I couldn't begin to explain—not in terms of Western science anyway. I'm sure a meditator like you has his own ideas. There's another voice he's been using, too, in impeccable Thai, very vernacular, much better than he speaks it himself. Who is that?"

"My dead brother," I whisper.

A shrug. "No *farang* would understand—but to us it's not so totally outlandish, is it? You better leave him now. As I say, he's very weak. You can come back tomorrow if you want."

Tears are pouring down Warren's cheeks as we leave the room.

In the corridor I say: "Is there going to be a next stage, or are you going to leave him like that?"

"Reassignment, you mean? That's entirely up to Fatima." To my startled glance: "That was part of the deal. She has the—ah—pieces under controlled conditions in her penthouse." A glance at his watch. "And she has about six hours left to make up her mind. So far she's been pretty damn negative and without the material there's nothing I can do. I think you are closer to Fatima than I am. Does she have Buddhist compassion? Do you have any influence?"

52

Two Months Later

Told you she'd be back. Here I am waiting at Bangkok International Airport, wearing my best khaki sleeveless shirt, black pants and hideous black lace-up shoes.

The Thai Airways flight from San Francisco via Tokyo and Hong Kong has been delayed by one hour, but now I see from the monitors that it has landed. Twenty minutes later Kimberley Jones appears in the arrivals area wearing a beige business suit (trousers). Her hair is her natural blond, cut short but not ruthlessly so. There are three earrings in her left ear, only one in the other. Her lipstick is a modest pink. When she presses her cheek against mine by way of greeting I inhale a familiar scent which for me has Mother written all over it.

"Van Cleef and Arpels," I say with a smile.

"You got it."

I am uncertain whether to help her with her trolley piled high with purple Samsonite cases. What is the etiquette here? A Thai woman would be deeply offended if I didn't push it, but an American might be offended if I did? I decide to let Kimberley push it to the taxi rank.

In the back of the cab Kimberley says: "Surprised?"

"That you bought shares in my mother's company? Yes, at first, but when Nong told me she'd been exchanging e-mails with you, it sort of fell into place. Are you on vacation from the Bureau?"

"I took an unpaid sabbatical." A crisp glance at my face and away. "White men aren't the only ones who find this city irresistible, so it can't just be the sex, can it?"

"What is it, do you think?" I ask.

"I don't know. The bottom line is it's so damn human." A pause. "Still nothing on Fatima?"

I cover my face for a moment before replying: "Nothing. Vanished after—after she made her decision." I make a slightly exaggerated gesture intended to convey terminal vanishing, so as not to spoil the surprise tonight.

"D'you ever wonder if there might be something in what she told you that time, that she's like your shadow, your dark side? That you need her in some way?"

I experience a need to change the subject. I pass Jones the front page of the *Bangkok Post*, which features a full-length picture of my mother in a black and white Chanel business suit which is not a fake. The subeditor has highlighted my mother's reply to a question from a reporter about the Old Man's Club, the official opening of which is tonight:

> This kind of Western hypocrisy disgusts me, quite frankly. Why doesn't the BBC make a documentary on the rag trade, with all those women working twelve hours a day for less than a dollar an hour? What is that if it's not selling your body? The West doesn't care about exploitation of our women, it simply has a problem with sex and at the same time they're using sexual titillation to sell their shows. They love to embarrass middle-aged white men who hire our girls. Western women can't handle it that their men get a better time over here. If they're too mean-spirited to give their men pleasure, that's their problem. The bottom line is that it's about money. Thailand makes very little income from industries like the clothing industry—Western companies take the lion's share. But in the sex trade we see a true redistribution of global wealth from West to East. That's what's got them so hung up.

Kimberley hands me back the clipping with a grin. "That's a real feisty lady. What's she been reading? I've noticed how her English has changed over the past months."

"She keeps taking business courses over the Net. Her line is that if sex is Thailand's biggest industry, we ought to set about modernizing and regularizing it, giving the girls a better deal, a new career after compulsory retirement at age twenty-eight, compulsory profit sharing. She's got all the business buzzwords. You know, profit centers, value-added, service industry, human resources. She claims the industry is still in the Stone Age and that the government should give assistance instead of being obstructive."

Thanks to the expressway we arrive at the Sheraton on Sukhumvit in under thirty minutes. A moment of mutual uncertainty, then: "See you tonight."

"Yes." Slightly flustered. "Tonight. You know, I've never been to a brothel before—even though I own shares in one."

I give her a reassuring smile before I leave. I'm quite excited. We had our first distribution of shareholder profits a couple of days ago and I couldn't believe how much we've made in a few short months, even before the official opening. I'm off to all those famous names in the Emporium.

There are cables all over Soi Cowboy and the police have shut off the street to traffic. Trailers with the logos of the world's media networks are parked at all angles and lights flash as we approach in the back of the Colonel's Bentley, his usual driver at the wheel. I've heard about the Bentley, of course, everyone has, but this is the first I've seen of it. Vikorn gave it to himself as a present for his sixtieth birthday: Continental T-class, with all the bells and whistles. From its formidable stereo system booms "The Ride of the Valkyries."

The Colonel, Kimberley and I merge into the crowd while my mother steps into the light of the halogens. The Colonel is wearing a double-breasted linen suit by Redaelli, a painted silk tie and crepe shirt both by Armani, loafers by Ralph Lauren, Wayfarer aviator sunglasses even though it's dark. If he were not a genuine gangster he would look ridiculous. As it is, he looks terrific. For once I am not jealous, however.

As we watch from the sidelines I realize my mother's status as a former prostitute has given her a moral authority which even the BBC finds intimidating (she is wearing a black silk trouser suit by Karl Lagerfeld, black cross-grained shoes with red satin bows by Yves Saint Laurent, a beige cotton blouse by Dolce & Gabbana with a floppy red satin bow to match her shoes—the effect is of a twenty-first-century *person* in total mastery of both yin and yang). CNN has already switched its line from disapproval to ambivalence and the BBC has had to follow suit. The French and Italian media were never more than halfhearted about moral outrage founded on the act of sex and are taking a predominantly humorous line. Even the Muslim networks from Malaysia and Indonesia are holding back on the heavy judgments, the Japanese are openly approving and the Chinese are intrigued.

"Our societies need to grow up," my mother is saying. She has become more fluent by the day and her English is almost flawless, with a charming Thai accent which comes across as faintly childlike and softens her new aggression. "Globalization has caused the biggest increase in prostitution in the history of the world. This is a big story the media neglects because it's so politically incorrect. Uncountable women are on the game not because they need to be but because they choose to be. University students from Moscow sell themselves in Macao to make some pocket money. Chinese from Singapore fly to Hong Kong for the Christmas vacation to sell their bodies. Shanghai is awash with girls chasing the fast buck. Women from all over South America trade sex all over the world, especially in Asia and the West. You see British, Canadian, American and Scandinavian women in the escort business all over Bangkok. Why hasn't the media told the world just how popular a little private body-leasing has become even with well-off young women from G7 nations?" The female BBC interviewer nods sagely.

"She's good," the Colonel whispers to me. "She's even better than you used to be."

Now the CNN reporter, also a woman, is holding a large microphone in front of Nong's mouth. My mother hardly pauses as she switches networks. "You tell every young woman in the country that it is her right to dress up, look sexy, have a mobile telephone, own a car, go on exotic holidays, and nine times out of ten there is only one profession that will bring her the money she needs to do these things. So who is the pimp, me or the West? I'm really about damage control, accepting the situation for what it is and giving the girls a better deal. Would I prefer a return to traditional Thai, Buddhist morality? Actually, yes, but it's too late for that, the corrosion has gone too far, we have to deal with reality. Even the Buddha believed that."

The CNN reporter turns away from Nong to interview a wiry old man in one of my mother's T-shirts and red and yellow striped shorts, perhaps in his early seventies, slightly stooped with sinewy arms and a grizzled face: he looks exactly like the caricature on the shirt. "Excuse me, sir, have you been a customer of the Old Man's Club while you've been in Thailand?"

"I sure have. Soon as I saw the web page I booked me a ticket to Bangkok, one-way. If I have to die out here, that's okay with me. I'm from Kansas and I've had three wives, and lemme tell you, I never knew till now what those women who lived off me for fifty years weren't doing for me."

"Were *not* doing for you?"

"Damned right. If I had the time I'd probably feel bitter, but I don't have the time 'cos I'm too busy bangin'—"

"Yes, thank you, sir. And you, sir, did you come to Bangkok expressly to visit the Old Man's Club?"

"Yep, and I'm too old to care if you and your viewers don't like it. I'm eighty-one years old and I played the game all my life, raised three ungrateful kids who never come visit me, lost me a wonderful wife to cancer, God bless her soul, then married a bitch, may she rot in hell, and if I got ten minutes more left to live I want to spend those ten minutes right here in the Old Man's Club. Might not be love but it's the closest I'm gonna get this late in the day. Sure beats contract bridge. Have you any idea how boring contract bridge gets once you know there's something more exciting waiting on the other side of the world?"

"It doesn't bother you that many Americans might find what you are doing politically incorrect, even immoral?"

"Does political correctness give protection from Alzheimer's? One thing about being old, you learn to cut to the chase."

The CNN reporter turns to two young women waiting to be interviewed. They are Nit-nit and Noi, whom Nong poached from the Jade Palace on my recommendation. To the camera: "Well, the customers certainly seem satisfied, but what about the workers? These stunning young women, who in another society might well be movie stars or models, spend their nights catering to these clients. Let's hear what they have to say."

Nit-nit: "I wasn't sure what to expect, but the customers are so grateful, you know, it's kind of sad. I think in your country maybe you don't treat old people very well. In Thailand we would never leave our parents and grandparents to stay alone year after year. I think they would die sooner if not for us."

Noi: "Usually they are very funny, like it's all a joke, which is the way

Thai people see things too, so it's not so hard to be with them. They're not demanding like younger men, they don't tell you do this, do that, they're just so happy to be able to touch you. It's like being a nurse, really. It's part of Thai culture to respect and help the old."

Meanwhile the CNN reporter directs the camera operator to focus on her for the wrap-up. "Well, as Walt Disney said in *Lady and the Tramp:* 'We are Siamese if you please, we are Siamese if you don't please.' So far the criticism of Madame Nong Jitpleecheep's new club is muted, and the praise high. Only time will tell if what we have here is a variation on a theme of exploitation as old as humanity, or a step toward emancipation. In the meantime, the thirty-year-old party which is Bangkok's nightlife continues, whatever the rest of the world may have to say about it. This is Celia Emerson, for CNN, Bangkok."

One by one the lights start to die and men in shorts, sweating in the night heat, start to roll up the cables while Nong looks on a little wistfully. It is time for all of us to enter the club. The Colonel and Nong go first, followed by Kimberley, who assumes that I am following her. Instead I pause at the door to watch a black limo draw up behind one of the media trailers.

I am wearing a four-button double-breasted blazer by Zegna, a spread-collar linen shirt by Givenchy, tropical wool flannel slacks and, best of all, patent leather slip-ons by Baker-Benjes. My cologne is a charming little number by Russell Simmons. Somehow I think my getup will be particularly appreciated by my personal and secret guest, who emerges with some difficulty from the limo, aided by two burly minders. She walks with the aid of a stick and her facial features will never be other than masculine. Her dress falls poorly, in my opinion, even though it is the very best from Giorgio Armani. On the other hand, the estradiol has done wonders for her hair, which falls in a heavy, luxurious curtain onto the collar of her dress. The minders leave her to approach me at the threshold.

"Nice threads," Pichai says to me, using Warren's vocal cords and scanning my new wardrobe with her gray eyes.

Inside, our live entertainment is singing "Bye Bye Blackbird."

John Burdett is a nonpracticing lawyer who worked in Hong Kong for a British firm until he found his true vocation as a writer. Since then he has lived in France and Spain, and is now back in Hong Kong. He is the author of *A Personal History of Thirst* and *The Last Six Million Seconds*.

A NOTE ON THE TYPE

The text of this book was set in Electra, a typeface designed by W. A.
Dwiggins (1880–1956). This face cannot be classified as either modern or old style. It is not based on any historical model, nor does it
echo any particular period or style. It avoids the extreme contrasts
between thick and thin elements that mark most modern faces, and it
attempts to give a feeling of fluidity, power, and speed.

Composed by Creative Graphics,
Allentown, Pennsylvania
Printed and bound by Berryville Graphics,
Berryville, Virginia
Designed by Virginia Tan